Stranded

By Emily Barr

Backpack
Baggage
Cuban Heels
Atlantic Shift
Plan B
Out of my Depth
The Sisterhood
The Life You Want
The Perfect Lie
The First Wife
Stranded

Stranded

Emily Barr

First published in 2012 by HEADLINE REVIEW
An imprint of HEADLINE PUBLISHING GROUP

1

Cataloguing in Publication Data is available from the British Library

Hardback 978 0 7553 8802 8
Trade paperback 978 0 7553 8796 0

Typeset in Garamond ITC by Palimpsest Book Production Limited,
Falkirk, Stirlingshire

Printed and bound in Great Britain by CPI Group (UK) Ltd, Croydon, CR0 4YY

Headline's policy is to use papers that are natural, renewable and recyclable products and made from wood grown in sustainable forests. The logging and manufacturing processes are expected to conform to the environmental regulations of the country of origin.

HEADLINE PUBLISHING GROUP
An Hachette UK Company
338 Euston Road
London NW1 3BH

www.headline.co.uk
www.hachette.co.uk

For James, Gabe, Seb and Lottie, as always,
with lots of love.

acknowledgements

Thanks first of all to my friend Vanessa Farnell for accompanying me on the research trip to Malaysia. Someone had to help check out those paradise beaches and you threw yourself into the assignment with admirable dedication.

Melissa and Cory Anderson won a competition to have a character in this book given a name of their choice, and named him after their son Jonah. He is the handsome one on the beach, as I'm sure he will be, in the real world, in years to come.

Thanks to the friends who keep me going on a day to day basis, and particularly to Kerys Deavin, Jayne Kirkham, Helen Allies and everyone I chat to in the school playground. Often you're the only people I speak to all day.

Thanks to Sarah Duncan, Liz Kessler, Sarah Moss and Craig Green for writerly solidarity. And to the children in the school writing club: you have no idea how much your enthusiasm and brilliantly lateral approach makes me laugh and inspires me.

Thank you to my local independent bookshop, the Falmouth Bookseller, and particularly to Ron Johns and Katy Lazenby for support, and also wine.

My family, as ever, have put up with my erratic hours and distraction as I was writing Stranded: James, Gabe, Seb and Lottie, thank you, as ever, for taking it all in your collective stride, as you always do.

Enormous thanks to Sherise Hobbs, Leah Woodburn, Emily Furniss, Veronique Norton and everyone else at Headline for the invaluable support and the spot-on editing and encouragment. Huge thanks to everyone at Curtis Brown, and particularly to Jonny Geller. There's no one in the world I'd rather have fighting my corner.

prologue

I roll over on to my back and open my eyes. The world has not ended overnight: the cloudless sky is pink where the sun is rising over the sea. I squeeze my eyes tight shut and try again. If I concentrate hard enough, perhaps I will be able to wake up at home.

I try with all my might to create my own bedroom in Brighton around me. The sand under my back becomes a mattress, the tatty sarong a duvet. The shifting, snoring people around me are transformed into my beautiful Daisy, sleeping just across the landing.

Much of the time I do not believe life on this island is real. I am strangely certain that I could pull myself home if I tried hard enough. I give it everything I have, this morning. If I wake up at home, I will appreciate everything I have like never before.

It doesn't work, of course. It never does. The beach is still there. The water that imprisons us here is still lapping on the shore like something from a travel agent's twisted brochure. I pull myself into a sitting position and look around. The sea is glimmering in the breaking dawn, and it is flat. This morning's air is perfectly still. The sand is exactly the way it always is. No boat is visible on the horizon. No one has come in the night to rescue us. Nothing has changed. We have been stuck here for many days. Nobody has counted; the time has drifted by. We are still alive, all seven of us, though one is ill and at least one other is mad. The rest of them are still sleeping, so I stand up and pad away, savouring time on my own. I walk to the edge of the jungle, listening to its sounds. Everything in there is waking up. The rainforest teems with life. From the smallest insect to the giant lumbering dinosaur lizards, the inhabitants of the island's interior are harmless, to us if not each other. There are no tigers in there, no rabid monkeys. What peril there is probably comes from the mosquitoes.

My hair is straw. I dread to think how leathery my face has become: it is peeling in places, though we still have a little sunscreen left. I am wearing the bikini and sarong I happened to have on when this started. If I had known what I was heading towards, I would have worn something sturdier and brought supplies. The sarong used to be pink with gold lamé at the edge. I was pleased when I bought it in Accessorize at Gatwick. Now it is greyish and the gold thread is broken and sticking out everywhere. There are three holes in it. This is a rubbish sarong. I never expected, when I bought it, that it would become the sole thing I owned.

If it weren't for Daisy, back at home wondering what has become of me, I would set out into the sea and swim until my body gave up. As it is, I just have to wait.

The day stretches ahead. All we do is find food and fetch water. We have no energy for anything but the struggle to stay alive. This is no life at all. I lean against a tree and sob. This is where I will die. We will all die here, and we know it. I hope it happens soon.

chapter one

Four weeks earlier

When the hotel spa opens at seven, I am there, my bikini under my clothes, ready to swim. I see no one but the man behind the desk, who smiles warmly and hands me a fluffy white towel before going back to his newspaper.

The floor is dark marble with a decking pathway leading to the pool to stop you slipping. I pass showers with heads the size of dinner plates. The areas are separated from one another by bamboo screens. It all feels hugely luxurious, a million splendid miles from my messy little terraced house at home. The warm air cossets me like a duvet. Everything is perfect. I have never been to a spa before; now I never want to leave.

I hope no one will notice that I am an impostor. I am not the kind of woman who comes to a place like this, yet I am doing, I think, a reasonable job of pretending to be one. Simply being a Westerner seems to be good enough. I stand in front of a mirror in the changing area.

It is dimly and flatteringly lit, and if I toss my hair back and pose in a certain way, I can make myself look like the person I want to be. I can pass for a confident traveller who is here on her own because she likes it that way. At least the divorce has made me lose weight. I had my hair coloured before I came away, and now I see that my disguise is adequate for the moment.

No one will look at me and guess that I am petrified of everything. It is, though, unusual for a woman in her later thirties to be wandering around Asia on her own, so perhaps an observer might briefly wonder what has brought me here.

I do not look like a middle-class drunk, a comically inadequate wife, a badly dressed mother who turns up at the school gates too late and who has to go and find her daughter sitting, mortified, in the office. No school office staff would wrinkle their noses at the smell of lunchtime wine coming off this woman. No husband would declare himself bored senseless by her stupid behaviour.

Rather than having a window, the pool is open to the outside world, high up where no one could possibly see in. I am on the second floor up here, and all that is visible is a few clouds and some treetops. The air is steamy and hot.

I test the pool's water with a toe: predictably, it is gorgeously warm. Soon I am ploughing up and down, counting so that I can make sure I have done it twenty times before I allow myself to succumb to the massaging jets that ring the pool's fringes. Then I try each of them in turn: the jacuzzi, the overhead shower with its magical water pressure that pummels my shoulders when I stand below it, the shelf to lie down on, just below the pool's surface, where hundreds of little jets spring up below and pound the body with a surprising force.

I lounge in the steam room for ten minutes, and wonder whether I could forget the grand plan and the paradise beach and spend the full three weeks right here.

I sit down to breakfast calmer than I have been for years. I now understand why women rush to spas squealing about 'pampering', a word that has always been guaranteed to lead me directly into homicidal rage. I would still rather poke my eyes out with the serious-looking fruit knife in front of me than be "pampered", but I can, now, see the appeal of the spa. It is a hugely indulgent misappropriation of the world's water and energy resources, but I cannot help loving it (and that is why humanity is doomed, encapsulated in one idle thought).

It is easy, now, to convince myself that I am enjoying the freedom of being alone. With the guidebook propped open under the edge of my plate, I work to renew my motivation to leave the city and head, tomorrow morning, towards the island. On the island, the sea will be my spa. Lying on the sand will be my pampering. And I will be in touch with nature, not cloistered away from it with other paying customers.

Theoretically, you should not have to fly thousands of miles and then set off on an epic land journey on your own, just to prove a point to an ex-husband who has told you you would be 'incapable of organising fucking Mass at the Vatican'.

'You couldn't organise Mass at the Vatican either,' I retorted, when he said that. 'Imagine the pressure. All those little things you'd have to get right. And you're not a Catholic – you'd have no more idea how to go about it than I would. We are both entirely incapable of organising Mass at the Vatican.'

Chris rolled his eyes. 'We are a match made in heaven,' he said as he walked away. He used to do the eye-roll whenever I spoke. I am here to show him that I am capable and brave; but I could have done that by staying at home and living happily without him. God knows, it would not be hard to forge a better life than his.

Coming here is completely out of character for me. I have never done anything remotely like it.

The reason I am in Malaysia, of all places, is because of a chance conversation I had at a party I gatecrashed. I decided to follow my instincts, or what I thought were my instincts (because I have never really been able to separate a good instinct from a self-destructive urge), partly to surprise everyone and mostly to amaze myself. As soon as I closed the front door, heaved my backpack on to my shoulders and started towards the station, I wished I had set my sights on something more attainable, like, for instance, exploring Scotland.

Happily, the hotel has an impeccable dining room, where no one looks at a lone woman. There is a wall of cascading water behind me, which is distracting, and I keep looking round at it even when I know exactly what it is. On the next table, a couple are arguing in quiet, deadly tones. I cannot understand their words, but the dynamic is as reassuringly familiar as an old fleece. When the woman's mobile rings they both half-smile in relief. She immediately starts shouting down the phone, taking it all out on whoever is on the other end, in what might or might not be Mandarin.

I know that, when breakfast is included in the room price, you have to eat everything you possibly can to see you through the day. With this in mind, I have a plate full of tropical fruit, followed by two pieces of toast, and a large helping of the Malaysian breakfast, which is curry and rice. I drink as much coffee as I can persuade the waitress to pour me, and then I remember that I have only spent half a day exploring this city, and that there are many more sights I need to tick off.

I write a text to Chris's phone, saying: 'FOR DAISY. Off out exploring the city again. Breakfast was great, the spa amazing, will bring you here next time. Hope you're having fun – love you lots and miss you hugely. Mum xxxxx' I imagine Chris picking up the phone and reading my message before handing it to her. Even read through his eyes it passes muster, so I click 'send'. Then I pack the guidebook back into my bag and head out into Kuala Lumpur.

Ninety per cent of me wants to spend the day in the spa, but this is my only full day in the city, and I have to see it. I have to do that so I can report back to Daisy, and so that Chris sees that I can not only manage without him, but that I can have adventures on a scale that would be entirely and unarguably beyond him.

I get over the main road outside the hotel, scurrying through the hot air in the wake of two young men. If I cross with people who look local, I am less likely to be crushed under the wheels of a bus. That is one of my maxims.

I have been staring at the Petronas Towers from my hotel room window, pleased to be opposite the sole Kuala Lumpur landmark that I had ever heard of. There is an air-conditioned mall at their base; its shops are Armani, Hermès and other designer names, far beyond my price range. The only place I can afford to buy anything is Starbucks, and I have had enough coffee for one morning. Instead, I buy a ticket to go up to the bridge later in the day, then exit the tower and head for the nearest Metro station.

All day I tick off the sights from the guidebook, and keep myself safe. I pound the streets, from one site of interest to the next. Yesterday I saw the area around the hotel, so today I ride on the Metro, which is inevitably cleaner and easier to use than the London version, from KLCC at the Petronas Towers downtown to Masjid Jamek. There I visit, first of all, a Hindu temple, where I watch people in brightly coloured clothes prostrating themselves before the shrine. Little girls with gold earrings smile diffidently, and I wave, as shy as they are.

I look at the confluence of two muddy rivers (and inform myself, thanks to the guidebook, that the words 'Kuala Lumpur' mean 'muddy confluence', so at that point I am properly at the centre of the city). On the spur of land where they join, there is a mosque, and while at the Hindu temple I felt welcome to hand in my shoes and join the throngs of people as an observer, I would not dare go anywhere closer to the mosque than I already am, leaning on a railing and looking at it across the water. I have no idea whether women are allowed in there at all, let alone unrepentant infidels who have just been divorced for unreasonable behaviour.

I walk around the old colonial cricket pitch, with its flagpole and its Christian church. I stroll into the church, where fascinating brass plaques commemorate young, dead colonists. Most of them died in their twenties and thirties, but only one memorial gives a cause of death, which is a fall from a horse. A honeymooning couple from the Punjab ask if I will have my photo taken with them. They make me feel like a film star. I try to smile a dazzling smile, though no doubt it comes out looking manic and odd.

The sun shines hard in the deep blue sky as I wander through Chinatown, where I am offered pirate DVDs and fake designer bags at every turn. I pause before a perfume stall, trying to figure out why anybody would buy a fake designer perfume. With a bag you can see the attraction, because it looks (presumably) like the Prada version. With a perfume, though, the bottle looks right but there could be any old rubbish inside it.

The stallholder mistakes my fascination for a potential purchase and starts haggling. I try to say no, but he calls me back with a lower price, and before I know it I have bought a bottle of pretend Britney Spears 'Hidden Fantasy' perfume for about four pounds, just to get away. This proves that I am still stupid and incapable.

I decide to stop for lunch, sitting at a table under an umbrella, at the edge of a food court. I order vegetable fried rice and a bottle of water, then on impulse add a can of beer. A few people say random hellos in passing, but I am left to get on with it, and I am extremely grateful for that. No one is interested. Everything I did in Brighton, everyone I was, has been left behind. For the first time in many years I have the space to breathe.

By the afternoon, jet lag is kicking in, so I take the Metro back to where I started and keep my appointment with the Petronas Towers. As I ride up in the lift with the fifteen other people in my group, I smile at a tiny beautiful girl of about three who is wearing gold earrings and a bright yellow dress, and she looks at me with frank interest. She is with her parents and a baby in a pushchair, who is so surrounded by blue things that there is no doubt about his gender. I seem to unnerve her, so she reaches for her mother's hand, which emerges from the folds of a niqab with beautifully manicured fingernails.

The bridge that links the two towers gives a dizzying view over the sprawling city. You could come here every day for a year and notice different things each time. I see parks, buildings, people, cars, all vanishing into the distance. Everything is vividly, almost violently green. So far I have seen only sun, but I know that when it rains here, it really rains. My hotel is easy to spot, and when I look hard I can even see my window. I left my lovely new sarong on the windowsill; and that smudge of pink marks my spot in this unexpectedly welcoming city.

I think about Chris, and instantly hate myself for letting him into my head. I have spent years struggling against him, but now, as I stand forty-two floors up, looking down on a cosmopolitan city thousands of miles from home, I find I can think of him kindly. Being magnanimous pleases me, because he would hate it.

Marrying Chris was one of my worst ideas. Had things unfurled in the normal way, I would barely remember him. We were two irresponsible slackers drawn together by a shared preference for speed when everyone else was taking Ecstasy. We would have stuck together for several weeks, for long enough to realise that when we were sober we had nothing in common, and then we would have gone our separate ways.

Chris was beautiful when I met him, with light brown hair that would have reached his collar had he worn one. His face shone with the possibilities of youth, possibilities that he was efficiently extinguishing by living solely for hedonism. His features were perfectly arranged, his cheekbones high, his eyes a warm dark brown. Now his hair is thinning on top and he has grown it long in compensation and wears it in a Slade-style ponytail. Then he was thirty-two. Now he is forty-three. Much has changed.

Neither of us could ever look back and regret Daisy's unplanned appearance in the world. I thought about aborting, but I wanted to be a mother, and when Chris drunkenly declaimed that we would be 'amazing parents', I decided to pretend he was right. We made all the conventional decisions, up to and including a pregnant wedding, in a rush of excitement at being grown up.

The thing that is inexplicable, when I look back from this distance, is the fact that we stayed together until last year. We managed to stretch out the misery like an implausibly elastic piece of old chewing gum; one that should have gone into the bin long ago. I suppose neither of us wanted to be the one to give up. I wanted to make him leave so that I could blame him. He, I am quite sure, wanted the exact opposite. We stubbornly waited in that limbo for a decade, until we succumbed together, six months ago.

I was afraid that when we told Daisy we were splitting up she would be upset. I was sure she would be insecure and worried. Instead, she grinned for days and kept saying: 'I thought you'd never do it. Thank you!'

Now we are actively divorced. I am keeping his name because I share it with my daughter, but that is all I have of him now: his genes in my child, and a surname.

chapter two

I have never walked into a bar alone before. I have drunk on my own many times, but always closeted away at home.

I am drenched with warm rain so that my hair (carefully washed and dried in anticipation of this outing) sticks flatly to my head and cheeks, and my long skirt and cotton top cling and look lewd, even though I chose them because they were the most modest clothes in my arsenal. As soon as I am across the threshold I close the door behind me to keep the driving rain out of this sanctuary. It shuts with an unexpected bang.

I look around, take in the battered leather chairs, the high ceiling with its fan lazily stirring humid air, the aged framed newspaper cuttings and cartoons on the walls, and smile to myself.

'This will do,' I mutter, and I squeeze the worst of the rain out of my hair by wringing it with both hands. A small puddle appears at my feet, and this makes me laugh.

There are three men sitting at the bar on high stools, and two men behind it. Otherwise, the large room is solely populated by empty chairs, sofas that would be called 'vintage' at home, and tables that bear the rings of glasses that have stood on them over many years. All five men are looking at me, and all laugh along with me at how wet I am. I sit on the stool they offer rather than retreating alone to one of the comfy chairs, and look at the laminated cocktail list that someone slides into my hand.

'Margarita!' I say, as my eye falls upon the word. I think I am safe having a margarita here.

Daisy would like this room. Daisy likes things that are straightforward and interesting. She hates anything girlie. This place is not girlie at all. It is overwhelmingly, testosterone-heavily male.

There is a room adjoining the bar, a dining room, and although the bar is nearly empty, the dining room is almost filled with people eating. The clatter resonates around, echoing off the high ceiling. I think I will be able to sit at a table on my own and get some dinner there myself: it does not look threatening. That will cement my triumphant day.

The barman is, I think, much older than me, and he looks as if his origins are Chinese. He smiles and inclines his head.

'Margarita? Certainly,' he says, in perfect English. He barks something at his younger colleague, who immediately starts to assemble blender, ice, salt and the right-shaped glass.

This, I am beginning to remember, is how life used to be. In my twenties I relished everything. I lived. I worked, I spent time with friends. I was outward-looking and sunny. I was not vindictive, nor bitter, and I was free.

When I concentrated, I was able to see my pregnancy, coming along serendipitously at the end of my twenties, as an exciting move up to the next stage. When we decided to make a go of it, we did it properly. We dashed headlong into playing at being grown-ups. Chris would stroke my bump and coo at the baby. I filled the cupboards with nutritious food and cooked dinner for us every night.

If I could go back, that would be the first thing I would change. No one tells you that if you think it's fun to play at being a wifey person, owing to the novelty factor, the recipient of your attentions will happily settle into the role of the waited-upon husband, and will become phenomenally grumpy when you get bored of pretending to be a woman from the 1950s and want to split the workload fairly. Whenever I hear of anyone planning marriage now, I want to tell them that. It is my sole piece of advice, apart from 'Are you sure?' Do not become besotted with the idea of yourself as someone's wife. Start living together in a way that you could imagine sustaining for decades. The novelty of being able to say 'my husband' wears off much more quickly than you might imagine.

My horizons narrowed. The world closed in. We had a daughter, and we were both in love with her and bewildered by the new world she brought with her. At first we would change her nappy together, wash her in a little basin, marvel in unison at her tiny nails and the complicated whorls of her ears. I would breastfeed her, sitting in splendid sloth on the sofa, while Chris brought pint glasses of water and bars of chocolate and plates of toast.

Then he started to go out. He would go for a drink, and come home later and later. Life settled down. Chris got a boring job at a bank, and resented me for it with every fibre of his being, every moment of every day. I cooked and ironed and washed up and resented him right back. Occasionally we went on holiday to miserable cottages in rainy villages, and both of us mainly communicated with, and through, Daisy. We rarely had money, and we never did anything. Part of me was bored senseless, but I subdued that part and lived in my imagination. I constantly planned ways to escape, but I never did anything about it, because I was certain that Chris was making the same plans and I assumed he would effect an exit first. In the end we gave up simultaneously, with a surprisingly fiery flourish.

I sit on my bar stool and look back through the window, splattered with raindrops, to the dark street. My clothes are still clinging, my hair is bedraggled, and outside the rain is still falling. I do not know a single person on this continent. The men sitting at the bar with me are the best friends I have.

'Where are you from?' asks the man on the next stool. He has a thick black moustache.

'From England,' I tell him, and hope he does not hate me for being an ex-colonist. This, I imagine, is the constant niggling fear of the liberal Englishwoman abroad. I instantly wish I'd said Britain, because people like Scotland and Wales better.

'Ah,' he says, beaming. 'England. Where do you live – London? Which team do you support? Manchester United?'

I think of Daisy, thousands of miles away, and I remember the way she forced herself to be a football fan as part of her quest for a bond with her father. I say what I know she would want me to say.

'I support Chelsea,' I pretend, hoping for no follow-up questions. I have no idea who is the manager, or the captain, and I could not name a single player. 'Stamford Bridge,' I add, sharing the sole piece of information that comes to mind.

'Ah, Chelsea.' He nods. 'Me, Aston Villa.'

'Aston Villa? Really?'

'Really. In Birmingham. You know Birmingham?'

'I've been there,' I tell him. 'Not for a while, though. And I don't live in London, but I live near, in a place called Brighton. Hove, actually.' I smile to myself as I say that, the local phrase that describes a particular area west of the boundary between the two towns. Hove-actually is a million light years from here, and all the better for it.

The older barman, who turns out to be the proprietor, is awe-inspiringly well informed. He grills me on British politics, and the royal family. He asks what I thought of Tony Blair and 'the one after Tony Blair'. I am shamed to realise that I have few equivalent questions about Malaysian politics for him. I ask about religion. 'The huge majority are Muslim, though KL is very cosmopolitan,' he says. Then he tells me about the history of his bar, which has been around for years and years. I am unexpectedly lost in tales of communism and colonialism, of men checking their guns in behind the bar.

My drink arrives. I smile my thanks and lean my elbow on the counter.

'So, you are on holiday?' he asks, after a while. 'With friends?'

I inhale deeply. The temptation to lie is almost overwhelming. It would be the easiest thing in the world to say yes, and to invent a friend or partner. Tell the truth, I instruct myself. I do not know these people and it does not matter what they think.

'On my own,' I say. 'I'm on holiday for three weeks.'

The man next to me looks confused. 'With friends?' he asks again. He glances around, just in case my friend might be hiding behind a chair, or on the other side of the heavy curtain.

'No.' I take a slug of my drink. It is sour and perfect. 'I really am on my own.' I carry on, before anyone can interrupt. 'I just got divorced, and my daughter is spending the school holidays with my ex-husband. I wanted to do something interesting, so here I am.'

This is the conversation I thought I would not be able to have with anyone in Asia. I thought I would be judged and found wanton. In fact, the men barely react.

'You're staying in KL?' asks the proprietor. 'For all your holiday?'

'No,' I tell him. 'No, I'm not. I am on the move. I'm on my way to an island.'

Three months ago, I was struggling. Daisy was with Chris for the weekend, and I could not bear being in the house on my own.

I was glad that Chris had gone to live in a squatty bachelor pad, but whenever Daisy went to visit him, I fell apart. The walls of my house were covered with Daisy's old paintings, even though she considers herself far too grown up for painting these days: both Chris and I would always sellotape any new picture to the walls, and only when the edges curled and the paint flaked off would we allow one to disappear. Likewise, neither of us ever took her old school photograph off the mantelpiece when a new one arrived, so they are still lined up there, a row of Daisys, from the four-year-old on the left (so innocent and brave that she makes me cry, if I am in the right mood) through to the Daisy of today (long-haired, attempting to look moody while a harassed photographer tells her to say 'sausages') on the right.

I could not stand being at home on my own while Daisy was doing whatever Chris does with her at the weekends. I went out at five o'clock, because when you have a child you can never really go out at five in the afternoon. That is the time of day when you have to be starting to cook and thinking about their bedtime, even when they are ten. It is the time of day when I miss her the most, when she is not there.

I had a drink and a Valium before I went out, just because, and I strolled into the centre of town and wondered what to do. I was feeling pleasantly fuzzy, and thought vaguely about going to sit on the beach and look at the sea, even though it was winter, and dark, and also raining. On my way to the beach, though, I noticed a party in a little art gallery in the Lanes. The lights and voices called to me, and I obeyed them, picked up a free glass of wine and started looking at the abstract paintings on the walls. They were mostly white and blue, and I liked them. They were easy to look at. The windows were all misted up and the people around me were warm. I found myself wishing for a cigarette, even though I have never smoked.

'Esther,' said a voice, and I jumped guiltily and looked round.

'Zoe!' I was delighted to see her. She is one of my closest friends. She kissed me on the cheek.

'It's lovely to see you,' she said. 'You should have told me you were coming.'

'Oh,' I said. 'I didn't know. You know. Daisy's with Chris . . .'

'Do you know Jessica?' she said.

'Er . . .' Everyone knows someone called Jessica.

'The artist. Didn't you know she's my niece? Over there. She's so clever. Look, this is Ally, her sister.' She grabbed an implausibly beautiful girl of about twenty by the arm and spun her around to face us.

Because she did that, I am catching the early bus out of Kuala Lumpur tomorrow morning.

Ally was tanned and gorgeous, with long honey-coloured hair and sparkling eyes. I felt myself age by a decade, just looking at her. I glanced at myself, clutching warm wine, oozing desperation. I was wearing a thin dress and I was still cold and wet from outside.

'Hi,' she said, bouncing around on the balls of her feet, and holding a little bottle of water.

'Ally's down for Jessie's exhibition,' explained Zoe. 'She's been away in Asia for a year and apparently getting back to civilisation is something of a culture shock. Remember, I told you about her?'

'Auntie Zoe, it's not civilisation,' Ally objected, with pursed lips. 'You know where I was five days ago? *That* was civilisation.' She looked around the room, at the loud drunk people. 'Five days,' she repeated.

'Where on earth were you?' I asked, partly because she wanted me to, and also because I wanted to know about a place that could make someone glow in the way she was glowing. I planned to adopt it as my next fantasy destination.

'I was in the most incredible place on earth,' she said happily, and I looked at the light in her eyes and I believed her. 'In Malaysia. The Perhentian Islands. They're like one of those fabled magical places. There are two of them, but the smaller one is the one to go to. Perhentian Kecil. You've got jungle in the middle, just thick unspoiled jungle, and then around the edges there are perfect beaches, lots of them, and huts to sleep in. The turtles lay their eggs on the beaches and they have done since millions of years ago. There's coral with little Nemo fishes, and friendly sharks, and the sun shines all the time. The beaches are covered in bits of white dead coral like bones. It's like, life is back to its basics. You eat fish, you drink a beer if you can find one, though you have to look quite hard because it's a Muslim country and they don't have the same reliance on alcohol that we do.' I felt her look at the wine in my hand. 'And you lie back and feel the sun on your skin. No one bothers you, everyone's friendly.' She smiled and looked a bit embarrassed. All the noise around us, the clinking of glasses and the loud conversations, seemed vulgar. 'Sorry. The place has got under my skin. There's still sand in all my stuff. I'll adjust soon enough.'

I smiled at her. 'It sounds wonderful. Doesn't seem to me like you should adjust. The Perhentian Islands? Maybe I should go.'

'Esther's recently got divorced,' Zoe told her, unnecessarily I felt.

Ally laughed. 'You *so* should go. All of Asia was amazing, but those islands were like nothing on earth. I'd be back there today if I could. I was wondering if I ought to marry one of the local men so I could live there for ever.'

Zoe and I both inhaled sharply.

'Don't, Ally,' said Zoe.

'You'd end up sweeping the floor and having babies,' I told her. 'Do it by yourself. Don't get married.'

'Yeah! Joking. I'm off to London the day after tomorrow, to get a job. My real plan is to save up enough money to go back for a few weeks next year.' She laughed. 'Get married! I don't think so.'

The conversation stuck with me. That girl had been happy and carefree, and I wanted some of what she had, even though I knew that it was almost entirely because of her youth, and that even the gorgeous Ally would be jaded when she was in her late thirties and burdened with responsibilities and cynicism.

The next night, I poured my usual enormous 'one unit' of wine, and sat down at the computer. Google corrected my spelling, and in no time my screen was filled with photographs of the Perhentian Islands.

I sat and stared at the screen, and as I looked at the photographs of sandy beaches and sun glinting off sea, my perspective shifted for the first time in over a year. Possibilities – self-indulgent ones, but all the more appealing for it – presented themselves. It occurred to me that there was nothing to stop me actually going. I had been stashing little bits of money for years, keeping a running-away fund. I could use it to go to these islands. Chris wanted Daisy for the Easter holidays. He always insisted on not taking his main holiday in the summer, because he said he loved it in the office when all the parents were away camping with their sticky children. That would give me three weeks. I tried to forget about it, but those islands presented themselves in my dreams and daydreams, day after day, week after week.

I knew with absolute certainty that if I went to this place, I would become happy and strong. Everything would be all right. It would be about the island, about the bigger picture, not the small one.

I wrote an email in the middle of the night, ten obsessed days later.

'I'm planning to go away over Easter,' I typed casually, 'since you've asked to have Daisy for the entire break. You can have what you want. The whole school holidays. Will you confirm that's OK?'

I sent it at 9.32 the next morning, to make it look like a piece of business. I was calling Chris's bluff, agreeing to the extreme negotiating position he had taken purely to annoy me. He made me wait three days before replying.

'Sure. Hanging out with Daze is always a joy. We'll need to know where you're going and when, of course, just in case.'

When I booked the tickets to and from Kuala Lumpur, I forwarded the email to him. That was as full as my itinerary was going to get, as far as the nosy ex was concerned.

*

For a second, I flash on to the way he would react if he knew I was here, in a bar, with a second margarita, somehow, in front of me, and five men mildly interested in my story. For the first time in a long time, I can imagine him smiling. This is how I was when we met. This was the way he liked me.

'Perhentian Islands?' asks the man with the moustache, the Aston Villa supporter.

I smile at each of them in turn.

'Yes,' I say, amazed that he knew. 'Perhentian Islands,' I repeat. The words feel like the most momentous thing I have ever said. I am going to heaven. I am going to find perspective, happiness, to remind myself of the things that actually matter in life. I am going to be all right.

'Ah,' they say, and they smile knowingly. The proprietor turns to me. I feel that something important is about to happen. I am wrong.

'If you would like to eat here,' he nods towards the dining room, 'then please do so. The kitchen will close at nine forty-five.'

'Yes please,' I say. 'And could I have another drink?'

Later, sleepless from jet lag and margaritas, I stand at my tenth-floor window and stare out at the city. I can see where the main road is, the one I crossed this morning, using locals as cover. A string of white lights moves towards me, and red ones move away. I wonder who is in those cars and where they are going. The lights on the Petronas Towers follow the curves of the huge building in tiers and make the massive structure look delicate. The footbridge is lit up. I wave at myself, earlier today, as I stood on it and looked back to this window.

I do not think I will sleep. I think I will lean on my windowsill and stare at this city all night. Yet somehow, hours later, I wake up in bed, smiling.

chapter three

I am in the back of a battered yellow taxi, and the meter is running, which I know from my perusal of the guide-book is a good thing, because when they don't use the meter is when you get ripped off, and I am looking out of the window, watching the city of Kuala Lumpur whizzing past. Next time I am here, I tell myself, I will have been to paradise. I will be, in a way I cannot stop imagining, fixed. I can picture myself: I will be wise, happy, emanating an unshakeable inner wisdom. Instead of skinny, I will be slender and elegant. My skin will have regained an approximation of a youthful glow. I will shimmer with health, and my attitude to Chris will be patronisingly benign. I will go back to Daisy and be the best mother in the world; because, God knows, she deserves that. Whatever it takes, I will do it. I will be different, serene, wise. I will be the mother she should have had all along.

I watch a woman driving in the next lane, and wonder why it seems strange to me that she can drive a car. It is,

I know, because she is wearing a headscarf that covers all her hair. I suppose the headscarf looks to me like a symbol of submission to some man (or, perhaps, to The Man), and driving a car looks like someone in control of a massive machine, and the two things together are confusing.

She seems to feel my eyes on her, and glances across at me, then turns away, unsmiling. I could not drive here.

We are leaving the city, along a main road, and suddenly I am wondering where we are going. I wanted the bus station, and on my map the bus station was not at all far from the hotel. The meter is reading thirty-nine ringgit, which is approximately ten pounds, and that is a lot more than this journey ought to be costing.

Be brave, I tell myself. Whatever is happening, you need to stop it. I lean forward.

'Er, excuse me?' I say, sounding like a ridiculous parody of an Englishwoman abroad, and one who has not even bothered to learn a single word of the language of the host country, coasting on the familiar notion that people who deal with tourists know how to speak English. 'The bus station? Bus to Kuala Besut?'

The man nods sharply, as if I am an annoyance, and carries on driving; and the highway just keeps going in front of me, and I know I am being taken to a place that I don't want to go to, and not only that, but I seem to be paying through the nose for it. I try to remonstrate, but again he shakes me off, and I sit, hating myself for my timidity, and wait to see what will happen.

Eventually he pulls into what looks like a mainly deserted multi-storey car park, stops the engine and looks at me expectantly. My heart is thumping. I am terrified.

'Bus station?' I say weakly.

He nods. Obediently, I get out of the car and slam the door, pleased by the idea that this might, in fact, be the right place, and delighted that it seems he has not brought me to an empty car park to rob me.

He winds down his window and waits. I hand him a fifty-ringgit note. He gives me change and speeds away. Then I stand on my own, pull my backpack on to my back and wonder where the buses are.

There are concrete pillars, a few cars parked a little way away and no sign of a human being, nor of any form of public transport. I feel that someone might be watching me from a distance.

This is all wrong. I live in Brighton. That is where I belong. Thinking I could come here, at the age of thirty-nine, and act like a backpacker was stupid. I am not one of life's backpackers and I never could be. I did not 'go travelling' in my youth, because I never wanted to. I cannot do this.

I step over a little wall and out of the car park. I look up and down the flat tarmacked road for a bus. The sun shines mercilessly on my head. There is nothing. I am lost.

Obviously, the worst thing to do would be to get into another taxi, with the person who came over to ask why I was crying, and see which bizarre spot I might end up in this time. All the same, this is what I do.

'Hello,' says the man. 'Please do not cry. Where you go?'

He is smiling at me, and he nods to his taxi behind him.

'I want the bus to Kuala Besut,' I say.

He laughs and points to a building beyond the car park.

'Here there is train to the airport or bus to Malacca. You want to go to Malacca? Very beautiful town.'

'No!' I sniff and try to pull myself together. At least there is a bus here. That makes things a bit better. What, I wonder, would the chances have been of me, Sussex working mother, sitting crying in front of this man, this Kuala Lumpur taxi driver? It seems so profoundly unlikely that our paths should ever have crossed; and yet they have.

'You need to go to Putra,' he tells me, and he is calm and authoritative, and when he walks off I duly follow him, nodding because I recognise the name from the guidebook. Again, I sit on the shiny vinyl of a back seat, and watch the meter climbing as we reverse my previous journey and head back along the motorway, into the city. I see the Petronas Towers up ahead, and the hazy skyline of the sprawling, friendly city, and I tell myself that a little misadventure does not matter. In fact, seeing the city from behind a cab window is a reassuring, safe thing to do, and I would rather go back and forth by cab all day than get on to a long-distance bus.

Stupid woman, I tell myself. I could have booked an internal flight, which would have taken about an hour. Then I could have got a taxi, which would also have taken an hour, and gone straight to the boat. I could almost be at the island by now. Instead, I thought, from the comfort of my terraced house in Hove, that it would be more authentic and interesting to travel by land and to see the interior of Malaysia in passing. And look at me: I cannot even bloody turn up at the right bus stop.

I have been saying 'mm', I realise, to the driver, without listening. That is a workplace habit, as well as a maternal one.

'Sorry?' I add, leaning forward. 'Can you say that again?'

He nods. 'I say, I take you to Kuala Besut? All the way to where you go. One thousand ringgit? We agree.'

Oh good God.

'No,' I say. I dredge up a firm and decisive voice. 'No, I don't have a thousand ringgit. Please just take me to the bus station.'

'But you agreed! You say "mm".'

'Which is not "yes",' I point out.

He shrugs. 'OK, how much you want to pay?'

'I want to pay whatever the bus costs. Because I want to go on the bus. I don't have spare money to take a taxi *all the way across the country*!'

'Eight hundred?'

'No!'

'OK. Seven hundred. That is the best price.'

I look out of the window, hoping we are not already on the main road to the east coast.

'Look,' I say, as sternly as I can. 'If you're not taking me to the bus station, why don't you let me out here and I'll pay you what it says on the meter.' Then I look at the meter and gasp. It says seventy-four ringgit. Last time I looked, it said seven. The taxi I just took in the opposite direction cost forty-one.

'The meter is *very* high,' I tell him, wondering how confrontational to be, and how best to get the hell out of this taxi. I know as soon as I have spoken that I should have gone for a furious approach.

The man is studying me stonily in the rear-view mirror.

'Is a very long way,' he says.

I take my mobile out and make a show of reading the sticker on the inside of the window, which tells me how to report an errant driver. I look for a number to phone, but there does not seem to be one, so I key in the email address instead.

He is still staring, unsmiling. I do the same thing back; but I am well aware that we are speeding along a highway in a car that is entirely under his control, and that even if I were able to leap out, he would still have my backpack in his boot.

'Nearly there,' he tells me. I narrow my eyes at him, though I doubt he notices. Neither of us speaks.

And then, all of a sudden, he has pulled over on the hard shoulder, and cars are zipping past right next to my door. The driver has jumped out and marched around to the boot, and so I check the meter, which is showing a massive eighty ringgit, and try to open the door on the pavement side. It will not budge, so I open the other one and step out on to the motorway, feeling my hair swept up by the breeze of the traffic that thunders past. Somehow, although I would be terrified to be inches from speeding traffic at home, this seems the least of my worries right now.

I hand him the money with a scowl. He accepts it gracelessly, and I notice, to my immense surprise, that I am next to Putra bus station. I hoist my bag on to my back and try to forget how badly I have screwed up the very simple matter of getting from my hotel (which I think I can see from the bus station doorway) to here. At least I am here, and it is 10.20, so I am in time for the bus. Nothing else matters. I make an effort not to translate what I have spent on taxis today into supermarket shops or child benefit.

The bus station is basic, with concrete walls, rows of plastic seats and a line of windows belonging to different companies, selling tickets to various places. The floor is dusty and tiled. Most people are clearly local: right now, if there was another foreigner with a backpack, I would march up to them and start talking.

This fact makes me smile, in spite of my frustration. When we were happy together, Chris and I made a show of not needing anything from the outside world. We were both happy to hide away in our own little universe. Neither of us is any good at starting conversations with people we don't know, and neither of us has advanced social skills. Yet now, dirty, not-drunk, and unnerved by the discovery that I am a truly terrible traveller, I would talk to anyone.

An electronic board shows that there is indeed a bus heading to Kuala Besut in ten minutes. I find the right ticket counter and stand politely, waiting for the head-scarved woman behind it to finish her telephone conversation.

I look down at myself. I am wearing a long batik skirt I bought yesterday, bright pink with flowers outlined on it in brown, with a black T-shirt from New Look, and a pair of pink flip-flops. My hair is tied back with a hairband, scraped completely off my face. I look like a grown-up backpacker. I *am* a grown-up backpacker. Chris would probably like me looking like this. Soon, I am sure, we will bear each other no ill-will. He is probably glad, already, to imagine me happy.

The woman is looking at me, her face open and questioning.

'Yes?' she says.

I wonder what it would be like to wear one of those headscarves. It carefully covers every bit of her hair, keeps her head slick and smooth as a Russian doll's. It is pinched closed tightly under her chin, so there is no danger of any stray lock peeking out. What, I want to ask her, is so shameful about hair? I have no idea, and touch my own head self-consciously. I get my hair cut so it's straight across the bottom every now and then, and then let it grow straggly in between. Does this woman think I am brazen and shameless? Do I think she is submissive and coerced? I have no idea, as we have not yet exchanged a single word.

'Hello,' I say, wishing I were able to do this in Malay. 'Can I have a ticket to Kuala Besut for the ten-thirty bus please?'

She nods, takes a ticket from the pile next to her and starts filling it in with a Bic biro. At the same time, she makes a phone call, then shakes her head and puts everything down.

'Sorry,' she says. 'Bus full.'

I bite my lip. 'The bus can't be full!'

Why did I say that? Of course it can be full.

'Sorry. Night bus, nine p.m.?'

The idea is not appealing. I curse the taxi driver once again.

'Anything else I can do?'

She shrugs. I look at the destinations listed in the window of her little booth. One of them rings a bell.

'What about this place?' I point to it, then hazard a pronunciation. 'Kuala Terengganu? That's on the way, isn't it? In the right direction?'

She nods. 'Bus at eleven fifteen. Six hours.'

I buy a ticket for this unknown place-on-the-way, and find a rickety plastic seat, part of a row of them, all attached to the same metal bar. I sit next to a woman who is smoking and has an enormous Louis Vuitton-style suitcase. She smiles at me as I dump my shabby backpack next to her posh case.

'Hello,' she says.

'Hello,' I reply, and get out my guidebook to look up the town in which I will be making my unscheduled overnight stop.

Malaysia rolls past the window. Kuala Lumpur's suburbs stretch on, and then give way to greenery. I have never seen anything so green. It looks like rainforest stretching away, with tall palm trees, small palm trees, fronds and jungly things. After a while, I begin to realise that it is going to be like this for the whole six hours, as this busload of people and I traverse the country.

It is exhilarating to know that I am on this bus, on my own; that I have got here by myself, made this happen (eventually) myself, and that I am thousands of miles away from my normal life. I like being on the move. It means I am not anywhere in particular, and am not having to engage with anything or anyone.

I behaved terribly recently, and I have taken myself away from my life. That is good.

I am not missing Daisy too much yet, because last year I had to train myself to allow her to go and stay with Chris without letting my heart break. It was horrific, but I am steeled, now, to spending time without her. She is with her other parent, I tell myself repeatedly, and that is fine.

I did love him, in a way. I loved it that he gave me Daisy. I loved it that he was as shambolic as I was, that we improvised our own little family.

Our wedding was a small civil affair in Brighton, with a party in a seafood restaurant afterwards. It was happy. Everyone else was drunk, and I was hugely pregnant. I overrode all my misgivings, as, it transpired, did Chris.

The bus rumbles on. I stare at the guidebook without reading it for a while, and then take out a novel and don't read that, instead.

We stop, after a few hours, for what I suppose is lunch, though it is hard to keep track of the time. The sun is hot, the ground dusty and the Malaysian version of the motorway services is delightful. A low concrete building, painted brightly in blue and yellow, houses numerous food stalls which face out on to a courtyard of long tables. I find the loo first, and then order some random food, by pointing, from a smiley woman. It all works. Even though I am not where I planned to be, and not heading where I planned to head to, it all feels OK. This is definitely the right direction.

chapter four

Cathy

May 1988
God's Village

There is something exciting going on. I don't know what it is yet, but I know they will tell us when they are ready. I can hardly wait to find out. Neither can Philip. We whisper about it and try to work it out, whenever we are away from them. I am In Love with Philip. It is hard work, but I *am*. We are going to get married when we're a little bit older and I will take on wifely duties. That is my destiny. I have always known it.

If the secret is something big, something amazing, then perhaps it will all be all right. Could it be something that will allow me to accept my destiny? All my hopes are pinned on that.

I am fairly sure that we are not even meant to know that there is something we are not meant to know. I do my best to do my work, to go to school, to go to church and bible study and carry out all my chores and duties, in as normal a manner as possible. Yet I feel my eyes darting around as I seek evidence or clues everywhere. Please, I whisper, internally. Please, please be something big. Be something life-changing.

Because as things stand, my life is about to close in on me. I will have no choice, soon, but to forget my ideas and curiosities and accept what I have been given by God.

I will take my exams soon, my GCSEs, and then I will leave school for ever. My first exam is next week: it is going to be physics. My last is on June the 17th: English language. In many ways I am not going to miss going to school at all. I will certainly not miss being taunted as a freak and having my beliefs laughed at by pupils and teachers alike. I see the teachers trying not to giggle, sometimes, when Philip or Martha or I express or explain our tenets. It is horribly unprofessional of them. *Laugh at the children from the cult*, they must think (NB we are not a cult!). *It's an easy way to get everyone else on side*.

I will miss studying, though. I would like to do A levels. I can't say that out loud, because apparently God does not want me to do A levels. Besides, not doing A levels will mean that I can spend my time here, where everyone understands me. When I come home every day, the relief of not being out in the world is so immense; it feels like climbing into a warm bath. So when my whole life takes place in this compound, then, perhaps, I will be properly happy. This is what I try to believe, all the time. There is nothing for me to do but be happy with my lot. If you are not happy with your lot, bad things happen to you. Victoria discovered that the hard way, and because of what happened to her, I know I am going to have to put up with my destiny.

Cassandra, my mother, says, about the way people are to us at school: 'These things are sent to test us.' I am secretly bored of that. She has been saying it since I was old enough to understand, and she will never elaborate on it beyond something like: 'Jesus knows, Cath. He sees your suffering in His name.' And I sometimes think, really? Does he, actually? But I can't say it, because one thing you cannot do here is question your elders. Another thing you cannot do is question Jesus. So I would be in double trouble.

I used to be surprised that Moses and the others let us go to school at all, but when I said that to Victoria, who was three years older than me, she said, 'Oh, we've only been going to school for a few years, Cathy. Before that they used to home-ed us, but the council kept checking up and it pissed them off so much that they decided school was the lesser evil.'

I remember gaping at the casual way she said the rudest word I had ever heard in the Village. I heard far worse words than that at school, of course, but school was an alien world and the rules were different for those children.

Victoria said worse words, too, and then she died. I knew she would, as soon as I heard her say the f-word out loud, on the actual Village compound. God was going to punish her for that, I thought, and indeed he did. When she died, the Villagers put a death notice in the paper. It did not say she had been struck down for swearing and other behaviour. They just said she had 'gone to be with Jesus' and left it at that.

I have to work in the Village and in a couple of years I will marry Philip, and we will continue to live here and do God's work, whatever He decrees that to be.

(I'm not completely sure I want to.)

I can't believe that, lying here in my bed at night, in our girls' cabin, I have had that thought. I could be struck down now: I really, genuinely could. I never swear, though, and I never have the wrong friends like Victoria sometimes did. All the same, if she could be struck down, I could be too.

I cannot help it, though. I *do* wonder what it is like, out in the world. It is, after all, God's world. Every day I fight the urge to ask if I can go and explore. It would be a stupid thing to ask, because I know what the answer would be. It is not His will for me to go out and explore. If they knew I was thinking about it, they would be watching me like hawks.

I am lying on my bunk, staring at the shadows on the ceiling that are coming in through the light of the lantern outside the window. The others – Martha, Eve and Daniella – are asleep. Martha is the same age as me (eleven days older, in fact), so we have to spend all our time together even though we don't like each other. The other two are younger, so one of our duties at school is to look after them.

I wish I could keep a diary. We are allowed to, but the Parents read them. As they only want to read about what we have done to serve God and the Village, that makes it pretty much the same as not being allowed to keep a diary. I need to write about my secret thoughts and fears, my fantasies about going into the world.

If I had a friend, I would be happier. Victoria was funny. I wish she was still alive. She wasn't my age, but she liked me, and I loved her and she made me laugh.

Instead I have Martha, who is (whisper it) boring and fat. And Philip. I love him, and I will marry him, and we will have children together. All the same, he is not my best friend (and I am not completely sure I love him in the right way). There are a couple of girls I like at school – Sarah, in particular – but I am not allowed to be friends with people from outside the Village. I live in my head, all the time. Sometimes I am sure Moses can read my thoughts, and is displeased. I see him looking at me, and I look away.

All the same, there is definitely something in the air. My hopes are pinned on it. The Parents stop talking if they think we're listening. Perhaps some new people are coming. New people would be brilliant.

The other girls are asleep. The shadows on the ceiling are moving a little. They are, I think, branches, swaying in the breeze. I will just lie here and stare at them, and sooner or later, I am sure, I will sleep too.

chapter five

'Hello!' Two boys are balanced impressively casually on a small motorbike that may even be a scooter. The one on the back is waving to me with both hands.

'Hello,' I say back, and carry on walking. If I were in charge of this town, the first thing I would do would be to make all its pavements flat, and cover the holes that I presume lead down to drains and sewage. In a minute I am going to fall down one. I know I am. It is exactly what ought to happen next: the sole white woman in town will grant everyone a cheap laugh by dropping down a hole in the street and landing in poo.

Above me, hundreds and hundreds of birds are swooping and diving, performing aerial acrobatics. Perhaps they are eating mosquitoes: I hope so, because the atmosphere is so heavy it is almost solid, and I am sweating profusely. There is so much moisture in the air that I can hardly breathe. It is mosquito heaven. The very thought makes me itch.

I stare down at the pavement, and keep walking. My

backpack pulls hard on my shoulders, and I am trying, ineffectively, not to be conspicuous. The guidebook called Kuala Terengganu a 'pretty fishing town'. I have not found the pretty part yet. The bus station was concrete and functional, but bustling. There was a McDonald's near it, and a KFC, both of which made me think I was spending the night in a metropolis of some kind, but they must have been for the sole benefit of the bus passengers, because as soon as I stepped away from the transit hub, everything became more challenging. More authentic, perhaps.

Still, I must nearly be there. I am following the road down to the sea, and when I get close, there should be a hotel called the Seaview, which has a nice write-up in my book. I plan to take a room there, look at the view of the sea and exhale.

'Hello!' shouts another boy, who is also on a moped with his friend. All the women here are covered up, with full headscarves and arms and legs totally clothed. My longest, most drapey clothing does not look as modest here as it would at home.

'Hello,' I say back, worrying as I do so that I am being terribly brazen and slutty. They cannot possibly be viewing me in a sexual way, I reason, because I am thirty-nine and they are about seventeen, and I am doubtless older than their mothers.

A group of three girls, teenagers with pastel-coloured headscarves, are walking towards me. I try a smile, in their direction, and the closest girl smiles shyly back.

'Hello,' she says. 'Where are you from?'

'From England,' I tell her.

'Oh, England,' says another one. 'You like Malaysia?'

'Yes, very much.'

'Have a nice stay.' They all giggle, in a nice way.

Where the Seaview Hotel must once have stood there is a building that is clearly not a hotel. It does not look as though it has ever been a hotel. It is a slab of a building, made from brown bricks, with shutters and bars over the windows and a few people sitting outside. I carry on walking, but now I am at the seafront, and there is definitely not a hotel anywhere nearby.

I turn back and walk past the spot again. My destination is still not there. I am crushingly hot and horribly sticky, and I want to put my bag down.

I passed a grimy-looking 'business hotel' back up the road on a corner. As I no longer trust the guidebook, I drag myself back to it, hoping that 'business hotel' is not a euphemism. I manage not to fall into a drain on the way, and though I can feel mosquitoes air-bombing me, I am hoping they might be paranoia-produced imaginary ones.

The business hotel is just about affordable, and they laugh when I ask if they have a room: I get the impression that I could book a separate room for every item in my backpack and the hotel would still be half empty. The man hands me a key attached to a huge slab of plastic and directs me to the lift, and then I am on the eighth floor, and then in my very own room. My tiny piece of Kuala Terengganu is small and crowded with furniture, with a view of the town and a tiny sliver of sea visible between buildings. I go directly to the window to contemplate the birds, which are still diving crazily out there under the leaden sky, but step swiftly back, because the window is smeared with something unidentifiable, right at my eye level. Someone else has stood here and looked out, and left a smear of what might or might not be snot or saliva. Someone else has not done a wonderful job of cleaning the room.

I retreat to the bed and try not to wonder when the sheets were last washed. The bathroom looks all right, but I give the loo seat a brisk clean with a cleansing wipe all the same.

I realise I am starving. In spite of the hearty bowl of curry and rice I had for lunch, I have built up a massive appetite by doing nothing but sitting on a bus, in a state of great excitement, all day. Even the secretions on the window cannot dent my need for food, so in some trepidation I decide to go out into what is now dusk, and see the town.

According to my unreliable guidebook, there is a Chinese restaurant called the Golden Dragon, where, in this very Muslim town, I will be able to find a beer. I would like one of those very much. After trying hard to to memorise the route, I grab my shoulder bag, and set off.

It feels more intimidating at nightfall, and before I have been outside for five minutes, it is properly dark. I stumble around, worried about the sewer portals in the pavements, and try to go the right way. Two men on a moped slow as they pass me and shout 'Hello!' I say hello back, but I don't look at them for long because I have no idea what that might mean, in a town this religious.

Around the corner, on a street that is almost deserted,

the same thing happens, and again I return the greeting with some reluctance. This time, however, the teenager on the back of the moped spits at my feet, and they roar off, laughing.

I stop, frozen to the unreliable pavement. There are tears in my eyes but I blink them back, furious with myself and with those boys. I see, suddenly, that every 'hello' has been sarcastic. Everyone here hates me. I am wearing a long skirt and a long-sleeved top: I am not acting wantonly. Yet they probably know, just by looking at me, that I drink alcohol, that I have had sex (though not for a while, I want to tell them) without being married. And that is immoral to them; and they have let me know about it.

I am sure this place has more to offer, but I turn around on the spot, and walk straight back to the hotel. I need to feel safe much more than I fancy a beer.

The hotel's restaurant is bland and shabby, and I am its only customer. My longing for familiarity is suddenly so strong that I order something the menu calls 'fish and chip'. The fish is breadcrumbed and cardboardy, but the chips are plural, and they are fine. I drink a glass of 7 Up, which I don't think I have ever done before, pay the bill and head to bed.

There I lie on top of sheets that do not smell particularly laundered, and listen to the occasional car that passes on the street outside and wonder how I came to be so far from my comfort zone. I wanted to leave it, but now I realise that I have come much too far. I don't even lie in bed and cry. This is just bleak: I need to get out of here.

I pick up my phone and look at photographs of Daisy – sensible, dependable Daisy, who is so much more grounded than her mother – until I fall asleep, wishing I was with her, back at home, wishing I was still married, for all our faults, to Chris.

chapter six

As I step down from the bus, into the sunshine, I laugh out loud. I draw attention to myself, but I don't care. This is why I came here. I have swung from misery to joy, because I have got out of that town, and now I am exactly where I ought to be: I am in the salt-scented, sun-baked town of Kuala Besut, the gateway to the Perhentian Islands.

As I laugh, I see a Western woman, sitting at one of a number of white plastic café tables next to the bus stop, look up and smile at me. I grin back. This woman has short brown hair and big dark eyes. She is wearing a white shirt and a long batik skirt, and flip-flops, and she is about my age. This is my genre of person: I have finally found my place. She looks back at the postcard she is writing, still smiling.

'This way to buy a ticket,' says the bus conductor, pointing to a semi-covered concrete corridor lined with stalls selling sarongs and garishly patterned beach towels. I follow the Scottish boy, Edward, who sat across the aisle from me on the bus, into an office. He gestures to me to go first, but I refuse: I don't want to be deferred to like an old lady. I am, after all, still in my thirties, just.

Edward is cheerful, and I know from our basic conversation on the bus that he is easy-going and chatty. This is the kind of person I should be hanging around with. He is, I hazard, about thirty. I look at his shapely legs, poking out from under khaki shorts, and listen to him buying a boat ticket to the island, from an extravagantly relaxed and friendly woman. He is, I think, a lovely-looking boy. I smile at my thoughts, because they fall somewhere between the maternal and the salacious.

'Where you going on the island?' the woman asks him, leaning back in her chair and putting her feet up on a nearby table.

'Long Beach,' he says. She nods and takes his money.

'Call us the day before you come back,' she instructs him.

I buy a ticket from her too, and thrill inwardly as I say the words: 'Paradise Bay, please.'

I want to sing. I am tingling all over. I wish I could keep this moment, bottle it up and get it out to examine whenever I need it.

The boat will be leaving at half past one. It is now, according to a wonky clock on a wall, nearly one o'clock. I sit at a white table, smiling again at the woman-like-me and trying to guess her nationality. Her hair is, somehow, too short for her to be English, and too geometrically cut. I am ready to guess that she is German or Dutch when she leans over.

'Are you on the half-one boat?' she asks, in a Radio Four English accent.

'Yes,' I say. 'I thought you were Dutch.'

She laughs.

'London all my life. But I think I'll take that as a compliment. You?'

'Brighton.'

'Oh, lovely. I've been there, of course. We all have, haven't we? Beach destination of every Londoner.' She looks around. 'If not quite as idyllic as this one. Where are you staying on the islands?'

I get to say it again.

'A little place called Paradise Bay. It was recommended to me by the niece of a friend.'

'That sounds nice. Random. I'm going to one of the more mainstream places, I think. Coral Bay. For the moment, anyway. I'm really just going to hang out and go where the fancy takes me.' She smiles. Her smile is warm and beautiful. 'I'm Katy,' she says.

'Esther.' I wonder if we should shake hands, but it feels too formal. She goes back to her writing, and I wander over to the counter and order some lunch.

Ten minutes later, I am eating spicy vegetables and rice, drinking warm water that tastes of the plastic bottle. There are now three boys at the table on my other side, and they are talking to me whenever I look up at them. They are Piet from Holland, a gorgeous man who introduced himself as 'Jonah Anderson from Canada', and Edward, who, as we have been acquainted for several hours, now feels like my oldest friend. They are kindly conversing with me as though I were not a lot older than them, and I am enjoying trying to convince myself that they haven't noticed the decade or so that separates us.

Katy is still on the other side, but she is lost in writing in a book now, a diary, probably, and is not joining in the conversation at all. This, I suppose, is why it's nice to be older. You don't have to try to get everyone to like you all the time.

In front of me, on my white plastic table, is my ticket to the Perhentian Islands. It has a picture of a beach on it. I pick it up and turn it over and over, marvelling at it.

'How long are you travelling for?' asks the Dutch boy, looking at me politely. He is tall and wholesome, and very courteous.

'Just three weeks,' I tell him, though I don't want to think about the fact that I will have to make this journey in reverse in the near future.

They all smile regretfully in my direction. I am apologetic.

'I know three weeks isn't long enough for proper travelling.' I am using my most humble voice, as if by coming here for so short a time I am breaking a rule or two. 'But I have a job, and a daughter, so it's quite something that I'm here at all.'

'Wow,' says Jonah. 'It certainly is. Where's your baby, if you don't mind us asking?'

Jonah is a proper, clean-cut Canadian, the sort who ends up in Hollywood with everyone thinking he's American. He has dark hair and chiselled cheekbones. I wonder if I am blushing when he speaks to me.

'Of course I don't mind,' I tell him. 'She's not much of

a baby these days. She's ten, and she's with her dad. We're not together any more.'

'Oh. Sorry to hear that.'

I giggle. I cannot help it: he is trying so hard to say the right thing.

'It's fine,' I assure him, and right here, right now, it is. 'Things are better this way, that's for sure.'

'Well,' says Jonah, 'good on you for getting yourself out here.'

I scoop the last of my rice on to my spoon. Just as I am admiring my perfectly clean plate, the woman from the ticket office strides past, shouting: 'To the boat, everybody, please!'

I now feel that I endured a horrible night in Kuala Terengganu just so that I would appreciate this. It is a speedboat, and it goes fast. As soon as we are out of the harbour, wearing our life jackets, the driver (or whatever you call someone who drives a boat) cranks up the engine, and we start leaping over the surface of the water. At home I would hate this. I would grasp the side of the boat and close my eyes, expecting at any second to flip over and die. Now I keep my eyes open, fixed on the bulk of the island in front of us, and my smile is so wide that it hurts my mouth. I relish every leap the boat makes, love the fact that the engine is so loud that conversation is impossible. Spray peppers my face whenever we go over a particularly big wave. The boat holds about fifteen people, including the three boys I just met, and Katy, and we are all sitting like this, staring forward at our destination. There are a few Australians, including a small, weedy man who tried to manoeuvre himself to sit with me, though I managed to outmanoeuvre him by asking someone to swap places in case I was sick. Most of the passengers, I think, are German. They are friendly and trendy and a bit intimidating.

As we approach the island, I know that I have done it. From the moment I met Ally in the gallery, I have been working towards this: Paradise Bay resort on Pulau Perhentian Kecil. I have a hut reserved, and I am nearly there. The sky is a deep blue today, the sun shining relentlessly, glinting dazzlingly off the waves.

It almost seems too soon when the engine slows and we start crawling towards the shore. The first place we stop is Coral Bay, where several developments of huts are clustered around a long sandy beach. I catch my breath. This is one of the 'built-up' parts of the island, yet it is beautiful, and I would be happy to be getting out here. There is a jetty on which heaps of supplies are waiting in the sun. Many boxes of eggs are piled up, and I find myself hoping they will be taken somewhere cooler soon. Moored by the beach, there are much smaller speedboats, some of them with taxi signs on them. People are lying on the sand reading, and sitting in cafés. To the left there is a very smart-looking development of bungalows with a big building at its centre.

Five people get off the boat here, including Katy, who grins and shouts, 'I like the sound of Paradise Bay – might see you there!' to me as she jumps on to the steps.

We turn left and head next to what I calculate to be the north of the island. Away from the beaches, there are large rocks at the water's edge, and behind them, jungle.

The thick trees cover the island. We pass a couple of beaches that are deserted but for one or two people lying on the sand, or sprawled on rocks. I can barely tear my eyes away.

At a tiny resort called D'Lagoon, three more people get off: they are met by a boat that comes out from the beach, and their backpacks are thrown into it after them. Then we stop at Long Beach, another built-up area that does, indeed, have a long beach, which seems to be peppered with diving and snorkelling outfits. Edward, Jonah and Piet get off here, shouting a cheery farewell. I hope I will see them again. We cross to the other island, the bigger one with the smarter resorts on it, and drop several people off there. By now there are only two of us left on the boat: a Japanese girl, and me. She is left at the fishermen's village, which looks like an actual place where people live, with administrative buildings, shops and a school.

Then it is just me and the boatman.

'Paradise Bay?' he says.

'Paradise Bay,' I agree.

'You have boyfriend?' he says, but I can tell his heart is not in it.

'Yes,' I say, automatically. He shrugs and laughs.

A man comes out from the beach in a smaller boat, and I climb in, as I have seen all the other people do, and wait for my bag to be thrown after me.

'Thank you!' I shout to the driver. He waves as he turns the boat around.

'Esther?' asks the man who has picked me up.

'Yes,' I agree, delighted that my reservation exists.

He drives the boat right up the sand, and gestures to me to step out first. I stare at the sight in front of me as I climb inelegantly over the front of the boat. This is a perfect white beach. It seems to me to be just the right size. There are wooden huts, nicely spaced out around it, with a bigger wooden building that is clearly the café at the centre. A bougainvillea with magenta flowers is flourishing in front of the café. Two people are lying in the shade. The air smells of seawater and flowers. I have found heaven.

I push my hair back from my face, trip over a rope and fall flat into the water.

When I stand up, I see the boatman, a man on the beach and a couple sunbathing all laughing at me. That is fine. I am laughing at myself. I would struggle to laugh at myself for falling over at home, but here it is fine.

'Thank you,' I say to the boatman.

'Have a good trip!' he says. We all laugh again at that. I notice that I have reflexively kept my canvas shoulder bag out of the water. That, I think, was clever of me. 'Welcome to Paradise Bay,' he adds.

I smile at him. 'Thank you. Thank you so much.'

My instincts were right. This place will be exactly what I need it to be. My new home is a small wooden hut on stilts. It is not one of the ultra-desirable ones at the edge of the beach; it is a little way up the hill, between a large rock with the sea behind it, and the jungle. I am tucked into a crevice. All I can hear when I am in there is the high-pitched chirping of insects. Even the sea is silenced by the rock. I have my own little veranda with a hammock on it, and a small table and two white chairs, and when I stand there, I look down past the other huts to the edge of the sand. The air hangs hot around me.

Inside, there is just a table, a chair, and a bed, over which a large mosquito net is hanging. I dump my back-pack next to the bed, change into my bikini and put a sarong on top. Within minutes I am coated in sunscreen, have my straw hat on my head and my flip-flops on my feet. My book is in my hand. I am ready.

It is three o'clock. I work out a schedule for the rest of the day. For the remaining daylight hours I will lie on the beach reading my book. Later, I will retreat to the café and sit by myself like a confident and carefree grown-up, and after that I will go to bed. Tomorrow I will repeat the procedure, and then I will do it again, and I will keep doing it until it becomes my everyday life.

On the beach, I am three quarters asleep, lying on my stomach with my head turned sideways, when a shriek jolts me back to consciousness.

I blink and yawn. It was a high-pitched female scream, coming from the direction of the sea. By the time I manage to turn around and look, it has been followed by male laughter, and it is quite clear that there is nothing wrong.

There are two people in the clear water, and they are obviously very much a couple. He is tall, dark and muscular. She is petite yet curvy, with slick blonde hair. They are toned and tanned, like film stars. They seem to be in the wrong place altogether. A couple like this ought to be cavorting in the Caribbean, somewhere where they might be picked up by the paparazzi. The rest of us look like kicked-back backpackers.

They are doing what swimming pool signs used to refer to, disapprovingly, as 'petting'. Oblivious to the fact that everyone in the area is now observing them (or perhaps not as oblivious as they look), they are snogging like teenagers, giggling, disappearing underwater and resurfacing in gales of laughter. I try to work out whether they could actually be having sex in the water. I have never tested the logistics of whether such a thing is technically possible.

A German couple nearby are looking at them too, though with less surprise than me. I catch the eye of the woman, who is completely cool, with long straight hair and a bikini patterned with little pictures of lemons that manages, somehow, to look stylish rather than stupid. She grimaces, and I nod and widen my eyes. We both look back to the couple in the water.

'Three days they have been here,' she calls to me. 'Three days! It's exactly the same each day.'

'They don't get tired of it?' I ask.

'It seems not.'

One of the men who works here comes and stands between us.

'They are just married,' he explains, as the woman's bikini top comes off. He seems torn between disapproving and approving very much indeed. 'This is very unusual for Malaysia, to do this.'

'Oh, for God's sake,' says the German woman. 'Topless in a Muslim country? How stupid is she?'

'Very,' I agree. I assume these people have not passed through Kuala Terengganu.

She turns to her partner, who is wearing board shorts and has long curly hair, and, as far as I can tell, admonishes him in German for looking at the topless woman.

'Where are they from?' I ask, hoping that they will not turn out to be British.

'Amerrrrrica,' announces the man from the café, who introduces himself as Samad. 'They are Americans, from Hollywood.' He waves to a woman who is walking across the beach towards him, carrying a tiny baby.

'Yeah,' I say. 'They look like it.'

The spectacle quickly becomes boring, and I turn back to my book. Samad is off, running across the sand towards his child.

Sitting in the restaurant alone is less painful than I feared. I have been travelling for five days now (and it seems incredible, now that I am here, that less than a week has passed since I left home, taking the train to the airport at five in the morning), so I ought to be used to it; and I am.

This place is, happily, so relaxed that I do not feel in the least bit out of place, as I sip a tall glass of watermelon juice and wait for the fish I have ordered to arrive. I read my book a bit, write a postcard to Daisy and try to relax in the here and now.

I am staying here for two weeks. That is, clearly, a long time. If I start to panic now because I am going to have to leave in fourteen days' time, I might as well not have come.

For a second I allow myself to imagine going home. I will, undoubtedly, be tanned. I will possibly look a little better, because the lovely food and the fact that I plan mainly to lie on the beach doing nothing means that some of my horrible splitting-up gauntness will have been softened away. I will have attained some perspective and wisdom, here on this beach, that will stay with me for ever. That is what I am banking on.

My journey back will be quicker. I am flying from Kota Bharu, which is somewhere to the north of here, on the mainland, back to Kuala Lumpur. Then I will hang around the airport for a few hours, or dash into the city for some last-minute present-shopping, before starting the international flight home. At some point, many hours after that, I will walk in through my own front door. The house will be empty, unoccupied for twenty-two days. The plants will be dead, of course, because it never occurred to me to get someone to come in and water them, though I could have done because I do, I remind myself, have friends. Even after everything that has happened over the past year, everything I have done, I still have some friends. Zoe, for instance, knows exactly where I am and approves of it.

I will walk in, and drop my backpack. There will probably be sand in it, from this very beach. Some of the sand I see now, when I look up from my postcard and out at the beach, will be coming home with me. Daisy will not be there. I will have a shower, put on some clean clothes and go to Chris's flat to collect her.

Meanwhile, however, I am here. I am here and, for the next two weeks, I have nothing to do but lie back and recuperate. I take deep breaths and remind myself to savour every moment.

*

Everyone seems friendly. I do not particularly talk to any of them. I eat my food and walk slowly up the small hill to my hut. Then I read for a bit longer, crawl under the mosquito net and go to sleep.

chapter seven

The days slip by. People leave the beach, and new people arrive. An Australian couple who are noticeable because they are older than everyone else turn up. Unfortunately for them, their names are Jean and Gene, and they seem to spend all their time fighting. I stay away from them, which is easy since they have booked one of the premium huts, at the other end of the beach, so I do not have to listen to them shouting obscenities at one another very often. Someone else's unhappy marriage is not a place I want to visit. I slip into a dream world, one in which I get to lie on the beach all day, eat my way through the menu, and drink fruit juice. The Americans stay there, still cavorting loudly on the sand and in the sea and enjoying their audience.

On the fourth day, I begin to think I should be doing something. I ought to be making the most of this time. People keep going out on snorkelling trips, and when they come back, they prattle on (if I can understand them, which I only can if they are native English speakers) about the Nemo fish and the turtles and the coral and the little friendly sharks, which sound like puppies the way they describe them. It is exactly what Ally said at the gallery. The trouble is, these snorkelling trips seem to last all day. I simply cannot force myself to spend a day away from my beach.

On day six, Edward, Jonah and Piet arrive. I recognise them at once from the boat trip. They wave to me as they jump on to the sand.

'Hi,' I say, barely bothering to raise my head from its comfy place on the towel.

'All right?' calls Edward, with a little wave and a lovely smile.

'Hi there, Esther,' says handsome Jonah, and I try not to simper.

I start to sit with the three of them sometimes, if I turn up in the café at the same time as them. They are easy company, and we while away the hottest part of the day playing cards or Scrabble.

A day or two later Katy turns up too and moves into the hut next to mine, though she keeps out of everyone's way even more than I do. I start to look at my life at home, and realise how screwed up it is. I suppose I need to go back and start getting it in order. This probably means I ought to start yoga and forgive myself for Daisy's messy childhood. She is, after all, fine. I text her and ring her, and I can hear from her voice that she is genuinely happy.

When I was pregnant, I used to imagine the baby being a girl. I have discovered since that most women assume they're having a girl, because it makes sense for a female body to grow a female infant: plenty of people I met on the baby circuit had been taken by surprise by the realisation that they had, internally, managed to grow a penis.

All the same, I happened to be right. Throughout the pregnancy, I had a very precise picture of what my daughter would be like. She would, I was certain, be a waif-like, sensitive creature who would be happy if she was curled up reading a book, or painstakingly practising her ballet. My imaginary daughter had fine blonde hair, and was tiny for her age, with pale skin and a button nose. I decided she had to be 'Daisy' because it was an appropriately pretty, translucent name for a fairy child: she would be my flower baby.

Chris said, 'Yeah, OK,' when I told him that I had been communicating with the baby from the inside, and that her name was non-negotiable. I think I would have had to announce a very outlandish name indeed for him to have bothered to object.

The moment she was born, before I even saw her, I knew that I had been entirely wrong. As soon as she was breathing air, I felt her presence on earth, her Daisy-like essence, and I knew exactly who she was. The fey fairy child melted into the corners of the room and evaporated.

Real Daisy shouted to me as soon as she was unleashed upon the world. She was solid and dark, and the moment she was in my arms she fixed me with a piercing stare, her brow furrowed into a frown. The real Daisy was, and is, a formidable creature. She hates all things pink and glittery, dismisses society's plans for her, rejecting ballet and Barbies and toy kitchens with barely a contemptuous glance. She holds on to the things she loves with a determined passion. She loves swimming, rap music and walking other people's dogs. She wears trousers and jumpers and anoraks, and if I didn't force her to let me brush her hair and tie it back, it would straggle across her face, the occasional tucking-behind-the-ears its only grooming.

The thought of her walking along the seafront from Hove into Brighton with a dog lead in each hand, struggling to speak authoritatively to her charges while her hair blows into her eyes (because her father will certainly not have bothered to brush it), makes me miss her intensely. She loves dogs. She doesn't mind picking up dog poo in plastic bags and disposing of it.

'I quite enjoy it, Mum,' she told me, laughing at my horror. 'Because it's the only time you ever get to pick up a poo.'

I long for her. I wrestle my longing under control, because apart from the thousands of miles between me and my daughter, the worst thing about my life at the moment is the fact that I am, before long, going to have to leave this island.

One night I am sitting alone in the café, drinking a rare beer which Jonah produced from a carrier bag after a trip to Coral Bay and handed to me. I am going over things in my head, wallowing in self-absorption.

'Mind if I join you?'

I look up and see that it is Katy.

'Of course not.' I push the other chair out with my foot, and she sits down.

'Sorry,' she says, with a warm smile like the one she gave me when we were waiting for the boat. 'You looked deep in thought, but all the other tables are taken. It was either ask you, or butt in on the honeymooning lovebirds.'

We both look over at the Americans' table. They are caressing one another's thighs.

'Yeah,' I agree. 'Better for you to sit here, I think.'

'So what brings you here on your own, Esther?' she says, declining half my can of beer. 'There aren't many of us lone women about. We should find some solidarity.'

I smile at her. 'Divorce,' I say. 'I spent my whole marriage imagining escaping like this. Then I realised I could actually do it. My daughter's with my ex, so there was nothing stopping me.'

'Good for you,' she says. 'And are you feeling nice and relaxed? You look it. I envy you, you know. Every day, just chilling with your book. You should be on an advert for this place.'

I grin. 'I love it here. It's put quite a few things in perspective.'

She looks at me with interest. 'Such as?'

I take a deep breath. I like Katy, and she is a safe stranger. I have not had a proper conversation with anyone since I have been away. It will be good to talk about this. She seems interested; and if I tell her my story, perhaps she will tell me hers. I would like that.

'When I was married to Chris – that's my ex-husband,' I say, taking a sip of beer, 'I was not at all happy. Nor was he. For some reason, though, we stuck together.'

'Because of your daughter?'

'If it wasn't for Daisy, we wouldn't even have stayed together more than a couple of weeks, I don't think.'

I remember Chris, pretty and carefree back then, without a care in the world. I remember myself the same way, dancing through the clubs of London in a short skirt. I was infatuated with him when we met, but I never even properly liked him, let alone loved him.

'But even with Daisy,' I continue, 'I have no idea why we limped on beyond her first birthday. She's ten. We split up when she was nine. We could have saved ourselves a huge amount of trouble. I know I never wanted to be divorced. It wasn't what I'd foreseen for myself – who does foresee it, I suppose? And Chris was from a very conventional background, and his parents would have been horrified. So we took the cowardly option, sank into a resentful misery and wasted our entire thirties on each other. I'm quite sure that he had affairs, but I never cared enough to find out. I should have had some myself, but I could barely get off the sofa most days. I suppose I was waiting for it to peter out.'

'And it did peter out,' Katy says, 'in the end.'

'It ended with a surprising bang, actually,' I say, draining the beer. 'A last flash of passion. I'd been drinking too much, and he'd been staying at work late, whatever that meant. One Friday night, he rolled in drunk at midnight, and I was passed out on the sofa, and something about the scene, even though it was one we had lived so many times before, set him off. We'd both had too much to drink. We hadn't spoken to each other properly for years. He looked at me and, he said afterwards, something snapped. He says now that it was because he could see the person I could have been, and instead there was this miserable person I'd become, and he felt responsible. I'm not sure he was really feeling quite so noble at the time, however. He started yelling at me. I woke up, and I started yelling back. Everything came pouring out, all the misery and the resentment; every single thing we hated about our life together. I can't remember the detail of it, but I remember feeling that a dam had been broken, and it was an enormous relief. My memories are hazy, but I must have got myself off the sofa. I don't know how long we were at it for. I do know that we were wrestling, pulling each other's hair, physically attacking one another and yelling abuse. And then I looked up and Daisy was standing in the doorway. Watching us. Utterly horrified and bewildered. It was the worst thing that has ever happened, the worst thing I've ever done by a million miles. I saw her there, and it was as if someone had injected ice straight into my veins. Our eyes met, and I was sober. I couldn't get Chris off me until I said "Daisy". Then he stopped all right.'

I have to stop speaking. I cannot confront this memory for a moment longer. I want to look at Katy, to see how shocked she is, but I am too ashamed even to raise my eyes from the table. There is a little beetle walking around the circumference of my glass. I watch it for a while. It goes all the way round. I wonder whether it thinks it's walking in a straight line.

'But Daisy,' she says. 'She's OK, isn't she? Children are resilient.'

At that I manage to look up at her, briefly, and smile.

'No one in the world is as resilient as my Daisy,' I tell

her. 'And I'm not just saying that to make myself feel better. She has her feet on the ground. She was massively upset, obviously. But she's the kind of girl who confronts things head on, thankfully, rather than bottling them up. Unlike both her parents. Who knows where she picked that trait up from? But I'm glad she did. So we had to talk her through it again and again. Chris moved out straight away. Both of us had had the wake-up call. We apologised to her, together and separately. And in the end, she forgave us. She announced it: "Mum, I've decided that I forgive you now. Just don't ever behave like that again, because you really let yourself down."'

Katy is laughing. 'She sounds wonderful!'

'She is. She was so relieved when Chris moved out and she got to spend time with each of us separately. Loads of her friends have divorced parents and apparently it's much cooler. She's been fine since then. I wasn't so great, I must admit. I've found it hard to pull myself into shape and be happy as a single woman at the end of her thirties. That's why I'm here, I suppose. To get myself together and look forward to the future, and be the mother Daisy deserves.'

Katy fiddles with the menu. 'Which sounds like a highly worthy project.'

'It is. And it's working. I hope.'

She strokes my arm. 'Of course it's working. Shall I tell you why I'm here? Just to remind you that no one has a straightforward life?'

I smile. 'Yes please!'

We order some food first, and wait until it arrives. The air is warm and I can smell the bougainvillea. I watch the

Americans get up from their table and hustle each other, giggling, on to the beach.

When we each have a plate of fish and rice and salad in front of us, and a glass of water, Katy looks to me, a lock of hair sticking to her cheek, and I nod.

'So,' she says. 'I recently split up with someone too. It's been incredibly difficult. We haven't got any children, so things are easier in that respect. Also my partner was a woman, so the dynamic was probably different. But we'd been together so long. And now we're not any more.' I see her make an effort to keep her equilibrium, and succeed. 'And that is quite hard, isn't it? When you suddenly have to see yourself as a lone person in the world again. Not part of a unit. At least you have Daisy. I suppose that means you'll always be part of a unit of some sort. Not me.'

I lean forward and touch her arm. She flinches slightly, but does not withdraw.

'It is hard,' I agree. 'Making that adjustment. I've found it almost impossible. Is it helping you, being here?'

She shrugs. 'Not as much as I'd hoped. No. You see, I still love her. That's probably the difference between my situation and yours.'

'So why did it end?'

Katy blinks hard, and I wish I had phrased my question more tactfully.

'She'd had enough. Essentially. I'm . . . well, I had a conventional upbringing, and I've always found it hard to reconcile the fact that I'd always been told homosexuality is unspeakable and horrible with my very pure feelings of love, and, indeed, lust. She hated the conflict I suffered over it, the fact that I couldn't tell my family to get stuffed. I adored her. I still do. I just couldn't quite be publicly proud of who I was. She felt that I was ashamed of her, that she was my guilty secret. It wasn't the case at all. In the end she'd had enough. She walked out on me and never came back.'

'Did you ask her to come back?'

Katy looks at me and laughs. 'Oh, I lost all dignity, believe me. I cried and begged and stalked. She'd made her mind up. Then she started seeing someone new. That was when I decided to get away.'

I sigh, and smile at her. She smiles back.

'I'm glad I met you,' I tell her.

'Me too,' she agrees, spearing a piece of fish and a red pepper with her fork. 'Solidarity in heartbreak.' Then something occurs to her. 'Hey,' she says. 'Have you done one of those snorkelling trips yet?'

'No. I've vaguely thought about it, but I haven't stirred myself to do one. You?'

'Well, I've been planning to do one. I was talking to Samad about it; you know, one of the guys who works here?'

I nod. 'The one with the little baby.'

'Yes. Well, he's actually thinking about setting up as a trip operator himself. He says that's where the money is. He also says the trips available here are all pretty identikit. He's planning a different one, something that shows you new stuff. He made it sound amazing.'

'Well, that sounds good. Can we go?'

She drops her voice. 'The best part? He wants to do a trial for the trip he's planning. Snorkelling, fishing, lunch on a deserted island. We can be his practice customers. How's the day after tomorrow for you?'

I look at her, and feel a smile spreading across my face.

'I wasn't going to tell anyone this,' I admit, 'but the day after tomorrow, I am pretty sure, is my fortieth birthday.'

Katy laughs and touches my arm.

'Then that's perfect,' she says. 'I'll talk to him again. We'll get it set up.'

chapter eight

Cathy

June 1988

They told us! I have never been happier. Everything I was worrying about has vanished, faded away. It is the truth, I know it. The truth is far better than anything I could possibly have imagined.

I no longer have to worry about a niggling desire to explore the world. I don't have to dread the mechanics of what marriage to Philip might hold for me. I do not have to pine about not being allowed to have a job, let alone a career, and wanting to go to university. None of that matters any more. I am completely free and I can look forward with happiness and excitement to unimaginable joy. Thank God for that – literally.

I am in the best place I could possibly be, the only place in the world. I looked at Martha's face last night, and I loved her. How could I ever have found her irritating and petty? I saw my feelings reflected in her: she loved me too, for the first time in her life. We are the luckiest people in the world.

Everything is about to change. 'Change' is too small a word for it. Everything is going to be transformed beyond all recognition.

Our arch-Father, Moses, the leader of our community and also biological father to many of us (including me), gathered the whole community together. All of us, eighty-three people, in one place. Children sat on the floor, adults on chairs, and Father Moses stood on the platform. Then he climbed up on to his chair and then stepped on to the table, and he stood on the table and put his arms up and shouted out.

I cannot repeat his words exactly, not even in my head, because they are too holy. But this is the Truth that he told us.

The Rapture is coming. The Lord is coming to earth to reclaim the faithful. On June the 21st, midsummer night, He will come. If I am worthy (and I know I am not, though I will try to be between now and then, a manoeuvre He will no doubt be expecting, but I believe him to be kind to repentant sinners, so it could go either way), I will be taken with the others to heaven, to dwell with Him for eternity. If I am not, I will be left on earth with the other sinners, and we will bear the effects of His wrath, which will be well deserved.

I would like to wish away all my previous heretical thoughts, but since God has seen them, of course, there seems no point. I am truly, truly repentant and I hope He sees this too. I wish I could control my mind completely. Sometimes I find myself thinking bad thoughts purely because I know it is of the utmost importance that I don't. I'll suddenly realise I've been daydreaming about going to university, and then I will kick myself. I don't mean to do it. I hope God realises that.

If I am left behind, I will know that it is what I deserve, and I will do my best for the other sinners when the Apocalypse happens.

What's more, Father Moses has given us work to do.

We have to tell the world the truth, to give the sinners a chance to repent. Father Moses says that Jesus, who visited him when he was watching the news on the television, told him that each one of us has to bring at least one former sinner into the compound. They have to be saved, to want to be saved. Each of us children has to bring someone from school, even Martha and me, who are just about to finish our exams and leave. 'No exceptions!' he roared, and we jumped in our skins, because it was the voice of Jesus speaking through Moses' mouth. At least, I think it was.

I am going to go to school tomorrow and give it my very best shot. A week ago, I would have felt myself being crippled with embarrassment at the very idea of trying to bring someone from school, a sinner from the outside world, into our Village. I wanted to belong in their world, not to bring them to ours. Now I know that it is the only way to save them. I cannot wait to get to school and talk. They will laugh, and for the first time in my life I can truthfully say that I don't care. I have never been this happy, never in my sixteen and a half years.

There are only seven days left until the End of the World, and that, it transpires, changes your perspective somewhat. I will go to school tomorrow and spread the word. Martha and I and Eve and Daniella will work together, talking to all the girls, while Philip, Simon and the others are going to talk to the boys. We sat in a huddle after the meeting, working out our strategy. It is important that every child in the school hears the future from one of us directly, because that will give each of them a chance to respond and it will leave less to the sort of stupid rumour that we can all too easily imagine.

We sat on the wooden floor in the vestry, all talking at once, all of us united, for the first time ever. I have never been as happy in my life as I was this evening, working together with my friends and colleagues. It would be lonely to be the only one at school. But we are going to work in pairs, and Martha and I are taking care of every girl in the fourth, fifth and sixth forms. Martha is my half-sister, although we are one big family here so the biological connection is less important than it is for people out there in the sinful world. We are not at all alike. I am taller than her, with light brown hair that used to be blonde when I was a child (and until now I have wished it still was, in my vanity). Martha is small and (though it doesn't matter, I am just describing her) fat. She has dark brown hair, which her birth mother, Judith, cuts in a pudding-basin cut, though I have always thought long hair would suit her better. But again, nothing matters now.

Oh, the months and years I have spent yearning for such shallow things as make-up and a stylish haircut: the best I have ever been able to do is to grow it long, and straight, and while I am supposed to have a centre parting, at school I part it on the left and pull it slightly over my face. Martha has enthusiastically reported back to the leaders and I have been in trouble for that.

I forgive her – of course I do, just as Moses and Cassandra forgave me my vanity. Because we are the only people who know the truth. The whole compound is filled with excitement and anticipation. The world is not going to end, but everything is going to change, at sunrise on the 21st of June. I cannot wait.

chapter nine

I wake up feeling happy, roll over in the semi-darkness and stare at the chinks of luminescent sunlight that are squeezing through the gaps around my shutters and making geometric patterns on the ceiling of my jungle hut. I can hear the rustle and chirp of the wildlife around me, and something scampers across the roof. That is probably what woke me up.

I sit up in bed in the tent of the mosquito net, and grin. This is my fortieth birthday. It is the day of the big trip. I am relaxed and languid, which is exactly the way I wanted to be when I reached this point.

I check the time – half past seven – and pull on my bikini and sarong for a quick swim before we leave at half past eight. I hope Katy has kept her promise not to tell anyone else about my birthday. I do not want the attention. I was delighted to be able to escape 'turning forty' at home. My well-meaning friends and my enthusiastic daughter would have demanded parties and fuss. I will telephone Daisy, at massive expense, much later in the day, when she is up. This will involve an exchange with Chris, who, although he is forty-three himself, I know will take the opportunity to mention middle age in a mocking tone as many times as he can possibly manage.

I unbolt my door. Every night, I carefully lock myself in, even though there is no glass in the windows – the very idea of glass in the windows of a cabin like this is ridiculous – and the shutters can only be closed by pushing them up against the window until they stick. Nobody could get in through the door without an axe or a battering ram, but anyone could push the shutter and saunter through the window. I make a conscious effort to dismiss those thoughts. This is a safe place and there are plenty of cabins nearby, and people would hear me if I screamed.

I love the feeling of the early morning. Everything is still and fresh. The air is warm, but cooler than it will be later. I walk down to the beach and stand on the sand and breathe. I close my eyes, and savour the warmth on my cheeks. The sea is pulling against the sand, making the most gentle lapping sound. It is completely different from the grey Channel at home, which, when it feels the urge, crashes against noisy, stony sand. This sand is so fine, so many millennia old, that the water barely whispers on it.

My sarong is crumpled on the white sand. I am in the embrace of the warm sea. I swim out, feeling the occasional tiny nips of whatever it is in the water that bites or stings almost imperceptibly, until I am level with the jutting rocks at the side of the bay.

Then I flip over on to my back and float at the mercy of the small waves, looking up at the sky.

'Happy birthday,' I whisper to myself. And I smile. It is going to be a very happy birthday indeed.

There are a few people having breakfast in the café by the time I get there, and I wish them all a good morning. The German couple whose names I have forgotten return my greeting, while the man out of the bickering Australians grins at me, and Katy invites me to join her. The excitement is written all over her face.

She leans towards me and stage-whispers: 'Happy birthday!'

'Thanks.'

'Ready for the day out? Have you got everything you need?'

I nod at the little bag by my feet. It is sagging emptily. This is because I cannot think of anything much that I will need at all.

I see that Katy has the remains of scrambled eggs and fruit on her plate, and I order the same. Katy's porcelain skin is tanned, and she looks relaxed and happy.

The German couple, the woman with the lemon-print bikini and her partner with the springy hair, are standing with their bags on the beach. As I watch, a water-taxi pulls up and they walk into the shallow water and throw their bags into it. The woman, whose name I have never learned, is wearing a short sundress decorated with pictures of cherries. Her hair is tied back to reveal a long, curved neck. She turns and waves to us.

'Have fun today!' she yells.

'We will!' Katy calls back. She looks at me. 'They wanted to come too, but they've got a plane to catch. Helga was really cross about it.'

'Who else is coming, then?' I ask.

'Oh, I'm not sure. Edward, the Scottish guy – he was keen.' Katy stands up. 'Anyway, shall we find out? Have you got everything?'

'Sunglasses,' I say. 'Sunscreen. Phone just in case Daisy sends me a birthday text. A bottle of water.'

She nods. 'That should do it. Travelling light.'

We meet at the end of the beach, close to my hut. Samad looks up as Katy and I approach across the sand, and gives us a huge grin.

'Katy!' he says. 'Esther! Thank you.'

The others all turn to us, and I am slightly dismayed to see that both the shouty Australians and Mark and Cherry, the amorous Americans, are here; apart from them, there is just Edward, Katy and me. It never occurred to me that either couple would join in a trip like this.

However, out of everyone on the beach, I would have chosen Edward and Katy to spend my birthday with. The others I will live with.

'Hi!' I say to everyone, and I make myself smile broadly around the group.

'G'day,' says the shouty Australian woman, though from her tone she might just as well have said 'I don't like you'. The others greet me in a more friendly way, and Katy grins and claps her hands.

'Everyone – it's Esther's birthday!' she announces, and

they all smile and say the right thing. I look at her, annoyed, because she knew I wanted to keep it secret. There is nothing I can do now, so I force a smile.

'All are here,' says Samad, and he turns and walks off. I follow at the back of the group. As we pass my cabin, the last one in the resort, an enormous lizard comes out of the jungle, makes a sharp left when it sees us and lopes off down the path.

'It looks like a dinosaur,' I say.

'They've been around since those days,' says Edward, turning in front of me. 'I'm sure I read that somewhere.'

I stop and stare at it. It is at least as long as Daisy would be if she lay down next to it; its legs are chunky, more like cats' than lizards' legs, and it is mostly powerful tail. It looks at me with a beady eye and stays absolutely still, as if frozen into place. The others walk on a little way. I am transfixed by the expression on its face. Daisy would have adored it. I take a quick photograph with my phone.

'Thanks,' I say. Then I realise I have been left behind. 'Bye then,' I say to the lizard. 'See you tonight.'

It turns and ambles back into the forest, moving more laboriously than you would expect from a lizard.

As I head around the corner and away from the cabins, someone behind me calls my name.

'Esther!' he shouts. I stop and look back, scanning the huts for the source of the cry. There are a couple of people on the beach. Then I see Rahim, who I think owns the resort, waving from the steps of the café.

He wants to talk to me. I lift a hand and wave over my head, then hurry after the others.

*

They are already on the next beach, climbing into a small fishing boat. It was clearly not built for eight, and the benches along the sides are already cramped. The cross Australians are on one side, the beautiful Americans on the other, and Katy and Edward are still on the beach. Katy has a collection of hut keys in her hand, all of them tied to large pieces of wood to make them unlosable.

'I'm going to go back and hand these in,' she says. 'Do you want to give me yours, Esther? I'll just say we're all off for a walk together. I can't bear the idea that they might fall into the sea.'

I laugh.

'I would never have thought of that.' I hand my key to her, and she runs off.

Samad is on the sand, eyeing up the boat.

'Esther,' he says, smiling at me. He is jumpy: I see his eyes flick anxiously after Katy.

'Yes, sorry. I stopped to look at the lizard.' I will not tell him, I decide, about his colleague shouting after me, because I do not want to make him worry about being in trouble. If Rahim says anything to Katy, she will be able to field his questions with more aplomb than I would.

'Edward – here,' Samad says, and Ed climbs aboard and sits in the appointed place. 'Katy will go there. Esther, we squeeze you in the middle. You are thin!'

'Cheers!' I will take my compliments where I can find them.

'Hop on in!' Mark instructs me. I have never seen the Americans up close before, though I have seen far more of their anatomy from a distance than they have ever seen of mine. Mark has glossy black hair and a rich, kempt look, while Cherry is perfectly toned and somehow, in spite of the lack of facilities here, manages to wear just enough make-up to make her look like a Hollywood actress playing the role of a woman on a paradise island. I wonder, in my jaded way, how long their marriage will last, and whether two years from now they will still be all over each other, ostentatiously being in love. I also want to know why they have come here for their honeymoon, rather than somewhere showier, but for the moment I let Samad give me a hand into the boat, and manage to park myself on the cross-bench perpendicular to Jean, who is skinny, with a bird-like face, and next to the space allocated to Katy.

'Ready to swim with the turtles and friendly sharks?' Mark says, fixing me with a dazzling smile. Up close, he even smells glamorous: he must be wearing cologne or something. It is jarring in these surroundings. 'And coral, and all the usual paradise paraphernalia? And we're stopping on one of those islands for lunch. Just us. Desert island. That's the thing that's swung it for Cherry and me.'

'Right.' I look forward to watching them having sex in a new location, then. From the corner of my eye I catch Jean having the same thought, and smirking.

Katy runs back smiling, and climbs in.

Samad starts the engine.

'You *have* got lunch,' Gene says to him, leaning forward. The Australian's ample stomach bulges over the waistband of his shorts, and wiry grey hairs grow out of the top of his T-shirt. 'We're not going to go hungry, are we?'

'Yeah,' Jean adds, rolling her eyes. 'You wouldn't like him when he's hungry. He's even worse than bloody usual.'

'Oh, will you listen to her?' Gene asks us. 'Don't marry, young Edward. You're not married, are ya?'

'I'm not,' Edward admits, and his reluctance at being drawn into the fight is almost tangible. I like him for that.

'Good job,' says Gene.

'Indeed,' Jean retorts.

I look at Katy, and then at Edward. I can see that all three of us are beginning to regret this.

The wind blows my hair back from my face. The engine whines and does not sound entirely healthy, but we move so I suppose it is all right. I turn back and watch the beach disappearing behind us. Soon we are round a corner of the headland, and it is gone.

I stare around without talking as we motor far out to sea, in waters that look almost deserted. Luckily for everyone, Jean and Gene lapse into silence too. Mark and Cherry are entwined and I try not to look at them, as it feels uncomfortable and voyeuristic to be so close. Sometimes there are other boats in the distance, but Samad explains that all the snorkelling trips visit the same spots, and that we are trying something different.

'They go to lighthouse, fishermen's village, romantic beach,' he says dismissively. 'They are lazy. Always "lunch in fishing village" because people say "oh lunch in fishing village is the real Malaysia". It is not! Just for tourists!'

'That's what I love about this,' Katy murmurs. 'The fact that we're not going along with the herd. Look at us – we're heading out into the ocean, to places that no one ever visits.'

'It is amazing,' I agree. 'Out on the water like this.' And it is. I could sit here and look around at the sea all day.

I am happy not to be on the circuit, meeting other boatloads of people at every spot we visit. When Pulau Perhentian Kecil is a barely perceptible line on the horizon, we stop, Samad throws down the anchor, and hands out snorkelling gear.

'You swim all around,' he says, sitting back and putting his feet up. 'You see everything. Then you come back.' He takes out a cigarette, hunts through his pockets for a lighter, fails to find one and puts it back in the packet.

'I haven't done this for years,' I say to Jean, who has whipped off the kaftan she was wearing, revealing a sturdy purple one-piece.

'Agh,' she scoffs. 'It's not exactly much of a skill, is it, darling? Just put the stick in your mouth and breathe. Like smoking!'

She pulls her mask down and grins at me. Then she turns to look at Gene, who is rocking the boat as he nearly trips, taking off his shorts.

'Oh for God's sake, you idiot!' she yells. 'You're going to tip up the bloody boat, you moron! Do you want to capsize us all? Is that it? Cretin.'

Gene turns and makes an ugly face at her. She juts her chin back at him and they glare at one another. I wonder if this is what the dying days of my marriage looked like to outsiders.

Instantly, I know for certain that the answer to that question is a resounding 'no'. Chris and I never had anything approaching the passion that these two share. I would have relished making scenes like Jean and Gene's. It was only the death throes of our relationship that took us anywhere near here, and no one witnessed that, apart from the sole person who would have been, and was, damaged by it.

I take a deep breath and jump over the side of the boat, into the warm, clear water.

It envelops me. I float on my back and stare up into the blue sky. There are a couple of wispy clouds, and nothing else at all. I feel the sun hot on my face, and am glad I am coated in high-factor sunscreen.

It is glorious out here. I adore being so far away from land, from everything. There is a twinge of fear that goes with it, but I can see the boat and so I push the fear away.

Edward swims up next to me, doing a businesslike front crawl. He stops and treads water. When he slicks his hair away from his face, water trickles down the back of his neck. Katy swims up next to him, smiling broadly.

'Out in the elements,' she says happily. 'That's something, isn't it? Just us and the sea and the sky.'

I am trying not to be afraid of all the water underneath us.

'The sharks they get here,' I say. 'They are OK, aren't they?'

Edward chuckles.

'You know what?' he says. 'When you said that, my very first reaction was to dive down and grab your leg. But I didn't do it! How cool is that?'

I frown at him. 'What, I'm supposed to congratulate you? For not acting like an eleven-year-old boy?'

'Yep!'

'Congratulations, then.' We both laugh.

'Thanks.' He swims away, then turns to call, 'By the

way, the sharks are fine!' before diving down under the water.

'There's nothing dangerous,' Katy says. 'Really, there isn't. Come on, do you want to have a look around together?'

I nod. 'Thanks. I don't normally get freaked out by things, but this is kind of odd. The huge amount of water under us, the fact that it's all full of creatures down there and we don't belong. And knowing that we're so far from anywhere where we could . . . I don't know, walk and stuff.'

'Oh,' she says, 'but that's the joy of it.' And she turns and starts to swim.

I am not one of life's swimmers: I did not even learn to swim until I was nearly twenty, and that was only when I realised everyone else could do it. I learned because I wanted to start driving lessons, and decided that you should not learn to drive without first being able to swim. The life skills do not come in that order. Swimming was more elemental, and also cheaper.

I was an au pair at the time, on the outskirts of London.

'We'll pay for you to do a course or something,' Mrs Tao offered, breezily, soon after I started the job. 'That's what our girls normally do, though ordinarily it's an English course, which naturally you, Esther, don't need! So what do you think? French or something?'

I smiled at her. I liked living in their house. It was spacious and airy, and I had the entire top floor to myself.

'Swimming,' I said. 'I can't swim.'

'Done,' she replied at once. 'And how on earth did you manage to grow up without learning to swim?'

She never waited for the answer, so that was all right.

I hated my lessons at first, hated standing in the shallow end with an odd cross section of the non-swimming population (an old man; a teenage boy from a land-locked African country; a nervous woman a decade my senior, and others), all of us watching the patronising instructor who started her first lesson with the words: 'Now, as you'll all be aware, this –' and she splashed the surface with her hand, '– is *water*.' Yet when I first made it across the pool, I felt as though I had won an Olympic gold medal. I drive without thinking about it now, but when it comes to swimming, I am still a little wobbly.

The sun is hot on the top of my head. I have been daydreaming, and Katy is swimming around slowly, her face in the water and her snorkel stick poking out.

When I swim over and join her, peering through the screen of my snorkel mask, I immediately realise what all the fuss has been about.

There is a cloud, a shoal, whatever you are supposed to call it, of tropical fish, directly below me. The clown fish are tiny, much smaller than I would have supposed them to be, back in the days when I used to watch *Finding Nemo* with Daisy. And there are millions of others: blue fish, gold fish, shimmering silver fish. There are huge ones and minuscule ones. Fish that are shaped like proper fish, and odd ones with lumps and bumps all over them. There is coral, utterly unlike the dead white coral that is all over the beaches: it is alive, bright, moving.

I swim away from Katy, away from everyone, my face still in the water. I get used to breathing through the snorkel. It stops feeling scary and starts being normal. Occasionally water will splash into the top of it, and the first time I panic when I inhale it unexpectedly, but when I discover how easy it is to bring my face to the surface and sort it out, I stop worrying. This is a glorious way to spend a day. I become entranced by the comings and goings in the deep. I want to see turtles, and even sharks, because nothing in this glorious place could possibly hurt me.

I follow one knobbly fish, swimming above it as it makes its way somewhere, purely because I like its spectacularly ugly face and its funny lumpiness. Its body sometimes looks brown, sometimes gleaming gold. It moves lazily from side to side as it swims, over coral, through the middle of smaller fishes. I lose myself completely in shadowing its journey, wondering whether it is aware of my presence. I must be cutting out some of its light when I am directly above it. Perhaps I am no more than a cloud in the sky would be to me. I focus on its world, the colours, the dangers and the predators. I wonder whether it eats smaller fish.

When it abruptly speeds up and darts away from me, I resurface.

I am alone in the middle of the ocean. At first I smile: this is proper holiday bliss. Then, treading water, I spin around, looking for the boat. When I don't see it, I spin again, scanning the horizon. There is an island in the far distance, though I have no idea if it is Perhentian Kecil or a barren rock, and a strip of land that may be the mainland, far away against the sky.

There is nothing else.

I feel the depths of the ocean below me. A hundred thousand fish are here, and me. The notion of sharks no longer seems charming. My breathing comes faster. I can feel the sun burning where my parting is, on the top of my head. I lie on my back and try to calm myself by looking at the sky.

I cannot have swum as far as all that, because I never swim far. I must be near the boat. I ought to be able to see it; but there is no sign of it. I remember the story of the divers in Australia who were left behind because someone counted the wrong number of shoes in the boat.

I know that something has gone horribly wrong. As I swing myself back to an upright position, I realise I have to try to swim to safety. The island in the distance is my only option.

chapter ten

I am trying to do a front crawl, because I am pretty sure that that is the only way to get somewhere fast, but the island is no closer and I am exhausted.

When I hear the distant whine, I hardly dare hope, and keep my face set in the direction in which I am travelling, keep chugging away at my woeful crawl, until it is too close to ignore. Then I turn.

'Esther!' Jean is yelling. 'For Christ's sake!'

'Going somewhere?' calls Mark, leaning over the side of the boat, his teeth glinting in the sunlight. Samad grins at me and manoeuvres the boat alongside me.

'You said you weren't a good swimmer,' says Katy gently, as the boat pulls up next to me and Samad reaches out to help pull me in. It is neither easy nor elegant, but I am heaved over the side in the end like a massive tuna, and we don't quite capsize.

'But you've travelled an incredible distance,' Ed says as I get up and sit on the plank. I am trembling all over, and I feel ridiculous.

'Sorry,' I tell them all, looking down at my feet. 'I had no idea. I lost touch with everything. It was like being in a dream.'

'You raced away so fast – you looked like a woman on a mission,' says Katy, laughing at me. 'What were you up to? What happened in your dream?'

They all look expectant. There is nothing to do but tell the truth.

'I was following a fish,' I admit.

There is a brief silence. Gene chuckles.

'Hey,' says Cherry. 'That's good enough for me. Was it a funny-looking one?'

I nod, staring at my feet with their chipped pink varnish.

Edward puts a warm hand on my still-wet shoulder. I lean into him, grateful.

'Where was it going?'

'I think it noticed me in the end and it swam away. Probably just as well.'

'Indeed,' says Gene. 'It would have taken you to the Philippines if you'd carried on that way.' Although I still feel remarkably silly, the atmosphere between us all seems to have lightened. We feel less like a random collection of people and more like a group.

'Sorry,' I tell them, but I am smiling now. 'I'm the stupidest person in the world. You were always going to find that out at some point.'

At the next snorkelling stop, I am careful to keep close to the boat. Katy stays with me, though we do not talk much. I keep bobbing up to the surface and checking where everyone else is. Mark and Cherry swim a little way away and giggle together. Jean and Gene head in opposite directions and ignore each other so pointedly that I know they must be thinking, obsessively, of one another. Edward goes furthest, but comes back before he goes out of sight, and Samad stays on the boat, lying back with his eyes closed and the sun on his face. I watch some fish, look for the elusive turtles, and when I get bored of it, I climb back on to the boat and sit back, with Samad, who is dozing.

'I am forty,' I whisper to myself. It doesn't feel that way. Has it always been like this? I wonder. Has forty always looked old when you're younger, and felt young when you get there? Some days I feel a hundred years old, but mostly, I am exactly the same as I was when I was seventeen. Forty is, after all, going to be fine.

It must be about midday. Daisy will be waking up soon. I look at my phone, hoping for a message from her. It has a tiny amount of reception, but nothing has arrived.

Samad's eyes open suddenly, and he sits up, perfectly alert.

'OK!' he says, grinning at me. 'Lunch?'

I am starving.

'Lunch!' I agree. My birthday lunch. He starts the engine, which is the signal for everyone else to swim back, and we set off towards an island on the horizon. It is the only piece of land we can see at all: this is the most remote place I can possibly imagine.

'How old's your baby, Samad?' I ask, as I am sitting next to him.

'She is five weeks old.' He is proud. 'Very good baby.'

'Five weeks!' I coo. 'Tiny! How gorgeous.' And it is gorgeous, I think. Having a new baby is like nothing on earth. It forces you to live in a strange hyper-reality in which everything revolves around the newcomer's needs.

'Do you have other children?'

'Yes. Two others. All girls. Four and two years old.'

'Wow,' I say. I sound impressed and jealous even though I am profoundly glad that I only did it once.

Around the other side of the island, he approaches the beach carefully, slowing the engine so we appreciate our first sight of our destination. This is a perfect place, a genuine desert island. With no landmarks at all, I am completely disorientated. There is no sign of the long Malaysian peninsula that is the mainland, and no trace of Perhentian Kecil. I wonder if this means we are facing due east, towards (according to Gene) the Philippines, but in fact we could be facing anything, and we are definitely facing nothing. Nothing is close enough to be seen. The island is small, and as far as I have seen, covered in dense jungle apart from this beach. It is an inspired place to stop for lunch.

On my fortieth birthday, I say in my head, I had lunch on a remote paradise island in the South China Sea.

We pile off the boat and on to the white beach. Everything is silent. This feels like a place that is not used to people. For a moment I wonder whether we should be here. This beach would have looked exactly as it does now, hundreds of thousands of years ago. There has never been electricity here, or a house or a shop or the internet. It is nature in its purest form.

The sand is white and hot, so that you cannot walk on it with bare feet. The water is clear, clearer even than it is back at the resort. The air feels different in my lungs, far from all sources of pollution apart from us, though I am quite sure I am imagining that.

Nothing feels quite real. The jungle is making the same chirping, rustling sounds as the one on Perhentian Kecil, and I decide to keep well away from it. I picture the dinosaur lizard I spoke to this morning, and imagine its bigger, more savage cousins living in the interior of this island. There could be actual dinosaurs. Anything could be there.

Samad bustles around setting up lunch, declining offers of help and shooing us away. He has unloaded four fishing rods, with the lines and hooks and everything that goes with them. We are, I think, supposed to attempt to fish for extra lunch, but I cannot be bothered with that, not least because he has clearly catered for the fact that we are unlikely to catch anything. I go to sit on the hot sand with Katy instead, and we kick back on our sarongs and talk, in a desultory and lazy fashion, about what it is that makes this scene – the desert island, the sand, the sun, the sea – the epitome of the idea of heaven in our culture.

'I wonder,' I say, 'whether we see the place where land and sea meet as "paradise" because life started by crawling out of the sea, on to the sand.'

Katy laughs.

'Um, probably not, Esther,' she says. 'And anyway, that's just a theory. I think it's probably because people go to beaches to laze around, and there's nothing much to do when you're on a beach, which really is many people's idea of heaven. I bet that people who live here – not here, obviously, no one lives here, but back on the main island – don't see it that way. I bet they don't look at the beach and say, "ahhh, bliss".'

'They look at the beach and see fat white people who fancy a beer,' I posit. 'They would probably see a completely different landscape as heaven.'

'What, though?' Katy wonders. 'It's hardly going to be central London, is it? My old street in Hackney? No one would sigh at that.'

'I think if you lived here, and if you actually had to work, you'd find yourself hankering after mountains. The Himalayas or something. Let's ask Samad,' I suggest.

At that moment, he calls us over.

'Everybody!' he says. 'Um, I am sorry. I have a question.'

We all wander over, ready to help. When we are within conversing distance, Samad smiles an embarrassed smile, and says, 'OK, I am sorry to say that I need to ask if anybody has with them a lighter, or perhaps some matches.'

He has set the lunch out on the beach, and I am impressed and surprised by the care he has taken over it. He is clearly serious about his new venture. He has brought an ice box filled with fish (on the correct assumption that we would not bother to try to catch anything) and pieces of meat, as well as a tupperware box of salad and a cardboard box of fruit. A second ice box contains bottles of water and cans of soft drinks.

He has brought a small barbecue, and coals and wood to burn in it. It is, however, useless in its current state.

'I don't understand,' he explains. 'I have a lighter this morning. I keep it in the packet. With my cigarettes. But it goes. I have the cigarettes. But no lighter. But it is always in the packet.'

'You must have left it on the beach or something,' says Cherry. 'Or it fell out. Did you check the boat?'

'Every inch of the boat. Every compartment. Every place possible. Anybody?'

'*We* don't smoke,' announces Mark, looking expectantly at everyone else.

'I tried to towards the end of my marriage,' I tell them, for some reason, 'but I couldn't. Just didn't like it. It was annoying. I wanted to be a smoker: it fitted in with my self-loathing. I had to drink instead.'

'Good girl,' Jean tells me. 'Gene's a smoker at heart but I didn't allow him to bring his filthy habit on holiday with us. Doesn't stop him sneaking off when he thinks I'm not looking, the underhand bastard.'

We all look at Gene, instantly elevated to being our best bet. He shakes his head, regretful.

'Not today,' he says. 'Knew I'd never get away with it. Wish I'd given it a go.'

That only leaves Edward and Katy.

'Sorry, guys,' Edward says. 'I may be a Scot, which of course means I have deep-fried Mars Bars for breakfast and brush my teeth with golden syrup, but I'm a relatively clean-living one. No smoking here.'

'And not me. I've never smoked,' says Katy. 'Although now you're all looking at me with those imploring eyes, I'm really, *really* wishing I did.'

The fish look fresh and tantalising in the ice box. Samad replaces the lid before the insects find them.

'I am sorry,' he says, and he looks mortified. 'I go back and find a light? One hour? You can wait one hour? Or you just eat the small lunch?'

'Let's have the small lunch,' I suggest, looking around. 'Look, we've got salad and fruit. It all looks beautiful. We're not going to die, are we, if we have salad for lunch? Don't bother to go all the way back, just for a lighter. We could always make a barbecue on one of the empty beaches when we get back later, and cook all this then. We don't need to waste it. And we could catch some fish of our own later, too.'

I look round the little group, waiting for back-up. Cherry agrees at once. Her skin is glistening, tanned and toned, and she is, I think, almost impossibly beautiful.

'Absolutely,' she says, and I am not sure her accent is Californian. I think I have been assuming she is from California purely because she is blonde and toned. 'Do not even think about doing that, Samad. We'll be just fine with what we have here.'

No one else agrees, least of all Samad.

'But,' he says, 'this is practice run for my new work. We must do it right. Now I learn: always check for the lighter.' He laughs, his face suddenly crinkled and bright, in spite of our predicament. 'Good lesson.'

'Maybe we should let Samad go,' says Katy, pressing her hand on to his shoulder. 'Let him have a proper run-through of his expedition. We don't mind what we have for lunch – of course we don't – but that's not the point. The point is that Samad needs to do this properly, because that's what we're here for, and what's an hour, after all?'

'I'm with you, Katy,' Jean agrees. 'He wants to go back for it, don't you, darl? So go back for it. Look around you! We can wait it out here, can't we? It's not exactly sitting on a shoddy plastic seat at Adelaide bus station at five in the morning – which incidentally we have done, and for longer than an hour, too, thanks to the way my husband organises his bloody trips. So we kick back on the sand for an hour? Lie back, bit of a siesta? Fine by me.'

'Yeah,' agrees Edward. 'It won't be an enormous hardship. Do what you want, Samad. But if you go, fetch, like, ten lighters or something. Leave them hidden all over the beach. Then this will never happen again.'

Samad laughs, a bit sheepishly.

'One hour,' he says. 'You wait. I am sure I have lighters this morning. But I will be back – with much fire.'

He steps into the boat and starts the engine, and we watch him motoring off, out to sea and round to the left. I glance at the others. Jean and Katy have both got books out of their bags and have settled back on the sand. I wish I had brought a book with me. I check my phone, which, unsurprisingly, has no reception, then I lie back on the hot beach and look at the sky. It is the darkest blue, with not the wispiest hint of a cloud.

When I prop myself up on my elbows, I see that Edward is swimming methodically around the bay. He swims out as far as the jutting rocks, across to the other side, back in, and across the shallow part. He does it again and again.

Gene is walking about, exploring at the edge of the jungle, which makes him braver than I am. I have a nagging fear that since the creatures in that jungle have probably never seen humans, they might attack us on sight. There must be thousands of them, so they would definitely win.

Mark and Cherry have disappeared by themselves, for which I suppose we should be grateful.

My stomach rumbles so loudly that I am sure the other two sunbathers must hear it, so I laugh and say: 'If he doesn't come back soon, I'm going to start on the fruit.'

'Go ahead,' says Gene, sitting down next to us. 'Grab a banana if you're hungry.'

This is the most I have ever heard him say in a normal voice.

'I might, actually,' I agree. 'It seems like ages since breakfast.'

The banana is black on the outside but just right on the inside. I try to make it last, but it is gone in seconds.

I lie back, close my eyes and wait. Samad will be here soon.

'The liar,' Jean says, and her voice wakes me up. I have no idea where I am. I wake up feeling hot, and aware that I am lying on my sarong, on sand. It takes me several befuddled seconds to make sense of anything. 'He said he'd be an hour. Anyone notice what time he left? It's certainly more than an hour ago.'

I remember. It is a beach, but not our normal beach. Even then, I don't begin to worry, not at all.

'It can't be much more than an hour, you fucking fusspot,' says Gene. 'Give the poor man a bloody chance.'

I am more concerned about the way Gene is speaking to his wife than about when Samad is coming back. None of us are worried about that; not at all.

chapter eleven

As the sun is starting to sink in the sky, and we are still waiting for him, the anxiety begins to niggle.

'He'll come,' says Katy, her eyes wide. I can see from the set of her jaw that she is strained, but she is determinedly optimistic. 'Of course he will. He'd hardly . . .'

I keep checking my phone, just in case, but it does not miraculously receive a signal. Ed and Cherry also have phones with them, and neither of them work either. No phone company would send a signal out here. There is nothing we can do but wait.

'I should have brought *my* phone,' Mark announces unhelpfully. 'I bet that would have worked. My phone is the greatest.'

No one bothers to tell him to shut up, though I see even Cherry roll her eyes. Here, perhaps, is where harsh reality starts to intrude on newly-wed bliss.

I am sure I am not the only one to have started cataloguing reasons for Samad's non-appearance, in my mind.

Reason one: the engine on his boat was definitely

sounding dodgy. I noticed that this morning. He could be drifting out at sea, unable to reach the mainland (this is by far the most likely scenario, in my opinion).

Solution: he had a phone with him. And even if he has no coverage, he will attract the attention of a passing boat sooner or later.

Result: he will come back, or get someone else to come and pick us up.

Reason two: he got back to the mainland, went to collect his lighters and suffered some kind of freak accident. He might, for instance, not have wanted to draw attention to himself at the resort, and thus he could have got on the moped I have seen him riding, and whizzed along the jungle path to his home in the village. He could have come off his moped and banged his head.

Solution: as long as he isn't dead, and does not have amnesia, he will come back for us.

Result: we might end up being here overnight, unless he is dead, in which case it might take a bit longer. Even then, his family will know about us and they will make sure we are collected. People only get amnesia in films, so we should be all right on that front.

Reason three: there was an emergency with one of his children, and he forgot about us.

Solution: he will deal with the emergency, and send someone to fetch us.

I stop the speculation, and tell myself sternly that people in real life are not at all likely to die out of the blue.

'He'll come for us,' I say, with all the desperate confidence I can muster.

'Of course he will,' Edward agrees. 'Now. What are we

going to do for food, while we wait? We've got all these lovely fishies. Anyone know how to make a fire by rubbing sticks?'

'Of course we don't,' says Mark, and this is the first time anyone has sounded angry. Until now, we have been ruthlessly polite to one another. 'Isn't that the entire fucking point?'

'Er. Gene and I have done it, in the past,' says Jean, sounding more hesitant than usual. 'But I'm not sure I could manage it. I'll have a go. The sun's still hot enough, at least.' She half-smiles. 'I don't suppose anyone has a magnifying glass?'

Mark snorts, and there is a general, sorry shaking of heads.

'If we had a fucking magnifying glass . . .' Mark mutters.

'No,' she continues, 'I thought not. No mirrors? In that case, may I use one of these cans of drink?'

The air is thick with scepticism as Gene hoists himself up from the sand and grabs one of the cans of Coke that Samad has left in a box on the beach. Together, without a word to each other or to the rest of us, they get to work, polishing the bottom of the drink can, using a small piece of chocolate from the side of the cool box, followed by the edge of Jean's sarong.

I sigh and lean back. The chances of this working are, surely, zero. I watch thin, blonde Cherry leading Mark away by the hand to keep him from heckling.

When she is satisfied with the (admittedly impressive) sheen on the bottom of the can, Jean hands it to me, telling me to 'Hold that and don't touch the shiny part,' and the two of them set off to the edge of the jungle. I sit, clutching the can, and wait. My eyes are still scanning the horizon, constantly. I think there is an exponentially high chance of Samad returning before they get back with whatever they have gone for, and this thought buoys me in an illogical way.

'He *will* come,' Katy almost whispers, as she sits beside me. I look at her, and see that her eyes, too, are fixed on the horizon.

'I know,' I say. We stare, side by side, both of us willing his boat to edge around the corner.

But it is Jean and Gene who come back, twenty minutes later, their arms full of dry leaves from the jungle.

'Not easy to find these,' says Gene, dropping them with a sigh. 'Lucky it hasn't rained today.'

Jean sits next to me, and takes back the can.

'You know what to do,' she says to her husband. I do not even really want to watch, as I am embarrassed for them, but it turns out that I cannot look away. She holds a dead frond of palm tree in front of the can, and angles it until the sunlight, which is coming strongly from disturbingly low in the sky, bounces off, and on to the leaf.

Edward and Katy move closer, too.

After a long, long time, the leaf starts to smoke. I lean in, kneeling up beside them, amazed as the smouldering leaf begins to glow. Then, suddenly, it is alight: the flame is tiny, but it is there. Jean shields it with her hand, cupping it and moving slowly to the pile of dry leaves.

Now it is as good as a match.

We all stare as she lights leaf after leaf, until enough of them catch fire properly. Gene has built a cage of sticks all around them. The sticks start to crackle. There is a fire. They have actually built a fire on the beach.

Gene grins up at us. We all gaze, mesmerised, forgetting everything else for a moment. There was nothing, and then there was fire. It feels as magical to me as it must have done to the cavemen.

'Don't just stand there!' he roars. 'Get to it! Dry sticks, twigs, branches, whatever you can find. And fast! Dry, remember! Dry!'

By the time we have a proper, roaring bonfire, the sun has vanished behind the bulk of the island, and the light it has left behind is fading fast. The flames are leaping up, and we are all making forays into the jungle, which is now alive with hissing, chirruping, otherworldly noises, and coming back with arms full of wood. Much of it is wet, but we bring it anyway.

I hate being in the jungle. It terrifies me far beyond reason. Yet I force myself to do it, sticking as close to Katy as I possibly can. I try not to let anyone see the depths of my dread and horror.

When Samad comes back, he will see the fire; it will allow him to navigate to us, in the darkness. That is why we are doing it.

'He's not coming.'

I wince at those words, and pretend Mark has not spoken.

'He probably won't be coming tonight,' Katy agrees, hesitantly.

'No shit,' Mark agrees, and he sits down, beside Katy, next to the fire. We are cooking the fish on it, and it smells incredible. I am starving. If I could be sure of being rescued in about an hour, I would be enjoying myself enormously.

'And you have to ask yourself, Katy,' Mark continues, 'why is he not coming tonight? Why in the world would he shoot off to fetch a lighter and never come back? I've been running over and over it in my head, and I do not believe there is a benign solution to this conundrum.'

As a mother, I automatically want to dispense comfort. Thus I cannot help myself stepping quickly in.

'I don't know what scenarios you're working on, Mark, but I think he's very likely to be back for us soon. Say he had an accident and is in hospital or something. He has a family. He was telling me about them. He has a wife and three daughters, and his brother and his family live with them too. He wants to set up as a tour operator because he wants to make more money for them all, and tourism is the only way to do that here. So he would not have set off with us, on his inaugural tour, without telling them what he was up to. Which means that, even if we have to camp out here overnight, someone will know we're here. Samad's wife and his brother. They'll come and fetch us, or send someone else to do it. Maybe his baby's ill and he's got caught up with that? He'll remember us. There's no possible scenario in which that doesn't happen.'

There is a little sigh.

'Thanks, Esther,' says Katy.

'Yeah, that makes sense.' Edward sounds grateful.

'Absolutely,' agrees Cherry. 'We'll have a little adventure, and enjoy being rescued in the morning. In fact this will be a night we'll never forget.'

'Uh-huh,' says Mark. 'Well, Esther, I do hope you're right. In every scenario, we are camping out on the beach tonight, yes? So we may as well get on with it. Try to make it into a great spiritual awakening, or something.' His voice is mocking.

Soon it is pitch black. The jungle is phenomenally noisy. An enormous lizard slinks out on to the beach, looks at us with a beady eye and turns away. Something yells 'Gecko!' so loudly that I jump: although I have seen and heard these geckos – lizards that are smaller than their voices sound – back at the resort, there they were an entertaining novelty, and now we are on their patch. They sound nearly human, and very creepy.

'The key thing,' says Jean, 'is not to let it spook you. This is not so very different from where we woke up this morning. All that's missing is the structure of the hut around you. We can all lie down here and sleep on the sand. It's good for the soul, and as Esther says, it's only until tomorrow. If you have a sarong, I'd put it over yourself, not under, to keep the mossies away. Don't get spooked. We're going to be all right.'

The sky is alive with stars. There are so many that I find it impossible, as I lie awake on my back, not to be happy. I am part of the cosmos, camping out on a beach, sleeping under the heaven's embroidered cloth for the first time in my life. I can picture Daisy at home, perhaps watching the same stars and thinking of me (in fact it is still daytime at home, and she would never look at the stars and think of me, but I am trying to create a cosmic connection and so must ignore inconvenient realities). She will be thinking of me, because it's my birthday. She will have texted or called, and she will be wondering why I have not replied. I try to send her a telepathic explanation.

There is no point staying awake in the dark, now that we have eaten all the food.

We lie around the fire in the warm night air. Mark and Cherry huddle up together, a little distance from us, under two huge beach towels. Jean and Gene pick spaces resolutely apart from one another. Katy, Edward and I lie in a line, our heads towards the fire, and Katy wriggles close to me so that her towel covers us both. It is more reassuring than my flimsy sarong.

I whisper my thanks, unsure of who is already asleep.

'When I wanted to do something different today,' I add, up close to her, 'this is not quite what I had in mind.'

She giggles. 'It's quite something, though, isn't it?' she whispers. 'Amazing things happen when plans go wrong. And you realise you can't control it all after all, and you just have to live in the moment and do what you can.'

'Yes,' I agree, 'though I'll be pretty happy to see that boat in the morning.'

'Oh yes,' Katy agrees. 'Bet you won't forget this birthday.'

'Happy birthday Esther,' says Edward, drowsily, and everyone joins in. I drift off to sleep with their words echoing around my fuzzy brain.

chapter twelve

Cathy

June 1988
Four days to go

They are all laughing at us: I leave school every day wanting to cry. I manage not to, however, because I know that my feelings are nothing. My tears, if I let them come, would be for the poor arrogant sinners who are about to realise the truth. They think we are ridiculous, and they point and stare and giggle at us all the time. They think I am upset about that. I am not.

They could be taken to heaven to sit with Jesus for eternity – they *really could* – but they are blind to the truth. They do not care. They are condemning themselves to eternal misery, just because it's easier to chuckle at the weirdos than it is to listen to what we say.

Now I know why Cassandra has the name she does. Although she was secular, Cassandra was condemned to tell the truth and never to be believed. I am Cassandra myself, now. We are all Cassandra.

I have realised the harsh truth of God's word. Life is not easy and most people are not good. The lazy path that you could unthinkingly walk is the one that takes you directly to damnation.

God does not make it as simple as people think He does. He will not take just anybody. He gives us our time on Earth to prove ourselves, and He does not hesitate to damn those who are found wanting. However, if I can save one soul (and after today I believe that I can), then I will have riches beyond anything any human can imagine.

I did my last exam today. I did my best because I wanted Him to see that I was good.

I have found one person who is interested in seeing the truth. Many others have pretended. Yesterday, one of the year four girls told Martha she was interested in finding out more. Martha brought her straight to me and we explained it. She asked lots of questions. We answered them all, falling over ourselves in our excitement, knowing that all of this would be worth it a million times over if we could save just one soul.

Then she started to giggle. After that, her friends, who had been listening from the other side of a door, all burst out laughing. The whole thing was a massive joke.

They thought it was at our expense. I started muttering prayers then and there, trying to intercede with God on their behalf. They have no idea what they are doing, I know. Since we found out that this was going to happen, I have felt myself possessed by the divine. I live on a different plane, now. I think that this is how other people feel when they are 'in love', but this love is a million times more intense.

Eva and Daniella have been having better luck with the younger ones. They have been banned from talking about it at all, because some of their teachers complained that the children were getting scared and excited and telling everyone the world was about to end. There was a lot of energy around at the lower end of the school, and when all mention of it it was forbidden by the teachers, that made it a thousand times more interesting to the other children. None of us have ever been subversive before. We have always been straighter than straight, squarer than square. Now we are a bit naughty.

'Oh for God's sake,' Mr Stephenson said today, and we boggled at his profanity. 'I do not want to hear one single word about the . . .' here he clearly censored himself, 'apocalypse!'

The teachers even spoke to Cassandra and the others about it.

'Mass hysteria,' they said. 'Highly damaging.' The adult Villagers were pleased with us.

Eva and Daniella have at least five new friends who will be joining us on Tuesday. I only have one person – but one is enough. She is Sarah. Sarah has white-blonde hair with black roots, and her ears are pierced three times in each one. I have always liked her, because she is kind and thoughtful, though I have never had very much to do with her because we live at opposite ends of the spectrum. Sarah often doesn't bother with her homework, she works when she feels like it and she is rude to teachers most days. I do everything I am supposed to do, put my hand up only when I am certain I know the right answer, and I never, ever misbehave. I would be in so much trouble at the Village if I acted like Sarah does. Before we knew about the Rapture, I used to envy her slightly.

But it was Sarah who walked up to me at lunchtime today, chewing gum, and said: 'The end of the world? How does that work, then?'

I looked at her, checked no friends were lurking ready to laugh and thought that she was probably teasing. I started to explain all the same. She listened and nodded.

'I've never been that into God and shit,' she admitted, popping her gum, 'but it's interesting. I mean, the world's got to end at some point, right? So maybe it *is* now. How cool to be around when it happens. I hope you're right about it. I quite like the idea of flying to heaven. And I have had this really, really strong feeling lately that there's something massive about to happen. Something bad. If you guys can turn it into something good, I'm there.'

She's coming home with me after school tomorrow to find out more.

'Won't tell my mum that's where I'm going, though,' she said. 'She would literally go apeshit.'

Martha is jealous that I've got Sarah. She hung back after school to try to catch a few more younger ones.

If I can save Sarah's soul, it will be bliss. Proper, full-on bliss. I am sure she will come. I am certain that she has glimpsed the truth, the light, the grace. In three days, everything will be unimaginably glorious.

I am positive about that. Nothing else matters. We are free.

chapter thirteen

I assumed it would become mysteriously cold in the night, as it apparently does in the desert. I was wrong.

When I wake up, the sun is rising over the sea. The sky is grey-blue tinged with pink. The air is still, everything suspended.

The jungle, however, is impossibly noisy, with birds and insects and creatures I shudder to imagine welcoming the day. The fire is glowing a tiny bit, just at its embers, and the light is soft and filled with promise.

Even at home there is something special about being awake at dawn; here it feels enchanted. This is the Garden of Eden. I look around, my limbs aching, and see that, during the night, I have kicked the towel back on to Katy (who is sleeping peacefully) and shifted myself away from the fire. I turn on my back and stare at the pink sky, wide awake, listening to the wildlife. My ears are attuned, immediately, for the sound of an engine.

It is far too early for rescue: I know that. All the same, he will arrive, and when he arrives he will be mortified.

He will explain and we will understand. We will tell him to stop worrying. I imagine myself saying, 'Samad, it's fine! It was the biggest adventure of my life,' so clearly that I almost feel he is here, on the beach with us.

The jungle life is unnerving, so I sit up, turn my back on it and look to the sea instead. The water is lapping on the shore with the gentlest of swooshes. Mark and Cherry are entwined around one another, and I suppose that this will be a wonderful honeymoon anecdote for them when they get home. Edward is not here, and everyone else is sleeping on the sand. I look at them, absolutely defenceless and unconscious, sprawled around in uncontrolled poses. Their vulnerability worries me.

For half a second I picture a huge prehistoric lizard strolling out of the jungle and burying its teeth in the flesh of the nearest person, Cherry. She would be succulent though muscly, and so probably gristly. My sole hope is that the creatures, whatever is living in there, do not realise that we are here before Samad gets back.

I stand up, aching in strange places, and walk down to the water's edge. I am glad we had this night. I even wonder whether Samad might have done it on purpose, to give us an unforgettable holiday experience. Perhaps this is part of his grand plan to create a bigger and better trip than anyone else's. It is audacious, but it has worked.

The warm water laps at my ankles, and I stare at the absolutely straight line of the horizon. I try to remember which direction we approached this beach from, but I have no idea, and anyway, we came from a snorkelling spot and not directly from the main island. When Samad left yesterday, I think he went to the left. I close my eyes and try to replay the moment. I am sure it was the left.

To the left of the beach there is a rocky outcrop. The rocks are big and easy to climb. I scramble up and make my way around, using hands and feet to grip the boulders, until I am perched at the top, with a view of the sea to the left and the little bay in front of the beach to my right.

There is nothing to be seen over here either: no view of the main island, no approaching boat, nothing but more placid sea and the same straight horizon. It is a good spot in which to wait. I pull myself up so that I am sitting cross-legged, shift around so that I am facing left and train my eyes on the water. I try to breathe deeply and calmly like I used to do in the yoga class I briefly went to, and I wait.

The sun is shining down on me, stronger by the seond. I try to empty my mind. I am suffused with optimism. Rescue will come soon: I know it.

Nobody wants to go far from the beach. We all want to be here, to watch the boat coming closer, to rush into the water and fire questions at Samad, if it is indeed going to be him. Perhaps it will be a friend or a member of his family, or somebody from Paradise Bay who has come out to look for us. Whoever it is, we all want to witness their arrival.

I sit on the rocks for a while, and then Edward calls to me from the beach.

'Esther!' he shouts, and I look down at him. 'We're going to divvy up the rest of this food! You'd better come and dig in.'

I scramble down.

'Is that wise?' I am trying to be sensible. Mark and Cherry are sitting at the back of the beach in the shade of the trees, and I see that they are eating bananas and sharing a can of Sprite. They are no longer caressing one another; in fact they are further apart than I have ever seen them, and their faces are tense and unsmiling. Cherry has black make-up smeared on her face, under her eyes; I hope Mark tells her soon. The fact that he hasn't makes me like him still less.

I watch them for a moment. Occasionally one of them will say something, and the other will barely acknowledge it. They are not looking at one another.

Being left here is disconcerting. We are in a place we did not choose to be, with people we would not have picked. It is a paradise island, but it is also shaping up as something of a hellhole. All we can do is wait. We are utterly powerless and devoid of choices.

'We're working on the basis that Samad or someone will be here for us today,' Ed says, as I approach. He does not look panicked, but there is a certain tension in his even features. Jean and Gene are busy dividing what we have into piles, and there is a horribly small amount in each: a few bananas, a can of drink between two, a pile of crisps that must equal a seventh of each of the two packs that were left.

'It's the only way to do it,' Gene says, nodding to a pile for me. 'You're sharing that can with Katy, darling. Because if we started trying to make it last we'd be left with absolutely bloody nothing. We'll be sampling the best of Paradise Bay's fare tonight in their café, you see if we don't. And young Ed here has volunteered to head over to Coral Bay for some beers when we get back, so we can all toast this little adventure. You get me?'

His certainty is infectious. I put a crisp into my mouth and immediately feel better.

'Sounds good,' I say, letting it melt on my tongue so it lasts as long as possible. 'Do we have any water?'

'Two small bottles,' Jean says, nodding to the closed ice box. 'But we thought we should keep them, drink the sugary stuff first. Just as a nod to the Fates, you know? Keep something in reserve. We're also lucky enough to have the fishing equipment that Samad left, so if the worst does happen and we end up spending another night, we can always catch ourselves something.'

Gene laughs at that, not in a pleasant way.

'Oh, listen to the master fisherlady!' he says. 'Like it's that easy. You know why people go out in boats to fish? Because that's where the bloody fish are. Out at sea. Not at the beach.'

She shrugs.

'That there is the ocean. Fish live in it. We have the equipment to pull them out. So shut your stupid fat face.'

They resolutely turn their backs on one another.

I pick up my share of the food and carry it to the very middle of the beach, where I sit alone and stare at the horizon. I cross my legs and try to will a small boat into view. I savour each shard of crisp, sucking the salt off it and only swallowing once it is soggy. When they are all gone, I start on a banana, pulling pieces off and appreciating everything. I am concentrating so hard on the food and on the ocean that I do not notice Katy arriving until she touches my arm.

I jump.

'Katy!'

'Sorry.' She is smiling. 'Didn't mean to scare you. You were miles away, weren't you?'

'Oh,' I say. 'I wish. Here, half of this drink is yours.'

'Thanks.' She takes the can and swigs from it. 'Mm, warm Sprite. The kind of thing you would actively avoid back in the real world. I'm sure we'll be off this island soon, and maybe for a while we'll stop taking things for granted.'

'For sure. Like, when we were at Paradise Bay – you know it felt like we'd left our normal lives behind and we were living so simply, all of that? When we had dinner together at the beach café – well I don't know about you, but I think I was happily ignoring the fact that there were so many members of staff in that place, all of them catering to our every whim. People cooking, people asking what we wanted and getting it made and bringing it to us. Someone else crushing up fruit into smoothies. They'd bought the fish from the fishermen, they'd made sure they were stocking everything they needed, all the spices for the sauces, all of it. And I did not really give any of that a moment's thought because I was so busy being pleased with myself for being there.'

Katy nods. 'I know what you mean. You take everything for granted without even knowing that's what you're doing, don't you? And it takes something like this to make you realise . . . But not even this, really. I mean, we're sitting here drinking a fizzy drink made by one of the world's biggest companies. We're eating processed food. We're still one step away from harsh reality. I do hope we don't really end up having to fend for ourselves.'

All of a sudden I am scared.

'Could we make a raft, do you think?'

We both look around. There are so many trees in this jungle, which, if it is the same as the jungle on Perhentian Kecil, will get thicker and thicker as you go back from the beach. There will be strong creepers and plenty of wood. There is ample material for a raft. In fact we could probably make a sail with some of the enormous leaves that are bound to be in there.

'We'd need an axe,' Katy says. 'Or something with a very sharp and strong blade, anyway.'

'Maybe we could find a sharp stone?' I try, looking at the fine sand that covers the beach. There is nothing remotely sharp on it. Everything here was washed smooth thousands of years ago.

Katy is rightly sceptical, but she kindly says, 'Maybe.'

We both look back at the horizon.

The sun is overhead and we are all lying in the shade of the trees at the fringe of the forest. Nobody is speaking. There is nothing to say.

I am drifting in and out of sleep. All we can do is wait. We have eaten every single crumb of our supplies. We are in the shade but still sweltering and dripping with sweat. I am very well aware that I have been wearing this bikini all day and all night, and that the sarong that is wrapped around me was also my blanket last night.

By the time I go to bed tonight I will be clean and

moisturised and full. All this will look like a bizarre adventure. I hang on to that thought as tightly as I can.

Sometimes I think I see something on the horizon, and I jerk upright to look, but it is just the flash of the sun on a wave, or perhaps a sea creature surfacing. It is never a boat. I notice other people doing the same, but they never say anything either. My head is throbbing at both sides, tapping out a rhythm to the afternoon.

'We could make a flare,' Mark says at one point.

'Using what?' says Cherry, her voice uncharacteristically sharp. Nobody replies, because it is too obvious. The fact that Mark, who until now has been the voice of mocking cynicism, could propose so ridiculous a plan makes me feel more hopeless than anything else that has happened.

By the time the sun slips behind the jungle, we all know that, once again, he is not coming. We are stuck on the island for a second night and we have no food left and only two small bottles of drinking water between the seven of us.

'He might still come,' Katy is arguing, but she sounds frantic, and seems to be arguing with herself more than with anyone in particular. She is furiously constructing scenarios. 'He might have had an accident and be in hospital. Of course they won't remember us for a while. Maybe they'll stay at the hospital for the morning and then they'll go home, or some of them will go home, because they'll have to, and when they get there, they'll remember us. And the people at Paradise Bay will be wondering where we are, and they'll all get together, maybe about now, and Samad will have told his family we're here, and they'll get straight into a boat and come and pick us up.'

We have been through all of those scenarios many times, out loud and in our heads, and Katy saying it now sounds more like someone reciting a ritual than anything else.

'Yes,' Jean says, but her voice is hollow. 'But why the hell are we still here? All of that should already have happened.'

We stare out to sea, just in case, but all those words have not made any difference. Nothing we do or say is able to change anything.

The sun is low over the rainforest. I wish this beach faced the other way. For one thing we might see a boat, and for another I would like the sun to set over the sea, rather than creeping behind the forest, leaving us to endure the inexorable leaching away of the day. Drama and colour would be better than this gradual fading-out of everything.

The fire is burning with a strong flame. We are still here. No boat will come in the dark, but we all make an effort and drag what leaves and branches we can manage on to the beach, just in case some fishing boat comes by in the early morning and sees our fire and comes to investigate.

We are almost silent. When I look at Ed he smiles warmly, and that makes me feel better. I edge closer to him.

'It'll be OK,' he says. 'It's still an adventure. Tomorrow, if we're still here, we can explore, see what it's like on the other side, light fires all over the place. I was thinking, we could get the whole bloody forest on fire, perhaps

– draw some attention to ourselves. Someone, somewhere would notice an island going up in flames. Someone would come closer to have a look. Don't worry too much, hey, Esther?'

'But what about water—' I am saying, when we are both distracted by a scream from the jungle.

At first my heart leaps: something is happening! In a fraction of a second I process the fact that it was Cherry's scream, that she might be hurt, that nothing good is going on and that rescue, if it comes, will certainly not arrive from within the island. Anything that came from within the island would be a horrible thing.

Ed is already starting towards her, when the scream becomes a shout.

'I know!' she yells. 'I am very *very* well aware of that fact, thank you!'

'Which does not help matters,' Mark is yelling back at her. 'Not one fucking bit.'

'This was not my idea, for your information.'

'Oh, wasn't it? It wasn't mine.'

Their voices are lowered after that so that, although we can still hear that they are arguing, we can no longer hear the words. Ed and I look at each other.

'Another warring couple,' he says quietly. 'This place is not a great advertisement for marriage, you know. There's Gene and Jean who loathe one another's guts in a way that I find startling and scary. You're divorced. Katy's recently separated from someone, hasn't she? And now even the honeymooning lovebirds are at it. I thought I could depend on them, at least, to keep the romantic dream alive.'

'What about you?' I ask, as Ed puts a handful of dry fronds on the fire. 'Is there a girlfriend wondering where you've got to?' I find myself slightly, ridiculously hoping that there isn't.

He shakes his head and laughs.

'There is not. Nobody has any idea that I'm here. There was a girlfriend for a while, of course. There've been a few. But there's not any more. And if she, Ellie, the most recent one, could see me here, about to admit defeat by bedding down for the night as soon as the sun sets and wondering how far our chances are diminished by the third day, she'd vaguely think she might call the coastguard but then something she liked would come on the telly and she probably wouldn't get round to it. We're not exactly a big presence in each other's lives. We never were really.'

'At least you don't positively detest each other. Which proves you weren't married.'

'There was never enough passion for that even to be a consideration,' he says. 'There was no passion at all, in fact. Do you think good passion turns to destructive passion? The evidence around us would suggest it does.'

'Not in my case. Chris and I just stumbled into one another. It was never going to work.'

Soon all of us are around the fire, back in our places from yesterday. Gene comes out of the dark, stumbling, but when he gets close to the fire we see that his arms are full of bananas. He hands them around.

'Several fruit trees in the vicinity,' he says. 'Come on, eat up.'

We pass them around. I eat a couple because I know I should. The strange thing is that I am not hungry at all. My head is pulsating from within, and I am trying not to think about water.

I put my head down on the sarong, and without saying a word to anyone, I let myself drift off to sleep. I dream so vividly that a boat lands on the beach and everyone goes away without me that I sit up abruptly in the middle of the night and look around, sobbing heaving great sobs. The moon is shining down from a starry sky, and the whole of the surface of the sea is gleaming silver. I cry harder as I realise that I cannot see the boat, that they really have all left without me.

When I notice that they are still here, sleeping around the glowing embers of the fire, I carry on crying because I cannot imagine being rescued now.

Katy is not where she should be, next to me. I scan the beach, but she is nowhere to be seen. After a while she climbs down from the rock at the edge of the beach, the place where I sat this morning. I watch her approach the fire.

'Esther,' she whispers, with a little smile. 'Not sleeping either?'

She lies back down next to me.

'I had a dream that everyone went away without me,' I whisper. 'I woke up and thought it was true.'

'Oh, Esther,' she says, and I can hear the smile in her voice even though I cannot see her face. 'My dream was that there was a little boat moored just beyond those rocks. I was so certain. I had to go and check.'

'No little boat?'

''Fraid not.'

She covers me with her towel and I shift closer. I don't think I can possibly be going to sleep because my head is pounding and I am trying to work out when I should have been leaving for my flight home. I lie and think and try not to cry because losing water through my eyes seems to make my headache worse and worse and worse.

chapter fourteen

Samad does not arrive in the night. He does not come in the morning. We share the last of the water, but it doesn't work because Mark gulps down half of one bottle in one go.

He is sorry, but not sorry enough.

'I couldn't help myself,' he says, uselessly.

I hate him. When I look around, I see that everybody hates him. We are all firing pure, shining arrows of loathing in his direction. He laughs a bit and puts his hands up. 'Hey,' he says. 'I'm sorry, OK? I didn't mean to.'

'You didn't mean to drink far more than your fair share of our last remaining lifeline, which is now gone?' Jean speaks for us all. 'Well. That's certainly all right, then.'

So we are on a baking hot island with absolutely no water. We are surrounded by it, but there is nothing to drink. Nothing at all. My tongue is big in my mouth. My throat is dry. The hunger is nothing. The thirst is everything. I lie back and look at the sky for a while.

'If it would rain . . .' I say, but my head is throbbing so hard that I cannot finish the sentence. I don't need to, because everyone knows what I mean.

'It's not fair,' says someone. I think it was Jean, but everyone sounds the same to my ears now. I know what she means, too. She means that it rained regularly when we were at the resort, and now we have been here for a length of time that is fuzzy but that includes, I think, three nights, and it has not rained at all.

I am glad that I am not able to work out when I should be catching the plane home. I see Daisy all the time, but I cannot properly think about her. There are all sorts of consequences for her of my being trapped on an island without water. But I cannot actually address them and I know that this is for the best because there is nothing I can do.

All the same, one moment I am looking at the defiantly blue sky waiting for it to rain, and then the sun is in a different part of the sky and I am curled up on myself, rocking to and fro and rasping the words 'my baby', over and over again. I must have been doing that for hours. She is right there, and if I didn't know better I would think she was with me on this island, because the image of her, in her baggy jeans and her yellow and red striped T-shirt, her long hair back in a messy ponytail, her face confused and concerned for me, is so vivid. She keeps reaching for me, and I stretch out a hand to touch her back, but of course there is nothing.

The sun is burning my shoulders and my face. I can feel it all becoming raw and cracking and peeling. I make an effort and sit up. My throat hurts so much, and my mouth is so dry. I heave myself to my knees and then wobble to my feet.

I sway as I stand, and when the black spots that cover everything shrink a little, I look around. Mark and Cherry are in the shade, lying in one another's arms. Their marriage, I think, is going to end here, on their honeymoon. They came to Malaysia for the paradise beaches, and it is the paradise beach that is going to claim them. At least they are together, I think, knowing how sentimental this is and not caring.

Jean is propped up against the boulder at the end of the sand. She sees me looking and lifts a hand, then lets it drop. Gene is lying beside her, his eyes closed. Ed is near me, asleep on the hot sand. He should come to the shade as well.

The fire has gone out. The last thing we need is a fire, unless we could somehow use it to take the salt out of the seawater. I have an untrustworthy memory of someone on TV doing that once, condensing it on to a piece of metal and letting it drip down.

Someone is moving around in the rainforest. I look for Katy, and when I see her, she is on her knees, licking a leaf. At least she is doing something.

I try to walk to the shade, but my knees wobble and buckle, and I end up crawling, dragging myself out of the burning light.

This place was going to be perfect. It was heaven. Look at the white sand, everyone said. Salty seawater. How perfect. How marvellous. This is paradise. The sun shines off the sand and I have to screw up my eyes.

'Ed,' I say. He should come too but I don't have the

strength to pull him. I change course and crawl towards him. The sand is so hot. I want to lie down but I know I mustn't. I reach him and put a hand on his chest.

'Ed,' I say. 'You need to . . .'

He opens an eye. 'What?' he mutters. He is completely disorientated, and I see in his eyes that he does not recognise me.

I try out the words in my head. They sound right, so I say them.

'Come to the shade.'

He frowns. 'What?'

'Shade.'

He props himself up and scowls around the beach. Then he tries to stand up. We end up crawling together to the edge of the rainforest.

When we get there, we look at one another. I cannot speak and he does not seem able to either. Everyone but Katy is collapsed, and she is nearly gone. We have no water. You cannot live without water. You die.

The sun shines off the sea and dazzles me. I turn my head away from that treacherous beach, the place that has taken us and beaten us, and lie down between two trees, on the edge of the sand. I want the dinosaurs to come out of the forest now, and eat me.

I should go and look for water. The creatures that live in the forest must drink something. But my head is pounding so loudly that I cannot hear anything else, and I am parched, and all I want is a drink and there is nothing.

I close my eyes. Perhaps I will just have a little sleep. The darkness descends rapidly.

chapter fifteen

Cathy

'Doomsday', 8 p.m.

Unless the Rapture has happened in an abstract and imperceptible way, with some kind of cosmic shifting that remains unnoticed by the people it happens to, then something has gone wrong.

We were ready, at dawn. We were so excited. We stayed up all night, praying and preparing ourselves. All of us were dressed in white, on Father Moses' orders.

'The Lord will appreciate you clothing yourselves that way,' he said, his blue eyes shining out.

It would have been nice if the end of the material world was marked with a clear starry night. Cassandra told me that God had more important things to worry about tonight than the weather and that I should not even think of complaining about it. No matter: the sky was filled with clouds and a light drizzle fell for most of the night.

Two television news crews came along shortly before dawn, and a woman with lots of make-up on poked her head around the door and asked if she could come in and film us 'being swept up to heaven'. Father Moses shut the door in her face. I could see that he recognised that she was beyond salvation. Sarah sat next to me, holding my hand, and my other hand was in Philip's. Sarah was wearing blue varnish on her fingernails, but I knew that God would not mind that. He might even have liked it.

Martha sat on Philip's other side. Cassandra kept looking over and smiling at me, probably because I am her only birth child. They say it makes no difference who your birth parents are, but it must do a bit.

Then we all started to sing. We sang a hymn that Father Moses wrote for the occasion: 'The Apocalypse comes tonight/ When our saviour shines so bright/ And all of us do pray/ That the righteous are taken away/ To heaven to dwell with God/ Like peas in their proper pod.'

(I can dare to think this now: I slightly felt I could have come up with some better lyrics than those, if he'd asked me. In fact most people could, but we were not invited.)

Because of the clouds, there was no first ray of sunlight. The hand of God did not reach down as dawn broke. Dawn was a smudge of grey, and gradually lightening clouds.

We waited. Philip's hand was sweaty in mine. Philip is, I think, nearly always sweaty. Sarah clasped me so tightly that I wanted to pull my hand away and rub it, but I bore it. I was tingling all over. Any second now . . .

And then, perhaps ten minutes after the light grey dawn began, I realised with a horrible sense of dread and betrayal that nothing was happening. If the righteous were being taken away, that meant we were not Saved. Not even

Cassandra, not Father Moses. Not even the babies were Saved.

Father Moses jumped up and shouted: 'Half past five,' and we pretended to believe that Jesus had beamed that message directly into his head. I knew it, though. My old misery and cynicism were creeping back. Everything I had banished with the expectation of paradise was suddenly there again, lurking at the edges of my mind. It was all I could do to hold them at bay, but I managed it until half past five came and went. The people from the TV were filming us through the windows, once it was light, and no one bothered to chase them away.

Sarah let go of my hand. I pulled my other hand out of Philip's and dried it on my white nightdress. People started to stretch and to look at one another in fear. Nobody wanted to be the first to point out that the Emperor was naked. We sat and waited. I was cramped and uncomfortable, desperate to stand up and walk around. I shuffled on my bottom. Everyone in the room, I suddenly knew, was waiting for someone to dare to point out the stark truth.

No one had planned for this (apart from everybody in the entire outside world). None of us quite knew what to say.

And as we waited, fidgeting and shifting and watching the drizzle stop and the clouds disperse outside the window, I admitted to myself that it had all been a lie.

I had made a fool of myself at school. I had allowed myself to be caught up in the idea of the Rapture because I wanted it to be true. I wanted to be taken up to eternal bliss. I had let Father Moses – my real father, I believe

– manipulate me. All those emotions, that exhilaration, had been real. Real, but founded on nothing. Father Moses had pulled it from thin air, unless he was suffering the biggest delusion of all. He had hypnotised us.

As the day unequivocally started, and it was completely light, I knew that I did not believe in his God. I was not sure I believed in any God at all. I was glad that I had finished my exams in spite of everything, because it would have been so easy not to bother, but now at least I will have my GCSEs.

I wanted to be sitting in heaven with Jesus. Instead, I am going to have to marry Philip. My destiny, from the moment it got light this morning, is to become a compound wife, sweeping floors and cooking stews and growing flowers and vegetables to sell at the market stall that has done so well in recent weeks as news of our impending Apocalypse had spread and people came from all around to buy our tomatoes and sweet peas and to laugh at us and take our photos and ask us giggling questions.

Now I desperately want to be one of the people on the outside, laughing. I do not want to be on the inside, fooled and tricked, contained and constrained. I stayed still because no one had told us to get up, but the tears poured down my cheeks.

In the end, Father Moses himself got up from his position on the platform, stretched, and said he was off to talk to Jesus for a minute. As soon as he left the room, we all stood up and the women started breastfeeding the little children, and some people lay down and went to sleep because no one had been able to doze during the long night of waiting. I assumed that when you were taken up to heaven, things like being a bit tired would not matter any more.

I lay down and slept on the hard floor, with Sarah next to me. Some time later Cassandra woke us, shaking my shoulder, and saying that God was not ready for us yet because there are more to be Saved than He was anticipating. I looked at her, and although I said nothing, she said, 'Catherine,' in her warning voice.

We went to bed and dozed all day. Sarah slept in my bed next to me for a bit, and then she went home.

She was not surprised that nothing had worked out the way it was supposed to.

'I thought it probably wasn't going to,' she said, 'but hey, it was worth a try. Are you OK, Cathy?'

'Yeah,' I told her. 'Well. Sort of OK.'

I watched her go. I longed to go with her. I wanted to run after her and grab hold of her and implore her to help me. I cannot marry Philip! I do not remotely fancy him. I cannot subsume everything. I can't stay here in this place, which, even though it is all I have ever known, I can see is not normal. I cannot just be a wife.

I am done with trying to convince myself. I want to get out of here.

This place is founded on lies, and I want to be normal.

chapter sixteen

It is the thirst. At least I think it is. I do not know anything.

I can feel my body giving up. When I look around this dry prison, I see other people with wide eyes and cracked mouths and sometimes I think they are feeling the same as me, and sometimes I hardly believe they are there.

We lie about, in the middle of this panorama that looks like paradise, and we wait to die. Paradise is an imaginary blissful destination that comes after death, so perhaps that is, in fact, where we are and what we are going through. Maybe it will all end in a minute.

Often I think we are dead. Everything I see, I see through a weird distorting filter. Sometimes I think it is a filter of thirst and hunger. Other times I wonder if something bigger than that has happened.

Maybe when I swam off by myself, following an ugly fish, I drowned as I tried to swim to shore. I contemplate that for a whole day, I think. At least, I start thinking it when the sun comes up and turns the sea a burning apocalyptic red, and by the time I stop it is dark. I may have eaten a few bananas in between. It is hard not to gag on them.

I followed the fish. I lost the boat. I would have been miles from that land I could see. There is no way I could have reached it. I died. That is what happened. I ran out of strength and I stopped swimming and every part of me filled with water. The fish are feeding on my body right now, sucking sustenance from me with their little gulping mouths. And as that happened, my conscious mind protected me by constructing this scenario. It imagined me being picked up, taken to the island and left here with the people I happened to be with at the end.

I wish it had let me have Daisy. If I try hard – if I concentrate with all my might – I can produce her, once again, on the sand next to me. But then I screw my eyes up and send her away again, because now when she arrives she is burnt and peeling and her features are contorted with starvation and thirst, and I cannot bear to see my baby like that. I try to get the Daisy in jeans back, but she will not come.

I try to send her home, then, to Brighton, to Chris's world with its baffling overabundance. She is in a world where, if you need something, you can go to the shops and buy it. Who cares if Chris is shambolic? Did I ever really care about that? Once I can peer down at her there, putting her hand up in the classroom, lying back on Chris's sofa watching *Horrible Histories*, walking someone's dog along the seafront, then I relax a bit further and know she is all right.

I have no idea how many days we have been here. I

rack my brains for the way this post-reality dream world began. A man went to fetch matches. That was it.

He left some food and some drink to ease us into the next world. We finished the food. We drank the water. We realised we could not drink seawater and that he was not coming back. We counted what we had left. Four cans of Coke. Four of Diet Coke. Two of lemonade and two of Fanta. There was a banana tree in the part of the inland jungle we could reach. Someone went further in and discovered papayas. We emptied the cool boxes and washed them out in the sea and put them in the middle of the beach to catch rain.

It did not rain.

We lit a fire and it went out. Some people tried to catch fish but nothing happened. The American woman screamed and cried and said she was going to kill herself if he didn't come back. I tried to say I thought that had already happened but I don't think I actually spoke out loud. My mouth is too dry to talk.

Somebody walks around sometimes. Someone peels a banana and feeds it to me. I am sure that has happened quite often. They put a can to my lips and I swallow but it is just something sugary and warm. It is not water.

I have forgotten what these people are called, if I ever knew. I don't think they are real.

She is shouting. People often shout. This time it carries on so long that in the end the words make their way into my consciousness.

'Water!' she is saying. Of course she is saying water. That was my mind. I made her say water because it is the only thing that matters. It is the element that surrounds us and keeps us apart from everything else, and it is the element that is killing us by its absence. Water is the enemy. Water is the only word there is.

'Water!' she keeps saying. I turn over to block her out. Yes, I try to say. I know about water.

Hours pass and she is still saying it.

Then hands are pulling me. I twist and push them off. They grab me and hold me down, and something is at my lips. I take a sip because that is what I do, but it is not warm Fanta.

I gulp it all down. The bottle is empty. It vanishes and then it comes back, and I drink it down again. Then I wrench my head away and throw up all over the sand.

'That's OK,' says a voice, and it is a gentle voice. 'It doesn't matter. It's a shock to the system. There's plenty more.'

I wipe my mouth with the back of my hand. I turn and look at the person who is speaking. It is a woman. I recognise her.

'Esther, it's all right,' she says. Behind her I can see a man trying to light a fire. He does not have anything to light it with and is pointing a Fanta can at it, which is unsurprisingly not working.

'What?' I think I say.

'Esther, it's me. Katy. Look, here's some more water. Keep this bottle. Keep it with you, and sip it slowly. Hold it, Esther. Hold it with your hands.'

'Water?'

The woman smiles. I remember that she is nice and I like her. Katy.

'We found a spring. I found it. If you follow the path all the way into the middle of the island, it's there. A spring. I thought I was hallucinating. I drank loads of water and I was sick, like you. Then I drank more. I thought I was sick because the water was poisonous, but in fact it is fine, I'm sure it is. I feel better. Much better. Weirdly. So does Ed, look. Everyone's coming round. I think we're going to be all right, you know. I think that God has looked after us after all.'

I cannot reply to her, so I follow her pointing finger. A young man – *that*, I tell myself, is *Ed*. He is nice – is handing a bottle of water to an old man. The old man looks baffled, but he is sipping from it. An older woman is walking down to the sea on wobbly legs. A tall man with black hair is sitting up with his eyes closed.

When I look in the other direction, there is a blonde woman, who is sitting on her own on the other side of the beach, crying.

'Cherry's had water,' says Katy. 'But she won't stop crying. Maybe when she eats something.'

I make an effort and nod my head, because that feels like the right thing to do.

'It's OK now,' she says in her gentle voice. She sounds like somebody on the radio, someone who reads the news. Somebody you can trust. 'You're going to be all right now. We'll find food and someone will rescue us. They will. I am absolutely sure of it.'

chapter seventeen

My turn to fetch the water. It is my turn to fetch the water.

That means I need to fetch the water. Katy told me I had to.

The sun has risen over the sea, and all the water is burning pink, and that means it is morning. Another day has come and we are still here.

I prop myself up on my elbows and decide to go right now, because then it will be done. Katy has organised a rota for water and food and fishing, and she tells us all what we have to do and when we have to do it, and as long as we do as she says we are just about surviving. This means I have to go and fill an ice box with water, even though I am not sure I will be able to stand up. Being marooned on a desert island is not the way it is in films. It turns out that rather than learning deep lessons about life and love and what really matters, all you actually think about is food and water. Katy organised what she calls 'latrines', a row of holes dug in a jungle clearing. It is all about the basic bodily functions.

Sometimes I try to remember what life was like before this. All I can think of is Daisy. Nothing else I have ever done has any significance whatsoever, it turns out. I had a baby. I did all sorts of other things but they are nothing. I spent too much time with a man I didn't like and with whom I had nothing in common. We got away from each other in the end. The only thing that matters from that now – the only part of it I can remember – is the look in Daisy's eyes when I did something that hurt her. Daisy is practical and funny, and she deserves the best of everything.

As castaways, we are not bonding and becoming lifelong friends. We barely have the energy to acknowledge one another's existence. No one is confiding in anyone. I don't want to talk, not even to Katy, even though I told her my secrets before we came here. To carry on baring my soul here, aloud, would be unbearably claustrophobic; and anyway, Katy keeps talking about God and trying to get people to pray with her. I don't want to pray. I just want a boat to come around the headland.

I stand up and stretch. My legs are wobbly. I take unsteady steps to the sea and walk straight into it. It is warm and cleansing and treacherous. I wish it would evaporate so we could walk back to life. All the same, I swim around in it, in the bikini I never take off, rinse my straw-like hair, and step back on to the beach. I wrap my sarong around myself – the sarong I bought at the airport that was so lovely and new and is now fading and ripped – and concentrate on finding and putting on my sunscreen.

There is nearly a whole bottle of it left. If it was just me, it would last me for longer than I want to be here, but since we have to share everything, there are several people using it, which means it will run out and we will get burnt and peel. Still, I put lots of it on, because doing that means that I am expecting to be rescued soon.

The ice box is in its place on the beach. We have to leave it out in the middle of the sand, Katy says, and Mark says too, and so does Jean. Because otherwise little bits of jungly things fall into the water and that is not nice. I pick it up. There is a tiny bit of yesterday's water left, so I tip it out and watch it vanish, leaving just a patch of clumpy sand behind.

It is easy to find the spring. You follow the path and it takes you there. In two places you need to remember which fork to take, but Katy and Mark have made it easier by blocking off the path you don't take with big branches. That means you just go without having to think about it. Katy showed me yesterday.

I stumble along. The jungle is much too noisy. It is filled with insects and things that screech and chirp and cry out. I do not like it. I hate being on their territory, but I do not have the energy I used to have to be properly afraid of them. I happily risk the jungle-dwellers ganging up on me and eating me alive. They cannot have any idea of how easy that would be for them, or they would have done it by now.

A lizard runs up the trunk of a tree beside me. Its tongue flickers out. I stick my tongue out back at it.

This is a world away from the landscape of the beach. The rainforest world is enclosed with a ceiling of thick frondy leaves. It is hot and humid in here, where the beach is always dry. And here I am surrounded by life, by plants and creatures that thrive in this odd place. Spiky vines arrange themselves across the path at head height, just to trap me. I duck under them, feeling bad for being on their territory, even though they are just plants.

The spring is bubbling away. It is a miraculous thing. Katy says that when we were all half-dead on the beach, she went exploring.

'I could do it,' she says, 'because I'd drunk so much water that morning that it took me a while to get dehydrated. At least I think that's why. Maybe it was just my body reacting differntly to the crisis. Whatever it was, I walked and walked. I knew there had to be water in here somewhere, because there's so much life. I couldn't see where I was going, and I blacked out a few times, but I kept finding fruit. It was as if there was a cosmic force or something, putting banana trees exactly where I needed them. I kept stuffing my face with bananas and there was probably some form of water in them or something. Anyway, I kept going. I walked on the paths, wherever they took me. And then I ended up at the spring.'

She was telling us this soon after we all came back from the dead, when she fed us water.

'Did you think it was a mirage?' I remember someone asking. It was Ed, I think.

'Of course I did,' she agreed. 'I was having every kind of crazy thought. But I sat down and drank it out of my hands. I threw up in the nearest plant. But then I kept going and it was all right. As soon as I had water in my system I felt wonderful. Alive again.'

'Thanks, Katy,' Ed said, and we all muttered similar things. She saved our lives. I am still not convinced that any of this is real, but I cannot deny that things were worse when we did not have water, even if that was just a worse nightmare than this one.

The spring is in a little clearing. It bubbles out of the ground and gathers in a pool. It does not go anywhere. I had vaguely thought that a spring made a stream which made a river which reached the sea; but this one does not. It feeds into a pool, and perhaps it has an underwater network nourishing the nearby plants. Certainly there is much wild and magnificently bizarre foliage nearby: huge flowers bigger than my head, and creepers with odd leaves, and tall, tall palms that reach so far into the sky that they can probably see land.

I tip the ice box up and fill it as far as I can from the spring itself. That makes it about a quarter full. Then I use the biggest water bottle Samad left us, which is a 1.5 litre one, to top it up. Again and again I fill it, and tip its contents into the box. It empties with agonising slowness, glugging away. Time does not exist here, so it does not really matter whether it takes an hour (which I feel it does) or half a minute (which, if I make myself think clearly, is probably closer to objective, previous-life truth).

After some time, anyway, the box is nearly full. I move it carefully to a level place and sit down with my legs in the pool. I close my eyes and enjoy the cool water on my sore feet. Then I dip my hands in and allow the water to cool the pulse points on my wrists. When that is done, I am in a state of bliss, and I throw some cool water over my face and hair and lie back on the boggy ground, my feet still in the pool.

*

'Esther?'

I yawn and shake my head.

'Esther, are you OK?'

With the greatest reluctance, I open my eyes. All I see is the rainforest canopy. I prop myself up on my elbows and look around.

'Huh?' I think I say. It is some noise like that, anyway.

'Esther!' It is the Scottish man. He is Ed. Such details are surprisingly hard to remember these days.

'Ed,' I say. 'Yes. Just lying down.'

'Oh, sorry. I didn't mean to wake you. You look so chilled. It's just, well, we wanted to check on you because Jean said she saw you leaving with the ice box just after sunrise but you didn't come back.'

'I just sat down.'

'I know. It's been a while. That's all. Come on, I'll help you with the water. We can carry it together. It should probably be a two-person job anyway.'

I stretch. I want to be grumpy and snap at him, but we are stuck on an island. I think of all the people on the beach waking up and having no water. I remind myself that I have to be nice, much as I would rather not be, because we all have to live together, to sleep together around the fire, to share water and whatever scraps of food we have. If I drift into vicious mode, people will stop sharing things with me and I will die.

'Sorry,' I force myself to say. 'I suppose I fell asleep.'

Edward smiles warmly. I remember that he had a handsome friend. I wish he was here too.

'Will your friends be looking for you?' I ask, as we take the long handle of the box and start walking. It is awkward, because the path is too narrow for us to go side by side, and avoiding spillage of precious water is difficult when you are walking one behind the other. I walk behind Ed; we take tiny steps and make agonisingly slow progress. Unexpectedly, I remember his friends' names. 'Jonah, I mean, and Piet.'

'I hope they will,' he says. 'It's funny, but now that we've all got a little strength back – come back from the brink, you know? – I'm starting to try to put myself in their shoes. We must have been gone quite a lot of days by now. I don't think any of us know how many. Katy may do, I suppose. She's been the most on the ball. But say we've been here five days, perhaps. Even a week, maybe. What will they have done?'

'Did they know you were going on Samad's trip?' I try to focus on this. 'You're the only one of us, aren't you, travelling with people who aren't on this island. You're the only one who's left friends behind who might raise some sort of alarm.'

'Yes. I'm sure they'd try to find out what became of me.'

I seize on the idea. 'Perhaps they've got boats out looking. If they hadn't seen Samad, they'd think we all capsized, wouldn't they?'

'I'm pretty confident they'd have got some boats out looking, yes.'

'And sooner or later they'll find us.'

His voice is warm as he echoes me.

'Sooner or later they'll find us.'

He turns and gives me a reassuring smile. I hang on to the warmth and the certainty in his voice.

*

There is a small fire burning on the beach. I smile at the sight of it. Smoke is drifting directly upwards into the still air. The heat is stifling today.

'Well done!' Ed calls. 'Look at that! Did you use a can again?'

'It bloody took long enough,' Jean grumbles, but she is smiling, pleased with herself. 'Mainly because that piece of chocolate I polished it with first time round is long gone down my husband's greedy gullet.'

Gene waves an irritated hand in her direction.

'Shut up, woman,' he mutters.

'So I had to polish it up with leaves and bits of cloth and whatnot and it took for ever. But yeah, we got there.'

Katy is kneeling by the fire, feeding it with dry palm fronds and a collection of sticks and leaves she has piled on the beach. She looks up and pushes a dark lock back from her face. She has lost weight since we've been here and her cheekbones are protruding like knives.

'Esther. You're back. Anyone fancy fishing?'

I think about that.

'I fancy *fish*,' I say.

'Well yes,' Katy concedes. 'I think we all fancy fish. But to get us to that point, someone needs to do some fishing.'

'I'll do some fishing,' says Gene. 'Maybe we can get the little fishies to come to daddy.'

'Yes, I'm sure you can, Gene,' Katy says, in the head-girlish voice she uses when she is organising us. 'Why don't you give it a go? I think we can dig for bait in the forest, you know. Worms and stuff.' Her voice is irritating, but I know that I do not have the mental capacity to make the most basic connections – for example, that before you eat fish someone has to catch them, and before you can go fishing you need some bait – that Katy is managing. That means I cannot complain about her bossiness; I have, instead, to go along with what she tells me to do.

All the same, it is annoying. I try not to let it show on my face.

She does not give me any chores, so I wander around the beach. It is a sandy prison, but instead of bars it has water to the horizon. When I pass Cherry, who seems mainly to be sitting and staring at the sea, she looks up.

'Hi,' she says.

'Hi,' I reply.

'This is fucked,' she observes with a sigh.

'The most fucked thing ever.'

'You have a little girl, don't you?'

I think of Daisy. I am almost certain that I should have been home by now. If Ed is right about how long we have been here, my fuzzy reasoning suggests I should be getting back round about today. Perhaps yesterday, or maybe tomorrow.

I imagine Daisy with Chris, waiting for a mother who is probably never coming. I picture her confidently expectant about my return, planning what she is going to tell me and what we are going to do. Daisy always has ideas about what we must do, when we have been apart. They normally involve her drinking hot chocolate with whipped cream and marshmallows in a café, and going to the cinema.

I imagine the hours passing as I don't turn up. I picture Chris getting around to calling Emirates, and his surprise and annoyance on discovering that I was not on the aeroplane. I see this bald fact through his eyes and know that he will picture me lazing on a beach and forgetting to go to the airport.

'Yes I do,' I say. I cannot think of anything to add. 'I don't want to talk about her though,' I say, looking at Cherry's expectant face.

'You're tough,' she says.

'I'm not. I just can't bear it.'

'Yeah. You . . .' I wait for her to finish, but she doesn't. A tear trickles out of the corner of her big blue eye. I wonder what she is crying about, since she has her husband with her. I decide not to ask.

'Hey, don't cry,' I say in the briskest voice I can manage. 'That wastes water. We'll get out of here. And Katy seems to be doing a good job of making sure we stay alive.'

'She's bossy as hell, that one.' Cherry has dropped her voice. 'I mean, hello? We're all adults. We don't need the bloody Queen of England to tell us do this, do that. Fetch water, catch a fish.'

I laugh in spite of myself. 'I know! She's very bossy. But at least she found the water and stuff. She saved us. I thought I was dead. It's weird, isn't it? Coming back from the dead. I'm not sure I'll ever be certain I've come back to the same place.'

'I almost wish she hadn't saved us. You know? Because she knows we owe her everything now. I don't like owing someone like that. It's like we belong to her.'

'At least you've got Mark.'

She shakes her head. She raises her eyebrows, then speaks in an odd tone of voice.

'Yeah,' she says. 'I've got Mark.'

I stare at the horizon with her. Both of us are waiting for the sight of a boat that is not coming. It is the most hopeless activity there has ever been, and yet it is the only thing we can possibly do.

chapter eighteen

There is limitless water, and it restores me. I am not the same person: I do not think I can ever be the same person. I am absolutely certain that I have been through a portal of some sort and come out somewhere different, being someone different. This stupid island looks like scenery to me now. I want to find the place where the illusion ends, to see what is hidden behind it.

All the same, my headache recedes. It is still there, my brain still throbbing with a pulsating ache as though there were a creature in my head struggling to get out. I often wonder what kind of creature it is. A sea creature, I think; perhaps a giant squid. It lives in my head and it pulses away, but I can live with that, or I will until the day it bursts forth.

And now, with the water from the spring, with the bananas and papayas that Katy and Ed have been gathering, I am almost strong again. My knees often tremble but they do not give way. I can climb the boulder to look out to sea. I can fetch the water without having to take someone with me to help with the carrying. I can, for the moment, survive.

Then Gene and Katy catch four fish. They are not huge, but they are, as Gene says over and over again, protein. He insists that protein will make us all strong. The fish have silver scales and staring eyes. Gene casually whacks them against a rock and they die.

We cook them on the fire, wrapped in banana leaves, which singe but mostly do not catch light. As the light of the day recedes, Jean eases Katy out of her way and takes the fish apart. She pulls the flesh from the bones and divides it into seven piles, each on a banana leaf for a plate, arranged on top of the ice-box lid.

'I am being scrupulously fair,' she says firmly whenever anyone gets too close. 'I'll show you how fair, in fact. You can come and choose your helping and I'll go last. That's how fair I am.'

Nobody demurs. We are like toddlers now, each greedy to look after ourselves, to meet our own needs before anyone else's. I take a leaf and retire to a place near the fire. We do not need its warmth, but the comfort it gives is unexpectedly immense. Without the fire we are just a collection of stragglers, abandoned in the most remote place possible. With it we are a small community of (so far) survivors.

Only in the glow of the flames is it possible to cast ourselves in anything approaching a romantic light. We have not chosen one another's company. We did not want to be here. We all want to be away from here. All we want is food, water and a boat. No one tells you about the squabbling that goes on on paradise islands, about the loo arrangements you have to make with holes in certain parts of the jungle, and with leaves. No one tells you that you while away hours at a time by silently choosing the person you would like to die first, so that you get to split up their portion of food. I would choose the Australians, along with Mark because he makes too much noise. I have not told anyone this; at least, I hope I haven't.

'So,' Cherry says when we have eaten our fish, accompanied by a lot of fruit. 'While we're here. While we wait. Does anyone want to tell us anything about themselves?'

I stare at Cherry. She is more animated than I have seen her for a long time. The fish seems to have woken her up: for the first time in a while she is not crying. I say nothing. I have no desire to tell these people anything at all about myself. The weighty silence strongly suggests that the others feel the same way. In fact the silence has the same effect as a loud and forceful 'No!'

Mark says: 'Honey . . .' in a warning tone.

'I mean,' she adds, after a while. She sounds less sure of herself this time. 'I thought it might make the time pass a little less slowly. Now that we have some food inside ourselves. And we have water. I'm feeling stronger. I want to talk. Wouldn't you like something else to think about? Someone else's troubles? I'll go first.'

'Cherry,' says Mark. 'Please don't. Honey.'

'Why not?' she says. Her voice is high and tight. 'Why can I not tell them, Mark? What does anything matter now?'

'It matters because—' He stops. Then he laughs, a horrible unhappy laugh that is drenched in bitterness.

'Oh, go ahead. Tell them everything. You're right. Nothing fucking matters. I'm not even sure any of this is real, anyway.' I nod at that, knowing exactly what he means.

'I want to talk,' she says. 'Sweetie. I want to tell them. No one can be bothered with lies any more.'

Mark lies back on the sand. 'Go ahead,' he says quietly. 'Do your worst.'

I am vaguely interested by this, but not enough to muster any words of encouragement. There is a little rustling around the fire, and an expectant silence falls. I think it is expectant, though it might be lethargic.

'Right,' says Cherry. 'I am pretty sure I will feel better if I put you all in the picture. Mark and I are married – you all know that, right?'

I murmur my assent, as do others.

'We can hardly have bloody missed that fact, young lady,' Jean says. 'You live on Long Island and you're just married. On honeymoon, can't keep your hands off each other. That's actually just about all I remember.'

'Yes,' Cherry says. 'We live on Long Island, right at the tip, in a place called Montauk. And we are married. Here's the thing, though: we are not married to each other.'

It takes us a while to compute that. After a loaded pause, Ed says slowly: 'So you're married to other people?'

'That's it.'

'Oh,' I say. 'Oh my God. Being here, then . . .'

'Not ideal,' Mark mutters.

'So how on earth,' Katy asks, 'did you come to be here on holiday, having sex all over the place and pretending to be on your honeymoon? Cherry, you were right. This is a fascinating story, and for the first time since we've been here, I'm actually interested in something other than our plight. Will you tell us?'

'Of course,' Cherry says. 'I'm sick of wishing it all away. I'll tell you the whole damn story and at least you'll get to share in the misery. And we might feel better for not having a secret any more. Lord knows, in the outside world we must be totally busted by now. There's no point keeping any secrets here, is there?'

'No,' says Katy, at once. 'Tell us everything.'

We shift in our places by the fire, which are the same places we happened to sleep in on that first night, and listen, agog, to Cherry's words. Her voice is hesitant at first but becomes stronger as she realises we are all rapt.

'I grew up in North Carolina,' she says, 'and moved to Montauk when I met my husband, Tom. We've been together for nearly seven years and we have two children. Hannah is four and Aaron is two. And now they've lost their mommy and it's all because . . .' She draws a deep breath. 'Sorry. I will do my best to stick to the story. I am not happily married. No shit, right? People tell me Tom's a good guy. I find him repulsive. You know when you start feeling that way about a person, and then every little thing they do makes you want to heave? That. He's overweight – yes, even for an American, you guys. His T-shirts have sweat stains under the arms that never come out in the wash, and he thinks that a clean pair of sweat pants constitutes making an effort with his appearance. And as it happens, the sportswear is redundant: he works out as much as Homer Simpson.

'But of course I am a million times, a gazillion times worse than he is. I know it; I can see you're all thinking it, even though I can't properly see your faces. Tom thinks Mark's a good guy; he's always said Mark is one of the best, though I doubt he's saying that right now.

'So I was bored, about to hit thirty, and waiting for Tom to notice how bad his cholesterol was and to go on a health kick so that perhaps I might fall back in love with him – or, failing that, to have a heart attack and do the decent thing and die on me. That was when the new family moved into the neighbourhood, into the house right across the street from us. We live in a little community close to the ocean and the harbour. Everyone knows everyone else. It's a big boat place, Montauk, and the beaches are to die for, plus they're joined up to the mainland, unlike this hellhole. So it would be impossible to become stuck there. I now value that about a beach. You know the movie *Eternal Sunshine of the Spotless Mind*? Not my sort of movie, but it was shot locally to us. Those big white beaches – that's us.

'I stood at my upstairs window and watched them moving in. Three beautiful boys, that was what I noticed first. Adam, Brett and Connor. They all have Mark's black hair, and their mother's huge grey eyes. They look like the same boy at different stages, don't they, Mark?'

I look to Mark for his confirmation, but his face is a mask. He is staring into the fire, not responding.

'They're stunning,' Cherry confirms for him. 'So I watched the boys for a while, and smiled and waved when they looked up at me. Then their mother – Antonia. She's an ex-model, very tall and limber, with long dark curls and those grey eyes. I smiled at her and felt a bit small and lacklustre in her shadow. Then Mark came along, directing the removals, and my heart literally skipped a beat the moment I set eyes on him.

'Anyway as he's right here and not joining in, I'll skip over that part. We got to know one another, in an entirely proper sense: our whole families were friendly. But I always felt there was something between Mark and me. Something unspoken, just a mutual appreciation, if you like.

'Then came one sunny day when I had just had it with Tom. I told him to lose some fucking weight and have some self-respect. I told him that I was taking excellent care of myself, putting the effort into not only losing all my baby weight, but maintaining the body I had at sixteen, and for what? I also reported that my friend Jess had said I looked like a trophy wife, and that when we were out together, people who didn't know us must think that Tom was seriously rich to have a woman like me on his arm. She said it to be kind to me, but it stuck with me and I shouted it to him in the heat of the moment. He said I was being discriminatory and sizeist and shallow and got in his car and shot off. That's Tom all over: why deal with something when you can walk away from it? Or drive away, in his case.

'It was hot, I was miserable. I saw Mark out in their yard attending to the weeds, so I thought I'd go over and apologise, because I knew he would have heard our quarrel, which I found embarrassing.

'I admit, though, that I changed into hotpants and a halterneck before I went. Aaron was scooting around the place on his little tricycle, and Hannah was indoors watching TV.

'I went over and smiled at him. He smiled right back.

'"I have to apologise," I said. "I know you must have heard Tom and me back then."

'He was charming and sweet and pretended not to have heard a thing. I caught him checking out my hotpants. We held eye contact for the longest time – far longer than people who were just neighbours having small talk would have done.

'"No one ever said it was easy," he said. "Marriage, that is. Please don't apologise. How are you doing?"

'"Oh, you know," I said. It was such a humid day. That was why I said: "Hot." And from the look he gave me, I knew it was just a matter of time. Mark, I wish you would join in with the story. Here I am talking about you, and there you are keeping silent.'

Mark grunts. 'Carry on. You're doing OK.'

'What happened next?' Ed speaks for all of us. We are collectively transfixed. I am lying on my stomach on my sarong, which is tattered and full of holes, propped up on my elbows, and I have almost forgotten our predicament.

'What next? Well, I perked right up. There was a spring in my step. I apologised to Tom for my words, and he promised to take care of himself a little better. We started living together amicably. As friends. I had not felt friendly towards him for the longest time, and now I made a point of being pleasant, and we were all of us happier. I could see the difference in Hannah and Aaron, when Mom and Dad were suddenly playing nice.

'I was a million times better to live with, because I was thinking of Mark. Our eyes would meet across the street, and suddenly I would be smiling and patient and loving to everyone.

'The day came, of course. You all know it did. On that day, we met in the street between our two houses. Tom was at work. Antonia was not around – I guess she was at work too. All the kids were at school or daycare. So there was Mark, and there was me. We spoke for a while about nothing in particular. Then he suddenly leaned forward and said: "Hey. Cherry. Do you ever feel like doing something risky?"

'And I said: "I thought you'd never ask."'

Cherry stretches out and smiles. 'And that was that. The big secret was born. The vows were broken. As soon as we did it once, we knew we had to do it again and again. It became something we did every week. I loved our Thursday mornings more than anything. The whole thing was completely addictive. I rationalised it all to myself in every which way. People do this all the time. I'm a nicer wife, a better mother. If I can look after my needs like this, there's less chance of the boat being rocked for the children. And so on.

'Every Thursday, Tom would leave the house for work at eight. He has an OK job – he's a chef at a diner, always busy through the summer. I would dress carefully, with my best underwear, and before I set off I would make sure I was thoroughly groomed all over. I would buckle Hannah and Aaron into the back of the car and take them to daycare, and then I would drive right out of Montauk, because staying in town would be like putting up a billboard announcing our infidelity. Anyway, Mark works out of town, a long way out of town, in Brentwood. So I'd head to Starbucks, and then to a motel close to his office.

'Mark says you have to keep as close to the truth as

possible if you're going to get away with it, don't you, Mark? He won't answer, but he does say that. He told his office, and even his wife, that he was using the motel as a work space every Thursday morning, a place where he could clear his head. He's a project manager, he needs to do the blue-sky thinking, so everyone believed him. In fact they thought he was damn brilliant to do something so maverick.

'I would park in the lot at the Starbucks and go in, so that if anyone saw me or my car there'd be no problem. I'd buy two coffees, then carry them direct to the door of our room, using a route that I knew kept me away from the eyes of staff. I kicked the door, which he left unlocked, and walked in.

'It worked. It just worked. Those mornings kept me alive. I didn't even feel I was doing anything immoral after a while. I felt that my home life was so much happier while I had this thing going on that in the overall scheme of things, what we were doing was a force for good. It's not exactly unknown, right? Marital infidelity. I started to feel that this was the way people lived, the great unspoken secret of everyone's lives, and I can tell you I loved it. It was like nothing I'd ever known. We could not keep our hands off one another. You noticed? There you go.

'But after a bit, the motel became stifling. Boring. We started planning to go away together. At first it was a fantasy. "Wouldn't it be amazing?" we'd say. "A foreign beach, palm trees, nobody we know, a place we could be together and proud instead of hiding away."

'One Thursday, Mark got out his laptop and started googling for a place to go. It had to be a tropical paradise.

It had to be a place where Americans don't go, so not the Caribbean, for instance. We needed there to be no chance of running into anyone. We thought about Cuba, but we'd have had to fly to Canada first, or Mexico, and it would have been complicated. We ended up landing on this place, and it looked perfect. Well, not *this* place. Obviously we did not plan for *this* fucking thing.

'I'm not sure when the fantasy started becoming real, but suddenly it was. We planned our cover stories. We looked at it on the web and emailed the Paradise Bay to book. We composed the email together, and when Mark wrote that we were on our honeymoon, I thought I would die of happiness. I could not get enough of staring at the photos on the web. The paradise beaches, somehow different from our beaches at home. The little wooden cabins. The day spent snorkelling with the turtles and the tropical fish. Yeah, that. The one that brought us right here.

'Mark got a new credit card and we paid for the flights with it. We were paying it back together. It was a store credit card so it looked as though those payments were just going to the store. We thought of everything.

'We felt that because we were daring to do this, we would be sure to get away with it. Every detail was planned. We flew out separately, via different routes. My cover was a break in California to visit my cousin Liza. Liza was fine with my using her like that. She likes an adventure and she's none too fond of Tom. She was the only person who knew about Mark and me. "All you have to do," she said, "is to promise to tell me all about it when you're back. Promise me that, and any time Tom calls you, I'll say you're in the bathroom." In fact, my cell phone worked at Paradise Bay, so I was able to check in every day and tell him what I was up to, before he called me. A careful bit of planning of time zones, and he was never going to question it.

'Mark's story was a work trip in Hong Kong. He even went to Hong Kong and had a meeting there before we hooked up in Singapore.

'And as soon as we met, at Changi airport, we could not stop laughing. We were having so much fun. It was the funniest, naughtiest, most wonderful thing I'd ever done, and I felt that nothing could touch us. We were the golden couple.

'I do believe in karma. That's why we're here. Sorry, guys. We're here because the Fates are out to get me and Mark. You guys just got swept up in it. We took too much. We overstepped the boundaries.

'The moment Samad didn't come back, I knew it. This was the universe getting us back. So my babies are at home without their mommy. I have no idea what day it is, but I do know this: I should be home by now. We were due to start our return journey the day after Samad's fucking trip. We left the snorkelling till last, so we would still have the salt on our bodies when we got on the plane. Any way you look at it, we should have been home quite some time ago.

'Which means Tom will have called Liza to find out why I'm not back. Liza will have called my cell a million times. In the end she might have cracked and told him everything. Or she might still be stalling him. I don't know, but if he doesn't know the truth yet, he is just about to.

'And Antonia will be waiting for Mark. I was supposed

to get home a couple of days before him. I would have been all tan from "California", and I would have run into Antonia on the street and chatted about my break, and I would have asked when Mark was due back from Hong Kong, and a part of me would have thrilled at that.

'But now there are five children without a parent. And we're stuck here and I can barely look at him, and I'm sick of fucking pretending. And now you all know what we're really like and you can think what you want about us. I don't fucking care. Even if Samad came back for us now, it would make no difference. Everything's gone. We've lost it all. Everything. And it's all our fault.'

Cherry is convulsed by sobs. I stand up and walk over to her, feeling a bit awkward, but no one else is making any move to comfort her. I sit next to her and put my arm around her shoulders like little girls do at school. She leans violently into me and cries into my shoulder, which feels weird as neither of us is wearing anything more than a dirty bikini, and it all becomes very slippery.

'Oh, Cherry,' I say, and I pat her back. I try to find some words of comfort, but none come. There is no possible good resolution ahead. Her best scenario is to be rescued and go back to face the music and see her children, but I suspect that will not happen.

'Well,' Jean says in the end. 'You probably wished at some point to be stuck on a desert island with your lover. Be careful what you wish for.'

'Yeah, I know.'

'It's awful for all of us,' Gene says, his voice gruff. 'In different ways. Believe me, this is just as bad for Jean and myself as it is for you. Not the same – of course we don't have a wife and a husband respectively stashed back in Australia; we are genuinely married to one another, more's the pity – but believe me, it's as bad.'

'When you have children,' I say, 'and you can't contact them and you know how bewildered they must be that you haven't come back – well, that's horrific, isn't it? And several of us are in that situation. The marriage thing is almost irrelevant. So Tom is hurt – but you must have known you'd be found out one day. Someone would have seen you walking from Starbucks to the motel with two coffees. You were probably lucky to get away with it for as long as you did. Tom would have got hurt anyway, and Antonia, and maybe you wanted that because it gets you out of a marriage that you sound like you really don't want to be in. I mean, you and Tom, Cherry. I'm not talking about Mark and Antonia because I have no idea what the story is there.'

I am more animated than I have been since we got here. Cherry's truth has transported me.

'They already did.' This is the first thing Mark has said for a while. 'They saw her, I mean. I didn't tell you, Cherry, but a colleague of mine, Jeanette Ogilvy. She saw you. Vaguely recognised you, because on Long Island, people do. Asked me about it. Knew I worked in the motel on a Thursday. Saw you with the coffees on several Thursdays. Put it together. I denied it, but it would have blown open.'

'Oh great,' she says. 'Thanks for telling me *now*.'

'And those cover stories,' he adds. 'They were held together with sticking plaster. One prod and they'd have been in pieces.'

'Yeah,' she says. 'Whatever.'

'How about you, Mark?' Ed asks. 'How are you doing?'

Mark says nothing. I watch the fire reflected in his dark eyes. Then he inhales deeply.

'Trying not to think about any of it,' he says. 'Was doing OK until my lover here decided to share the joy with you all. My wife does not deserve any of this. Obviously. She will be better off without me. She's a wonderful woman, intelligent and, as Cherry says, beautiful. She could do better than some dick who's off fucking a neighbour every Thursday. Going away with another woman pretending that *she*, not Antonia, is my wife. Sleazebag. And the boys. They could use a better role model than this one. I know Antonia and I know for sure that there'll be no second chances. She has self-respect. She won't let me back through the door. All I hope is that I get to go back and be a McDonald's dad to them. Have them at weekends, try to make it up to them. Rather than just vanishing for ever like this. How am I doing?' He pauses. 'Crashing remorse and self-loathing pretty much sums it up.'

'They'll think we've run away together,' Cherry says suddenly. 'I didn't think of it before, but they will. If . . . if nobody ever comes. If we live here for the rest of our lives, however long that might be. Not long. Then Tom and Antonia will think that Mark and I have run away. That we never intended to go back. That we're starting a new life without a word.' Her voice is wobbling all over the place. 'And Hannah and Aaron, and Adam and Brett and Connor. They'll all grow up thinking we . . .' She cannot say any more, and once more I cradle her as she sobs uncontrollably on my bony shoulder.

'That won't happen,' Katy says firmly. 'Certainly you will have a lot of explaining to do. But I am completely confident we'll get away. We have drinking water. We caught fish. At least we're not stuck up a mountain or something. In a way we're lucky. We'd have to be here a long time before we came anywhere close to running out of fruit, and the sea's all around us and we'll get better at catching things from it now we've done it once. We can survive here. We can live. Somebody will come and pick us up. We'll keep the fire going. Don't worry, Cherry. I promise you, as far as I possibly can, that we won't be dying here.'

'What makes you so sure of that?' asks Jean, her voice dry. 'If one might ask.'

Katy hesitates before she says: 'I just believe it. I know most of you don't, but I believe in God and I have complete faith in Him to look after us. And believing gives me strength. You can choose whether to expect the best or the worst. I'm choosing to expect the best. We can only guess what happened to Samad – goodness knows, we've exhausted speculation on that front – but I cannot see that seven people can disappear, just like that, and no one ever looks for them. I was sure there would be water on the island, and there was. It's the same thing. I'm sure we will get away, and we will. People do not just get abandoned and die all forgotten.'

'To be fair,' Mark says, 'it's you, Katy, that's kept us going. The rest of us were bloody useless. If Katy hadn't kept at it and found the spring, we'd all be dead. That is an indisputable fact.'

We all nod. It is sobering to have to acknowledge that

only one of us had the presence of mind to find the thing we needed to survive, while the other six lay down with no fight whatsoever, and gave up.

I look at Katy in the firelight. She is better than all of us. We should not snipe about her being bossy, and I vow not to, ever again.

'It's probably easier when you don't have children, you know,' she says lightly. 'I'm single. I'd split up with my partner not long before I came here. I don't have anybody who's going to be devastated by my failure to return. That is actually a huge burden not to have. I know that you guys, Jean and Gene, have children. Esther has her little girl. Now we know that there are a load of kids in Montauk wondering where Mummy and Daddy have got to. It's just me and Ed who haven't reproduced. So I think Ed and I can see more clearly than the rest of you, and all I can see is that we need to do everything we can, because every day that we survive, even thrive, is a day closer to the day a boat comes and picks us up. And even if that never happens, we may as well live here as best we can. Food makes a difference. You can see that tonight. Cherry had barely managed to say a word in days, and actually having something close to a proper dinner gave her the strength to tell us her story. Which I would say has done all of us good, in an odd way.'

'Maybe,' I hazard, 'like Cherry said, we *should* all share our stories. It might make the time go quicker. I feel better for thinking about other stuff. I'd never even heard of Montauk but I really liked that *Eternal Sunshine* film and now I feel I can imagine the place. And some of the things that go on in it.'

Neither Cherry nor Mark responds to this, but I see Jean and Gene looking at one another.

'We will,' Jean says quickly. 'But not tonight. I, for one, am going to have to work up to it. For quite a while. Let me think about it, OK? But we have a story to tell you all. That's for sure.'

chapter nineteen

Cathy

July 1988

Life in the Village appears to be carrying on as if nothing happened. Everyone seems to have forgotten that we ought to be playing in heaven by now, talking to Jesus, enfolded in His love for ever more. It did not happen, because it was a lie.

They can carry on with their stupid lives, living by arbitrary rules, obeying no omniscient God but a control freak who calls himself by the name of a prophet and who gets to make all the women pregnant whenever he fancies it. I do not plan to live out the rest of my days in this screwed-up excuse for a community. I am seeing it through new eyes, and it is a revelation, the very opposite of the kind of revelations they pretend to have round here.

I catch Cassandra watching me, and I know that she can see it. She is shrewd with people, my birth mother, and she takes a particular suspicious interest in me.

We should not officially know who our parents are. They are all 'the Parents'. We are all supposed to be children of God, not of men. Everyone knows, though. Cassandra and Moses are my biological parents. Moses is a common factor uniting most of the under-twenty-fives in half-siblinghood.

Cassandra played her trump card this morning.

'Catherine,' she said. 'I can see you are restless, so I have arranged a wonderful surprise for you, my dear.'

I knew better than to be excited.

'What?' I asked, when she stared at me for so long that I knew I had to say something.

'Marriage!' she exclaimed. 'Moses has agreed. You and Philip are old enough now. Your wedding is to be held as soon as we can arrange it. He says the middle of August will be suitable.'

I felt sick, because I had feared she would do this to me.

'I'm only sixteen, though,' I complained.

'You are an adult. You are educated. You are ready.'

'I'm bloody not,' I muttered, and she slapped my face, hard. 'Sorry,' I said, out of habit, hating her.

'Cathy,' she said, when we had both calmed down. 'When you are married, you will feel differently about your life. Your priorities will shift. You are behaving like a petulant child. That will change when you have a child of your own to think about.'

I looked at her, concentrating hard on not looking like a petulant child, nor like someone who could conceivably, as it were, be a mother.

Cassandra looked back with her clear grey eyes. She has long straight hair like mine, and fine bones and pale, almost translucent skin. Sometimes when I look through magazines that people leave lying around at school, I think that my mother could have been a model. She is tall and skinny and, I suppose, beautiful. Instead she has devoted her entire life to this place. She came here as a young adult. I sometimes try to imagine choosing this over everything else, and that is when I know we will never understand one another.

'You've never been married,' I pointed out, realising as I said it how sulky it sounded.

'That is because I was chosen by the Father,' she said. She meant Moses, not God.

'And you've shared him with most of the women here.'

She pursed her lips and seemed about to slap me again. Then she inhaled deeply. 'Well,' she said quietly, 'that's one thing you will not have to suffer, as you grew from his seed. And you should be grateful that I have found you a suitable husband. It took a lot of work on my part to have you, rather than Martha, chosen for Philip.'

'Yeah,' I said. 'Lucky me. I am so, so *incredibly* lucky.'

Philip and I have known we were going to marry for many years, and I have tried hard to look on him as my 'boyfriend'. It doesn't work: he repels me. The sight of him makes me feel sick, when I think about what we are supposed to be going to do together. There are a couple of boys at school I could feel the right way for: Sean Holden in particular. Sean likes me and often talks to me, and when he does, I find myself smiling and chatting back and wanting to meet him after school and go to the cinema and all the things ordinary people do. This, in itself, feels like a miracle (if I may say something so blasphemous, which I may, in my head) and makes my feelings for Philip (best described as cold revulsion at the moment) impossible to reconcile with my destiny.

I freeze when Sean speaks to me, if there is any chance at all of Martha seeing us together. If there isn't, then we laugh and talk and I feel myself becoming someone completely different. I turn into the person I want to be.

Philip is the same height as me, but with thick shoulders and fat arms. He sweats. His spots are nearly gone now, but he still smells a bit rancid. I remember when we used to dress him up in girls' clothes and make him be a princess in our games. If I marry him he will have total control over me. He will become my boss. I will have to do what he tells me to do.

'Catherine,' Cassandra said. 'Listen to me. You will marry Philip and have his children, because that is what God wants for you.'

'You just said,' I was unable to stop myself pointing out, 'that you had to work hard to get me chosen for him. So it's more what *you* want than what God wants.'

'Enough! You will not complain. Is that understood? I do not want to hear one more word.'

I sighed. I know when it is time to stop. 'OK,' I said. 'Sorry, Cassandra.'

She hugged me awkwardly. 'That's better,' she said. She pulled back and looked at me with those all-seeing eyes of hers. 'Good girl.'

I am acting from now on. I am not going to marry Philip. I do not believe in Moses, or his version of God, any more. I do not want to live here. I am ready to throw it all away and find something else. Anything will do.

chapter twenty

Gene and Katy spend the day sitting on the rock together, fishing. They make an odd pair there, side by side above the edge of the beach. Gene is wearing the faded sunhat he was sporting on the fishing trip, and Katy has improvised a head covering by wrapping her sarong around her head like a turban. It leaves her arms and legs and back exposed, but we still have supplies of sunscreen, and she says if she can stave off the headache, she can live with everything else.

I stare at them for much of the day. They talk to each other almost constantly, but I have no idea what they can be saying. I find it difficult to talk to Katy now, because I defer to her in everything. She is so much more together than I am. Gene, on the other hand, talks intensely, normally looking very serious, and they are forever passing their water bottle back and forth, and sharing fruit.

From time to time they land a fish. That is the greatest sight in the world. Protein is, indeed, the thing that allows you to function. If I ever got away from here, I would revere protein for its quasi-magical restorative powers. I would also never eat another banana again for the rest of my life.

Getting away from here is not going to happen. This is where I live. This is where I will die. These are the people with whom I will spend the rest of my life. This stretch of sand, and the rainforest behind it, is the universe.

At least I am with tolerable people. I can live with all of them, and I admire Katy, and Ed has, somehow, become my best friend.

I wander into the warm sea and float on my back for a while. Doing that used to be relaxing when it felt like a treat, when I was on holiday. Now it is just another way of passing the time. I save it up. The sea keeps us clean, but it also keeps our skin salty and scaly, and my hair is so dry it seems about to crack. I look at the sky. I spend a lot of time looking at the sky. It changes: sometimes it is light blue, and other times it is dark blue. Sometimes there are clouds, but they are always white and fluffy, and they blow away. It has not rained. I would like it to rain, very much.

'You look almost happy.'

I spin around, putting my feet down on white coral. Ed is standing next to me.

'I didn't notice you arriving,' I say. 'You positively startled me.'

'Sorry.'

'Don't be. I thought nothing surprising was ever going to happen again. It's good to be startled.'

He smiles. 'Right.'

I look at him. Ed's face is burned and his nose has

peeled. I'm sure mine has too. Everyone looks ravaged by the sun. He has lost weight and his ribs are sticking out. And, like all the men, he has a beard that is growing wilder and more Robinson Crusoe by the day. All the same, I love to look at him.

It comes on me suddenly, the realisation. I have not felt any form of attraction to a man for a long time. Now my legs actually weaken beneath me, as I realise. I look at him and feel breathless with sudden desire, and I try hard to arrange my features in a way that will hide it. Get through this conversation, I tell myself, and think about this later.

Ed is the person here I want to have beside me, all the time.

'Are you OK, Esther?'

I force a smile. 'How old are you, Ed?'

'Guess.'

'Oh, don't. I'll only have to say something younger than I think. Younger than me. Maybe ten years younger than me? Maybe you're thirty? So let's log my official guess at twenty-eight.'

He laughs. 'Thirty-one. Close. But it's just a number here, isn't it? We're all in the same boat and it makes no difference whether we're eighteen or eighty-eight.'

'In the same boat? Unfortunate turn of phrase, that.'

'It is, isn't it? Oh, to be in the same boat. Apologies.'

'I realised this morning that I have spent every single night of my forties on this island. It's another "be careful what you wish for", isn't it? I would have casually said that such a thing would be heaven, before it happened. You know: "Stranded on a desert island as a birthday treat? Yes please!"'

He laughs. 'Any idea how many nights it's been?'

'I completely and utterly lost count right back at the start when we ran out of water. You?'

'I'd guess ten, but I don't know. We should have made a tally chart or something. Or Katy should. She's the only one who would have kept count properly.'

'She probably knows exactly how long we've been here.'

'I expect she's not telling us because it would be bad for morale. So what do you make of Mark and Cherry?'

I stifle a laugh. I cannot actually laugh at them because of their children, but I almost want to.

'I would never have guessed. Never. I completely believed they were newly-weds on their paradise honeymoon.'

'I did too. I suppose when someone tells you they're married, you don't go around thinking: "Hmm, but are you *really*, I wonder?"'

'Or, "Yes, but are you married to *each other*?"'

'I feel for them. I really do,' Ed says.

'Me too. That guilt is awful.'

'In fact, I feel much worse for those of you with children than I do for me and Katy. She's right, I can see it in all of your faces. If you have a child at home, this is infinitely worse than if you haven't.'

'No babies in your life then, Ed?'

'Oh, Christ no. No youthful indiscretions that bore fruit, absolutely not.'

We are swimming out to sea together, without having discussed it. I am doing a slow breaststroke. Slow is the only speed we have.

'What would happen if we carried on?' I wonder. 'How far would we get before we ran out of energy and just stopped trying?'

'Not very,' Ed says, and he stops and spins around towards me. 'Look, Esther. Can I say something? This is going to sound weird, so I apologise in advance.'

My feet do not reach the ground. I am treading water, and becoming very tired very quickly.

'I can take weird,' I tell him, suddenly alert with adrenalin. I hope that it is going to be what I want it to be. I hope that it isn't. 'What isn't weird?' I add.

'Well.' He bites his lip and laughs. 'OK. Here goes. I wasn't going to say anything, but now I think, what the hell. When I first saw you, back on that bus in that other lifetime, I thought you were incredibly beautiful. I knew at once there was something special about you. That's why we came to Paradise Bay. Jonah and Piet were laughing at me because I wanted to go to where you were. Even though I thought it was Jonah you liked the look of, not me. And I only came on this trip because Katy said you might be going. And even now, after all we've been through, I still think you're the most beautiful woman I've ever met. I'm not meaning to proposition you or anything. I just thought I should tell you. That's all. I wanted to say it, just like Cherry wanted to tell her secrets. Sometimes you just have to.'

His sunburned face is even redder than it was before. He looks away from me, as shy as a child on his first day at school.

I have no idea what to say, but I know that I am smiling.

'Really?' I manage in the end. 'Seriously, Ed? Because

that is not how I see myself at all. In fact that's as far as you could possibly get from the way I see myself. I'm amazed. Sorry, that's why I'm not managing to be gracious. Seriously? You're not joking? You're not just saying this for a bet with Mark . . . ?'

He smiles. 'Don't be silly. I'm not joking. Honestly I'm not. But the last thing I want is for you to worry that you've been stranded on an island with an obsessed nutcase. As I said, I'm not saying this as a prelude to anything. I'm just saying it. Because I was tired of not saying it. And because you were there, in front of me. And so it just came out.'

I look at him. He looks back. Something inside me tightens up. We gaze into each other's eyes for a long time. I am still treading water. I want to savour this moment, but I cannot.

'Can we swim in a little way?' I gasp. 'I can't keep this going any longer.'

'Of course. Sorry. God, I'm really sorry. You should have said.'

We swim together until we can both touch the ground. When my feet find the coral, even though it is spiky, I am so relieved that I feel myself nearly buckling.

I am acutely conscious of Ed, of everything about him, and of the small but significant distance between us. Should I say it? I wonder. I know that I will. There is, after all, nothing else to do.

'Well,' I say. 'Since we're being honest. I've liked you all along. You know I have. And I was thinking, just now, that . . . Oh, fuck it.'

I walk right up to him, so that our bodies are touching,

and I put a hand behind his neck and pull his head forward so I can kiss him. He kisses me back. I had forgotten how it feels to explore someone new. For precious minutes I forget everything else and lose myself in the moment, in Ed.

We pull back and smile at each other. His hands are on my waist.

'Promise it's not just because I'm the only single straight woman here?' I say, making an effort not to look back at the beach, where I know Jean is staring and Gene and Katy are pretending not to have noticed.

He takes my hand and holds it tightly. 'And not because I'm the only eligible man?'

'Promise.'

It starts to rain before the fish have finished cooking. Gene and Katy have caught six today, and we are sitting around the fire waiting for them when it happens. The sun has already disappeared behind the forest, but the sky is still light. I have been vaguely aware of clouds sweeping in, but have not paid the changing light and the static air much attention. I am too distracted.

'Did anyone feel that?' Cherry says. She puts a hand out flat. 'A raindrop. I'm certain it was a raindrop.'

'I felt one too,' Ed says a moment later. I shuffle a little closer to him. This is not an environment for secrets, but I am pretending that no one has noticed. Nobody has said anything, and I have blanked out the little looks and the fact that his arm is around my waist, so we have, in fact, no secret at all. I am glad. I want to shout about it. I want Katy to ask me a leading question so I can talk about Ed.

I am like a schoolgirl with a crush, desperate to steer the subject around to my beloved.

And now, at last, it is raining. The water we need so much is splattering down from the sky, in drops that are immediately fat and huge. The sensation of being rained upon is so novel that it makes me laugh aloud, and then I jump up and throw my head back and savour the drops falling on my face.

Water is falling from the sky. Even though it would have been so much more welcome a few days ago, it still feels like a miracle and it almost makes me believe in a supreme being. The same one who stranded us here is now showering us with fresh water.

The rain gathers momentum, and soon it is falling so fast that it becomes an attack. My hair is drenched, the salt washed right out of it. The bikini and sarong that are all I own are clinging to me. I notice people bustling around the fire, grabbing the fish out of it. Raindrops are bouncing off the sand like bullets.

There is only one thing to do. Ed grabs my hand and we turn and run for the shelter of the jungle, where we stand under the canopy and listen to the rain pounding on top of the forest's leafy roof, and watch it blasting the sand in front of us, putting our fire out and destroying our dinner.

I look at him and he smiles down at me.

'Quite a day,' he says, and puts an arm around my shoulders.

I step closer and do the only thing I want to do in the world. I turn and kiss him again.

chapter twenty-one

We sit in the forest, but as close to the edge of it as we can because of the noises the bugs and creatures are making in there. I still hate being on their terrain. I cannot stop imagining the massive lizards strolling all over me as I sleep, taking bites out of my face and pulling my hair out to put in their nests. More realistically, the place is full of mosquitoes, and even though the practice nurse back in the other world told me that this was not a malarial area, I do not trust the little chart she pulled up on her computer. This island was not on it, for one thing.

There is nothing we can do to keep them away, now we are in the rainforest. Nobody brought insect repellent with them when they came on the day trip; Jean says she did, but she left it in the boat and so it has gone to wherever Samad ended up. None of us bother to speculate about him any more.

We sit in a gap between the trees, closer to each other than usual. Without a fire, everything is more frightening. The high whine of mosquitoes is a counterpoint to the pounding rain. I recall myself in Kuala Lumpur, crashing into a bar to escape rain like this.

'Here you go.' Jean is passing out little parcels, wrapped in banana leaves. 'It's not going to be tasty, but it should keep you going.'

'Tell us about dinner, Jeannie?' asks Mark. She smiles at him. He flatters her, I think, and she has warmed to him now she knows his real story. She hated the idea of him being blissfully married to Cherry. She loves the extent of their fuck-up.

'I present you: partly cooked sushi made from a fish whose name I don't know. Drenched in a rainwater coulis.'

'Yum,' I say. 'Thanks, Jean. Thanks for rescuing it when the rest of us were just feeling the rain in our hair.'

'You're welcome, darling.' She hands mine to me. 'But you, you grumpy old bastard, you can go last.'

'Fine,' says her husband.

The rain clouds suddenly cover the moon and we are plunged into absolute darkness. It is only when that happens that I realise it has not been properly dark in all the time we have been here. The sky has always been clear and at night the moon and the stars have shone down on us without stopping.

'Oh,' says Katy.

'Who turned out the lights?' says Gene. He says it in a jokey voice, but no one laughs.

I reach for Ed's hand, and squeeze it when I find it. He squeezes back, so I assume I have got the right person. The rain is pounding more heavily than ever. The mosquitoes are around us in a cloud, and when I put my other hand in front of my face I cannot see it, not even when it is before my eyes.

'I don't like this.' Cherry sounds as scared as I feel.

'Neither do I,' Ed admits.

'Well.' Katy draws a deep breath. 'There's absolutely nothing we can do. Nowhere we can go. We just have to sit here and wait for as long as it takes. At least we're together. The mozzies are going to feast on us all they want. I don't fancy actually sleeping here because of all the . . . wildlife. So we might have to sit here all night.'

'At least it'll get light in the morning.' I am trying to be positive, but it just sounds stupid. I wanted to spend tonight with Ed. I wanted to slip away with him.

'As far as we know.'

'What does that mean, Mark?' Cherry demands. 'I mean, what the hell? Why wouldn't it get light in the morning?' Her voice is rising.

'I just mean . . . Maybe it's not that Samad didn't come back for us. Perhaps something bigger has happened. I've been thinking this for a while.'

'Something bigger, such as?' Jean's voice is sharp.

'Such as? OK. Here are some options. Don't tell me none of you have thought of any of this, because I won't believe you. There are rogue Russians out there with nukes pointed all over the place. It's always been poised on a hair trigger. Maybe that's happened. Maybe they accidentally nuked Alaska or something. Perhaps there's been a nuclear war. It wouldn't take much for that to engulf the world. That could be the sun going out for ever. This could be radioactive rain.'

'Oh Mark, shut up.' I hear myself saying it, though I

hadn't planned to. 'You're being stupid. I don't think the sun goes out from a nuclear exchange between America and Russia, does it? Not in Malaysia?'

'No,' he says. 'I know we all like to think that Samad fell over and banged his head, because that's a lovely benign, local explanation. But if they started throwing nukes around, India and Pakistan would have joined in. We're not so far from that. Also, Japan's just over there. Anything could have happened.'

The rain is still falling. I cannot believe we longed for this. I force myself to swallow pieces of half-cooked fish even though they are cold and wet, and pick bones out from between my teeth whenever I find them. This is not the moment to choke. I shuffle right up close to Ed and wonder if Mark and Cherry and Gene and Jean are doing the same with one another.

'You can shut up, Mark,' Gene says suddenly. 'There is no point scaremongering like that and it's a stupid way to talk. Whatever has happened, we're stuck here and there's not a thing we can do about any of it. If anyone wants distracting . . . well, I'm prepared to follow Cherry's lead from last night and let you all know why it is that you'll have noticed Jean and me not getting on harmoniously much of the time. Katy's already heard the whole tale while we've been fishing, so I hope she'll put up with hearing it all over again.'

'You know I will, Gene,' she says in the most gentle voice I have ever heard her use. 'Of course I will.'

'Jeannie, you don't mind?'

'If you must. But I'll be correcting you if need be.'

'Don't I know it.'

Everyone is silent for what feels like a long time. Ed's body is warm and comforting next to mine, and in spite of everything I want to lead him away quietly into the rainforest, away from everyone. But I don't.

Things fly and creep, cheep and crack twigs all around us. The rain intensifies. Drops are coming through the forest canopy and splashing on to us.

'Well,' says Gene. 'We've both kept a lid on it because we agreed not to talk about it while we were here. But I can tell you this: none of you besides Katy here knows either of us at all, because you cannot know us without knowing about what has gone on in the last two years.'

'You know we have three children?' Jean says. 'A girl and two boys. Two little granddaughters too.'

We all murmur our assent. We do indeed know this.

'Well, there is something we haven't told you about one of our boys.'

'Jeannie!' Gene is annoyed. 'I'm telling it. Butt out.'

'Well don't expect me to let you present it all your way.'

'*I know*. Let me start at least.'

'Go on then. We'll let them judge, shall we?'

He sighs.

'I'll tell you the tale. Jeannie will tell you I'm wrong. You can do your best to work it out. But my way's the right way. Here goes.'

And, in the absolute darkness, he begins to speak.

chapter twenty-two

We listen to Gene's story in total blackness, to a background of unsettling jungle creatures and pounding rain. I am gripped from the very beginning. Ed's arm around me is my anchor to safety, and I wish we had got together earlier. It suddenly feels as if we have wasted too much time.

'We both agreed to come to Malaysia, and not a second has gone by that I haven't regretted it. Of course, there's being stuck here, but even before then it wasn't working out as it should have done. Not the healing and refreshing break. Turns out – and I don't think Jeannie'll disagree with me on this one – that if you go away from the thing that is central to your life, you see what's become of your relationship and it isn't necessarily going to be pretty, hey?

'We would never in a million years have come to Malaysia. When we went on holiday, we stayed in Australia. It's a country you don't need to leave. You've got the beaches, the mountains, the interior, you've got cosmopolitan cities and—'

'Gene,' says his wife, her tone withering. 'You're not the fucking tourist information centre. Get on with it.'

'Yeah. I've not always lived in Australia, you know. That's why I like it so much. Anyway, we weren't meant to be here. It should have been Ben. Our youngest. Little Ben. He was the one coming here, and he was coming on a trip of a lifetime with Samira, his fiancée. I'm going to say what happened quickly, to get it over with, because even though we're his parents, which means we're meant to be the strong ones, the ones in charge, neither Jeannie nor me is very good at dealing with the reality of this. As we have discovered since we've been away from home.

'Ben had been in hospital for two years and fifteen days when we came on this little jaunt. I hate the fact that I've lost track of the days. I want to know what day it is, because I want to think about it being the same day where he is, in Brizzie. I know this, though: he has had two birthdays and two Christmases in there, and by now it's probably been his third Easter. I always had the highest level of health insurance, because I worked on the basis that you had to be ready for the unimaginable to strike.

'And the unimaginable did strike.

'Ben was thirty-one. Now he's thirty-three. So there he is: a thirty-one-year-old man, engaged to be married to Samira, who is a lovely girl, and we're looking forward to some more grandchildren coming along. Jeannie and Samira and Samira's family are planning the wedding, which is going to be part Hindu, part secular Western style, which all seems to be an excuse for a mammoth party that lasts weeks. All of which is fine by me. More than fine. Perfect. Ben lives in Brisbane, in West End, which, believe me, is a cooler place to be than Chapel Hill, where his old parents live, but not so far away. He comes over to see us every week or two. He's a good boy, the best: handsome and clever and great at everything he does. A hell of a rugby player. We used to worry about Ben and his rugby, didn't we, Jeannie? All those injuries you hear about. Broken necks. But he seemed untouchable. No broken bones, never been X-rayed before. He never caught the flu, never got the vomiting bugs that went around. He used to get awards at school for perfect attendance because he was never sick.

'And then it all caught up with him at once.'

'Oh Gene,' says his wife, and now her tone is completely different. 'Do you have to say it? I don't want to hear it, not here.'

'It's a bit late now, darling.' His attitude to her is different too. He is much gentler. 'Come on. Me saying it isn't going to make it real. It's already real.'

'Don't tell us if you don't want to,' Ed says.

'No, I've said I'll tell you, and I will. I want you to know. It was the quickest thing to happen. When you realise that however much you try, no matter what you do, you can't go back and undo something, that destroys you. It should be the easiest little thing: you should be able to go, "no, that wasn't right – we'll go back and do it differently". If there was any way in which I could turn back time and put myself there in his place, then I would. I would do it a million times over. But I can't, and that is the bleak truth of the universe. When we washed up here, I felt the cosmos had skewed itself and I hoped that might give me a chance to hop over into Ben's life, but no such luck.

'So he was crossing a road. That was all it was. Crossing a road like everyone does every bloody day, except in a place like this, of course. It was a busy road in Brisbane at rush hour, and he was a bit closer to the corner than he would ideally have been, but the traffic was practically at a standstill and he was just walking between the stationary cars.

'The motorbike was weaving its way between them, as they do, beating the traffic by fitting through the spaces between the cars. Now don't get me started on that. If a biker wants to be treated as a driver when it comes to how much space you give when you overtake, then he should bloody act as a driver and wait in the traffic like anyone else.

'It was the work of a second. Ben steps out, the bike is right there, it smashes into him and he and the rider are flung into the cars. The rider had all his gear on, of course, so he just gets up and brushes himself down. Ben doesn't. It takes far too long for the ambulance to reach him through the traffic, but he hangs on.

'They call us. I pick up the phone, expecting anything but this. Some people say you know when something's happened to your child, but you don't. It hit us like a bolt from the blue. He's in a coma, they say. But it's Ben. I hang on to that. It's Ben, so I know he'll be OK. Jeannie's in a terrible state as we go to the hospital, but I keep saying to her, it's fine, he'll be fine. I think I have a parent's instinct. I bloody promise her we'll get there and he'll be sitting up in bed asking to go home. I believed in God, up until we got to the hospital and found that I was wrong. I had a very God-fearing past. I lost it all, in that instant. Gone.'

'Whereas I almost began to believe again,' Jean's voice says quietly, from the dark. 'It's tempting.'

'Yeah. We get there and they take us into a quiet little room and Jeannie's just saying over and over that she wants to see him, and I suddenly think: they've brought us in here to say he's dead. That's what happens on the TV. You get there and it's too late and they take you into a little room.

'But he's not dead, they say. He's in a coma. He might wake up, or then again . . .' His voice tails off, and Jean takes up the story while we all pretend not to be able to hear Gene struggling to compose himself, or Katy whispering words of comfort to him.

'Samira,' says Jean, her voice sharp. 'We knew she was a lovely girl, but now she showed us what she was made of. She's sat by his bed almost as much as we have, over the past two years. We said to her, look, Sammy. Go out there and have some fun. You don't have to be in here all the time. We wouldn't blame her, would we, Gene? If she went out and met someone else. She's the same age as Ben, and that means she wants to get on with the babies. He'd want her to do that. He'd understand. She's not there every day but she still goes in three times a week and sits with him and holds his hand and talks to him. Your heart just breaks for her, it really does. That's the father of the children she should have started having by now, hooked up on all of that. He's in a private hospital, thanks to Gene's insurance, and he has the best care you could ask for. He just doesn't wake up. We sit and stare and wait, but nothing happens.'

'I'm sure he can hear us,' Gene interrupts, composed again. 'Jeannie says he can't. I know, Jean. I know you say you're being realistic. But I am certain he's listening. I've sat by his bed every single day for two years and fifteen days. I've told him everything. He knows it all.

'Now before the accident, he and Sammy were planning their honeymoon. They were going to come here. Not actual here, not to the fucking jungle in a mozzie cloud in the rain. But to where we were, the island with the guest houses and the cafés. We had just bought their tickets as a wedding present when the accident happened.

'And then, when the two-year anniversary was coming up, we started to think that we should do something with the tickets, because the airline had said that under the circumstances they'd let us rebook whenever we wanted. We offered them to Sammy, of course, but she said no. I think we're starting to irritate her a little, to be honest. And then Jean decided we should come away together. I thought about it for a while, and I decided she was right. We did this for Ben, came here so we could go home and tell him all about it. That was the plan. As we've discovered, the gods like to laugh at plans.

'It was Jeannie who thought of it, as I say, but I could see where she was coming from. We could not possibly have contemplated a holiday in the normal run of things – how could we leave our child like that and go off camping like we used to do? – but this was different. This was Ben's trip. I asked him about it, when it was just him and me.

'"What if your mother and I went on the holiday for

you, eh, Ben?" I said, staring at him, waiting for a reaction. "To that island."

'And I saw a flicker behind his eyelids. I am sure I did. It was the first movement I'd seen from him, in all that time.

'"Nurse!" I yelled. They never come when you do that. Only on the TV does that work. I went and found someone, beside myself with excitement and anticipation. "Nurse, he moved! His eyelid. He moved his eye behind it."

'They came when they heard that, all right. I sat for the entire morning waiting for him to wake up. Nothing happened; but all the same, I knew what I had seen.'

'And that,' says Jean, 'is why we're here. It seemed like the thing to do. Both of us needed a change of scene, a bit of perspective, and we were doing this for our little Ben, our baby. We were doing it so we could tell him about it, whether he would hear our words or not. We were here so we could go back there.'

'It hasn't worked out so well for us, has it?' says Gene. 'Even before this fucking thing happened. I don't think either Jeannie or I realised, until we got away, how much our lives had become about Ben and only Ben. We hated being alone together. Just the two of us with nothing to do? No thank you. Laze around on the beach when our son is hooked up to a machine? Why would we want to do that? We turned on each other. As you noticed.' He clears his throat. 'For which I suppose we should apologise, hey, Jean?'

'Oh, I don't think so,' she snaps. 'They were hardly enormously inconvenienced in the scheme of things. This, here, now – this is enormously inconvenient. I'm not going to say sorry for anything.'

Gene actually laughs at that. 'Fair play to you. We're not sorry, it seems. So when we realised we couldn't stand each other's company once we were away from our lives in Brisbane, we tried to do our own thing, separately, and in spite of myself I started to wind down a bit. I could not reconcile my lying on the beach with Ben lying in the hospital – that was never going to happen. However, if I kept busy, trekking through the jungle, running along that concrete path around the coast to those bigger places, swimming as far as I could in the sea, I found it was doing me good.

'The day trip to this bloody place was supposed to be a reconciliation for Jeannie and me. I was feeling ready to go back. It was nearly time to see our Ben again, and I had so much to tell him.

'And then this happened. I considered, and I still do, that the way that arsehole never came back was a direct message to Jean and me from the universe. I haven't yet figured out exactly what the message says. Sometimes I think . . .' His voice wobbles, but no one interrupts while he composes himself. 'That Ben's dead,' he says, finally. 'And that we are too. Or if not, we soon will be. My body's giving up on me. I welcome that.

'And maybe you're right, Mark. Maybe it *is* something huge that's happened in the outside world that's kept us here. Those of us with families out there will be hoping it's something very local, and I can't for the life of me think of a credible event that would have affected folk from Brizzie to Paradise Bay but not us here. So I'm not letting myself think that everyone but us has somehow vanished in a puff of nuclear smoke.

'The only thing I cannot bear . . . just cannot fucking bear . . . is the idea of Ben thinking we couldn't hack it and have abandoned him. And Steve and Cassie doing the same, thinking we'd asked them to sit with him for ten days when all along we were planning to up sticks and never come back. I hope they look for us properly. I hope they realise. I hope they haven't stopped being beside him, haven't gone back to their normal lives and left him there, on his own in his room with just the nurses.

'And the thing that keeps me going is the fact that we're trapped here the same way Ben is trapped wherever he is. Sometimes I think he's right here next to us, in spirit. I start to wonder if I'm actually in a coma the same as he is, and this is the place my mind has made for me.

'But if I was, Ben would be here, and to be honest with you, I wouldn't have stranded myself with you people – Katy here aside. No offence, but if this was in my mind, I'd have Ben with me, and I'd have a doctor, a survival expert and a foraging chef. Plus some books and magazines and flares. So I can only assume it's real. And that's that. My wife has barely interrupted me at all, so that proves it. That is our story.'

chapter twenty-three

Cathy

July 1988

I am more scared than I have ever been in my life. When I thought I was about to leave this planet and go to live with Jesus, I was less scared than I am at the prospect of relocating by a matter of miles.

Tomorrow is the day. Everything is ready. I could still back out now, but it is unthinkable.

I have woken early and there is no chance I can possibly go back to sleep. My life is about to change for ever.

Sarah shrugged it all off when the Rapture never happened, said it had been interesting anyway and went back home. The TV people pushed their cameras in her face but she walked right on through them without even turning to look.

It was Sarah I went to when I realised I needed to leave.

I am sixteen. That is most of the way to being grown-up. They thought I was old enough to be married. I say that I am old enough to make my own choices. I choose not to become a Village wife. I choose the wide and sinful world. Whatever happens, it is the only choice I can make.

Nobody has ever told me not to leave. No one has said what a sin it would be, and that anyone who tried would be struck down by God and then hunted down by Moses and brought straight back. No one has said that because they do not need to. I am about to attempt something that is unthinkable.

The way I feel at the moment, it is either this or kill myself. If one does not work, I have made fallback preparations for the other.

For the past week, I have taken a few things to school, at the bottom of my bag, every day. Although GCSEs are over and we don't have to go in, I have told Cassandra and the others at the Village that I want to go, to read quietly in the library and prepare myself for my wedding. And to be honest, everyone is still trying so hard to act normally after the non-Apocalypse that no one has bothered to question me.

Sarah has met me there every morning, and she has taken away the things I have given her. If anyone looked in my wardrobe and drawers, they would discover that half of my clothes, such as they are, and all of my toiletries and books have disappeared. I will walk out of here this evening with nothing, and I will never come back.

Although no one has ever left, people have died. Victoria died. We had her funeral here. It was awful. It was in the paper and everything. Now I wonder whether God struck her down because she was leaving, rather than for swearing as we were always told.

I am trying to cleanse myself of thoughts like that. God did not strike her down. A car did.

Although this fact makes me wonder who was at the wheel.

I have left a note for Cassandra and another for Philip, because it seems only fair to tell someone personally if you are running away a month before you are supposed to be marrying them. I told Cassandra I was going to Scotland, but I only said that because I'm not.

I'm going to go to school in a few hours, and Sarah will meet me there, and we'll go straight back to her house. Obviously I have no money, but her parents (who I haven't met because I've never been allowed to go to anyone's house) are going to help.

'Turns out they got a bit of a scare,' Sarah said, 'when I joined you because the world was going to end. And they were so pleased that I came back again – they thought that Moses guy was going to make us all commit suicide when it didn't happen. Can you imagine? Turns out they were absolutely bloody beside themselves. That makes them want to help you get away too. They're desperate to save you.'

I smiled at that. 'Saving' me by helping me leave the Saviour? The world has turned on its head. It is scary but thrilling.

'You can't stay in the town,' she said, 'or those people will come along and haul you back. You know that. I know that. We all do. So we're going to drive you to the services, and my auntie Michelle will pick you up there and you can go and stay with them in London. They live in Isleworth. You can live with them for a while, then get a job and a flat or something.'

I just nodded. I cannot imagine staying in Isleworth (I had to look it up in a street atlas at school just to find out how to spell it), and I cannot imagine Sarah's auntie Michelle or the uncle Steve who goes with her, or the twin cousins Joe and Max. I can certainly not conceive of myself with a job, or a flat. It is petrifying but amazing, and it is hard to express just how determined I am. The world is opening up before me, and I am trusting the goodwill of strangers.

I need to do some A levels, and I need to earn some money. I need to become myself.

For the moment, however, I just need to get out of here. This is the strangest thing: as the sun rose that morning, and the Apocalypse never happened, everything inside me changed completely. I look at 'Moses' (and one day I will find out what my father's real name is), and I see a power-hungry charlatan. I have read about people like him in my English texts (Richard III, Lady Macbeth, for instance). I hate him. I despise everyone who is taken in by him, not least myself. No wonder there are so few people in this community. No wonder everyone at school laughs at us. They are right. We are wrong.

I have had a Damascene conversion in the other direction. I do not believe in God. I certainly do not believe in the Village's God. I want to evangelise my new-found atheism. Perhaps, when I get out there, I will.

I listen to the other girls breathing. I wish I could take

them with me. I ought to give Martha the chance, because somewhere beneath her placid exterior, I sense that she is not happy either.

I fear I cannot trust her, however. I must do this on my own. This is the last time I will wake up in my top bunk in this stupid cabin. In a matter of hours, I will be gone.

chapter twenty-four

I have fallen asleep without meaning to. I know that because I can see my surroundings by a dim and dappled light, and the rain has stopped, and the jungle around us is phenomenally noisy, with screeches and tweets and chirps. Every leaf seems to be quivering and unfurling. New flowers, I think, have opened. The air is clean and clear.

I move Ed's arm off me as gently as I can and, holding a thin tree trunk for support, stumble to my feet. All my muscles are aching, particularly at the top of my back, and when I stretch, everything hurts. There are angry red bite marks all over my arms, and when I start to think about them, I find them on my legs, my cheeks, every exposed part of my flesh.

Ed and I slept right where we were sitting last night as we listened to Jean and Gene's heartbreaking story. It is disconcerting to be here in this new, fresh world: one moment I was sitting up all night unable to see a thing and listening to relentless rain, and the next I am here in the Garden of Eden.

Katy is asleep near us, and I skirt her unconscious form as I pick my way to the beach. I see Jean up on the boulder, sitting cross-legged and looking out at the sunrise. There is no sign of Gene, Mark or Cherry.

The water is as flat as it always is. The sand is pockmarked all over where the rain has attacked it. This makes the beach look completely different. It has been defined by its powderiness until now, and suddenly it is heavy, darker, and all stuck together. When I walk on it, I leave deep prints.

I can see Jean's footprints coming out of the rainforest and walking straight over to the foot of the boulder where she now sits, her back straight as a rod. There are other footprints that wander around, down to the water, back again, and back into the jungle. I walk over to examine them, and decide that they belong to Mark and to Cherry.

The old fire looks pitiful. It has been battered so hard by the rain that the half-burned leaves and branches have been blasted away from one another, and all that is left of it is wan grey bits of forest scattered over an area of beach. It will be difficult to light a new one: everything is covered in water now.

I walk down to the sea and stand in the shallows. That, at least, has not changed. It is as warm and soothing as ever.

We eat fruit and drink from the rainwater that filled both ice boxes overnight. Ed and I make a sandcastle with the newly suitable sand, and lose ourselves for hours in forming towers and bridges.

'That's a novel courtship ritual,' Gene observes when he strides out of the forest and over to us. 'Building sandcastles together. Quite the little lovebirds.'

I smile up at him. I wonder, now, how it was that I never saw the pain in his eyes. I thought his misery was just because of his fractious relationship with Jean. Now it seems obvious that it is something bigger: something huge.

'Come and join us,' Ed offers. 'We need a gatehouse. What do you think?'

'Hmm.' Gene sits down and surveys the random edifice we have constructed. 'Well, for one thing, this place needs a better floor plan, but that's your business. For another, it would be good if the ocean here was tidal so the moat would fill up. All the same, I'll give it a go.'

Gene is soon absorbed in his work, constructing a perfectly round tower at a short distance from the castle, and making a straight road joining the two.

'That makes our castle look seriously crap,' Ed muses.

'It really does.' Gene's house is perfect in every detail. Ours is like a haunted house from a cartoon but far more random. 'Shall we try to make it better?'

'Why don't we knock it down and start again? On a much bigger scale. Look, if that's the gatehouse, then we need to be *way* bigger than it.'

We set to work. The sun is high in the sky, and Katy is fishing alone, before we even look up.

When Mark and Cherry emerge from the jungle, I take no notice. They run over to us and I look up, rather annoyed to have my dead-coral roof-laying interrupted.

Then I see Mark's face and I know something has happened. He is radiant, pink and breathless; alive in a way none of us have been for a long time.

'Come and see!' he says. 'Ed. Esther. Gene. Everyone. We've been exploring the island. From the inside. Following the paths around to see what there is. You know we thought you couldn't get through the jungle? We thought you could get to the spring and that was all? Well that's not true. You can reach another beach! And guess what we've found? Come and see. Leave your castle. You won't believe it. You have to come with us.'

I hardly dare hope. My stomach turns over and my heart rate speeds up. Ed says it before I can.

'A boat?' he asks.

I can hardly bear this. Another beach, and one that has a boat on it. It has to be that. Nothing else would be this exciting. I jump up, imagining a fishing boat pulled up on to white sand, or bobbing in a bay. I see the seven of us climbing into it, the engine miraculously starting, or else all of us fashioning oars from branches and rowing away. Whatever happens, a boat will get us out of here. We would not have to go far before we were able to see land. I picture us meeting another vessel out on the water, being pulled aboard and taken back. Jean and Gene are at their son's bedside, and he has woken up and is talking to them. Mark and Cherry are with their children, confessing, dealing with the consequences. Ed and Katy are going wherever they would have been going next.

And I am with Daisy. She runs into my arms and I catch her, stumbling back as she thumps heavily into me. I bury my face in her hair. It feels so real that I cannot believe it is not happening yet.

*

I have to make an effort and refocus my thoughts before I look at Mark's face.

'Oh crap,' he says, and he passes the back of his hand over his forehead. 'I made it sound too exciting, didn't I? Sorry, guys.'

I do not trust myself to speak. Ed mutters something and Mark replies, and I do not even hear what the great discovery actually is. They start walking.

Katy is at our side. She has left her fishing rod carefully on the rock. She is talking to Mark too. I don't listen.

Ed turns back. Even the sight of his face, smiling at me, does nothing for the blackness that has descended.

'Coming, Esther?' he says.

I nod and walk, but hang back so I don't have to speak to anyone. Gene overtakes me to walk with the rest of them, and I think, as I watch him, that he does indeed look as if he is in physical pain. He does not walk well. He limps and holds his body oddly. I try to recall him walking before, but I cannot picture it. We have not really had anywhere to go, and when it is his or Jean's turn to fetch the water, they do it together, holding the box between them. I have never paid much attention to the fact that they are so much older than the rest of us; in fact, they are probably the hardiest of the group. I just had no idea they were carrying around all this sorrow.

I am wondering whether I should suggest to Gene that he sits down and rests rather than exploring his way through the jungle when I realise someone is next to me.

'Hey, Esther.'

I look at her and force a smile.

'Hello, Jean. Are you OK?'

'Oh,' she says. 'You know. Within the parameters. Can't recommend sleeping in the jungle at my age, I have to say.'

'Did you sleep where we were? I don't even remember lying down. I just woke up all disorientated. Last time I did that, it was wine-related.' I remember a Brighton night, me stumbling around the streets in the way I used to do, as though hoping I might bump into a better life.

'Yeah. I do recall moving off a bit and finding a space to stretch out, but I don't think I slept more than a half-hour. I was surprised even to do that. I woke with a bloody great lizard standing that far from my face, looking at me.'

I shiver. 'That's why I keep out of here if I can.'

We are back in the rainforest now, following Mark, Cherry, Ed and Gene through the undergrowth, even though there is no real path.

'Where are we going, by the way? It looked interesting, and I was hitting a dead end as far as meditation was concerned, so I jumped down to join you all. Didn't want to miss out on an outing. Something to do.'

'Mark and Cherry found another beach. Mark is very excited about it.'

'I see they were back to their old ways last night.'

'Were they?'

She smiles. 'Oh yes. At first light, when I saw that lizard staring at me with his beady little eye, the next thing I saw was those two in a state of great undress, cuddled up nearby. Sleeping it off. They got up a while later and giggled and headed into the forest together. It made me feel almost nostalgic.'

I laugh. 'I was just thinking this morning it was like the Garden of Eden.'

'Indeed. Very apt.'

We walk in silence for a while, concentrating on climbing over roots and under branches and vines. Spikes and pointed things reach out and scratch us in fury at our passing through their territory. Five minutes pass, maybe ten, and then Jean starts speaking again.

'Look, Esther. I let Gene have his say last night because he needed to tell you all about Benjamin. I forced myself not to interrupt the way I wanted to. But it's not quite the way he said. He makes out that I'm the flinty one who has no faith in our son to wake up. It's not just me. It's the doctors. The thing Gene has never been able to accept . . . I can see why. It's much easier to keep hoping. But the thing is this: there *is* no hope. Last night he was daring me to step in and say this, and I didn't because it would have blown right up. But the doctors, the second opinion, any number of consultants – all of them say the same. Ben's dead, Esther. He's being kept alive by the machines because of Gene's top-notch medical insurance, because it's up to us to tell them when to switch it all off. And while Gene's alive, that'll mean never. He tracks down stories of miraculous reawakenings and prints them off and waves them in my face. He actually has a scrapbook of newspaper reports, going way back in time, that he has found on the internet. Just to prove it could happen. A whole fucking scrapbook. And he's glued a photograph of Ben on to the front of it.

'Gene treats every day as a new chance. Every day, for him, is the day when Ben's going to snap out of it and we're going to get our darling bright, beautiful boy back. And it breaks my heart over and over again to be the one to say "Darling, that ain't going to happen." In fact I stopped saying that more than eighteen months ago because I could not bear it. I want it as much as he does. I'm his mother; I grew him, I gave him fucking life. And there was Gene putting me in the position of having to say, over and over again, "But he's not going to wake up." I have never told him we should switch the machines off. No mother is going to take that side in that battle. But a whole heap of what he said about Ben twitching his eye which meant we were OK to go on this holiday is a figment of his imagination. He believes it all right, but that doesn't mean it's real. I was there. It didn't happen. It was just Gene's way, probably subconsciously, of finding a way for it to be OK for us to go away.'

I hold up a prickly vine and Jean edges through the narrow space it leaves.

'Thanks,' she says.

'So all the fighting you've been doing?' I ask timidly.

'Yeah. That'll be him fighting against me. He has to blame somebody, and there actually isn't anyone else. I'm the nearest. We made our peace with the biker long ago, and anyway what motorcyclist doesn't zip through sluggish traffic? That poor man paid a horrible price for doing what everyone else does all the time. Gene can't hold Ben responsible, of course. Neither of us can. There's nobody else but me. Of course he doesn't say the accident was my fault, but he lashes out. I genuinely thought it would be a positive thing to do, to get away to Malaysia, to go to the island on Ben's behalf. It wasn't. Gene was picking fights all day every day, because there's only one place in the world where he wants to be, and that sure as hell ain't here.'

There is a huge bushy thing in front of us which is prickly. It is definitely impenetrable, and I stare for a while, trying to work out which way the others went when they reached it.

'Here,' says Jean, and following her finger I see the path they must have taken, going off to our left. A few broken branches, a vine wrenched aside, the smallest indications that people have passed. She takes the lead and talks back over her shoulder. Something moves noisily close to us and I try not to jump. Sweat is pouring off me. The feeling that the world had been cleansed by the rain has long gone.

'I got furious with him,' she calls back to me. 'I mean, we were here, at this beach, and for myself, the reason I'd wanted to come was so I could sit still in this place that he never got to visit, and be still and think of him, of my little Ben, the youngest child, the one who got away with anything. To say goodbye in a way. To do it for him. I did not get one second's peace because Gene was needling at me non-stop, the entire time. He wanted to be at home, and didn't I know it. So I gave as good as I got for once. That's never happened before. It's not our ordinary dynamic. We've always had a traditional family set-up, where I did everything for the children and ran the household, and Gene went to work. I never fought back at him. I just took it all. This time I couldn't.'

'Jean, I'm so sorry. It's awful what you're having to deal with.'

'Yeah, I know. One of those things the universe throws at you. What do the Americans call it? A curve ball?'

We walk the rest of the way in silence. The others are out of sight but we can hear them ahead from time to time. It is hard work, and by the time we see the horizon through the trees, I am ready to drop.

They are standing on the beach, Mark and Cherry, Gene, Katy and Ed. Mark is grinning again.

'Ta-dah!' he says, and he gestures along the beach. I am almost too tired to turn my head, but I make an effort and look where he is pointing.

'No way,' I say.

'Way!'

Cherry is bounding along the beach. 'Isn't it great?' she says. 'Isn't it just the strangest thing you've ever seen? Who would have imagined it?'

'Well,' says Jean, in her usual dry tone. 'This certainly seems unlikely.'

We start walking, together, Ed beside me. He takes my hand. I squeeze his gratefully.

'It's probably going to need some work,' he says, 'but hell. We have time, if nothing else.'

This is the way Paradise Bay would look, the way any one of the guest houses on the main island would look, if they were left alone for a long time. It must be years since this place was used, but all the same, it is a collection of cabins. They have walls and roofs, and although some of the wood is visibly rotting, much of it looks fine. I count six cabins in a semicircle at the end of the beach, with a main building in the middle of them, three on each side. All have been reclaimed by the jungle to a certain extent, but they are far from derelict.

'Houses,' I say. There is something deeply creepy about the scene. I try to shake that feeling.

'And there's a well,' Mark says, as proud as he would be if he had dug it himself. 'With a bucket on a rope. And there's stuff lying around. Seriously: look at this – look what I found. It's almost ironic.'

He opens his hand and there it is: an orange plastic cigarette lighter. It looks insouciant in his hand, casual.

I walk closer and look at it. This is just a mass-produced piece of rubbish, from a factory somewhere here in Asia, no doubt. It is the kind of thing you can buy for pennies or cents, anywhere in the world.

It does not look like the sort of object that could cause seven grown adults to become stranded on an island indefinitely. All three of us stare at it.

'If we'd only had you a week or so ago . . .' says Edward to the lighter.

'More than that,' Mark corrects him.

'Is it?' I ask. 'I have no clue any more.'

'Anyway – you see what I'm saying, guys? I just found this, under the steps to one of the huts. If there's a lighter, there'll be more stuff. We can move in here. Sleep indoors. Make it our new home.'

Their enthusiasm, his and Cherry's, is infectious. I find myself smiling tentatively along with them. When I look at Ed, I see that he is just as pleased. In my mind I am making us a bedroom, though where we are going to find the mattress and bedside table, candles and vase of flowers that feature in my imaginings, I am not quite sure.

Katy's eyes are screwed up and she is clearly thinking it through. I look at Jean, and see she is uncertain. Gene, however, is the first to speak.

'Yeah,' he says. 'Fascinating and everything. But if you don't mind my asking: why the hell would we move here when, if that bloke comes back for us, he'll be going to the other beach? Are we fucking giving up here? Moving here to make some set-up where we lie about until we die? Is that it?'

I listen to Mark arguing, talking about leaving messages written on the sand at the other beach, making arrows out of twigs and bits of coral to show which way we have gone, keeping a fire burning day and night here so that we will be just as likely to be rescued, 'Because face it, guys, if anyone finds us, it's not going to be Samad coming back. That ship has sailed.'

And I realise I don't care any more, because I no longer have any expectation whatsoever that we are ever going to be found.

chapter twenty-five

Gene and Jean flatly refuse to move into the new home. They announce that they are going back to the original beach, where they will carry on exactly as we were before. They will relight the fire and wait for a boat. Nothing any of us says will deter them, though we try very hard indeed.

'Won't you do it for us?' I try, desperately. I can hear how ridiculous it sounds. 'We want to do everything we can to keep you safe. And there are buildings here. There's stuff. There's a lighter, there's wood, there's a water supply . . .'

Jean snorts, but kindly. 'Esther, I like you. You know I do. But I'm not going to do the wrong thing just to save you some anxiety, you idiot.'

'First rule.' Gene is breathless, purple in the face. 'If you're lost, and you can't make your own way to safety. Then you bloody well stay put. OK? Everyone knows that. Surely even you fools do.'

'We are staying put, though,' Katy says. She has been quiet until now, apparently taking it all in. Her voice is gentle: she and Gene are friends, often talking and even laughing together as they fish. '*This island* is where we are. If Samad came back, which we all know is unlikely now, he would hardly just check the one beach where he left us, would he? He'd search the island. We're far more likely to be rescued by a passing boat, and for that purpose, no one beach is better than any other.'

'Maybe, maybe,' Gene says. 'But all the same. It's a no from us. Don't worry – you guys do what you like. I can see you're all excited by the change of scene. We'll be neighbours. Keep a fire burning on both beaches, double our chances.'

Katy is worried. 'We'll come and visit you. We'll bring you fish.'

'We'll bring *you* fish, more like,' Gene says with a laugh. 'I'll split the rods with you. Come over in the afternoon to compare notes. Cocktail hour.'

Nobody says anything for a while. Splitting up like this seems to be madness, but neither side is going to back down.

'If he comes for you,' Cherry says, hesitantly, 'you will come and fetch us?'

There is a tense moment, before both Gene and Jean laugh.

'Of course we will, darling. You idiot.'

After that, the tension is broken, and we start on the process of moving most of the camp.

By afternoon, the freshness of the rain-drenched jungle has gone: everything is, if anything, more humid than before. It is hard to breathe because the air is so stultifying.

The move involves attempting to build a new fire, despite the fact that everything on the island is still soaked through by the rain, and transporting one of the two ice boxes from one beach to the other. We have our water container, and Jean and Gene have theirs. Already there are resentments building: they have one for the two of them, whereas the rest of us have one between five. However, they will have to make the long walk to the spring to collect their water every day, whereas we now have our own well, and it seems to work.

I stand back and watch Mark pulling up a very old-looking rope. At last a bucket appears on the end of it; it was probably once red, but now it is a faded and patchy pink, with areas that have been bleached competely white. Water is dribbling out of a crack in the side of it, but not fast enough for that to be a problem.

Cherry holds up the ice box and he pours the water into it. They grin at one another. It is painfully obvious that Mark and Cherry have resolved their differences. They are almost back to the way they used to be, when all they seemed to do was rip each other's clothes off in public. They, like me, appear to have given up all hope of rescue entirely, to be making the best of the world they have.

'We have a water supply!' Mark shouts, and I smile at Katy, who grins back.

'What do you think, then?' I ask her quietly, gesturing around. She steps closer and leans in towards me, confiding.

'It's a change. It's something to do, I suppose. I want to have a good look round those huts before I commit myself. I might go and join the oldies if it's too grim inside.

I mean, we've not really checked them out as bedrooms, have we? And I'm not sure it's going to be an improvement on sleeping on the sand.' She pauses. 'I suppose you'll be sharing with Edward?'

I feel slightly awkward about the fact that Katy is the only one of us who is alone.

'Mmm,' I say, nodding slightly. 'Anyway, shall we have a poke around?'

The six cabins are in various states of disrepair, and as we walk from one to the next, it is instantly clear that four of them are unusable. The floors are rotten through, and as they are raised above the ground on stilts, they have gaping holes with two-metre drops. The wood is smelly and horrible. Sleeping on the sand would be a far better option than trying to make a home in one of those hovels.

The two that are closest to the dilapidated main building, however, have new-looking floors made out of a far hardier wood. They are sturdy and perfectly habitable, with a bit of remedial cleaning.

'One for the American lovers,' says Katy drily. 'The other for you and Ed, I suppose.'

'That's not fair,' I say. 'We'll sleep on the sand, and you have this one.'

I hope she will refuse this offer, but she does not reply at all. She paces around the interior of the hut. It is just a floor, a roof and four walls with two windows. There was never a bathroom or anything here. Yet as I picture it with the animal poo removed, the torn-up paper taken out of the corner, the whole place washed down on the inside, I realise how much I have missed shelter. The idea of having a place of one's own is fundamental. The fact remains, however, that three habitable huts would have been better than two.

Katy is standing by the glassless window. I look at her back. We have all been wearing the same clothes for so long that I cannot imagine Katy without her blue T-shirt and cream shorts. Her T-shirt has faded as the days have passed, and now it is pale blue with white lines in it where sea salt and sweat have dried out. Her shorts are no longer at all cream.

'Share this hut with us,' I say quickly. 'We're all in this together. Share with Ed and me.'

I am not sure what Ed will say about this, but there is no other option. I have held off from actual sex with him because I am scared. This, I know, is the perfect continuing excuse. Katy turns around and pushes her fringe back out of her eyes.

'Thank you,' she says with a small smile. 'That's kind of you. It would be hard to sleep on the sand on my own, I think.'

'We'll make it as homely as we can.'

'Yes. I'm not sure how, but we will.' She walks closer to me. 'You can tell Daisy about this, Esther,' she says, 'when you're back,' and her kindness makes hot tears spring to my eyes.

'I wish I believed that,' I say, struggling suddenly. 'I did at first. Now I don't think I'm ever going to see her again. I can't bear to think about it. Daisy. You know, she sleeps with her polar bear at night. He's called Poley. When Chris and I split up, he bought her a new one that was exactly the same as the old one, so she has a Poley at both our houses.'

Katy's hand is on my shoulder.

'Did she mind the new one?'

'No. She was fine with it.'

I hear her draw in a long breath.

'Esther? I wish we could find some kind of spiritual comfort in all this. Do you believe in God at all?'

I swallow hard. 'No. I sort of wish I did.'

'Can you believe in something? The Fates, maybe? But I think that the universe, that God in some form, will take care of us. And I'm certain that we'll be all right, you know. I think we're all here for a reason. Those two' – she gestures towards the distant sound of Mark and Cherry's laughter – 'because they were behaving terribly badly. It's been a wake-up call, though admittedly they both appear to have learned to override it now. Still, when this is over and they have to go home, they will have learned some lessons and they will have to deal with the consequences of their behaviour. Gene and Jean will be finding peace with each other and with their son. They're getting there, they really are. You – well you told me, didn't you, about what your life was like in Brighton, the way you lost control and let Daisy see you fighting with your ex. So this will end up doing you a world of good. I can see it already, Esther. You're learning to rely on yourself and trust your instincts. And you've found Ed, and happiness. You wouldn't have let down your barriers enough for that to have happened if you weren't here, would you? I don't know enough about Ed, but he's clearly strong and this will not do him any harm, even if it ends up just being a great story to tell. I truly think all of us have washed up here for a reason.'

I ask the obvious question: 'What about you? What's your reason?'

I hope my scepticism is not too obvious. I think Katy is talking rubbish and I wish I hadn't offered to share a room with her, because I am now afraid she is going to start going on about karma and spirituality. I am sure that if she had a child, she would not see any benefit in being washed up on a random island indefinitely.

'Me? Oh, to test me in every way,' she says lightly. 'And also . . .' She looks at me and smiles warmly. 'The relationship I was in, that I mentioned? Well, since I've been here, I've been thinking about her a lot. It all seems simple with this perspective. Of course I love her. I love her completely. So I'm going to go back, when the opportunity arises – which I firmly believe it will – and give the relationship everything that I've got. I can do that, I think.'

'Right,' I say. 'OK. That sounds good.'

'Oh, it is,' she says, beaming. 'It really is. The world is a wonderful place. I know we're hungry all the time and we all have diarrhoea and every day's a struggle for food and all that. But the fact is, seven of us, none of whom have any survival skills or medical training, have managed to survive this far, however many days it's been. It's got to have been two weeks. And we're all skinny and sunburned, but we have been given fresh water and trees that are laden down with fruit, and we're surrounded by an ocean filled with swimming protein. Imagine getting stranded in Antarctica, say. We'd have been dead the first night. Nature is looking after us.'

I laugh, and head for the steps down to the beach, because I want to find Ed.

'That's true,' I admit. 'Remind me never to go on holiday to the South Pole, or if I do, never to go out on a day trip with someone who's forgotten his matches.'

Mark and Cherry have been exploring the biggest of the huts. It must once have been the admin centre and restaurant, but now it is almost completely rotten, with a peeling painted sign with the words 'Moonlight Beach' just about legible on it. There is a big open area up a ladder, and I can imagine it dotted with plastic tables and chairs, little candles on the tables at night and Malaysian cuisine served by waiting staff who would have been almost entirely taken for granted by the customers. This is such a long way from the mainland: did people come all the way here for a holiday? Perhaps, I think, we are not as far from civilisation as we think. Samad could have brought us in a loop.

Now there are huge holes in the floorboards, and creepers from the nearby jungle have pushed through every gap and crevice. This building, more than any of the others, has been reclaimed by nature.

A lot of the rotten wood is now laid in rows on the sand, drying out until it is ready to be used as fuel. They have methodically pulled away everything that can be pulled. Ed is not here: according to Cherry, he went back to the old beach to check on Jean and Gene.

I join in, wrenching old wood away from nails, and adding it to the rows on the sand. It is strangely exhilarating. I am aware as I work that I am hungry, that we have not eaten for a while, but the excitement of our new surroundings makes me keep postponing the boring business of looking for food.

Cherry is nearby, doing the same job as me, while Mark tries to get a fire going. Suddenly she cries out.

'Esther! Oh my GOD!'

I run to her. It takes me a while to process her discovery. It seems so incongruous here.

'Look at that,' I whisper. She takes my hand, and I squeeze her small, rough one in mine.

'Food,' she says reverently.

Cherry, it seems, wrenched the spongy door off a larder which was stocked with tinned food. There were eleven tins in it, left behind, I suppose, when the operation was abandoned. Either they were forgotten, or they were not considered worth bringing.

We now own four cans of plum tomatoes, two cans of peas and five incongruous tins of baked beans in tomato sauce. While there is not a tin opener visible anywhere, Mark has found some cutlery and gets to work with the sharpest knife he can locate.

'I'm going to trust you to do this,' I say to him, 'because I cannot bear the idea of having tinned food and not being able to access it.'

'Fear not,' he assures me. 'I will get to these peas if it's the very last thing I do.' And although it takes him several hours, he does.

By the time Ed comes back, carrying two mackerel as a present from the Australians, it is nearly dark. We have a puny spluttering fire, because nothing has really dried out enough to burn convincingly, and we are heating up baked beans on it.

Ed is gratifyingly impressed.

'No way!' he says. 'Fish and baked beans? All we're missing are the chips.'

To sit under the stars eating just-warm baked beans from a tin with a fork feels like the ultimate luxury. I lean on Ed, and smile at him, and take comfort from the warmth of his arm around my shoulders, and I can almost forget the bigger picture. I am nearly happy.

'Oh dear,' says Katy, lying on her back. 'I could eat all of that twenty times over, you know?'

'Yeah,' Mark agrees. 'I know what you mean. I was wondering if we could catch one of those giant fuck-off lizards tomorrow. Roast it on the fire, actually have something to eat with some substance to it.'

Nobody protests at this plan. Instead we fall into a discussion about the best way to go about trapping such a creature.

chapter twenty-six

Cathy

July 1988
D-Day

WOW.

Pull yourself together, Cathy.

Get a grip.

Stop crying.

I am in Isleworth. It turns out to be a place with lots of terraced houses in lots of streets, and some shops and a station. It is, I suppose, normal, though what do I know about that?

I am going to stay with Michelle and Steve for as long as I need to. That's what they said. I think they were a bit shocked when they met me, because I heard Michelle saying to Sarah's mum: 'Are you sure she's sixteen?' Apparently I look younger. I don't think I do, though. Probably I looked younger right then because we were drinking coffee (disgusting, it turns out) at a noisy, smelly place which was the motorway services, and everything had the texture of a dream. I must have looked like a child because I felt like one.

I want to wake up from that dream now. I miss home. At the Village, we had so much green space, and it kept us away from other people. This room I'm in now is a 'box room', apparently, and it feels like a box itself. I'm living inside a box. At the Village there are log cabins that the founders built in a circle, and you knew everyone who was close to you. Here, I know there are strangers on the other side of one of my walls, and that's weird. And the other people in the house are almost strangers, too.

But I have to be strong. Even though I feel I want to go back, I know really that I don't.

The plan almost went completely wrong at the last minute. I was ready to abort it (now a part of me wishes we had).

I set off for school exactly as usual; but as I was leaving the compound, I heard footsteps running up behind me. My heart was hammering: I knew that I had been discovered. I turned round almost crying, and there was Martha.

'Cathy,' she said. 'Why are you going to school?'

'I want to do some reading,' I told her. She knew that already, so I had no idea why she was asking, and I was scared.

'Cassandra says you should be reading here, not at school. She's worried that you're reading unsuitable things there.' She smiled. 'I think it's only just occurred to them that the school library has loads of books in it that they'd burn if you brought them home.'

I did not trust Martha.

'Well,' I said to her. 'I'm going to school today. It's the last time, though.' If it had been anyone else interrogating me, I would have pretended that I had to go in for something school-related, but since Martha was in my class, I could not.

'Cathy,' she said, her voice dropping. 'You're doing something. What are you doing?'

I looked at her, trying not to appear guilty, knowing that I was failing.

'What do you mean?' I said quickly. 'Um, maybe I *am* reading the wrong sort of books. Don't tell, though.'

She squinted at me. I wanted to tell her not to squint, that it did her no favours. But I did not. I will never see Martha again, so she will never know.

'You're not reading books,' she said scornfully. 'I'm not *that* stupid.'

'Well what do you think I'm doing?'

'I think,' she said, 'that you're seeing a boy. And I think it's Sean Holden. And you're promised to Philip, so that is really, really naughty of you!'

She giggled a little, and I relaxed.

'Well,' I said. I smiled and looked down, acting my part. 'I don't know how you know, but . . . Look, Martha, cover for me today, tell Cassandra and the others that I have to go in for something, to help clean up the field or something, and tonight I'll tell you everything. OK?'

I looked over at the cabins. Cassandra and Miriam were watching us. In a minute they would come over to see what was going on. Time was short.

Martha followed my gaze.

'All right,' she agreed. 'But you really do have to tell me everything, or I'm going to go straight to them. I mean it.'

'Promise,' I lied. 'Thanks, Martha. You're great. I'll be back this afternoon.'

I wanted to say something else, but how could I tell her to have a good life? For a couple of seconds I desperately wanted to ask her to come with me. We looked at each other for longer than we had ever looked at one another before, and then I turned and went.

I got away with it. I walked up the drive, swinging my almost-empty school bag, and left Martha's life, and God's Village, for ever.

Sarah was waiting outside school, and her parents were both nearby in their car, which was parked at the end of the yellow zigzag lines.

'All right?' she said.

And I had to say yes, even though I was not really feeling all right at all. She smiled and squeezed my arm, and I suddenly hugged her, because she was the only person I had.

Sarah's hair is really brown, but she dyes it herself, whitish yellow. It looks funny because she has big dark eyebrows, but I think it's quite nice that she doesn't match up. I looked at her brown eyes, and I knew she was my only friend.

'I might just go back, actually.' I said it without wanting to, said it before I knew what I was doing.

'No,' she told me, and steered me to the car. 'Cathy, you can't. You can't go back now, because you need to leave. You know you do. They're nutters. I'm sorry to say it, because they're your family, but we're getting you out and there's no way you're going back.'

She opened the back door of the car and shoved me in. For a second I felt that I was being kidnapped. There was so much that was scary now, and nothing that was normal, and I ached to be back in the cabin, living a life with tight boundaries.

Sarah's dad started the engine, before Sarah had even shut the door.

'This is the third time I've been in a car,' I said, because I wanted to say something.

'What were the other two?' Sarah was interested.

'School trips,' I told her. 'Once we went in Mrs Harris's car when she gave me and Martha a lift home because we came back from the theatre late. And once when Tom's mum dropped us off because it was raining. We got in trouble both times, though.'

'Well,' her mother said, 'you won't be getting in trouble like that any more, Cathy. You're about to be free.'

I sat in silence as they drove out of our little town, past everything I knew, and into the great unknown. We kept going for what felt like hours, though I was watching the clock and it was actually fifty-four minutes. I stared out of the window, watched as it started to rain. After a while Sarah's mum said, 'Cathy, I know it's scary. You're a free agent. Give it six months. You can probably stay with Michelle for six months if you need to. And after that, when you've seen how the rest of the world lives, if you still want to go back then you can. You know they'd be happy to see you. The prodigal daughter and all that. It's not as if you can't go back. Just give it a bit of time. Will you do that?'

I nodded. 'OK.'

They handed me over to Michelle and Steve, and I sat in the back of the car, in the middle, between two car seats that contained Joe and Max. Those boys are only two. They're quite noisy, and the one on my left kept saying, 'Cathy? Cathy?' and when I answered, he just went 'Cathycathycathy.' Still, I talked to them and I think they're going to be useful, because there's always something to talk about with them in the house.

It only took us twenty-three minutes to get to Isleworth from the services. I cried saying goodbye to Sarah, and we all promised to keep in touch. Sarah and her parents are coming over on Sunday for the day, so that's something to look forward to.

When we got to Michelle and Steve's house, Steve went out somewhere and Michelle and I sat down at the table with a pot of tea. That was when I discovered that she's fascinated by everything about my life so far. I think she loves the fact that she's helping me escape, and she keeps calling the Village 'the Cult'. I wish she wouldn't.

'It's not really a cult,' I told her at one point, because I could not bear to hear her say it again. 'It's a religious community. They don't try to brainwash people or anything.'

She looked at me kindly. 'Don't they, Cathy?' She poured more tea.

'Well, everyone grows up shaped by what their parents believe, I suppose.' I was feeling like I wanted to defend the Village by now. It was just so odd not to be in it. At this point there were still a couple of hours to go until I was going to be missed, and I was not looking forward to watching that moment go by. I was pretty sure that 3.45 would be the turning point. We were always home by 3.45.

'Yes, you're probably right,' she said. 'It's just that Steph and Jon were so frantic when Sarah had her little flirtation with Doomsday. They actually felt they'd lost her, lost their own child, because once she got hooked, she was like a different person. Fair play to that Moses bloke, though: we were sure he'd make you all drink the Kool-Aid – do you remember that? No, of course you don't . . . Anyway, we thought there'd be a mass suicide and that was going to turn out to be the Apocalypse he had in mind. And when it didn't happen, it was like the spell had broken for Sarah. Thank God.' She looked a bit embarrassed. 'Or maybe not God. You know.'

I struggled to reply. Part of me was resisting her so hard, and wanting to run away, right back to the Village. The rest of me was desperate to engage with someone sympathetic, an outsider. Also, I was as interested in her life as she was in mine, even though she has no idea that there is anything intriguing about her.

'It was like that for me too,' I admitted. 'I was so sure that it was going to happen. We'd all been on a bit of a high – just a natural adrenalin one, nothing else – for weeks. I was truly expecting to be pulled up to heaven. I mean, I just knew it. It's hard to explain. Nothing mattered, none of the details, just being taken to heaven with Jesus.'

'If that man had given you a potion that would have taken you to Jesus, would you have drunk it?'

I did not even need to consider this. 'Yes,' I said. 'I'm sure I would, if he'd timed it right. As soon as the sun was up, everything changed for me. Before that. Yes. Sure.'

'I knew it. Why didn't he?'

I shrugged. 'Probably because he believed so strongly that it never occurred to him to help things along.'

'Gosh, you poor, poor girl, you know? Look, you're only sixteen, I don't know if we need to get you deprogrammed or anything. There's a number I'm going to ring for advice, it took me ages to find it. Boys! Joseph, put that down *right now*! Max, do you need the potty? Do you?'

I've spent most of the time since then in my room, just trying to accustom myself to the fact that I have no rules or boundaries. I am allowed not to believe in God. Moses is just a control freak, a petty dictator of his tiny domain. The fact that so many people go along with him is inexplicable. I am not sure what I do from here. One day, I suppose, at a time.

chapter twenty-seven

I lie on my back and look up, not at the stars but at the peeling ceiling of the hut, illuminated only slightly by the moonlight that creeps through the two windows. Katy's breathing is deep and slow, and she is snoring slightly every time she inhales, a sound so intimate that I feel embarrassed to be listening to it. For a while I lie still and imagine the woman she loves, sharing Katy's air, listening to her gentle snores. I wonder about that woman, whose name I do not know, and about whom I know solely the fact that she does not appreciate Katy's values. Ed, next to me, seems to be unconscious, and his breathing is almost inaudible.

I have been here for hours. I have no idea how I assumed I would be able to sleep on hard floorboards. I think I had taken for granted the idea that houses are comfortable, overlooking the small fact of the lack of any kind of mattress. Every part of me that is in contact with the floor feels bruised, and I am craving the sand.

In the end, I stand up as unobtrusively as I can, wrap my tattered sarong that is now more hole than fabric around my shoulders, open the door as quietly as possible and tiptoe down the rickety steps to the beach.

The fire has gone out, probably because it was impossible to find any fuel for it that was not at least partly damp. All the same, the sky is clear and the sand, though still clumpier than it has been, is soft between my toes.

I sit beside the remains of the fire and stretch my legs out in front of me. The rainforest, for once, is quiet; the only sound is the lapping of the waves on the shore. It is odd to be here, at night, on my own. I am not used to solitude any more. The moon is nearly full, and it lights the water so brightly that I almost believe I could walk across it, all the way home.

When I lie down, I feel the reassurance of the familiar. This is my home: the beach at night. The sensation of the sand beneath my body makes me instantly sleepy. I close my eyes.

'Esther!'

I pretend not to hear, although I know it is Ed, purely because I was on the brink of blissful slumber and I do not want to have to make the effort, even for him.

'Esther,' he whispers again, and I sense him sitting down next to me. Then he puts a hand on my shoulder, and I am compelled to open my eyes.

'What?' I ask ungraciously.

'Couldn't you sleep?'

'No. It was the floor. Sorry if I woke you.'

He laughs. 'Don't be silly. I think I turned to grab you in my sleep and there was no one there, and then I realised I was bunking up with Katy, and that didn't seem quite right, so I thought I'd try and track you down.'

'I was easily found.'

'You were. It's actually nicer out here anyway, isn't it? It smells in there.'

'And Katy snores.'

'I was trying to be gentlemanly. I wasn't going to mention it. I never noticed it when we slept outside.'

'The confined space probably amplifies it. It echoes off the walls.'

'Doesn't it just?'

I am awake now, so I sit up and yawn and look at him. Ed feels like a part of me now. There is something rock-solid in all of this. I know his face far better than my own. We have all changed to the point of, I imagine, unrecognisability since the start of this adventure. When I try to picture my face, the woman I imagine is not the woman whose contours I feel with my fingertips. In my mind I am a cosseted Westerner with rounded cheeks, skin that is well nourished and moisturised, and nice white teeth. I know, though I choose not to dwell on it, that in fact my skin must be blotchy and rough, my contours haggard, and I dread to think what my teeth, cleaned only with a stick fashioned into the most basic sort of brush, look like. Everyone else's look grim, and mine must too. At least they have been untroubled by anything sugary.

I lean into his bony body. Ed is the truest ally I have ever had. Something occurs to me.

'Ed?' I say. He looks at me, eyebrows raised, his face craggy in the silvery light. 'I don't really know anything about you. In fact this is what I know: you're Scottish. You're lovely. You're thirty-one and you were travelling with Jonah and Piet, but only because you met them in

Thailand. Whereas I know a hell of a lot more than that about Mark and Cherry, and Jean and Gene, and even Katy, actually. And you know everything about me. I'm sure you know far more than you want to about Daisy and about Chris.'

I look at him, suddenly doubting that I know this man at all. I run over our conversations in my head. They have, every one of them, been either about the immediate predicament, or about me. He has divulged nothing whatsoever about himself.

He laughs, and leans back on his hands.

'The thing is, Esther,' he says, 'that I'm not remotely interesting. I wish I had a grand story to tell like everyone else. Do you want to know about me? It'll put you to sleep, so I'm happy to be of service if that's what you want.'

'Yes,' I tell him. I lie down on my stomach, loving the feeling of the sand beneath me, lean up on my elbows and wait. He copies my pose and leans in close to me.

'I'm almost tempted,' he says, 'to make something up, just to give me some more cred. But I won't. I'm the middle one out of five boys.'

'Are you? That's interesting already. Five boys?'

'Yes. And I suppose I'm the classic useless middle child. Patrick, David, Edward, James and Joshua, that's us. James and Josh are twins. My parents never planned to have five. They only planned to have three, I think, but then they decided to go for one more, after I turned out to be so disappointingly male. They wanted the wee girlie, but they got twin boys instead. There was a certain crashing inevitability about that, wasn't there? Patch and Dave are the super-achievers, the alpha boys. Patch is thirty-six now, getting married this summer to Alice, his fiancée. They both work in finance, and in spite of the recession and all that shit, they're loaded. I like Alice and I like Patch, but I kind of despise them both too, I think, because they just know they're the greatest. They're so confident. He's six foot three, head boy at school, Oxford degree, nice flat in Clapham, has always had a cleaner, never done his own dirty work, all that sort of thing. Massive sense of entitlement, and the world has duly stepped up and handed him everything he was expecting. Alice has the long blonde hair, the skinny jeans; she looks like she'd snap in half if there was a bit of a wind, but she wouldn't, of course, she's as tough as anything and she gets exactly what she wants from life. Anyway, that's them, and in fact, that's when the family will notice I'm not there: the wedding, on May the seventeenth. It can't be May yet, can it? It was only the middle of April. But if we were still here on May the seventeenth, they'd find themselves one usher down, and they'd start to say, "Actually, has anyone *heard* from Ed?"

'So Patch is a banker type. Dave is a maths teacher and housemaster at our old school. Loves it. Loved the place, still does. He's a weirdo for being obsessed with his old school, but the kids adore him, and he's a brilliant teacher apparently. On track for headmaster. So that's his thing: he's devoted to school, though I've always wished he'd managed to push himself a bit further and make a difference to less privileged lives. He has girlfriends, but, as he always says "no one serious", and I actually suspect him of being somewhat closeted. We'll skip over me, because you know me, and we reach the twins. Also known as "Mummy and Daddy's ickle boysies". They're massively subsidised and indulged, and they get to do whatever they like. They must be twenty-eight now, but you'd never know it.'

I am fascinated. 'Really? Where do they live? What do they do?'

'Oh, Mum and Dad bought them a flat in Edinburgh,' he says, and without looking at him, I can hear his smile. 'God, I forget how privileged life is until I hear myself saying a thing like that. It's a nice flat, too, New Town, big windows, high ceilings. Dad said something about "all the money we're not spending on school fees any more" to justify it. They have four bedrooms, because they "need a study each". God, it's ridiculous, and the parents don't even flinch. You would never in a million years have caught them doing that for any of the rest of us. Oh, and because the parents live an hour and a half's drive away, near Pitlochry, Mum pays for a cleaner to go in twice a week, since she can't manage to keep popping in herself. And since the twins are so fucking useless.'

'No way!'

''Fraid so.'

'Who does their washing and all that?'

'The cleaner. And their ironing, too.'

'And do they work?' I laugh as I say it, because I know the answer.

'Do you think they work? Do they sound like hard-working people? Of course they do, officially, "work". James is "an artist", and Josh is "a screenwriter". They lounge around smoking and drinking and shopping, but

James has an easel and a load of expensive paints in his "studio", and Josh is constantly getting a new Mac with all the gadgets, but keeps forgetting to use it to write his long-trailed Hollywood blockbuster. They are the living embodiment of why the word "spoiled" is so apt. Both parents mollycoddled them so much that they'll never be able to do a thing for themselves. As human beings, they have properly been spoiled. Ruined. Destroyed. I should feel sorry for them and relieved it wasn't me, but somehow I've never got there.'

'That is weird,' I say. 'Your parents can afford to subsidise them that much?'

'Yeah. While I'm filling you in on my delightful family, I should tell you that the money comes from evil, not from good. At least, Dad's an executive at an oil company. One of the massive ones. He runs their European operations. We all went to good old Scottish boarding school and had music lessons and did a million different activities and all that, but with me, Patch and Dave, they did that spartan, stand-on-your-own-two-feet thing. By the time the twins came along, it had somehow changed. There had been marital ructions that I've never quite put together, mainly because I haven't wanted to. But the end result was Mum pouring everything into the babies, and Dad guiltily paying for it all. I presume he had an affair, but it's equally possible that she did. Cherry's story made me see that. And it's not really a thing you want to think about your parents doing anyway, is it? So I'm happy to gloss over it and accept that the family dynamic was different by the time Josh and James showed up, for one reason or another.'

I turn to him, and put my face up close to his.

'And still, Ed,' I say. 'Still. Now I know all about your brothers, and your parents. And I still don't know about you. What's happened in your life? Boarding school, lots of activities. Then what?'

'Oh, I'm not interesting,' he says. 'I keep trying to tell you that, Esther. I'm Mr Average. I did OK at school. I went to university in Glasgow. I studied French and history. Spent a year in Paris. That was cool. I got some lovely French girls while I was out there and I probably had a glimpse of the possibilities that could exist for me away from my family. But I wasn't brave enough. I moved to London, worked and had an average sort of time for my entire twenties. Never quite settled. Never pushed myself forward. I felt I was doing all right if I just . . . got by. Stuck to the rules. I wish I had a grand drama to share. I really do. The rest of you – you've all been out there and made life happen.

'I think that's what I did by coming out here. I'd been going out with Ellie for a while, and then I knew we were getting to a point where we should be starting to think about settling down, and that sooner or later we should want a baby. Not that she expressed much interest, but I knew it was the next conventional step. That scared the life out of me. Because I like babies, but the last thing I want is one of my own. My own stupid family have stopped me wanting anything like that. I'd have no idea how to be with a child. Whether to ignore them or coddle them, and whether or not there's anything in between. I discovered, thanks to the Ellie situation, that I don't want children, so that was something good, and it gave me the push that, perhaps, I needed. It got me running fast away from responsibility. I actually did something, for the first time in my life. I gave notice on my flat, sold some things, bought myself a ticket to Asia.'

'What did your parents think of that?'

He shakes his head. 'Honestly? They barely noticed. I half hoped they'd be furious and tell me I was throwing my life away. If I'd been Patch or Dave chucking it all in to go travelling, they would have gone apeshit. If I'd been Josh or James they would have nodded approvingly and given them a credit card. But it was just me. They never really care what happens to me.'

'Ed! They must do, really.'

'Maybe. They keep it well hidden, if so.'

'It must be partly because they trust you, and they know they don't have to worry about you.'

'Hmm. It's true they've never worried about me. Perhaps I should have tried harder to give them cause for concern. If I had a different character, I'd have played the hellraiser and forced them to factor me into the family. But I just wanted everyone to approve. And I've never been as accomplished as the big boys, or as cute as the small ones. I told you I was boring.'

'You're not boring.'

'I am. I can see it in your face. Completely fucking dull.'

'No! That's not what you're seeing in my face at all.'

'So what am I seeing?'

'You're seeing respect. Appreciation. The realisation that if we were to get off this island, which I am completely certain we won't, then you and I might actually have had a chance together. You're the person I need, Ed. I can say this because it's just a dream, but I need someone grounded, like you, who hasn't had a random and crazy life. And you need someone like me, because I will be the person who makes you see how special you are. Sorry for the cliché, but it's true. Also, you don't want a baby. I certainly don't want a baby. I have the most amazing one already, and she'd love you. That is what you're seeing in my face. Realisation.'

He does not reply to that. When I look at him properly, I think he might be close to tears. Then he laughs.

'Oh, it's great, isn't it? You meet the perfect person, and you don't get to see if you can make it happen. I want to do everything with you. I want us to go to films and plays, and walk around London and Brighton and visit bars and cafés, and hang out with Daisy taking people's dogs out, and everything. I want to do everything with you that people who are together do. And instead . . .' He is laughing too much to be able to speak. 'Instead . . .'

I am giggling too.

'Instead,' I finish for him, 'we're washed up on a tropical island. The precise thing we would be wishing for if we were squeezing on to a rush-hour Tube train, or walking someone's dog in the rain.'

'We'd be saying: "Oh, if only we could go to an island where it was always warm, and there was white sand and balmy water, and no shops."'

'"And nothing to do,"' I continue, '"and a rainforest fringed with the most spectacular beaches, and we could get our water from a well."'

'"And catch fish from the sea, and eat bananas from the trees! Wouldn't that be blissful."'

We look at each other in the moonlight, and the hysteria builds up in me, and then I am laughing so hard that I am worried about waking Katy and Mark and Cherry. Ed and I laugh until we cry at the absurdity of our situation, and then I fall asleep cuddled up to him, our bones jarring against each other whenever we get too close.

When I wake up, Mark and Cherry are also lying around the dead fire, sleeping. I surmise that only Katy was hardy enough to make the cabin into the magical new home we all wanted it to be.

The sun is surprisingly high in the sky. Ed is not here. The other two are dozing. I feel happy, properly happy, for the first time. Whatever happens, Ed and I could work together. This is the first relationship that has felt this way for me: at the grand old age of just-forty, I have found the right person. That certainty puts a spring in my step and a smile on my face, in spite of everything.

I shake out my sarong and head to the jungle, towards what passes for the toilet facilities. As soon as I get to the edge of the forest, however, I hear someone crashing towards me.

She is out of breath, and looks stricken. I am aware of something in her hand, but I only want to look at her face.

'Jean?' I say. 'Are you all right? Is Gene OK?'

'Oh yes, yes.' She sounds impatient. 'Well, in a way. But look. Everybody. Where are the rest of them? Oh, sleeping. Well they need to wake up. Where is that young man of yours? We need to get everyone together, Esther. And now. Because this . . .' She holds it up. It is a telephone, but it is bigger than a normal mobile, and there is a huge antenna sticking out of the top of it at an angle. 'This object. Is a satellite phone. Found it buried in the rainforest. Purely by chance. A phone. And my bet is, somebody here knows a lot more than they have been letting on.'

I do not hear a single word beyond the phrase 'satellite phone'.

'It's a phone,' I whisper. 'Jean. Does it . . . ?' I cannot finish the sentence. A phone. An actual phone.

chapter twenty-eight

'It doesn't work,' she says over her shoulder as she strides to the bones of the fire. 'No batteries in it. Sorry, Esther. We were excited too. But the question, of course, is . . .' Jean claps her hands, twice, three times, impatience on her face as she watches the Americans stir.

'Wake up,' she snaps at them. 'Come on. Wake up. Wake up and tell us if you know anything about this.'

I watch both of their faces as they attempt to focus on the phone. Cherry's mouth forms a perfect 'o' when she sees the handset, but she does not say a word. Mark frowns at it, then leaps to his feet in one bound.

'That's a sat phone!' he says. 'Have you tried it?'

'No batteries,' Jean tells him, staring into his face as if they were playing poker, apparently gauging his reaction. 'Though we can only assume that there are some, somewhere on this island. Because this is not an old satellite phone.'

Cherry is on her feet too. The four of us stand around the phone and gaze at it. It looks very like a normal mobile. Only its antenna marks it out as different.

'Where did you find it?' I manage to ask.

'Yeah, there's the thing.' Jean nods to me. 'We found it by the purest happenstance. The rest of the crew, you people, were gone, and Gene is not steady on his feet. In fact, the walk over here and back as good as finished him off, where his legs are concerned. All he wants to do now is sit by the fire and talk to Ben, aloud, until either he dies or that bloody boat arrives. So I thought, to save his poor legs, I would make a new lavatory area, closer to the beach. After all, the rest of you are not there to complain about hygiene or whatnot. I went into the forest and found a place where the soil was soft and it looked as though it would be easy to dig. I started digging at it with a stick, but in fact the earth was so loose that I was able to pull it away with my hands. I thought nothing of it. I assumed some ants or similar had been through. It was only when my fingers hit the metal that I realised there was something buried.'

'And then you pulled out that baby.' Mark's eyes are shining. 'What the fuck?'

'Precisely,' Jean agrees. 'And it raises, you must agree, a number of questions, starting with the very one Mark just articulated.'

'Forget the questions.' Cherry is excited. 'It's a telephone. I've seen those ones on the television news. The reporters use them when they're somewhere that normal phones don't work. Afghanistan. You know. So that, in your hand, is a telephone that would actually get us off this island. Before we get all "what the fuck", why don't we scour the place until we find the batteries, and get ourselves a fucking boat?'

'Yes.' I can barely speak, but I need to add my voice to hers. 'I don't care why it's here, if we can make it work. If that can get us home . . .' I force myself to finish the sentence, because in my head I am only with Daisy. 'Then that is the only thing in the world I care about.'

'Yes, yes,' Jean tuts. 'I know, you two. I'm a mother too, I had the same reaction. Of course Gene got off his poor old backside and together we dug up everything we could find. I walked through the entire jungle, it felt, looking for loose patches of earth. And of course we can continue with that, but it's not an efficient use of our time. Because we could carry on looking until we die. Far better, in my opinion, for the person among us who brought it here to tell us where the batteries are hidden. Where's young Ed? Where's Katy?'

We all turn and scan the beach, though neither of them, clearly, is here.

'Ed and I slept by the fire,' I say, 'because the hut was horrible. I just woke up about ten minutes ago, and he wasn't here. I'm sure he's around somewhere.'

'Hmm.' Jean is suspicious instantly. 'And Katy?'

'I don't think she's awake yet.'

As if summoned by our collective will, Katy emerges from the hut, her sarong knotted around her waist, blinking at the daylight. She stands at the top of the steps and yawns loudly.

'Ahh,' she says. 'Well. The indoor life is not, it transpires, everything we'd hoped for. Morning, everyone. Jean! Hello. What is . . .' She suddenly runs, almost stumbling, down the unreliable steps. For a moment I think she is going to fall, but she lands on her feet on the sand. 'Is that a phone?' she says. 'What on earth . . . ?' Her eyes are wide as she joins the respectful group marvelling at the bizarre object.

'Yes,' Jean says. 'It is a non-functioning satellite phone. It is inconceivable that it was brought here by anyone other than one of our group. We need Edward.'

'I'll find him,' says Mark, and he strides away towards the buildings and forest behind them, calling Ed's name.

While he is gone, I try to make sense of this.

'You mean, someone here has hidden this? I just can't get my head around it. Surely it was left here when this place' – I point to the dilapidated buildings – 'when this place was abandoned? I mean, of course none of us has a secret phone. Because all of us are desperate to leave.'

'Yes.' Katy is nodding, and I can see from her face that she is still trying to compute the situation. 'It's impossible that we brought it. What makes you think we did, Jeannie? It only makes sense as something that was already here.'

Jean is shaking her head. Her cheeks are hollow, and the bones of her face all jut out. She looks like a skull draped with skin.

'I'd love to think that,' she says. 'I would. But this place has been left to the elements for some time.'

'Do you think, though?' asks Cherry. 'I mean, sure, there's creepers growing through everything and the wood has rotted. But might that not be something that happens very fast around here?'

'I don't think so.'

We stand in silence for a while, waiting. I try to run through it in my head. Jean's idea is nonsensical. She seems convinced that somebody among our small and close-knit band is conspiring against the rest of us. That cannot possibly be true: in fact, the idea is laughable.

When Mark and Ed come back, I smile with relief. Mark's arms are filled with bananas and papayas, and Ed is carrying, rather gingerly I think, a large dead lizard. He puts it carefully down on the ice box lid, and walks over.

'Mark told me,' he says, looking at the phone. 'We have to make this thing work. It's like a bizarre and miraculous lifeline, isn't it?'

'Yes, yes.' Jean is scathing. 'Can we now take the fact that it's unexpected as read. I want to know which of you people brought it here, and more than that, I would like to know where you're keeping its batteries.' She stares around the group, looking from face to face.

'But I don't think any of us brought it here,' Cherry says again. 'Like we were just saying. We can't have done, Jean.'

'You can't *not* have done. What I am saying is that I no longer trust a single one of you. Until we discover who brought this, all of you are under suspicion. I have no idea what's going on, but I am absolutely certain that this phone, new and shiny as it is, belongs to somebody here.'

Mark is almost laughing. 'But why, Jeannie? Who here would hide a satellite phone, and what would the big conspiracy be? I absolutely do not understand how that would work.'

'No. It's beyond me too, because there is something going on about which I have no idea. But look at it this way. Who knew each other before we got here?' She sits down, and the rest of us sit too, staring at her as she speaks. 'Gene and me. Mark and Cherry. You other three, you'd vaguely met over on the main island. All we know about each other is what we've told each other. We can't check anything from here. So Mark, for instance: you're a married father living on Long Island. Are you, though? Cherry says you are. But who is Cherry? Do you see what I mean?'

'Jean,' I say. 'Jean, thinking along these lines is awful. It'll destroy us. Maybe Samad left the phone there. If there's any sort of conspiracy, it would surely involve him, the man who brought us here and never came back. If we start to pull apart each other's stories, we won't last five minutes. I want to trust you all and I'm going to carry on trusting you all.'

'Is that right, Esther?' says Jean, turning her bird-like stare on me. 'Is it, now? What do we know about you? Absolutely nothing, in fact. Is there a Daisy? Is there a loser of an ex-husband? Did your story about staying unhappily married for a decade ever actually ring true? Why are you really here, Esther?'

I am aghast. 'Jean! I thought you and I were friends? What are you talking about?'

'I'm just saying that I am not taking anything for granted any more. Ed, you're more private than anyone here. You have shared next to nothing about your life. The rest of us have all been open. Not you. Why?'

'Oh, fuck off, Jean,' he says with surprising venom. 'Don't do this. You're being absurd, and as Esther says, you're dismantling the only thing we have, which is camaraderie. Don't do it.'

'But we have to do it, Ed,' Jean says. 'I know it's not

good for morale. But it's not me destroying the morale. It's the owner of this thing.'

'I'm with you, Jean,' Mark says suddenly.

'I am too, actually,' Katy says. 'I mean, I don't want us to start turning on each other. But at the same time, this is an actual phone. I don't know about these things, but is it not, like Cherry says, the only type of phone that would actually work out here? This is probably a crazy and stupid thing to say, but several of us have mobiles that don't get any reception. Would any of their batteries work in this thing?'

Mark smiles. 'Nice thought. But not a chance.'

'Not even worth trying?'

Jean holds open the battery compartment 'Look. Completely different from a standard mobile, I'm afraid.'

'Oh. Right.'

'But,' says Mark, 'here's the thing. We need to work out what it's doing here. Because I have a feeling that everything has just changed. If someone knows where the battery is, and if we can make it work, then we can get away from here.'

'And we need to,' says Jean, 'because Gene, I have to tell you, has just about given up. I've left him lying in the shade with a bottle of water, but I'm not even confident he'll make it through the rest of the day. He doesn't want to. So this is me, begging you all. Imploring you. If you know how to make this thing function, please, please show us.'

We have shifted about, unconsciously, so we are sitting in a circle, a little way away from the dirty remains of the fire. Jean, who has taken it upon herself to run this inquisition, stares first of all at Ed, who is sitting to her left.

'Edward,' she says, looking into his eyes. 'Did you somehow bring this telephone to the island in secret?'

Ed laughs, but in a bitter way. He has always been far calmer than me, but now he is, I can see, incensed.

'Of course I didn't,' he says, his fury visible to everyone. 'How would I have done that, Jean? And why? I mean – why? Why would I do that? It makes no sense at all. We all got on that boat together. None of us had a secret phone in a bag, did we? That thing is bigger than a normal phone. It wasn't on the boat, and that's a fact. I don't understand why you're doing this, Jean. Why are we not just searching the fucking island until we find the things that will make it work, if they're here?'

'See,' she says. 'You've gone right on the defensive. Esther?'

I squint at her. 'What?'

'Is this yours?'

'No, Jean.' I cannot even dredge up the energy to fight her. 'It's not mine. If I had a working phone, we would have got off this island a long, long time ago. Believe me.'

'You and Ed are sure you didn't know each other before we came here?'

'Sure,' I say, apathetically. I feel Ed bristling beside me, and try to calm him with a hand on his arm. I see Jean notice this. I cannot be bothered to say anything more. The whole scene has become too surreal.

'Katy?' barks Jean. 'This wouldn't be yours, would it?'

Katy laughs, a short, abrupt laugh. 'Oh, believe me,' she says. 'This is the thing I have been praying for. I wish it was mine, if that meant I knew how to make it work.'

'You need to be a little more specific in your prayers,' Mark tells her. 'Next time ask for the battery too.'

'I'll give that a go,' she says. 'It's horribly tantalising, isn't it? The very thing. Inexplicably here. Yet useless.'

I nod at that. Jean turns her attention to Cherry.

'Not mine,' says Cherry. 'Oh my God. I'm like Esther. I'm a mom. And even though I cannot think of any reason why anybody would hide away a thing like that, I can assure you that I *absolutely* wouldn't. I mean, deliberately keep us all here, away from our babies? So that Mark and I are discovered and divorced and gossiped about and hated? Why the hell would I make that happen?'

Jean shrugs. 'We only have your word for it, you know. Yours and Mark's.'

'Excuse me?'

'We can hardly check your story, can we? Any of you. Any of you could be lying blatantly about your lives away from here. Don't take anything for granted.'

'Oh, Jesus Christ, Jean,' says Mark. 'Enough of this. Stop playing Scooby-Doo. Fucking hell. Who's to say that you and Gene are what you seem either? For all we know, you've already called a boat and Gene's gone off on it. You probably haven't even *got* a son.'

'We have. I know that and Gene knows that. All I want to say is this: I am convinced that one of you knows more than you are letting on. I have my suspicions about who it is, but let's say this. Just get the missing battery, and put it in a place where we will easily find it. No need to say anything. Do that by sunset tonight. No more questions asked.'

She looks around at each of us in turn. When she stares into my eyes, I find myself shifting and fidgeting, wilting under the heat of her fierce suspicion. Then she stands up and walks off, carefully taking the phone with her.

Katy looks around for a moment, then says: 'This is all so odd. I'm going to go with her and check on Gene. Anyone else coming? I'm not sure the two of them should be on their own.'

Everyone is disconcerted. First Katy goes after Jean, and then Cherry does. Mark paces by the shore, deep in thought.

'She thinks it's us,' I say to Ed.

'She's lost the plot completely.' He is dismissive. 'Clearly, whatever that thing is doing there, it's been around longer than we have. She's found something to fixate on, that's all. She can fuck off. I think we should go after her, actually, because otherwise you know what she'll be doing. She'll be holding court to Katy and Gene and Cherry, constructing outlandish scenarios that involve you and me and some dastardly plot. Ridiculous. Come on. Let's go and stand up for ourselves.'

I heave myself up. 'OK. We'd better take that dead lizard.'

'Now there's a sentence I'll bet you've never uttered before.'

I smile at him. Ed carries the lizard, and I take the fruit, and we stumble through the humid rainforest, our legs scratched, unseen creatures rustling out of our way as we go. We leave Mark standing still and staring out to sea.

chapter twenty-nine

By sunset, we are all, except Mark, slumped on our original beach. Ed's lizard is cooking on an improvised spit over the fire, and smelling outrageously appetising. I search myself for any residual feeling of revulsion at the idea of eating a huge lizard, but there is none. My whole body is crying out for meat, and I wish I could have it all for myself.

Unsurprisingly, the battery does not appear by Jean's deadline. The mood of the camp is wrecked. There is almost no cooperation. Gene is lying by himself, his breathing shallow, holding a mumbled conversation with (I assume) his comatose son. Jean and Katy attend to him from time to time, one of them propping him up while the other holds a water bottle to his lips. Even the water bottles are close to giving up, their plastic stretched and cracking. Jean wipes Gene's face with a sunhat dipped in water, and murmurs to him, sharing, I am sure, her paranoid suspicions.

I do not want to be infected by the new suspicious

mood in camp; and yet I find that, in spite of myself, I am. Mark and Cherry's story is implausible, however you look at it. I trust Jean and Gene, even though I heartily dislike Jean at the moment and would love to be able to blame her for whatever it is we are accusing people of. Ed is suspicious of Katy. In my worst moments I even wonder about Ed: as Jean said, he is the only one of us who has not volunteered much about himself, and he only offered his tale of being the neglected middle child when I repeatedly pressed him.

I catch myself thinking along these lines and make an effort to stop it. I love Ed. I trust him completely. Yet I am not sure that I should depend on my own judgement. It has not always been good in the past.

Nobody is speaking. We are all sticking around the fire because, I think, everyone knows that to head off alone would be to invite suspicion. We stick together, and try not to look at each other. Suddenly there is nothing to say. Mark has not arrived from the other beach. I see Cherry looking for him, often. I wish I had had the confidence to stay there too. The atmosphere here is stifling and poisonous.

'It makes no sense,' Ed says, out of the blue. 'I cannot think of any scenario in which that phone is legitimately here. And yet, here it is. Could it be a collective hallucination?'

Katy shrugs. 'Could be. That's as plausible as anything else. I think the lizard might be done, guys. Shall I do the honours?'

'I'll get some plates,' I say, and I feel all their eyes on me as I head into the jungle to pick banana leaves. I want to turn and clarify that I will not be locating the battery and making a mysterious telephone call, but I manage to stop myself. If I said that, it would only confirm my guilt, in their eyes. I find the leaves I need, make sure I have one for everyone, including both Gene and Mark, and head directly back to camp, ensuring that no one can possibly think that I had time to do anything else.

'Here we go,' I say, handing them over. Katy has put the lizard, which is now charred black, its eyes exploded out of their sockets, on to the lid of this beach's ice box.

'Thanks,' she says. 'We're waiting for it to cool down.'

Ed, Katy, Cherry and I sit and stare at the lizard. Jean sits and stares at all of us. Ed suddenly turns on her.

'For fuck's sake, Jean!' he yells. 'Stop looking at us like that!'

She raises her eyebrows, but says nothing, and goes to sit next to Gene instead.

The lizard is the most delicious food I have ever tasted, and I thank it profusely for giving itself to feed us. I want to say grace, to thank not a divine provider, but the food itself. I manage, however, to restrain myself.

'Did you kill it?' Katy asks Ed, through a mouthful. It is properly dark now, and there is a cloud over the moon. 'I meant to ask, but we were rather overtaken by events, weren't we?'

'Yes,' he tells her proudly. 'I wouldn't have just brought back a dead one, because it would have poisoned us all. I was off collecting fruit, and it was on the ground at the bottom of a tree, doing that thing where they stand completely still and hope you don't notice them. I jumped on it. I didn't think for one second it would still be there once my feet landed, but it was. It started hissing at me, which was very disconcerting. I didn't have a weapon to hand, obviously, so I just stamped on its head until it died.'

'Wow,' says Katy.

'Respect,' I tell him.

'Ed,' says Cherry. 'You are a hero, and I don't care what Jean says.'

'I too,' he says, 'do not care what Jean says.'

'Me three,' I mutter.

Katy looks awkward. 'I know where you guys are coming from,' she says quietly. 'I mean, of course that phone doesn't belong to one of us. It's impossible and ridiculous. It was obviously here for some reason before we were – that is completely clear to everyone but Jean. But look at her. Her husband's about to die. Tonight, I would say. Her son, to all intents and purposes, is already dead, but Gene won't let him go, so she hasn't been able to process the grief. When Gene dies, if she gets away from here, she'll have to deal with switching off Ben's machine. I can see why she's clinging on to the suspicion thing, can't you? So let's give her a bit of a break.'

Ed nods slowly. 'When you put it like that. Yes. Sorry.'

'Hey.' I see Katy smile warmly in the starlight. 'Don't apologise. You provided the lizard. You're safe.'

'I can see that too,' I say. 'About Jean. I think I've been too wrapped up in myself. I could be a bit kinder to her, even though she does seem to think I'm plotting in some unspecified way to keep us all here for ever, and never see my daughter again.'

'That,' says Cherry, 'is because she doesn't believe you have a daughter. Poor woman. Of course she's losing it.'

We all watch Jean stroking her husband's hair back from his face. He is still mumbling an undecipherable stream of slurred words under his breath. Jean is speaking urgently, right into his ear, looking across at us from time to time. It is clear that she is talking about us.

Mark comes back just as I am drifting off to sleep. Suddenly he is standing over us.

'I've been thinking about this,' he says, his voice loud and portentous, bringing me instantly to complete consciousness. 'I think we do have a traitor in the camp. I know who it is. And do you know how I know?' He does not wait for an answer. 'I saw a boat!'

Everyone stirs at that, though I instantly disbelieve him.

'Honey,' says Cherry's voice, uptight and worried. 'What are you talking about?'

I manage to twist myself around and look at him. The sky is now so dark that it is almost impossible to make him out.

'I saw one. A light out at sea. What does that signify? A boat. Ship. Vessel of some sort.'

'So where is it?' I ask him.

He pauses. 'It went away.'

'Oh,' says Ed. 'Great. You're sure about that, are you?'

'Yes. I am sure.'

I lie back down. There is no point engaging with this. I suspect that Katy is following the same plan. Jean is sleeping away from the rest of us, with Gene. I block out the sounds of Mark's increasingly unhinged conversation and do my best to focus on sleeping, but I wake up again when I hear him saying to Cherry: 'You don't want to know who the traitor is, then?'

'No,' she says, with unusual vehemence. 'I actually don't.'

'Well I'll tell you anyway. Then you can be wary. It's Esther.'

I almost laugh. I nearly turn around to defend myself. Then I decide I cannot be bothered with any of it, and I force myself to escape from it all by drifting into blissful, straightforward unconsciousness.

chapter thirty

Cherry wakes us in the darkest part of the night, by yelling: 'Boat! A real one!' She is standing right above me, screaming.

The clouds have blown away from the moon, which is nearly full. The stars make me feel grounded. Cherry is pointing at the sea and shouting the same word over and over again.

As ever, it takes me a few seconds to orientate myself.

Ed is quicker. He is sitting up, and then his deep voice is joining Cherry's high excited one.

'It *is* a boat!' he says. His voice grows louder. 'There is! You're right, Cherry. There's something out there.'

Katy and I spot it. 'There! It's there!' We all shout at once. There is a light, an electric light, somewhere close to the horizon. I am aware that it is the first electricity any of us have seen for weeks. All of us are shouting at the tops of our voices. Jean joins us, looking around beadily.

'You see?' she says. But then even she joins in the shouting.

I stare at the light, willing it to change course and come closer. Ed ushers us all away from the fire and throws more fuel on it. I realise that this is the only thing to do, and join him, grabbing leaves and branches from the forest and running back, past Gene, who is so still that I wonder, briefly, if he has died yet. We throw everything we can on the fire, and the leaves, luckily, are dry now, so they burn brightly though quickly.

'Will they come?' Katy sounds breathless. 'Is there anything else we can do? Anything at all?'

Mark is next to her. 'No,' he says. 'There's not. The fire is all we have. They'll see it and come closer, because there must never be a fire out here. Which means they'll want to check it out.'

I suddenly remember Mark announcing me as the traitor, and I walk away from him. I have no desire to learn what it is about my behaviour that led him to judge me like that.

Ed takes my hand and we stand and watch the light, desperate for it to grow, for the shape of a boat to form around it.

It does not happen.

The next thing I know, someone is running into the water and swimming away.

'Cherry!' Katy shouts. 'What are you doing?'

'Cherry!' Mark yells. 'Don't be an idiot! You can't swim that far!'

But she is not listening. I stand rooted to the shore, and watch her splashing through the moonlit water, swimming with surprising strength in the direction of the light.

'She can't do that,' Ed says. 'We need to get her back. She'll drown.'

'Are you guys strong swimmers?' Katy asks. 'I'm not bad and I'll give it a go unless one of you wants to.'

'I'll get her,' Mark says. I catch sight of the sceptical look Katy gives him, before they both walk into the water together. After a moment, Ed follows them.

'Did my lifesaving course back in the day,' he says. 'I'd feel terrible if I didn't give it a shot.'

My swimming is far too weak for me even to try. I stand on the shore and watch in terror as three of my allies and one bizarre enemy disappear out to sea. They cannot, I think, leave me here with a dead man and a paranoid woman who thinks I am plotting against her. They have to come back. I feel entirely abandoned by them, just as we were by Samad.

The sea is lit up like a shifting silver cloth. I stare at the three heads that are ploughing away from me, feeling that I can keep them safe if I never take my eyes off them. Cherry is out in front, swimming purposefully towards the light. She is like a moth, I think, compelled to throw herself at the electricity. Two of the others are gaining on her, though I have no idea which two they are. The other is slowing down, and whoever it is, I am willing them to turn and come back.

As I stare, the single figure stalls. The other two reach Cherry. It is hard to see from the beach, but there is flailing, an obvious struggle. I stare in horror as they seem to pull and fight one another for an impossible amount of time. Then, finally, the figures start to head back towards the shore. It takes them for ever to get here.

*

'Don't worry.' Jean has crept up to me so quietly that I never noticed. She puts a claw-like hand on the top of my arm, and I want to shake her off but, somehow, don't. I cannot think of anything to say to her, so I just stand and stare out to sea instead. The figure that stalled is swimming back to the beach, and as it comes closer I see that it is Mark. Mark, the most self-consciously alpha of us all, is not who I expected to see. By the time he reaches the beach he is gasping for breath, clearly beyond exhausted, and he staggers past Jean and me without a word and throws himself on the sand beside the fire.

We stand and wait for the other three. I dread what is about to happen.

Cherry is still alive. We put her beside the fire. She is shaking violently, and her eyes are closed.

'She wouldn't come back.' That is all Ed manages to say. I sit up close to him and hold him as best I can, but he has no reserves left. Katy is shuddering and gasping for breath, not speaking to anybody.

None of us has commented on the fact that the boat has continued on its trajectory and passed out of sight.

Nobody says a word for hours, not even Jean. We sit up in the tropical night, and keep the fire burning, and nobody has anything left to say. Much later, when it is nearly morning, Ed mutters: 'She didn't want to get to the boat. She wanted to die.'

'You saved her,' I tell him.

'What right did we have,' he mutters, 'to do that?'

*

We all sleep late into the next day. We wake up burned by the sun and slick with sweat. I am acutely aware that Ed and Katy saved Cherry's life, against her will, while I stood on the beach and did nothing. If it had been just Cherry and me, she would have died. I am useless.

I fetch bananas for breakfast and attempt to cook them slightly to make them taste nicer. As I do so, I try to be reassuring.

'Whoever was on that boat last night,' I say, 'will have seen our fire.' I announce it as if I mean it. 'To be out in a boat at night, that probably means they're fishermen, which means they know the area, which means they know this is an uninhabited island. So they'll know there are people here, and in the morning they'll tell someone.'

A dubious silence greets this hypothesis.

'Or,' says Katy, 'they're out at night because they're up to no good, smuggling or something, and the last thing they'll do is tell anybody. Because if fishing boats ever passed this way, we would be long gone from here.'

'Yeah,' agrees Edward. 'Or that.'

chapter thirty-one

The boat does not come back. Nothing happens. Nothing else turns up on the horizon and there is no sign at all of anyone coming to pick us up. I did not expect it, but the glimpse of electricity and everything it implies, coupled with Cherry's crazed swim and set against the background of the satellite phone, has conspired to turn our camp into a snakepit of paranoid despair.

I have had enough. I do not like these people. I don't care about them any more. I do not have the choice, but all the same, I know that I have used my reserves, and that everybody else has too. I can no longer push Daisy out of my head. She is with me all the time, looking at me with her face furrowed in confusion, reaching out to me. I stretch out and try to touch her, but our fingers never meet.

'Esther,' says Mark, crouching down next to me and using a surprisingly gentle tone. 'Look. We have no idea what's going on here, but I know that the phone is yours. Tell us where the rest of it is. Or go and make a call and get someone to pick us up. Either will be fine.'

I look at Daisy. She vanishes.

'Fuck off,' I mutter. I cannot be bothered to defend myself.

'I won't.' He still sounds gentle, which is unnerving. 'Just tell me, Esther.'

'Why? Why would it be mine? It's not.'

'It fucking is. This is why I think so.' He seems to experience a surge of adrenalin, and suddenly leans forward so his face is right in front of mine. I pull back and he follows, his face so close to mine that I see his features, which I once thought were handsome, in double. He looks ugly and, I think, deranged. 'Number one. It's not Jean and Gene's. They found it, for a start, and also he's about to die. Number two, I know it's not mine and I can vouch for Cherry. That leaves you, Ed and Katy. Katy's the practical one who's taken care of everything. She would make that call if she knew how, and get us home, sooner than anyone else would. Ed's too much of a nice guy. You can tell by looking at him that he's too normal to pull a stunt like that.'

'And that leaves me, does it?'

'It does. You're the one that makes sense. You have a dark side, anyone can see that. You say you're divorced with a child, but what proof is there?'

I cannot let that go. 'What proof is there of anything any of us say? Isn't that the whole point? We don't know each other.'

'No. We don't. But I think I'm starting to know you a bit.'

'Mark! You're being completely mad. What is your scenario, then? Why would I have brought an incomplete satellite phone to the island, mysteriously carrying it here without anyone noticing? Tell me what I'm up to. I'd love to know.'

He scratches his head. 'I haven't completely worked it out yet. Here's one idea: you visited the island before we came on the trip, and left it behind. You'll use it to get picked up at some point, which I hope is going to be soon. As for why, I can't say, as I don't know what your real life is like, in the outside world. Who you really are. I'm thinking you've done something terrible, and you need to lie low without anyone being able to find you. This is a pretty good place to do that, don't you think?'

I retreat from him further, but he follows me, staring at me with possessed eyes, wanting me to crack and confess. Ed, I see, is still lying comatose on the sand, exhausted from battling Cherry back to shore. He will not be coming to my aid. Nobody is in a position to help me, and I am not sure that anyone but Ed would do it if they could. I touch Mark's chest with both hands. That is strange. I have never touched him before. Using all the strength I have, I push him away. He staggers, taken by surprise, and looks at me in triumph.

'See!' he crows. 'That proves it.'

'Oh, Mark.' I lie down next to Ed. 'Just stop it. Stop talking and leave me alone. You moron.'

I cannot sleep. Most people here, I realise, think the same as Mark. They think that I am the bad guy, that for some mysterious reason I have set up this whole situation. I wonder whether, if I swam out to sea, anybody would come after me. Ed would, I remind myself. But he has just done that for Cherry, and he has no strength to do it again. I could get into the water and swim away and nobody would be able to stop me.

I could just swim out a little way and put my head under, and breathe the water into my lungs. I would be gone before anybody noticed. That would be better than staying here. Our diet of fish and fruit is sustainable, and we could, I know, live here, amid recriminations and divisions and accusations, indefinitely.

I try to find Daisy in my mind and send her messages across the world. 'Tell them to go and check the islands,' I urge her. 'The islands out in the sea, near Perhentian Kecil.' She is awake. She is in Brighton, maybe at school (working that out is beyond me), sitting in a classroom and wondering where her mother has gone. Perhaps she will receive my message in her head. Maybe she will pass it on. She could call the British coastguard and get them to alert the Malaysian one. Someone could come and look for us. They must have noticed that we are all missing. In fact, it seems impossible that, over the past few weeks, absolutely no one has been out here looking for us.

The fact that a telepathic message to my ten-year-old is my best plan for getting off the island means that things are hopeless. Mark is sitting a little way away, staring at me and muttering under his breath. Ed, Katy and Cherry are flat out on the sand, and I have no idea what state any of them are going to be in. Jean is leaning over Gene, stroking his forehead, wholly absorbed in him. The fire is low. The night is bright. Nothing is going to change. There is no one here I wholeheartedly trust, and nobody trusts me.

*

I must drift off, because when I open my eyes it is light. There is a tinge of pink above the horizon. I check immediately for Mark. He is sitting up, staring at me with crazy eyes. When I look at him, he comes closer.

'Leave her, Mark.' It is Jean, who is standing over me, looking down on me.

'Why? If she's the one . . .'

'And what,' says Jean, 'if she's not? What if that thing was already here, or what if it belongs to someone else?'

I close my eyes and block out their endless paranoid speculation. I lie still and wish myself anywhere in the world but here. I retreat into my head and talk to Daisy. I hallucinate food. I refuse to speak to anyone or to open my eyes.

Even when I hear things happening around me, unusual things, I do my best to block them out. The sounds I can hear must be in my mind. The gasps and the excited voices cannot be real. The sound of an engine, approaching the beach in broad daylight, is definitely not something I could really be hearing, so I assume I am dreaming it. The excited shouts, the splashing of people running into the water; none of that can be real. It is a dream I like, however.

Then someone is shaking me.

'Esther,' says Jean. 'For God's sake. Get up. There's nothing wrong with you. Or do you want to stay here?'

I look at her.

'What?'

'It's happened, Esther. Someone's come for us. Open your bloody eyes, woman. It's a boat.'

I do.

And it is.

chapter thirty-two

Cathy

January 1989

I haven't thought back on it for the entire six months I've been here. I chose not to, because I wanted to close my mind and get on with life. I only dealt with the day ahead of me, and that was how I got through. No dwelling allowed.

It worked, most of the time. Better than I expected it to work.

I have been, I think, like a foster daughter to Michelle and Steve, and I don't think they've minded having me here. I've done lots of babysitting and I pick the boys up from nursery more often than Michelle does. Apparently they told their nursery staff the other day that I'm their cousin, because they got me confused with Sarah. It's nice being their cousin, and no one has corrected them yet.

It feels like a lifetime ago that I came here, fresh from the Village. I do my best never to look back at it, and certainly I do not allow myself to wonder what ripples my departure might have made. Sarah comes over every month or so – she gets the train into London from Hampshire, and then out to Isleworth. I love it when she comes to see me. We go out for coffee and cake, because her mum gives her the money for it.

She tells me about Martha.

'They went straight after Sean Holden,' she told me that first Sunday after I left. 'According to Martha, you were seeing him on the quiet. She went to Moses and told him that. So poor old Sean's got the whole of the Village on his doorstep demanding to know what he's done with you, not believing him when he has no idea what they're talking about, and actually pushing their way into his house and searching for you until his mum called the police.'

'Yeah,' I said. 'That was a bit of a red herring. Martha started it.'

'Well it was good. It took the heat right off us. They haven't a clue.'

'Didn't they tell the police I was missing?'

'Not yet. They want to find you themselves.'

'That'd be right. They don't like the police at all.'

'Listen to you!' she said. '"That'd be right"? That's a very un-Cathy thing to say. Where did that come from?'

'I've been watching *Neighbours*,' I admitted.

In the end, though, they did call the police. Martha told Sarah, she told her parents, and Sarah's parents went to the station and told the police the truth. Two police officers came to visit me here. I had to sit in the kitchen one evening with Michelle and Steve and go through my story with them.

It ended with them saying that I was clearly well cared for and happy, and leaving me alone. They even promised not to tell Moses or Cassandra or any of them where I was.

I was surprised to think that Moses had no power over the police. They weren't scared of him, I could see that. They thought he was pathetic. One of them called him a 'tosser' when he thought I wasn't listening. That was a revelation to me. Perhaps he was just an old man; perhaps I didn't need to live in fear of him tracking me down. Perhaps I had a right to live how I wanted to live.

They never did come after me. I have been living here, going to college, studying. Michelle found out that I could get some benefits, which I did, by filling in some forms, and I have had a little bit of money of my very own for the first time in my life. I am studying, just for one A level, at evening college. I chat sometimes to a couple of au pairs at the boys' nursery.

And it is that which has led me to the next thing. Michelle bought me a copy of a very odd magazine called *The Lady*, and she has helped me apply for jobs as a live-in au pair. There is one based quite near here, in Teddington, and I'm going for an interview on Tuesday.

'You'd be living with a family,' she said, 'and doing what you do here, but they'd be paying you properly for it. Which I wish we could do, Cathy. I thought you'd be difficult and that I'd regret taking you in. You were such a mousy thing. But you've been no trouble at all.'

That was nice of her. I told her that I'd been brought up to be no trouble at all, and she said that perhaps, in that case, I was still brainwashed.

I'm not, though. I don't think I ever was. I think I was following my community's traditions without ever questioning them, in the same way ordinary people do. My community just had stranger traditions.

I went to a normal church once, to see what it was like. It was weird: there were parts of the God I knew, but not enough to make Him recognisable. Everything was half-hearted. The idea of going to a normal church just for an hour on a Sunday morning and living a free life the rest of the time freaked me out.

I have not been back.

chapter thirty-three

The morning is clear and clean, and we are leaving.

It is a small boat, but bigger than the one we arrived on. There are two men on it, local men, and they are gaping at us and talking to each other using words I do not understand. Seeing new people is confusing, and I do not know how to respond to them. One of them smiles kindly at me, and I look away. Their faces are clean-shaven, and they are wearing proper clothes that do not have holes in, and that are clean. One of them, the younger-looking one, has on a T-shirt that is so white it hurts my eyes.

The only thing to do is to get into the boat.

Ed wakes up when I shake him. Katy was awake before me. Cherry is still weak from last night, and I think about how close she came to drowning herself, and how horrible it would have been, the night before our rescue. Mark tries to carry her to the boat, but he is not strong either, and in the end the bigger of our two saviours picks her up and puts her on board. It looks easy for him. She looks as if she weighs nothing at all.

We gather up our paltry possessions: the two books we all read several times, long ago, the towels, the sarongs. We throw the water bottles into the ice boxes and take it all away, conscientiously leaving no trace. I even drop the satellite phone in, despite all the trouble it caused.

Ed and I walk down the beach together for the last time. We hand an ice box to one of the men, who slings it on board. Ed takes my hand and we look back at the world we are leaving. This is no paradise. The beach is an expanse of grit. I long for electricity and progress and every little convenience that exists in the world.

More than anything else, though, I long for Daisy.

Mark, Cherry and Katy are on the boat, sitting in a row and looking dazed. Katy is managing to smile. Mark's eyes are darting around. I can see his mind ticking over. Mark trusts no one, and he is, transparently, wondering who these men are and where they are going to take us.

Jean and Gene are still on the sand. Both the men are standing over them.

'We should go and help carry him,' says Ed, and we both walk back up the beach, even though I am terrified to turn my back on the boat lest it should vanish.

As soon as we are close enough to hear her, Jean calls out.

'We're not coming,' she says.

'Jeannie.' Ed kneels down beside her. 'Jean, this is the thing that's going to save us all. It'll save Gene. We can get him aboard.'

'No.' She is adamant. 'He wouldn't last the journey. He's staying, and I'm staying with him.'

'You're not!' I tell her.

'We are, and there's not a thing you can do about it, young lady. Get yourself back to that daughter of yours. If she exists.'

'She does.'

'I believe you. Also, I don't care. Go on, be off with you.'

'But Jean.' I cannot think straight. 'You can't stay. You can't. We can't let you.'

'Oh shut up. I'm not moving him. Look at him.'

We do, and I stare for a long time before he takes a shallow breath. He is slick with sweat, but his face is so white that it is almost yellow, despite the sunburn.

The reality of us somehow picking him up and getting him on to the boat is, I realise, unthinkable.

'We'll get someone to come and pick you up,' I tell her. 'From a hospital, I mean, or something.' I had, I realise, forgotten all about hospitals. 'A hospital,' I repeat. 'That's where Gene needs to go. Isn't it?'

I look to Ed for confirmation. He is nodding.

'We promise we'll do that, Jean,' he says. 'You two stay here then, and we'll send someone out to get you.'

'If you like.'

'Of course we will,' I tell her. 'It'll be the first thing we do.'

'Well. We'll see. We'll just stay here, the two of us. We have water. We know where to find food by now. No rush.'

I look at her in bewilderment. Then I step forward and kiss her leathery cheek. She pulls away and frowns.

'No need, Esther,' she says, drily. We walk back towards the boat, which is still there, waiting for us. Then we are aboard, Ed and I sitting opposite the other three. The bench below us is smooth planks of wood, five of them in a row. It is the simplest thing, and yet it is miraculous. I stroke the wood, imagining the machinery that has made it the right length and texture, the process of fitting it into the boat.

Ed's hand is on mine. The engine starts. All of us look back to the beach that has been our home for an indeterminate amount of time. Jean and Gene are in their place by the treeline. Jean holds up a hand. We all wave back to her. Then we start to move. We pull away from the sandy prison, through the clear water, heading back through millennia of progress to the twenty-first century.

Soon the beach looks small. Then we are around the corner of the island, looking at a vista we have never seen before. The sun is already high in the sky and the water is golden. The sea is perfectly still. It feels as if the waves have stopped, the whole natural world on pause, while we make the transition from one time and place to another that is entirely different.

I grip Ed's hand as tightly as I can. I cannot say anything. This is so abrupt.

Our rescuers are asking us questions, but we speak almost no Malay, and they speak only a couple of words of English. No one is able to tell them our story, and we are unable to ask them if they know Samad. I watch Katy try his name out on them, saying 'Samad? Samad?' over and over again, but there is no reaction.

Eventually, one of the men conveys, through the medium of mime, that they were out fishing, and that they saw us. At least I think that is what he is saying. I want to ask why no one else has been past in all this time, and how often they come fishing this way, but the language barrier is unsurpassable. The fact that they are here, picking us up, suggests that Mark's worst Armageddon scenarios were not true.

I look into my fellow passengers' faces. Mark, Cherry and Katy are more familiar to me than anyone has been, ever. At this moment I know them better than I know my own daughter, because I have no idea what Daisy is doing or what state she is in. Until I see her, I will not believe she is all right. Until she sees me, she cannot possibly *be* all right.

I wonder if we will all drift apart and head in our own separate directions. Perhaps the past however-long-it-has-been will instantly seem unreal. Maybe we will all go home and deal with the ramifications of our absences, forget about each other and let our time on the island fade into insignificance.

The little boat bounces across the water. I try to convince myself that this is the beginning of the journey that will take me back to Daisy. Soon we will be on Pulau Perhentian Kecil, where there are phones.

I might hear her voice. The thought of it makes me retch with nerves.

Nobody speaks. We spent so much time fantasising about exactly this, and now it has come.

The engine of the boat is wonder enough. Soon we are going to be in a place with generators and electricity, with computers and the internet, with mattresses and sun cream and petrol, a place in which it is perfectly reasonable to plan to get into a metal vehicle and expect to be carried safely through the air to a place that is unimaginably far away, and, when you get there, to find your daughter.

There is a long strip of land in the distance. Beyond it is a longer one, that takes up the whole horizon.

One of the men points. 'Pulau Perhentian Kecil,' he says. I realise that the land behind it is Malaysia itself. We plough through the small waves, coming closer and closer to land.

All of us are tense. Mark and Katy look shocked as we all realise we are nearly there. Nearly back. About to step into the world we left.

Then we are approaching one of the bigger beaches on the island. There are huts and hotels all the way along the sand. It is still early, but there are people around: two runners in shorts and vest tops, a man and a woman, are making their way along the beach, and I remember that people do, in the real world, expend valuable energy just for the sake of it. A man in a white apron is carrying cardboard boxes of food from a small boat like the one Samad had towards a building. He puts a tray of eggs carefully on the sand. A white woman sits on the beach and leans on a backpack.

We come closer and closer until we are able to climb from the boat directly on to the wooden pier. I remember, suddenly, my arrival on this island, and some of the passengers getting out here. Everything looked charmingly primitive then. I try to see it with my old eyes, but I cannot.

This is time travel. We have been plucked from a world

in which we drank from a spring and roasted a lizard, and brought to this dizzying place, and it is impossible not to be overwhelmed to the point of nausea. Now I really feel that I have no reserves: all I want to do is stay on the boat, and stare at the land, and rock to and fro. I only manage to step back into the modern world because of Daisy.

The woman with the backpack looks up at us, as we are helped, one by one, from the boat. She looks again. She frowns and stands up.

She looks odd to me. Although she is, I suppose, probably not a person who would be classed as fat, everything about her is excessive. Her cheeks are smooth and plump, and between her short T-shirt and the waist of her long skirt, flesh bulges rudely out. Her hair is jaw-length, neatly cut, and a slide in the shape of a flower holds it back from her face.

There is nothing remarkable about this woman. She is a bog-standard backpacker, right down to the bag that has just fallen over at her feet. She is also entirely exotic: this is the person I was, without realising it, a few weeks ago. Even though I knew we had all changed, I find her astonishing.

My legs tremble as I step from the side of the boat on to the wooden steps of the pier. One of our rescuers, the younger one, grabs my hand from the land side of the operation and pulls me to stability. When we are all off, they usher us along the pier to the shore.

I sink down, back to the sand, enjoying its familiar safety at the same time as noticing tiny pieces of litter and cigarette filters in there. Although I am aware of activity going on, people talking to us, the backpack woman asking questions of Katy, the men who picked us up talking on mobile phones and everyone beginning to notice us, I cannot focus on any of it. My head hurts.

Jean and Gene are still there, still on our island. The two things I can hold in my brain are: send help to them, and call Daisy. There are many other things we will need to do. We will, I suppose, find out why we were left there. We will make arrangements to go home. We will find our old bags.

When I look at Ed, though, he smiles down at me.

'It's OK,' he says. 'Esther. We're safe. It's over.'

chapter thirty-four

It happens in a blur. People talk to us. They talk about us. They stare at us with concern and horror. News of us spreads around the resort, and people come to look at us. People from all over the world stand in front of us and take photographs. I do not even try to tell them not to. We are curiosities, and I understand that.

When I see a man staring at the picture on the back of his camera, I want to ask him to show it to me, but then, at the last second, I don't want to know. Somebody takes control; I have no idea who they are, but it is a man and a woman, local people I think. They lead us along the beach and into a building that has miraculous tiled floors, smooth and manufactured and incomprehensible. The café they sit us in has walls that are not there, open to the elements apart from the supporting pillars. We have a view of the sea and the beach. It is not, for any of us, a compelling view. I am far more interested, astounded even, in looking at the furniture, and the people, and the food and the drink. I stroke the back of the plastic chair

Ed is sitting in. The processes that led to its existence seem impossible. I do the same with the table, the plates, the clothes people are wearing and everything else I see.

Customers arrive in twos and threes. I glance at two women in sundresses sitting at a nearby table, and when I look back to our own table I see, again, that we are skeletons. The women look at us with as much curiosity as I am gazing at them. We look like concentration camp survivors next to these people. Mark and Cherry have remained, as far as I was concerned, the pinnacle of glossy physical perfection throughout our time on the island. Now, when I look back to them after staring at the random people at the tables around us, I wonder how I could possibly not have noticed them losing their shine. The five of us on our table look like extras from a horror film.

The owner of this place, I presume, comes over, bearing a tray of white china cups. The two men who rescued us pull up chairs.

'I bring you coffee,' the man says, smiling. I stare at the coffee. I had forgotten all about it, but now that I see it, I remember, dispassionately, that I used to love this drink. I drink it white, I remember that much, so I pour some milk in from the little jug.

'I call the police,' the man adds. 'They are coming. So tell me what happens?'

I take a sip from my drink and wince. This, I think, is what coffee tastes like? I look quickly to Katy, because she is sitting directly opposite me. She has the same reaction. We catch each other's eyes and smile. I put the cup down and push it away. It turns out that I have not been craving coffee at all. I thought I had.

I am not going to answer his questions. If I talk about this, it is going to be to the police.

A waitress arrives, looking at us with barely concealed horror, and puts a plate of food in front of each of us. We did not order, but they have brought us eggs and fried potatoes, toasted white bread with little foil-wrapped pats of butter and tiny plastic containers of jam. This is the food we dreamed of. It is the stuff of our hallucinations. A few hours ago, on that beach, we would have killed for this, for a plate of eggs and potatoes. It was the simple things that held the most appeal, I see now. We never dreamed of anything gourmet. It was just chips and eggs and easy things, bits of food that were almost, but not, attainable.

Now it is in front of me, and I am not hungry. I look at Mark, the most conspicuously hungry of all of us, and watch him gingerly load up his fork with food. He puts it in his mouth. All of us are staring. He chews it. He smiles with his mouth but not with his eyes, and gulps it down.

'That,' he says, 'is going to take some getting used to. There must be more calories here than we would have managed in our whole time on the island.' I realise that he could be right. In all that time we had no fat at all, beyond whatever might have been in the fish. The fried potatoes are swimming in oil and it is making me feel queasy, a reaction that is tempered by hunger.

'Oh,' says Katy. 'We are blessed to have been allowed to step from that Stone Age existence into this level of civilisation. It's like walking through the whole of human development, and ending up here, just a few miles from where we were, in a place where they have restaurants and cooked breakfasts, and knowing that that's just the start of it. It's . . . not easy, though. Is it?'

We all nod our agreement.

I force myself to eat a piece of toast. It is all I can stomach. Then I have a second piece and dip it into the egg, just because I know that Jean and Gene are still on the island, and I know that Jean must still be dreaming of food. I eat the egg for her, and after a while it feels good.

'Have we asked someone to go to Jean?' I say suddenly, terrified that we have all simply forgotten, in our befuddlement.

'Yes.' Cherry speaks for the first time since we set foot on this island. 'Those guys there. They sorted it out. Katy did too.'

Katy nods. 'It was the first thing we did. Made sure there was medical help going out to them. It's all in hand.'

Ed looks at the men sitting with us, and says to the owner of the café: 'Do you know a man called Samad?'

The man frowns. 'Samad?'

He turns to our rescuers and they talk to each other in what must be Malay. None of us says anything more to explain our plight. We wait for an answer. In the end, he turns back to Ed and says, 'You know Samad?'

'Yes,' Katy says. 'You?'

The man nods his head.

'I do not know Samad,' he says. 'Not myself. But know his friends, his family. Three, maybe four weeks ago, he is dead.'

*

When two policemen stride into the café, I put my fork down, scared, all of a sudden, of whatever it is that might be about to happen.

chapter thirty-five

Cathy

February 1989

Until today, I have been getting on with life, living quietly, doing my best to make my way in the real world. I think I have been doing well. I have a routine, and I love it.

Today, though, two things happened that have shaken me up.

A letter arrived for me. It came to college and I picked it up from my pigeonhole. It was handwritten, addressed to Esther Godschild, and there was a Hampshire postmark.

That scared me. I didn't want to open it, but then I knew that if I didn't, I would spend forever wondering what was in it. In the end, I felt that whatever it was, it wouldn't be as bad as anything I was imagining, so I ripped it open on impulse.

There was no letter inside, just a newspaper cutting. I unfolded it with shaking fingers, knowing before I looked at it what it was going to be. I suppose I suspected they would do this all along, but I never wanted to think about it very much.

It was the deaths column from the local paper.

The death is announced, it said, of Catherine Esther Godschild, aged 16, beloved daughter of Moses and Cassandra Godschild and child of God. April 16th 1972–July 14th 1988. May she Rest in Peace.

That was it. Seeing my name, and the date of my death, chilled me to the core. I don't think I will sleep tonight.

I am telling myself that I have been away for eight months, and all they are doing is trying to intimidate me. I knew I would be dead to them when I didn't go back. I was never going to see any of them again anyway.

But now I know they have been spying on me. They know I go to college here. They know I am calling myself Esther. They probably also know that I have changed their chosen surname of Godschild into Goodchild, because it sounds more normal. Occasionally other students even snigger at that, because it sounds funny to them, me being called Good Child, and I want to explain to them how very much more normal it is than anything else in my upbringing, but I don't. I relish the fact that I no longer stand out too much to risk it.

Hannah, who I'm quite friendly with on the course, saw me reading the cutting and came over. I put it away quickly.

'It's nothing,' I told her. 'Just some stupid thing someone sent me. About my family.' And I ripped it into pieces and put it in the bin, which felt good.

I said 'my family', but I don't feel that way about them.

As far as I am concerned, my family are the family I

work for, the Tao family, whose three daughters I take to school every morning and pick up every afternoon, fitting my college work around them. Both the parents, Eric and Melissa, work long hours in the City, and they have high expectations of their daughters, which means I spend between three thirty and six every afternoon taking them to swimming and music classes.

I enjoy it. I like it that, at eight, nine and eleven, they are old enough to chat to, and I am getting quite good at cooking for them. The house is huge, and I have the attic all to myself, with a television and a bathroom of my own. I know that Melissa and Eric like me to spend the evenings up here, and so I try not to hang around them too much. All I really want, though, is to feel like a proper part of the family.

So that arrived this morning. Then this afternoon the next weird thing happened. This has been quite a day. I was at home, writing notes for an essay about *The Tempest*, when the doorbell rang.

I put my pen down and skidded across the slidey parquet floor in my socks to answer it (I love that floor). I was expecting to sign for a parcel delivery. Instead, there on the doorstep was Victoria.

I knew her at once, but I could not believe what I was seeing. Slowly, I realised that she was 'dead' in the same sense that I was 'dead'. We were both dead only to the Village. I cannot believe I didn't think of that before.

She looked different. She has short hair now, and she was wearing a pair of round glasses. Her nose is still covered in freckles. She had on tight black jeans and a shiny purple top, and shoes that were pointy and purple.

She was smiling. She said, 'Hello, Cathy,' and I couldn't think of anything to say apart from, 'I like your shoes.'

She hugged me, and straight away I was crying into her shoulder. My hair was wet and I pushed it out of the way.

'Hey,' she said. 'It's OK.'

'I had no idea, Victoria,' I said, when I managed to pull away and control myself. 'I truly thought you'd died. Why did I believe that? I should have known, shouldn't I? Oh, I can't get my head round it. Look, come in. You look amazing. The same, but different.'

'You're looking good too. I don't call myself Victoria any more, by the way. I changed my name to Karen. Are you still Cathy?'

'No. Esther.'

'Your middle name.'

'I suppose I should have just picked a brand-new one, but it would have felt a bit weird. Karen.'

She laughs. 'Yes, it did at first. Didn't exactly protect me from them either. Anyway, I've pieced your story together. I saw your death notice. It's quite handy, watching that column, to see if anyone else has escaped. They always put the death note in about six to nine months later and post it to the person in question. It's Moses and his special brand of control freakery. So when I realised you'd gone, I got in touch with a couple of people from school, and they said Sarah knew where you were. I followed your trail from there.'

I put the kettle on. 'I'm so glad you did. I would never have thought to look for you, you know. God, I'm stupid.'

We both smiled, and I felt so warm inside, so immeasurably comforted to be able to share all of this with someone who had trod the same path.

I made us both a cup of tea, proud of the gorgeous house I lived in, knowing that I still had over an hour before I had to leave to fetch the girls. And I asked Victoria/Karen to tell me her story.

She had done a more dramatic flit than me. This is what she said, more or less.

'I didn't plan it, Esther. I just packed a bag and stashed it under my bed, because luckily I had the bottom bunk, and then that night I ran. It was urgent because . . . Did you have this? You didn't, did you, because Moses is your natural dad. They were going to marry you off to Philip instead, weren't they? Believe me, you're lucky. I was born outside the Village, and my dad wanted nothing to do with it. And girls who aren't his children are fair game to Moses. He dresses it up as being what God wants, and to give him his due, he does wait till they're legal, but essentially if he considers you attractive and you're over sixteen, he's going to have you, and you're going to have yet another one of his children. I didn't find that an appealing prospect, you know? And I was seeing Sam at school, and I knew it was coming. My own mother was trying to prepare me for it. Hideous.

'So I ran away. I just waited till about one in the morning, when I knew everyone should be asleep, and I got dressed under the covers, picked up my bag, stepped into my sandals and left. I'd oiled the hinges of our hut door, and I just opened it, walked through it and closed it behind me. Then I walked as quickly as I could over the grass to a bit of the hedge, not the main gate, and crawled through, and ran across a few fields. I knew where the station was, and I didn't want to get Sam into trouble or let anyone at all know where I was going, because it seemed easier that way, so I walked to the station, checked the time of the first train and went and sat in a hedge nearby to wait it out. The first train is nice and early, half past five, so I was pretty sure I wouldn't have been missed, and I just walked into the station and got on it with all these commuters. They ignored me because they ignore everyone. I went and stood in the toilet when the ticket collector came around, and so I found myself in Waterloo station, all alone in the world, with no money whatsoever, at sometime after six in the morning.'

'What did you do?' I asked her.

She grinned. 'I phoned my dad, reverse charges. He was annoyed at first to be called so early in the morning, but when he realised it was me and that I'd run away from the Village, he woke right up.'

'Did he look after you?'

'He did. He was quite confused and he didn't seem to know what to say to me loads of the time, and I could see that he felt bad that he hadn't tried harder to get me out of there when Mum met Moses and took me in. But he did what I needed him to do.'

'He helped you see how the rest of the world worked.'

She grinned at that. 'It's strange, isn't it? All those things that people assume everyone knows about. And you wonder whether to draw attention to yourself by, for instance, admitting that you never bought anything in a shop before you ran away from home at the age of sixteen, or whether just to ride it out.'

'Michelle and Steve – Sarah's aunt and uncle – used to get me to tell their friends all that stuff. I never minded. The more you're open about things, the less you feel bad about them, I think. They used to get me saying all of that: never went to a shop, never looked at a screen let alone watched TV, never saw a newspaper except in school, had no idea about music and concerts and other religions. They must have hated sending us to school.'

'They managed to withdraw us from enough lessons, didn't they? I think the school was so afraid of being accused of religious intolerence that they pretty much did what Moses told them. You know, we didn't just miss assembly, did we? We missed general studies, anything to do with politics, anything to do with current affairs, anything where we would have had to wear a PE kit. Morons.

'Anyway, so two years or so later, I saw the entire national media ridiculing the Village because of the impending Apocalypse. I saw Moses addressing the TV cameras, stupid self-important prick that he is, with no idea whatsoever that everyone was laughing at him.'

'He was on TV? But he made such a big thing about not letting any of the cameras in because he was afraid the media might be the tiniest bit cynical and sinful.'

She just raised her eyebrows at that.

'I did expect more people to leave after that, I must admit. I thought the Apocalypse not happening was surely as concrete as proof could get. But there was only you, Cath. Esther. Just you.'

'There are more of them who want to. Even Martha kind of does. I could see it in her eyes. I didn't dare tell her I was going, though. I nearly asked her to come with me, but I couldn't, because she might have stopped me.'

'Poor Martha,' Karen said. 'I'm not sure she'll ever dare to do it. Horrible to be stuck there wishing you weren't. One day we could go back for her, maybe.'

'We should. Have you met any others?'

'Oh yeah,' Karen said. 'Quite a few, actually. There's a group at the Cult Information Centre. You should come along and meet them. We get together occasionally because it's nice to be with other people who understand.'

I smiled at her and sipped my tea. 'It certainly is.' A cult. After fighting against Michelle calling it that, I am now happy to use the word. It diminishes its power almost entirely.

So that is what happened to me today. I discovered I was officially dead, and I met someone I thought was dead. Victoria/Karen. It has been interesting.

One thing she said has stuck with me, though.

'Some of the others are older. Jack – remember him? You probably don't. He's twenty-nine, he's got a baby now, and do you know what they did? They actually tried to take his baby a month after he was born. Jack has no proof that it was them, but he's certain it was. Because the same thing happened to Cecilia. She's got two little children, and one of them was actually kidnapped when she was about six months old. The police only got her back because this woman stopped at the motorway services and took the baby into the shop, just after the story had been on the news, and the guy who was working there recognised the baby and called the police. Can you imagine? He kept the woman talking – she sounded a lot like Cassandra, by the way – pretending to have a problem with the cash register so she couldn't pay for the stuff she was buying, until the police turned up. When they did, she just put the baby on the counter and ran out the back and ended up getting away. So if either of us ever has children, Esther, we'll need to be very, very careful.'

That was horrible. I know how much I like the children I've looked after. I can't imagine a baby of mine being stolen. They wouldn't be able to keep it because we would know exactly where to go to find them, but I would hardly trust Moses not to harm it just to get back at someone who has run away from him. That is definitely something I need to remember for the rest of my life.

chapter thirty-six

We talk to two policemen. One of them looks to me to be unimaginably fat, though in reality he is probably on the plump side of normal. He has a little beard, and it is trimmed so neatly that I realise how wild Ed and Mark's facial hair has become. I have not given it a moment's thought, but they both have proper shipwrecked beards.

The other policeman is small and wiry, and his eyes dart all over the place, looking from one of us to another, roaming all over our ravaged skin and our hollowed cheeks.

They explain to us, carefully, that nearly a month ago, Samad was killed on the island. Somebody stabbed him in the back and dumped his body in the jungle, where it was found half-eaten.

They both insist that this is unusual.

'On this island,' they say, 'nobody is killed. People die, but murder – no. Crime is people stealing tourists' bags from beaches, and that is all.'

'Poor Samad,' whispers Cherry, her eyes brimming with tears.

'And nobody knew about us,' Katy says softly. I think of all those hours we spent assuring one another that Samad's family would know where we were; that if something awful had happened to him they would send boats out to look for us. We were wrong: either they didn't know, or, most likely, they assumed that since he was back on the island, we were too.

I want to think about poor dead Samad, but suddenly my head is filled with nothing but Daisy.

'What do we do next?' Mark asks.

The fat policeman raises his eyebrows.

'You were staying at Paradise Bay?' he asks. 'We will take you there. Find your bags, ask them why they did not report you missing. Then we get you home. You want to go home?'

I close my eyes tightly. I long for my daughter so much that I cannot answer.

New clothes and toiletries materialise from somewhere. I feel odd wearing a strange T-shirt and a pair of shorts. I never wear shorts. They never suited me before, but now I have my new skeletal figure, I can wear anything.

I smear sun cream on to my face. It stings.

We go by police boat to Paradise Bay, all of us. We step into the shallow water and on to the beach. A generator is humming. There is a café with laminated menus, and people are lounging around on chairs, having the food they choose cooked and delivered to them.

There is a garden here, a well, and rows of vegetables.

This is what we would, ideally, have recreated on our own beach. I know, now, that it is impossible without the back-up of the outside world. You cannot grow potatoes or any other edible item if you do not have a potato plant in some form to grow it from. There is a laptop computer with its lid closed, and I know that the entire world is available there at the click of a button.

I am feeling a little bit stronger. I start looking around for a telephone.

The man at Paradise Bay is apparently dumbstruck at the sight of us. He peers into our faces, recognition growing. Soon he and the policeman are arguing. At last they turn to us.

'You did *not* leave your bags in the rooms,' the man says, switching languages but clearly continuing the argument. 'You paid for your rooms and they were empty. We were sad you left like that, and it is unusual, but we never knew something was wrong. Never! You must believe this!'

'We didn't pay for the rooms,' Ed says. 'I didn't pay for mine.'

'Nor me.'

'We didn't either,' says Mark, and Katy shakes her head.

The man screws his eyes tight shut, then opens them again.

'Not yourselves,' he says quietly. 'But they were paid for.'

'Who paid for them?' I ask.

'I was not here at that moment,' he says. 'It was Ali. My brother's boy.' He turns and shouts in the direction of the kitchen. I look at Cherry, because she is beside me.

'What's he talking about?' I ask quietly. This makes no sense.

'He's lying,' she says at once. Her face is blotchy with tears but her voice is firm. 'He's covering himself. They were paid for? I mean, what the hell? Did you pay? No. Did we? No. Of course we didn't pay.'

A boy in his late teens is produced from the kitchen. He twists the corner of his faded green T-shirt and shuffles his feet. When he speaks, his English is halting.

'A man come and pay the bill for the five rooms,' he says. 'I not know why. But I take the money and he say bye. I not ask anything.'

The policeman lets rip with a stream of dismissive words. Mark talks over him.

'What did this man look like?' he asks.

The boy talks to his uncle, who says: 'My nephew says he was an old man, perhaps sixty or seventy years old. He have white hair. He was very certain that he was paying the bill and he did not explain except to say he was a friend. When I come back, we went to the rooms and saw that they were empty, so we clean them and put in the next guests there. We think all you have gone.' He gestures in the direction of the mainland. 'You know, we have many guests. There is always someone who wants the room.'

The policeman turns to us. 'Do you know such a man?' he asks.

'Not Gene?' I wonder. We look at one another. Why would Gene have doubled back and paid for our rooms? He did not want to be on that island, stranded and unmissed, any more than anyone else did. In fact, he has come out of the ordeal far worse than the rest of us.

'Before we left,' I remember, 'Katy brought all our room keys back and left them with you. Do you remember that?'

'Yes,' says the boy. 'One woman. I remember.' He clearly does not recognise Katy.

'Yes, I dropped them off,' she says. 'I handed the keys in. Then we got in the boat, and we left.'

I think of poor Samad, killed on his brief trip back for the lighter. I think of the satellite phone, and a man who looked like Gene ensuring we would not be missed. Nothing adds up.

'Can I use your telephone?' I say, because it doesn't really matter any more what happened. The only thing that matters is getting away.

It is dark in the back of the staff area, where the phone is: there are no windows in the dark-wood walls. A white T-shirt hangs on a nail above the phone, and a single faded yellow flip-flop is in the corner, by my feet.

In the half-light, I press the keys on the telephone handset. Two zeros to get me out of Malaysia. Two fours to get me into Britain. Then 1273 for Brighton. Then the six digits of Chris's number, which, happily, I can remember.

After some clicking and buzzing, the miraculous British ringtone starts to sound. My vision blurs. My heart pounds throughout my body. Every fraction of a second stretches on as I wait for someone to pick up.

Daisy could answer. I have not got anything ready to say. I know it would be better if Chris picked up, but I long to hear her voice.

It rings and rings. I stare at the dusty floor. When the click happens, it is the answerphone. I do not even get to hear a familiar voice on that, because he has not bothered to change it from the electronic woman who came with the machine.

'I'm sorry,' she says, not sounding sorry in the least. 'The person you are calling is not available. Please leave a message after the tone. When you have left your message, you may hang up, or press one for more options.'

There is a clinical bleep, and I try to speak.

'It's me,' I say. I stop, take a deep breath and try again. 'It's Esther. Mummy. It's a long story. I'll call again in a bit. I want to try your mobile but I don't know the number.' I stop and hold the phone out in front of me, staring at it. Then I think of more to say and hastily pull it back to my ear. 'I'm in Malaysia,' I add. 'I was stuck. But I'm coming home.'

Then I put the phone back down, deflated, and go to tell Cherry it's her turn.

Ed, Mark and Katy are sitting on the beach. I go and join them. It is peculiarly comforting, to be on the sand with these people.

'As if some mysterious man strolled up and paid for our rooms!' Ed is saying as I sit down next to him. 'Here's what happened: Mr Paradise thought we'd bailed on him and threw our bags into the sea.'

'Helping himself to what he wanted first,' Mark suggests.

'Yes. That.'

'And this older man who came along?' asks Katy.

'Well,' Ed says. 'I would imagine he's a version of Gene, probably because poor old Gene isn't here. It's a story they've made up to hide the truth: they thought we did a runner, and were more concerned with renting the room out to other people than anything else.'

Katy is restless, unfocused. 'But I don't care,' she says. 'It's sad about Samad. The rest of it? So what? We're back. I'm not going to hang around talking to the police, who are clearly out of their depth. Nothing is going to happen, because the person who left us there is dead and the whole thing was an accident. I want to get as far away from here as possible. I'm going to head off on my own and get to grips with everything, and go home in my own good time. If I melt away, don't worry about me.'

I understand Katy's position entirely. 'I wish I could do that too,' I tell her. 'I'd come with you in a second. But I need to get a passport and get home to Daisy.'

'I know you do.' She puts a hand on my arm and smiles. 'And you will. You'll be back in a day or two, I know you will. Just keep the pressure up.'

She leans over and kisses me on the cheek. Then she gets up and walks away from us. I wonder whether we will ever see her again. If anyone can look after herself, alone in Asia without a bag or any documents, it is Katy.

Cherry joins us. Her face is puffy and red, and she is trembling all over.

'I just told him we have lots to talk about,' she says, lowering herself to the ground and conspicuously not sitting anywhere near Mark. Mark's jaw is twitching, and he is trying to mask his anxiety by talking too quickly.

'What did he say? Did he say anything about me? Did he mention Antonia? What's going on back there?'

She shakes her head. 'I didn't talk for long. Just said

I'd had a mishap and would explain when I got home. He didn't say anything about you. He was crying just to hear me. I could hear the kids in the background.'

She is looking away from Mark, out to sea, the direction all of us looked in whenever we could, just in case.

'Mark?' I ask, to distract him. He looks at me. Soon, I think, his beard will be gone and he might be a little bit more like the smooth newly-wed he once appeared. 'Do you still think I'm some sort of traitor?'

He smiles and looks embarrassed. 'I apologise for that, Esther,' he says, looking at his own fingers, flexing them experimentally. 'No. Of course not. I was just . . . I suppose it was getting to me.'

I laugh at his understatement. 'That's OK then. It's fine. I just wanted to check.'

'You were pretty crazy there for a while, Mark,' Ed tells him.

'We all were,' I add, quickly. I do not want any rifts reopening now, not here, where we are safe again. 'Forget about it. I wish we knew where Jean and Gene are and what's happened.'

'I don't think Gene can still be with us,' says Ed. 'He didn't want to be. I hope Jean's OK. I hope one of her other children is coming out to take care of her.'

I call Chris again, but again I get the answerphone. I leave a stream of consciousness, explaining as best I can what has happened to me. I try to ring his mobile, but I get the number wrong and end up having a flustered conversation with a woman in South Wales. I try to remember his work number, or the numbers of anyone I know. They are all gone. I try my own home number, but when I hear my voice speaking from an earlier era on the answerphone, I hang up.

Things become strange. I exist from one moment to the next, no longer trying to make sense of anything. Sometimes my vision goes blotchy, and my head hurts. Whenever I eat, I will the food to stay down. I cannot cope with the noise, or the people. I cannot cope with the fact that Daisy is not there, and nor is Chris. I feel that I am failing. I barely notice someone organising beds for us. I don't care what happens, as long as I can get home.

chapter thirty-seven

I wake up confused. There are noises outside. My heart leaps at the prospect of rescue, and then I realise I am lying on an actual bed, one with a mattress, and as consciousness returns, I remember it all.

I roll over and yawn. Ed is next to me, fast asleep. He has shaved, and this has made him look different. Soon his face will fill out again and he will be back to the way he used to be. I look at him for a while, feeling an unbearable tenderness, and wonder if I will see him after we get away from here. I reach out to stroke his cheek, and he stirs slightly, but does not wake up.

We are in a hut at one of the resorts at Coral Bay, halfway down the island. The roar I can hear must be a generator. The voices belong to people I don't know.

This hut even has a bathroom attached, so before I leave I go in there and shut the door. I must have been in there last night, but everything was such a blur that I cannot even remember it. I think we were so stunned and exhausted that we barely took anything in at all.

There is a real loo. That is nice, though it seems crazily luxurious. There's a white shower cubicle, and when I turn the dial, actual water flows into it in a cluster of tiny needles. Before I stand under it, I glance in the mirror above the little basin.

The first thing I think is that this is not a mirror but a window, and that there is a woman staring through it at me. I switch the shower off and step closer to it. She comes closer too. I make a few faces and she makes them back at me.

I am forced to conclude, in the absence of any other possibilities, that this is what I now look like. I avoided mirrors yesterday, but now I have to face myself. This woman with blotchy sun-battered skin, with brittle haystack hair, with startled eyes, is nothing like the way I imagined myself, even in my most pessimistic moments. I splash my face with water but it makes no difference. Weeks of island life have ruined my face.

There are a few toiletries in the shower, and I set to work, washing my hair over and over again, cleaning my salt-dried body, trying to find the real Esther underneath the destruction wrought by a month under the sun. There is a tiny bottle of conditioner, and I have used it all before I remember Ed, sleeping next door. He will want to condition his hair too. I had better go and hunt some more down.

I dry myself with a limp white towel that was hanging on a hook. The luxury of a towel! Then tentacles of reality begin to reach through my befuddlement, and a revelation arrives.

Daisy! I am going to see my daughter again. Chris will

have received my messages and he will have told Daisy that I am safe. Alive. Today I will talk to her. It will be shocking for her, because I am weeks late and she probably thinks I'm dead, but I'm not. I am really, properly alive.

Ed is still sleeping when I leave the room and step out on to a veranda. We are, it transpires, high up above the resort of Coral Bay, in a row of wooden huts reached by several sets of makeshift-looking steps. I lean on our railings and stare out, phenomenally disorientated. After a while (I have no idea how long), a door opens somewhere behind me, and a voice says, 'Esther.'

I look round, and there is Katy emerging from the door next to ours.

'I thought you'd melted away,' I tell her. 'You said you were going to.'

She laughs. 'I know I did. The practicalities of real life ambushed me. It's hard to melt away when you've got nothing.'

'No Apocalypse, then.' I gesture to the normal beach life below us. 'No nuclear meltdown. No war. Nothing.'

'No,' she agrees. 'It wasn't the world. It was just us. How are you feeling?'

'Strange.'

'Yes. Me too. I'm not sure I slept. It's the thing we were longing for, and then it happened, and there's a part of me thinking it would be so much easier if we were still out there.'

I do not reply to that. She comes and stands next to me.

'Anyway,' she says. 'I spoke to my family. And I spoke to my ex. They were a bit surprised. Understatement.'

'It's not often you get to be a dead person calling in, I suppose. I'm going to try home again now.'

Katy smiles. 'Yes – you're bound to get them this time.' She gives me a little wave, and sets off down to the beach. I watch her go, down steps that are built on wooden supports above massive uneven rocks. She grips the handrail as she goes, and she looks as nervous about being out in the world as I feel. As I watch, she talks to a man on the sand, gestures up towards me. The man walks her to a boat that is waiting on the sand, and she gets in it, and I hear the whine of its engine as she disappears in the boat, around the corner. I imagine her going back to Paradise Bay to try, again, to find our bags.

Ed finds me in the café, all showered and cleaned up, and we smile shyly at one another.

'I had no idea what I looked like,' I feel obliged to say apologetically. 'That mirror was shocking.'

He laughs and kisses me. 'What are you talking about?' he demands.

'Well, I am completely ravaged by the sun,' I explain. 'I look terrible. Ancient and with awful skin.'

'Don't be ridiculous. You looked lovely then and you look gorgeous now. Esther, stop it with that talk, OK? Living without mirrors is good for the soul.'

I roll my eyes. 'OK. I need to call Daisy, but it's still night there. But I could still call. I think I'm holding back a bit because . . .' I'm not sure why. Because I am never going to be able to make this up to her. Because she might never believe that I didn't abandon her on purpose. Because I will break down uncontrollably if I speak to her and I'd rather just get on a plane and appear in front of her where I can hug her. Then she will really believe I am back.

'I know,' Ed says. 'The funny thing is, I'm the same for different reasons. It was easy yesterday, when we were all freaked out, to say I was letting people with kids do the phoning first. Today I'm going to have to do it. But I know that if I make a grand announcement about being safe, they'll be confused, because they won't even have noticed I was missing.'

I squeeze his hand. 'Try them. You might be surprised. It will have been your brother's wedding by now, won't it?'

'I'm not sure. I don't think so. Can you remember when I said it was?'

'May the seventeenth.' I remember this clearly, for some reason.

Mark appears, his eyes darting around, clearly unsettled. He grabs a chair from someone else's table without asking, turns it the wrong way round and straddles it. Once I would probably have been mortified to be sitting with someone who does this, but now I could not care less.

'OK, Mark?' I say. 'Did you sleep?'

'Oddly enough, I did,' he replies. 'I slept in a bed, for the first time in weeks, and I slept like a fucking baby. Better than one of them. Much better. It was like I was in the Queen of England's best feather bed at Hogwarts Castle, without her Majesty beside me or I might have been a bit distracted. Enjoying your eggs there, Esty?'

'I am, Mark,' I confirm, 'and I will never take an egg for granted ever again. We are blessed by the chickens. I'm eating them slowly so I can enjoy them. And so I don't throw up.'

A waitress has appeared next to Mark, and he says, loudly, 'I'll have what she's having,' nodding at me, then smiles at his little joke.

'You're in a better mood today,' I observe.

'I know. Bravado. Time to face the music. I've eaten. I've slept. I've screwed up and I'm going to deal with it.'

'Seen Cherry?' Ed asks. Mark nods.

'She's on the phone at the reception desk,' he says, jerking his head backwards. 'Crying down the phone again. Trying to keep Tom there until she gets back. At least he's speaking to her. Fuck.' He shouts the word, again and again. Ed and I look at one another and wait for him to finish, which he does in the end. 'Hey, sorry, guys,' he says, addressing the room. 'We've just been stranded on an island out there for twenty-nine days. Twenty-nine days!'

His food arrives and he starts eating. Cherry comes along, her face red and blotchy.

'My babies,' she whispers. She is so wretched that I shift my chair over to hers and put my arm around her shoulder, and she buries her face in me and sobs. I find myself blinking back the tears, fighting myself fiercely to stay in control.

'You'll be back with them soon,' I mutter into her hair. She sniffs and visibly exerts control over herself.

'Yes,' she whispers. 'And you'll be back with Daisy. Tom's known for weeks that I was with Mark, and maybe he'll divorce me now. That'll be OK as long as he lets me have

Aaron and Hannah. Aaron and Hannah.' Their names have been a mantra for her the whole time we were stranded, and they still are now.

'Anyone seen Katy?' Mark says, clearly keen to change the subject.

'Yes,' I tell him. 'She was in the room next to ours last night. I saw her this morning. She hadn't slept. I saw her get in a boat and go around that way.' I point in the direction of Paradise Bay. 'I guess she'll be back, or we'll see her there. Or we won't. Anyway, she's fine.'

'We need to go back and look for our bags,' says Cherry, with a sniff. 'Typical of Katy to be ahead of the game.' And we all get up to go and make a fruitless search for the backpacks that vanished a month ago.

chapter thirty-eight

Chris does not answer the phone this morning either, and I start to feel a heavy dread in my stomach. Something has happened to him, or to Daisy, or to both of them. I ask around for a charger that might fit my useless mobile phone that contains all the numbers I do not hold in my head, but before anyone can find one, we are gathered up by the two policemen and told to get on a boat.

Katy has vanished, as she said she would. I imagine her taking her own path around South East Asia until she feels ready to go home, and mentally I wish her luck. The police tell us that Gene has died, and that Jean's daughter and her other son are coming out to look after things. I wish we could see her, but apparently we have no time.

Everyone else has made their calls. Things have been arranged without my having done anything. The embassy in Kuala Lumpur is organising flights home for Ed and me, and Mark and Cherry are being looked after by their embassy.

Ed's parents are coming to Heathrow to meet him. 'They sounded a bit baffled,' he said, 'and I suppose it would be slightly odd to have an emotional call from someone you hadn't realised was missing. We're going straight to the wedding, apparently. Mum said: "Oh, it sounds as if you've had an adventure. That'll be a good story to tell at the reception." The instant downgrading of that experience into a wedding anecdote.'

A group of people gather to watch us set off on our journey back to Kuala Besut. As well as the four of us, there are about fifteen other people, normal people, making the journey. Most of them are holidaymakers, with a few locals thrown in. Every single one of them stares at us for the first few minutes, and then a man who is sitting next to Cherry turns to her. He is, I think, German.

'What happened?' he asks. He has a goatee beard and curly hair, and he looks both kind and insatiably curious.

She shrugs. Cherry, more than any of us, hates the attention. She turns away from him, on the brink of tears again.

Mark steps in. 'We were stranded,' he says. 'On one of those islands.'

'And how did that happen?' asks a woman.

'It just did,' Mark tells her. He looks across to Ed and to me, and we all smile. We do not owe these people our story. We do not owe them anything. None of us says another word for the short boat trip to the mainland.

It is good to be travelling. This is the first part of our journey home.

*

I stare out of the window of the taxi which is taking us to the airport. I look at the houses and shops we pass, and already the sojourn on the island is feeling like a dream. Our driver likes overtaking at speed, while Boney M plays at top volume, and a month ago I would have been frightened by his reckless driving, but today it does not seem to matter. Every fibre of my being longs to see Daisy. The fact that Chris is not answering the phone is the only thing on my mind. I screw my eyes tight shut and try to remember the phone number of anyone I know in Brighton. If I can tell someone that I am alive and heading home, they will be able to tell Daisy.

We are in a slightly more built-up area when it comes to me.

'Three-one-nine-two-one-zero!' I say.

'I'm sorry?' asks Cherry, sitting next to me.

'My friend's number. I've just remembered it. That's Zoe's number. Her niece was the one who told me to come here. She'll be able to find Daisy for me.'

Ed places a warm hand on my shoulder. 'Well done,' he says. 'You can call her from the airport.'

I sigh, relieved. 'Yes. I will.'

Mark reaches back from the front seat and ruffles my hair.

'Good job, Esther,' he says. 'See, you'll find they're absolutely fine. They will have heard your messages by now anyway.'

I smile back at him. 'Thanks, Mark. Christ, it's going to be weird not being with you guys all the time. What am I going to do without Mark, Cherry and Ed?'

Ed and I look at one another. We have not discussed

this, but I know we have no future in the real world. It was perfect on the island. Ed was my saviour. But the age difference between us is suddenly there again, and besides, I live in Brighton and he lives in London and Scotland. I have a child and he does not. He has a busy life and I do not.

'You guys have to come to the States,' Cherry says firmly.

'Yeah, come visit our street.' Mark roars with inappropriate, self-mocking laughter. 'Come meet my wife, and Cherry's husband. Nothing will be awkward *at all*. You'll love it.'

'We should, though,' Ed says. 'I'm not coming to Long Island to visit your families, but Esther and I could make a trip to Manhattan sometime, come and meet up with you. Talk about old times.'

We all smile. 'The stars,' says Cherry.

'Keeping the fire going,' says Mark. 'Christ, but I was good at that.'

'Cooking the lizard,' I say.

'Watching the sun rise over the sea,' says Ed. 'Look at us – we're romanticising it already. I could also have said: waiting for Gene to die. Imagining us all starving to death one by one. Carrying that bloody water through the jungle. Being sunburned. Being scared. Being hungry.'

'Yes,' I agree. 'It was mainly about missing people and being hungry. In fact, that's all it was. Missing people, being hungry, being scared and waiting.'

I stand in the small airport, huddled towards the phone, watching Ed, Mark and Cherry sitting on a row of plastic chairs on the other side of a shiny marble-effect floor.

Zoe's phone rings. It rings some more. I begin to wonder if some catastrophe has befallen Brighton when, just as I am about to hang up, she answers.

'Hello?' she says. She sounds breathless.

'Zoe,' I say. I make an effort to keep my voice from cracking apart. 'It's Esther.'

She is silent for a while. Then she says, in an uncharacteristically timid voice: 'Esther? The real Esther?'

'Yes.' I am half laughing, half crying. 'The real Esther. Zoe, Chris isn't answering his phone. Is Daisy OK?'

'Yes. I'm sure she is. But . . .' She stops.

'I know. I got stuck, Zoe. It's a long story, but I couldn't get back. And now I can. I'm on my way home.'

I see the others standing up. If they had bags, they would be gathering them up. All three of them look across at me. I know it must be time to go upstairs to the departure lounge.

'I'm at the airport,' I say quickly, 'and I have to go. Zoe, can you find Chris for me? Can you tell him I'm coming. I'll be a couple of days. I'm not quite sure yet. All my stuff has gone, so the embassy are sorting it out for us. But I'll keep trying him, all right? And can you tell Daisy . . .'

I stop. She knows what I mean.

'Yes,' she says. 'I can tell Daisy. Just get yourself home and we can make it all OK.'

'Thanks Zoe. Got to go.'

I catch up with the others, and we walk up the stairs into a departure lounge that is full to bursting and so hot that it is hard to breathe. A television screen advertises our flight to Kuala Lumpur. People are starting to surge forward to get to the plane. I take Ed's hand and join the throng.

We are descending into Heathrow. The cloud parts to show us London spread out below us. It is huge and exciting, and I grin at the sight of its roads and sprawl. I am ready for everything now. I am on my way to find my daughter.

We said goodbye to Mark and Cherry in Kuala Lumpur, and left them shakily waiting for their own aeroplane.

'Antonia doesn't want to know,' Mark said glumly after his third conversation with his wife. 'I can, of course, hardly blame her. It's going to take all my powers to persuade her to let me see the boys from time to time. She slammed the phone down so hard that I felt the reverberations from here.'

Cherry was pale. 'Tom's the opposite,' she said. 'He keeps telling me to get back safely and we'll work it all out. Can you believe it? He won't even leave me after *this*!'

'You can leave him, though,' I reminded her, and she nodded.

'I'll just have to hope that he doesn't go for residency,' she muttered. 'I'm not exactly going to come across as Mother of the Year in court proceedings. Hannah and Aaron. My babies.'

We have sworn that we will keep in touch. I am sure we will: our shared ordeal is too vivid to be forgotten. Now Ed and I have been on a plane for what feels like days and nights on end, and all of a sudden the journey is about to finish. I am glad I have had him by my side, because the inside of this aeroplane is so much the exact opposite of the island that at times I have had to ram my fingernails into the palms of my hands to stop myself standing up and attempting to run away. It is only now, as the journey ends, that I feel excited.

There are hundreds of people, all crammed into a confined space, all breathing the same air, with no connection to any place on earth. On the island we were seven people, with air and water and beach and jungle, all pristine, all around us. On the island we scrabbled around for enough food to keep us alive. On the plane we just have to sit still and be good, and mass-produced food is handed to us on a tray.

'Is it weird,' I asked Ed at one point, 'to be slightly pining for the island?'

'No,' he said. 'It's not. I know what you mean.'

The woman on the other side of him gave us an understanding smile. I forced a smile back. She clearly thought we were unhappy to be returning from our holiday. I opened my mouth to explain, then closed it. We do not, at least, look so weird any more. In KL we were able to smarten ourselves up, and neither of us looks like anything more unusual than a beach bum now.

By the time we get through passport control and walk straight past the baggage reclaim, with nothing to collect, I have forgotten the aeroplane altogether. My heart is pounding, my legs actually feel weak, and I grab hold of Ed's arm just to force myself to keep going.

I left long and detailed messages for Chris and for Zoe, from KL, telling both of them what flight I would be on, and when it was going to land. I have not, however, spoken to anyone at home since my truncated conversation with

Zoe. I desperately hope Daisy will be here to meet me. Even if Chris hates me for disappearing, he is not unreasonable. He will let Zoe bring Daisy to meet me. I begged them both to let her be here.

Ed squeezes my arm. 'She'll be here,' he says. 'She's in the same building as you right now.' I force a smile, trying to believe him.

I step through the automatic doors, and scan the waiting crowd. My knees are weak; my breathing is erratic. I look at every single person. I look past the drivers with boards bearing names written in marker pen. I stare greedily at the children, glancing at one after another, discarding them. There is a girl with light brown hair who makes my heart leap, and I take a step towards her before she turns slightly and I see that she is not Daisy. I slow myself down, keep walking, look from face to face, desperate to see the only person in the world I want to see. She must be here. My daughter has to be here, somewhere in the crowd.

chapter thirty-nine

When I vaguely notice a woman calling, 'Edward!' in a posh voice, I let go of his arm so he can go and see his family. I stretch my fingers out, realising how hard I must have been gripping.

I check the grown-ups. Nobody is Chris. His balding head and ponytail make him easy to identify, and he is definitely not here. None of these people is even Zoe. My only hope, the owner of the sole phone number I managed to remember, is not here.

The airport staff look at me in a strange, almost nervous way, but they do what I ask in the end.

'Your daughter?' asks a uniformed man, raising his eyebrows. 'Well, yes, that's what we're here for.' I could swear that he looks at a colleague and widens his eyes, but perhaps I am paranoid, because he does not know me and his job is to put out tannoy messages for people, so there is nothing odd about my request.

'Will Daisy Lomax and her father or companion please

report to the information desk at arrivals,' he says, and he repeats it a few minutes later. 'There you go,' he says. We are at the information desk, but I find his manner odd, so I walk a little way away and look and wait. I cannot stand still, so I walk up and down, and round in circles, then go back.

After half an hour, I have to accept that Daisy is not here.

I have no money. I have nobody to collect me. I have no working phone, no credit card and nobody to help. There are no options. The only thing I can possibly do is wait.

I try to fill in the Daisy-shaped gap. She's fine, she's with Zoe or another friend. She's fine, she's with Chris's mum. We may never have liked one another, but I could entrust Daisy to her care. She's fine, she's at school. I had not thought about school, but I suppose it is termtime now. We must be somewhere in the first half of the summer term. There might be a school play. Daisy might have a part in it. She always wants a part in the play; ideally, one that involves singing while dressing as a man.

The hand on my shoulder takes me by surprise, and I jump, my heart leaps and I turn around to gather her into my arms.

'Sorry, Esther,' says Ed, and I blink away the disappointment. I cannot cry because she must be somewhere, and I need to find her. This is not a time to feel sorry for myself.

'Ed,' I say, blank and hopeless. 'Didn't you go with your parents?'

He smiles. His arm is around my shoulders, and I lean in gratefully.

'We've got a connecting flight,' he says. 'To Edinburgh. It's from Terminal One in a couple of hours – it's Patch's wedding the day after tomorrow, so we're not going home first. Apparently they've got clothes for me and stuff. It will be a little surreal. But I didn't want to go anywhere till I'd seen you with Daisy. I wanted to meet her. I took the parents into Costa, to their horror, and then I heard the tannoy announcement.' He looks me in the eyes. 'She's not here.'

'Nobody's here,' I admit. 'No one. Not Chris, not Zoe. And I don't know where to go or what to do and I haven't got any money and . . .' I stop, for no other reason than because I cannot talk any more.

'Can I come to Brighton with you?'

'No,' I tell him. 'You have to go to your brother's wedding.'

'Well, I can obviously miss that. I wasn't planning on going, was I? Not when we were on the island. Let's go to Brighton together. It's just near here, isn't it?'

I smile despite myself.

'No, it's just near Gatwick. This is Heathrow. And you have to go to Patch's wedding, Ed. I'm a grown-up. I'm forty years old. I'll deal with this. I can always phone you. Can I?'

'Of course you can, you idiot. You've got my home numbers, and look, the parents have their mobile, so I'll write its number down for you. Ring on this any time. You know that. And call me when you find her, OK?' He stops, then turns me to face him and looks me directly in the eyes, his hands on both of my shoulders. 'You do realise this is your ex getting back at you for not coming home? Once you're face to face, you can explain the bizarre truth and get everything back to normal. And Esther, here's some cash. I got it out with Mum's bank card. It's yours. You're not paying it back.'

He hands me a thick wad of folded-up notes.

'I am,' I tell him. 'And Ed. There aren't enough words to say . . . Without you, I don't know what . . .'

He holds me close and kisses me. I kiss him back, dreading our separation and the fact that I am going to have to do this on my own. I wish I had let him come with me.

As I turn to walk away from him towards the bus stop, I see the people who must be his parents watching me from a distance, unsmiling.

I have to take a bus to Gatwick, where I get on to a little train to Brighton. The Brighton to London line is so familiar that I feel sick. I look around at the other people on the train. It is not a commuter train: most of the other passengers look like students or travellers. I wonder what their stories are. I bet that not one of them has been abandoned on an island for twenty-nine days.

Already the experience seems so unreal that I wonder if I could have imagined it. In all our shared fantasies of rescue, we never supposed that we would return to the outside world to be met by profound indifference.

Brighton station is the same as it ever was. I am home, but it is not home until I have Daisy. I see her in the crowd, see her face everywhere. I see her in the adverts. Every little girl (and there are, I instantly establish, three in the station) is Daisy for a second, until she is not. One girl looks the way Daisy did when she was about three. For a few mad seconds I think it might be her. Everything is so odd that the idea of time moving backwards while we were on the island is as good an explanation as anything. Every possible man is Chris, and then not Chris.

There is nobody here that I know. In my paranoia I imagine that people are giving me disapproving looks, frowning at me like Ed's parents witnessing their ignored middle son kissing a woman a decade his senior. I walk out into the grey mist, and follow the well-worn path home. Turn right, up the hill, and onwards until, fifteen minutes later, I am standing outside my house.

It is in front of me, small, white and terraced. Even the house seems to be giving me a judgemental look.

'I got stranded,' I tell it, grumpily, before realising that, since I have nothing, I have no key. The neighbour, Marjie, has one, and I bang on her door. She opens it quickly, the phone tucked between shoulder and ear. When she sees me, she frowns, but does not stop her conversation.

'Yes,' she says, 'but if you're meaning that I need to back-pay it from November, then I'm afraid you've another think coming.' She looks at me with some distaste, and I wish I could take her phone away and explain why I have only just come home.

'Key?' I ask instead, miming the unlocking of a door, and being brief to fit the amount of attention she has for me.

She nods and takes if off a little hook on the wall, while

saying, 'I assure you I do *not* owe anything like that amount.'

She hands it to me, shaking her head, and slams the door behind me.

It is a ghost house, exactly the way I left it six weeks or so ago. Six weeks is not even a long time, though it is, conspicuously, long enough for the kitchen to start to smell. The air inside is musty, and although I am cold, I open a few windows. There are no sheets on my bed: I remember bundling them all into the laundry basket before I left, Daisy's and mine.

Daisy's room is empty. She has not been here. Her cuddly bear, Poley, is missing, as are the clothes she took with her to stay with Chris. Poley should be here, though. She has a spare one at Chris's house. I stand in the centre of the small room and look at the evidence of my daughter.

There are posters of animals on her walls. I love it that she is still childish enough for her pin-ups to be puppies and horses. There are toys spilling out of her toy box, and her books are haphazard in her bookcase, slumping on top of one another, piled up horizontally on top. I look at the titles: they range from some of the picture books she liked as a toddler, the special ones she has kept for sentimental reasons (*The Very Hungry Caterpillar*, for instance), through a collection of Laura Ingalls Wilder and Harry Potter, to her current favourites, which mainly feature vampires and werewolves.

I put new sheets on her bed, taking care to make it perfect, and arrange her things so she will have a home to come back to tonight. I open all the windows to air the house. Then I call her school to let them know that I am home and that I will be collecting her this afternoon.

That, at least, is the reason I give myself. In fact, I just want to know for certain that she is there. It is either call the school or go up there and demand to have her pulled out of a lesson.

'Hello,' I say, when the office staff answer. I put on the most grown-up, least wobbly voice I can muster. 'This is Esther Lomax, Daisy's mum.'

'Oh,' says the woman in the office. 'What can we do for you, Mrs Lomax?'

I think I hear a reaction in the background when she says my name, but then I realise I am paranoid and confused and must be imagining it.

'Well,' I say, struggling to be poised. 'I'm home from Asia, rather later than planned, because I got stuck on an island for a month.'

'Stuck on an island,' she says drily. 'I see. Quite a hardship.'

'And I've just got back to Brighton and I can't find anyone, and so I just thought I'd let you know that I'll be at school to pick Daisy up this afternoon.'

There is a lengthy pause. Then the woman says:

'But Mrs Lomax, Daisy is no longer a pupil at this school.'

'What?' I struggle to respond to this. 'Yes she is! What happened? Where are they?'

'Your ex-husband withdrew her.' I cannot frame a response to that, and after a few seconds she continues. 'You signed the paperwork, Mrs Lomax. That is to say, I have here a piece of paper with your signature on it. We were led to understand that you were spending a lengthy period of time abroad.'

'Not through choice!' I try not to shout, pause, and take a deep breath. 'I was stuck. I had no choice. Where did he take her?'

'It says on the paperwork . . .' I hear it rustling in the background, 'that she was moving schools. That is all we know, Mrs Lomax.'

I slam the phone down. There is nothing else to say to this woman. Before I have even drawn breath, I am halfway out of the front door. I remember that I am still dressed for the Asian beach, and that I have all my clothes in the wardrobe upstairs, but I cannot bear to go back and change. With nothing in my hand but my keys, and a pair of flip-flops on my feet, I run to Chris's flat as quickly as I possibly can. I tear across roads trusting that they are not busy and that nobody is going fast enough to pose a proper danger to me, and somehow, no car mows me down. I swerve around pedestrians, glad to be in a place where no one pays much attention to someone who is behaving oddly. I nearly crash into a heavily pregnant woman as I round the last corner, but she manages to step out of the way. I do not see the look she gives me, but I can imagine it from her exclaimed 'Fucking hell!'

Chris lives in an upstairs flat in a big house in Albany Villas, close to the seafront. I run up the sturdy front steps and press his buzzer, not bothering to take my finger off it. I know he will not answer, and indeed he does not. I try his neighbours, but none of them answer either, even though I know that his upstairs neighbours are a retired male couple and that one or other of them is in the entire time.

Back at home, I try to stem the panic. I am her mother. I have to be rational. Mothers sort things out. They do not fall apart and do random things.

I charge my phone up, finally, enough to be able to switch it on. Chris's number is in the address book.

It rings.

After three rings, it is picked up, and my ex-husband's voice says, in tones of obvious astonishment: 'Esther?'

chapter forty

'Where is she?' I demand. There is no time for explanations or small talk.

'Where are *you*?' he counters. 'And what the hell? I never thought we were going to hear from you again. Until you left those mad-as-hell messages on my machine at home the other day. Zoe said you spoke to her. Esther, you can't just bugger off and then come back and shout at *me*!'

'I didn't bugger off!' I yell. 'I was left on a fucking island without anything at all, for a month. Where is our daughter? She's not at school, Chris. What is going on?'

He pauses.

'Oh,' he says, too late for his casual tone to be convincing. 'Well. Considering what you said earlier, you're in no position to complain. She's with her grandmother.'

I exhale in relief. 'Your mother? But why on earth did you pull her out of school? Can't your mother drive her in from Haywards Heath? Anyway, Daisy's not going to be with your mother for ever. And what do you mean about what I said earlier? I don't think I said anything earlier, did I? Apart from "where's Daisy"?'

'Um.' I hear him take a deep breath. He is suddenly deeply uncomfortable. 'Um, Esther. We probably need to talk. It's not my mother she's with. It's yours.'

And every fear that has been bubbling under the surface, every terror that I have repressed, suddenly rises up and explodes.

'Chris,' I say. 'What the hell have you done?'

He says he will come straight over. I go upstairs to Daisy's room and sit on her bed, and know that I have failed her utterly.

'Sorry,' I whisper to the puppies and ponies on her posters. The places where the pictures are ripped around the edges, where the corners are bending upwards, are unbearably poignant. I take a jumper out of her drawer at random and bury my face in it. I climb into her bed.

I knew that one day they would try to do this. I wanted to believe they wouldn't, but now it seems crashingly inevitable. I will have to untangle what has happened, and how; but before that I need to rescue my poor baby daughter.

It is important to be practical. A shower is the first step, to be followed by clean and presentable clothes. I will dry my hair and track down my make-up and see if I can remember how to put it on. Shoes, I think, vaguely, too. Shoes are good. I know where I am going, and I need to look confident to carry this off. The moment I step back there I am going to want to turn into a sulky teenager again.

Chris hammers on the door while I am wearing nothing but a dressing gown. I run down the stairs to let him in, and his face immediately gives away the fact that he knows he has screwed up completely.

'Come up,' I say, over my shoulder. I was married to this man for nearly a decade. He can see me getting dressed.

'Blimey, Esther.' He sits on the bed, our bed, and looks at me. I look back, wondering if he reads the fury in my eyes. He does, I am certain, but it is not that he is recoiling from.

'What?' I demand, pulling on a clean bra that is now too big for me and doing it up on its tightest setting, to no avail.

'Esther. What has happened to you? You're a fucking skeleton.'

'Yes. As I said.' I pause. Did I say? 'I went on a fishing trip. We stopped on this completely remote island for lunch. And the guy went off to get his lighter and never came back. Twenty-nine days later, a boat spotted our fire at night, as far as I can tell, and the next morning someone came out and rescued us. Twenty-nine days, Chris.'

He says nothing for a long time. Then he sighs.

'I believe you. I completely believe you. That is a much more Esther thing to do than deciding you were going to stay on some paradise beach shagging a young man indefinitely and that you didn't want to be a mother any more.'

I turn and stare. 'What?'

'Well.' He sighs and puts his feet up on the bed, and even though he has horrible clumpy boots on, I do not complain. 'You did email me and say that was the plan.

It came from your account. You set up that Hotmail account before you went, right?'

'Yahoo. No one has Hotmail accounts any more, do they?' My mind is whirring, trying to work this out.

'Oh. I think the emails came from a Hotmail account. Actually, I'm sure they did. Because I thought that too. That Hotmail was a bit, you know, 1999. But you'd said you were setting up a new email, and there were emails from you, with your name on them. And they said you were blissfully happy on the island, and Daze and I wrote back saying that was good. Because I was totally being the responsible guy here, you know? Doing my fucking best. I was rising above your tone and helping Daisy to write back to you with the stuff she wanted to tell you, all her news, the dogs, I took her riding, she did a swimming thing – you know.'

'I don't,' I tell him. I am chilled to the bone. 'I absolutely don't. I sent you emails from Kuala Lumpur. Twice. The first few days I was there. There was no internet on the island. So I didn't send you anything, apart from texts.'

Chris twiddles with his ponytail

'Yeah,' he says. 'Daze liked the texts. She said you sounded nicer in them. Like her real mummy.'

'That's because I was her real mummy.' I button up a workish blouse that I wore for one of my many and boring admin jobs. 'Daisy knew, then. She knew what was me and what was . . . someone else.'

'I guess.'

The blouse flaps around me like a tent. It is silky and extremely secretarial. It will do. I flick through my skirts, searching for one with an adjustable waist.

'Chris,' I say over my shoulder. 'Have you got your car?' He nods. 'Tell me when we're on the way. What happened. Because if I stop and think about it now . . . You do, though, remember me telling you that Daisy was never going to have any contact with my so-called family? Remember that they were never, ever allowed to know she existed? Remember you wanted to put a birth announcement in the paper, because you were being Mr Fucking Conventional, and I stopped you because I could not bear to take the risk that my birth family might find out about her?'

He nods, apparently unable to answer. He is avoiding my eyes. The seconds tick by.

'I dropped her there,' he says, eventually.

I am ready. 'Let's go and see, then, shall we?'

He leaps up from the bed, his face set.

'Come on, Esther. Let's do it. Let's go and find her.'

chapter forty-one

Chris has parked around the corner. There is a cool breeze coming from the direction of the sea, and it blows into my face. For the first time ever, I am glad that I do not have a sea view. Not having to look at a watery horizon is a refreshing idea.

'So you're just off the plane,' Chris says.

'Got back a couple of hours ago,' I tell him. I look at the sun. Although I have lost track of time, it seems to be the middle of the afternoon.

'Knackered? Jet-lagged?'

I shrug. 'Least of my problems.'

'Let's pick up a coffee on the way. Take it with us.'

'Oh.' I think about that. 'I don't like coffee any more. But yes. Why not?'

I sit in the front seat and buckle up my seat belt. My ex-husband looks across at me.

'You never told me anything,' he says, looking away, putting the key into the ignition. The engine roars into life. I look at a woman walking past, holding the hand of a toddler who is stopping every few seconds to examine something: a snail on a wall, then a tiny weed growing through a crack in the pavement.

'I know,' I say. The indicator clicks, and we pull out into the traffic. Chris turns left on to Church Road, past the hall in which I did pregnancy yoga, many years ago. 'I thought I told you enough. Obviously I didn't, though. It's my fault.'

He is staring straight ahead, driving much more carefully than usual. 'Don't be silly,' he says.

'I was married to you. We have a child. Once I was out of there, I decided, in the end, that I would never talk about it again. But I should have done, to you.' I attempt a smile. 'One of the myriad reasons why we didn't work, no doubt.'

He drives for a while. We are almost out of town when he says, 'A symptom, not a cause, I'd say. You didn't feel you could share something fundamental about yourself. Should have been a clue that I wasn't the one for you. Can you fill me in now, please?'

I think about Ed. I would happily tell him the whole sorry story. I only didn't on the island because I could not bear to start dwelling on it. Having the Village in my head while trapped in the remotest place in the world with nothing to do would have been a recipe for madness.

'Yes,' I say. 'Get out of Brighton. I'll tell you everything.'

After the services on the M23, I have a paper cup of coffee in my hand. It is too hot to hold. I take a sip.

'Oh,' I say. 'This one only tastes of hot milk with a bit

of coffee flavour. It's not like the one on the island at all. This one I can drink.'

'Knock it back, then.'

I take a few sips. Chris puts his drink down between the two front seats, and starts the engine.

'You tell me,' he says. 'And then I'll tell you.'

And so, as quickly as I can, I fill him in on my childhood living in what is, unequivocally, a cult. I tell him about my escape, and my death, and the Village's habit of child-snatching as the coldest, most vicious form of revenge. I do not look at him as I speak, because I do not want to see his face.

When I finish, he says nothing. Silence stretches out. We are on the M25. He overtakes a stream of lorries, then makes a sound like nothing I have ever heard before; it is inhuman, the sound of an animal separated from its young. I do not know what to do, so I close my eyes and wait for it to stop.

'Esther,' he says, eventually. 'If I'd had the faintest fucking idea . . .'

I look at him. His face is green.

'I know. Truly, I do. I'm sorry. Will you tell me what happened now? I just need to know before we get there.'

Both of us are sober and grim. Chris gives a curt little nod. He takes a deep breath and composes himself.

'Right. I cannot believe I bought into it. She was . . .' He collects himself, visibly. 'So, Daze and I had a few weird emails from you. She's getting a bit worried. She loves it when you text but she hates the emails because they're all about not wanting to come home and imagining a new life for yourself in Asia. I was befuddled by them too. But you didn't write them.'

'No.' I am not ready, yet, to think about who did write them, though I know. 'Then what?'

'So this woman calls me at home. She introduces herself as Cassie Godwin. "Does that name mean anything to you?" she asks. She sounds nice. Older. Friendly. "No," I say. "Should it? Sorry." Because, of course, I instantly think that she's someone I've forgotten and that I'm being awfully rude. "There's no reason at all that you should know me, my dear," she says. "But I'm Esther's mother." That threw me. I knew you didn't speak to your family. I knew that you held them in the highest contempt and that you would never tell me anything about them. I had, of course, no clue about what her agenda might have been. And I did know how much you didn't want them to know about Daisy, but I was pissed off with you. So I was a little intrigued that she'd surfaced once you'd buggered off.'

'I can imagine,' I tell him. 'Of course. And . . . ?'

The traffic is heavy, as, I recall, it often is. We did not sit around on the island fantasising about being stuck in traffic on the M25.

'And she started to talk. She sounded very hesitant. She said you had disowned your family and run away as a headstrong teen, and they had decided to leave you to it and wait for you to come back. "You know Esther," she said. "She does what she wants and there is really no point in trying to stand in her way. We decided, her father and I, that we would not contact her. We would just wait. I thought she would come back, but she never did." Fuck. It sounded bizarre to me. It didn't sound like you, not the way she was telling it. I should have gone with that instinct.

'"Did she ever mention our religious views?" she asked.

'"She never mentioned you at all," I told her. And she started to spin me her bloody story.'

'What did she tell you?' I demand, fury rising hot through my body. 'Did she explain that I ran away to avoid having to marry some random spotty boy, chosen solely because he wasn't my half-brother, at the age of sixteen? Did she tell you about the time we all sat up all night waiting for the Apocalypse?'

He stares at me for so long that I reach over and touch his cheek, to turn his head back towards the road. The pain on his face is impossible to look at.

'No,' he says. 'She did not. Obviously. You told me all that in fifteen minutes. You didn't tell me in ten years. That Apocalypse thing. It was in the papers, wasn't it? Years and years go, when I was eighteen or so. I remember it.'

'Yes. You do. That was me. That was her. That was them.'

He screws his eyes up. 'It was one of those things that stick with you when you're that sort of age, because you're so open to the idea that it might be true. I remember the build-up: the end of the world is nigh, all of that. Everyone was half hoping that it might actually happen.'

'Yeah,' I say. 'Not as much as I was hoping it. I knew it was going to happen. It had to, because we'd all been brought up with God's word as the absolutely unquestionable thing. And this was, supposedly, God's word. Then the world went on as normal. The sun came up. It was the biggest betrayal of my life.'

'Esther. Why the hell didn't you tell me any of this

before? You just clammed up about your family and said you'd tell me about them one day.'

'I realise that.' I try to focus. This is crucial. 'So how did we get from Cassandra posing as a poor ignored mother to you sending Daisy to stay with her? How did she pull that off?'

My heart rate is galloping. It is the caffeine. It is the past catching up with me. It is the fact that, finally, they have stolen my child.

He sighs.

'She said that she and your father had been keeping an eye on you from a distance, just to make sure you were OK. She knew about Daisy, however much you might not have wanted her to. She knew where you lived. She knew we were no longer together, and she also knew you were on holiday in Malaysia.'

'And did it not seem a little freaky to you, that she knew all that?'

'Remember that by this point, you were pretty much saying you weren't coming home. I was, stupidly, glad of some support. And she sounded nice, Esther. She really did.'

'Yeah. I bet.'

'She asked if she could meet her granddaughter.'

'At what point did she admit that she lived in a cult?'

Chris moves expertly into the outside lane. He is a much better driver than he used to be.

'She said she lived in a "spiritual community". I had the impression it was a bit new-agey, and also that she'd only moved there recently. She said she wasn't with your dad any more.'

'Ha!' I say to that, suddenly sixteen again. 'She *wishes* she'd ever been with him. She had to share him with every other woman in the place, plus anyone else he happened to take a fancy to. He treated her like scum, and she took it because it was God telling him he was special and the normal rules didn't apply.'

'Yeah. Obviously she didn't mention that. She just asked if it would be possible for Daisy and me to meet her somewhere, just so she could have a look at her granddaughter. I'd just had an email from you that I'd kept away from Daze, talking about this Canadian bloke that you'd met at that resort. So I was feeling a bit "fuck you", to be honest.'

'She was writing those emails.'

'Well, yes. Clearly. At the time I didn't suspect that. We met her at the park, St Ann's Well Gardens. I recognised her as soon as I saw her because she looks exactly like you, Esther. It was freaky.'

'Does she? What does she look like?' I am biting my lip so hard that I expect to taste blood any second. I have consciously not thought about Cassandra for more than half my life. In my mind, she is tall and skinny with a disapproving face and long blonde hair. Now that I think about it, I can see that, perhaps, I have grown to look like her in the past twenty-four years. The thought has never occurred to me.

'She's not as thin as you are now. But she nearly is. And everything about her – her hair, her face, her cheeks, all of it – is exactly you. If I'd seen her walking down the street, I'd have said "that's Esther's mum". Grey hair, though. In some sort of bun affair. She looked like a granny. She looked, actually, like you will look in the future. Daisy warmed to her at once, I could see, because she was the next best thing to you.'

'Oh, fuck.'

'And she was lovely to us. She did a good job. She played us properly. She was warm and sweet and concerned. She walked around the park with us and watched Daisy on the big slide, and she bought us a drink at the café. Daisy liked her, though I think she was a bit baffled that she'd had no idea that she even had a grandmother.'

I know we will be there before long; I need to hurry this along. 'A trip to the park,' I say. 'This was when you were still expecting me to come back?'

'A couple of days before we were expecting you, yeah.'

'Then?'

'Then we had that day. Oh Christ, Esther. It was the worst day. You'd sent all these emails. Or whoever had sent them. And they'd been full of your new life and how much you didn't want to come back, and it had been fucking alarming, you know? It didn't sound like you, so I was afraid you were cracking up. Part of me knew you wanted to stay on that beach, but I never thought you actually would. I was glad you were coming back: it's hard work, making your life revolve around a child. Respect. I was looking forward to going back to sharing the childcare, though it seems crap to say that now.

'So Daisy was properly excited. She woke up saying "Mummy's coming home!" She got dressed at six, and because she wanted to make a fuss, we bought you some flowers.'

I look at him. He is staring at the road.

'You bought me flowers?'

He nods, without looking at me. 'That'll be a first, hey?'

'I'll say.' I imagine the flowers wilting and dying. I would have been on the island for nearly a week by that point, longing for Daisy with all my being.

'She wanted to go to the airport. I told her if it'd been Gatwick, maybe, but there was no need for us to schlep over to Heathrow. She made me agree, though, that after you called to say you'd landed we'd go and meet you at Brighton station. That much I could manage. We sat by the phone. After a long time, a very long time indeed, we decided to go to the station anyway. Probably your phone wasn't charged and you didn't have any money for the payphone. You know.'

'Yes.'

'We got a drink on the station and waited.'

I can imagine the scene more clearly than I want to.

'And I didn't come.'

'Obviously by this point I'm realising I have to step up and be the responsible guy. I take her home, tell her your plane must be late and start googling for crashes. That seemed to me the obvious, though horrible, explanation. Though there was nothing on the news or anything. Then, as I'm on the phone to Emirates, trying to get them to tell me if you were on the plane or not, since their website is bloody adamant that it's landed, an email comes through.'

'From me?'

'A very fucking breezy one, saying that you've made some life-changing decisions. I deleted it because I was so furious, but this is what it said. "I need time out from motherhood. This break has made me see that. I'm going to spend the next couple of years looking after myself."'

We are on territory that is so familiar now that I keep my attention focused inside the car. I want to ask whether Daisy read the email before he deleted it, but time is running short.

'Then Cassie came back.'

'I was glad to see her. She timed it perfectly. No shit, right? She asked to take Daisy out for a pizza. I told her to be my guest. I was stringing Daisy along with lines, ironically as it turns out, about you being trapped in Malaysia because of a boat not working.'

I almost laugh at that. 'Right.'

'But she was confused. You know. She's not stupid.'

'No,' I agree.

'They came back, Daisy having had a lovely time. Cassie asked if I was OK. She wondered where you were. Et cetera. I got Daisy out of the room and confided in her. She was massively sympathetic.'

'It fitted with the story she'd told you about me stropping off in my teens and ignoring my poor innocent family for ever more.'

'It did. She offered to help out with childcare. It's not easy, when you've got a job, to manage a child at school too. She suggested taking Daisy out of school until things calmed down. It sounded like a good idea.'

'So she stepped in and became a concerned granny. Just her? No one else from the Village?'

'No, very much on her own. Daisy went out with her

a few times. Then she started asking for Daisy to spend the night. I brought her to visit. It's a nice-looking place.' He is defensive, looking at me pleadingly. 'I think we'll get there and she'll be fine. And very, very glad to see her mum.'

I look at him, then away. 'Well that's because you didn't grow up there. I vowed never to speak of them again when Karen moved to Australia. But I should have done.'

'Who's Karen?'

'A woman like me. She said she'd only feel safe if she was on the other side of the world from them. I should have listened to her. Anyway, that doesn't matter. How long has Daisy been there?'

'Two nights.'

'Right. They'll be expecting us.'

'Not until tomorrow.'

'No. Now. They are going to be expecting us now.'

Then Chris is indicating and pulling into a driveway. I am sixteen again, waiting for the Rapture. I am Daisy's age, ten, beginning to realise that we are different from other people, starting to envy them and knowing I must not admit it. I am an awkward teenager trying to make myself believe in Moses' version of God because it would be so much easier to conform. I'm holding Philip's sweaty hand and trying to convince myself I could love him. I am bristling at being in Martha's whining company all the time.

The memories overwhelm me, and I lean back in the seat. I want to close my eyes, but if I did that I might miss Daisy. The only thing that could possibly have brought me back here is her: my funny, dependable daughter. She is a girl who deals with everything life throws at her. That attribute will be being tested right now.

I shudder at the idea that she will have met Philip, if he is still here, and Martha.

'Be strong,' I whisper to my daughter, 'and don't believe anything they tell you about me.'

There used to be a white sign with 'God's Village' painted on it in wobbly black letters, and a looming black cross. It used to fill me with grim ennui, coming home after school. Sometime over the past couple of decades, however, it has been replaced by a larger sign with a rainbow on it, and the words: 'Welcome to the Community of Peace'.

This could be a yoga retreat, or a Buddhist centre. They have tarmacked the drive and put speed bumps into it. There are wind chimes hanging from branches, and little mirrors and dream-catchers tucked away in the trees. The buildings, I soon discover, have been done up too, though they are still essentially the same: the log cabins are still grouped around a central courtyard, with a longer two-storey building at one side. Flags fly from the eaves, the sort of silky flags you see on people's tents at festivals, and a banner draped on the main building says 'WELCOME' in multicoloured silk letters. There is even a gift shop, which makes me boggle, and a big noticeboard in the courtyard is covered in posters and 'Information for Visitors'.

There is a bad sculpture in the courtyard that shows a woman cradling a baby. I glance across at it.

'Someone else's baby,' I say, as we turn into the car park. Chris frowns, not following.

There are four other vehicles in the little car park. Three are small, cheap cars, while the fourth is a green-and-red hand-painted minibus that looks spectacularly cultish. Chris reverses into the space directly opposite the road out. He nods at it.

'We can make a quick exit if we need to,' he says.

I look at Chris, suddenly fond of him. He let Daisy come here, but that was my fault for not telling him anything about this place. All I ever said was that I hated my family and would never speak of them. The fact that he believes me, that he has brought me here to collect Daisy, gives me the strength I need.

'You ready?' he says. He is nervous. 'I'll just say we've come to get her a day early because you're back. It'll be fine. No drama.'

She will not be here.

'Maybe,' I say, and try to smile. We look at each other for a second, and get out of the car.

chapter forty-two

The atmosphere of the place presses down on me. They can put up all the flags and mirrors they like: this is the same place it always was. I can feel its essence, and every fibre of my being wants to turn and run.

They have Daisy. I am not going anywhere.

Chris and I walk in silence to the main building. When we are on its doorstep, I turn to him.

'You dropped her off here?'

'Yes. Cassie told me to come to this door to pick her up.'

He knocks quickly, as if to harness the optimism.

When, at last, the door swings open, I see, first, that neither Cassandra nor Daisy is on the other side. The man who stands before us, looking at us with a challenge in his eyes, has a greying beared, cut pedantically close to his chin, and sandy hair. He is stocky, with a belly that strains against the buttons of his checked shirt. I watch his gaze flick dismissively over Chris, then come to rest on me.

'Philip,' I say.

'Catherine,' he replies. He looks at me, waiting.

'Where is she?' I try to keep my voice calm. The only thing that matters is my daughter.

He smiles. 'Where is . . . ?' He raises his eyebrows, pretending to have no idea who I am talking about.

'Come on Philip.' I make a huge effort to control myself. He wants me to break down and scream and cry. I will not. 'Daisy. My daugher.' I look at Chris. 'Our daughter.'

'Daisy?' He pretends to think about this. I always hated Philip, and now I am biting my lip and using every ounce of self-control I possess to avoid thowing myself at him, scratching and kicking and biting.

Chris steps in. Chris still thinks it might be all right.

'Yeah, mate,' he says. 'Daisy. She's been staying with Cassandra for a couple of nights? While Esther was away?'

'I'm sorry,' says my former fiancé, smiling at me in triumph. 'I'm not sure who you mean. Cassandra's out at the moment. Would you like me to give her a message?'

'Tell her we will fucking find her,' I say, and I pull Chris's sleeve. 'She's gone. They've got her.'

'They might just be out,' he says, desperately.

'Of course, there will be an explanation,' says Philip, with an undisguised smirk.

I wonder how many times Cassandra and Moses have told her that I don't love her, that I never want to see her again. I wonder whether they have started to implant their God in her mind. We love you, they will say. We are your family now. Our twisted God loves you, and one day soon, he will be taking you to heaven to sit at His right hand.

I remember Sarah's parents' fears of a mass suicide.

'You can fuck off,' I tell Philip.

'God bless you, Catherine.' He closes the door and bolts it.

We sit in the car, but we do not go anywhere.

'We'll just wait until they get back, shall we?' Chris asks, though I can see that he does not expect that any more than I do. 'And while we wait, Esther. Please. Tell me anything that might help us find Daisy. Anything about being a child here. What was it like living here as a kid?' His voice is urgent, terrified. 'You haven't stopped shaking since we arrived. And biting your lip. Do they still wait for Doomsday?' I shrug, unable to speak, and he changes tack. 'That man was Philip, then. The one you were meant to marry. Why did he keep calling you Catherine?'

I look at him. 'Did Cassandra not call me Catherine?'

'No. Of course not. She called you Esther.'

'Right. Well. OK.' I take a deep breath, and tell him all about my old life here, in bunk beds, being sent to school and being a weird outsider. They will not be able to do that to Daisy, because as soon as she is back, we will come and get her.

I mention my fears when Daisy was born, my determination to have only one child so I could better protect her from them, my occasional certainty that they were keeping tabs on me.

'Esther,' he says, his pain palpable. 'I know we were never the great romantic couple. I know we would never have been together if it wasn't for Daisy. But I'd thought we both gave it our best shot. I did. I tried as hard as I could to make it work with you. It was never going to, I see that, but I wanted it to. I thought you did too. But you didn't trust me with . . . well, with anything. If you'd told me, I'd never, never, never have . . .'

'I know. I'm sorry. This is my fault, Chris. Not yours. I recognise that.'

'And you getting stuck on that island?'

'Yes. Somehow that will have been them. Let's find Daisy first, though.'

'Let's call the fucking police. That's what we'll do.'

I put a hand on his arm. 'Not yet. They'll lie. They'll turn it back on us. The police would terrify me.'

He is not happy, but he lets it go for the moment.

At last I see a figure I recognise, sticking a notice on to the information board. After all these years I know her at once, just from the way she holds her head. I open the door and bolt towards her.

Her hair is still short, and I briefly think what a waste that is. I hope that at some point in the past twenty-four years she grew it long, but I doubt it. Gravity would have worked wonders on Martha's hair. It would have made her pretty. She is broad and heavy, and though I know we are both forty, she could easily be fifty-five. She has sunk into middle age. Her clothes are baggy and shapeless; they are old-style Village-wear. No one has told her that, to keep up with the cult's new image, she should now be wearing tie-dyed trousers and a rainbow jumper.

I look at her. Her face is lined. Mine, I imagine, is worse.

'Martha,' I say. I put a hand on her arm in an attempt to make her engage with me.

'Oh,' she says, her voice flat. 'You're here. Philip said you would be.'

'I'm here for my daughter,' I say. 'Daisy.'

She smiles with her mouth, but not her eyes. 'Are you?'

'She's not here, is she? They've taken her. Cassandra and Moses. They took her, didn't they, right away, so I won't be able to get her back. Martha. Do you have children?'

She looks away. 'That's none of your business.'

'Of course you do. Wife and mother, that's your job. Do you know, there's a whole world out there? It's a mad, weird, sometimes bad world, but it's full of adventure. And out there women don't have to be just wives and mothers. You can have a job, a career. You can do things on your own. Be yourself. It's not too late for you. Life begins at forty.'

She snorts at that. 'Oh, thank you for the greetings-card wisdom, Cath. You leave me behind when we're sixteen, come back when we're forty, solely because you think I'm the only idiot who you might be able to persuade to help you.'

'I didn't *leave you behind*, Martha. You didn't want to come.'

'Oh?' She arches one eyebrow. I wish I could do that. 'You asked, did you? I said no, I don't want to, did I?'

'I assumed you wouldn't want to. I couldn't ask you outright because I thought that if I told you what I was doing, you'd have gone to Moses.'

She bites her lip. 'I would not. I knew you were leaving. I half knew it. I watched you walk up the drive, swinging your bag, without looking back. If you had asked, Cathy

. . . I would never have been brave enough to do it alone. I would have gone with you then. I would have swung a bag and not looked back, if we'd been together. After that Rapture. That was the only time when I was desperate enough.' She looks away from me. 'All I ever wanted was to be your friend.'

'You hated me.'

'No. You hated me. You must have really hated me to leave me behind. I had to pick up the pieces. Marry your fiancé. We all had to pretend you were dead. I guessed after that that Victoria had run away too.'

'That's right. I met her in London, and some others. She's called Karen now. She moved to the other side of the world, years ago, because she said she never felt safe when she was near this place. I should have done the same. Look, Martha. Did you see Daisy when she was here? Was she all right?'

As she gazes at me, I can sense her trying to decide what to say. My heart is pumping hard, and I cannot stand still, so I am shifting my weight from one foot to the other. I can feel my body wanting to collapse, but I only notice it fleetingly because the sensation is entirely overridden by terror.

'She's fine,' she says in the end. Her face softens. 'She really is, Cath. You know, growing up here wasn't that bad. I mean, nothing really terrible happens. It's unusual, but it's not . . .' She tails off.

'She can't grow up here, though! She's mine. Where have they taken her? Tell me, Martha, and I'll do anything. I'm sorry I didn't ask you to run away. I wished I had, as soon as I was out. I've had a niggling regret about it ever since.

'It's not too late, though. You're married to Philip? I just met him. He's a wanker. I know that and you know it. Martha, you can jump in the car and come with us. I'll help you with everything. Just tell me where to go to find my baby.'

I have to stop talking because there are tears coursing down my cheeks, and I have to wipe my snotty face on my polyester sleeve.

'You left her, though,' she says. 'Cassie could never have got her otherwise. You were out of the country. Where *were* you?' She looks apologetic. 'I'm afraid they really don't tell me anything. There are strong women in this Village, but I don't get to be one of them.'

I have to steel myself to tell her. The story sounds less plausible every time I repeat it. I have to remind myself that it really happend. Less than a week ago, I thought I would be on the island until I died.

'I was stranded,' I say. 'On an island. I went on a day trip. We were dropped off, and the boat never came back.'

'Oh,' she says. Scepticism drips from her every pore. 'I see.'

'It's true, Martha. And I half think you know about it already.'

She glances around. 'Look, Cathy. Only because I have children too. They don't tell me anything, but I'm not happy with what they're doing. Goodness knows, I've done as I've been told my entire life. Back when Moses was in charge, I did what he said. Then Cassandra, and our new leader. Since I was seventeen, I've had to do whatever Philip's told me to do. And now my own sons have authority over me.'

'It sounds like it's time you rebelled.'

'I'm not going to leave with you, because I couldn't walk away from my children. But I'm going to tell you, very quickly, a few things I've overheard. They have never let me in on any of the secrets. I'm too unobtrusive. No one ever even thinks of Martha. Boring, fat old Martha.

'Our leader's been away for a while. Philip and Cassandra between them have been in charge. Philip is the golden boy. I've tried to piece it together, because as soon as I realised the little girl was yours, I started to pay attention. I've always looked on you as the one that got away. Always wondered what would have become of me if I'd gone too. Philip's still here, holding the fort, as you know. The others set off early yesterday morning, by car. I woke when Philip got up to see them off. It was still dark. Later, I heard him on the phone. He definitely told them to take the M5 and the A30. I believe they were going to Devon or Cornwall, to lie low with your little girl until they had fully assimilated her into the ways of the community.'

I make an effort to control myself. This is crucial. I must do it.

'Are you sure you don't want to come?' I say. 'Because we're leaving right now.'

She looks at me with scorn. 'Of course I want to come, Cathy. For crying out loud. I won't, though, as I said. Because of my boys. I could not bear to be dead to them.'

'Can you find out where in Devon or Cornwall? Can you, please? I'll write down my number, if you can call me.'

'Don't,' she says at once. 'If Philip sees you, there will be trouble. We've been talking too long already. Someone's going to be watching. He'll want to know exactly what you said so he can report it onwards. Our leader is very interested in you, even though we are still supposed to think you're dead.' She bites her lip. 'Tell me your number, Cathy. Tell it to me, and I'll remember it. I keep my phone on me, so that it stays private.' She smiles suddenly and nods downwards. I follow her gaze.

'You keep it in your bra?'

I never thought I would hear Martha giggle, but she does, almost imperceptibly. 'That's one place Philip is guaranteed not to find it.'

I tell her my mobile phone number. She repeats it twice and nods.

'Got it,' she says. 'I'll send a text if I can find out any more details. I won't say it's from me, though. I'll use a code name. In fact I'll say I'm Sarah, like your friend from school. She used to tell me, you know, that you were OK. I never went back to school, but I would see her in the town sometimes, and if no one else was about, I'd ask.'

'I'm sorry,' I tell her, and I am. I can hardly bear to think of Martha's bleak life. I want to ask about the new leader she keeps mentioning, but we need to get going. 'How old are your boys?' I say instead.

She smiles. 'Eighteen and sixteen,' she replies. 'All grown up.'

'They still live here?'

'They do. They're their father's sons.'

'If you change your mind,' I say, 'I'll come back for you. Any time. You know I will.'

'I know. Thanks, Cathy.' She looks away. 'I appreciate that more than you can know.'

*

Chris has switched the engine on before I reach the car.

'Devon or Cornwall,' I say. 'M5 and A30.'

He drives straight out of the compound.

'We'll head to the M4,' he says. 'Get on the M5 at Bristol. A30 at Exeter.'

I look at him and smile, suffused with a sudden optimism.

'Chris Lomax. How the hell do you know a thing like that? Did you keep a secret *Top Gear* fetish hidden from me for the length of our marriage?'

He shrugs. 'Some things you just know.'

'Those emails.' We are back on the M25, and the traffic immediately slows across all the lanes. I force myself to try to fit the pieces together. 'Oh God. We've got hours in the car, haven't we? I'm going to have to address this.'

'Yes. Someone wrote them. I should have known it wasn't you. Look on my phone, and you should be able to find them. I deleted them all off the computer at home so that Daisy wouldn't read them, but I made sure I had them on the phone, for reference.'

I pick up his iPhone and scroll through. Most of his emails are junk. Some are from Groupon. Others are work-related. My own name jumps out at me and I open the thread and scroll down to the bottom, to read it in the right order.

'Hi Chris,' I have apparently written. 'Hope you two are well. I'm having an amazing time. The beach is as wonderful as I hoped. I've met some cool people. There are some Americans who are all over each other, and lots of Germans, plus a lovely Canadian called Jonah. It's just paradise. I may be here some time! Look after Daisy. If I don't come back when planned, don't worry about me. I will be in touch. Best wishes, Esther.'

I look over at him.

'You thought I'd written that? Seriously? That is a terrible impression of me.'

He shrugs. 'I was hardly going to be suspicious, was I? Just thought you were being extra nasty on purpose.'

'But,' I say, and I am suddenly very cold, 'there *was* an American couple all over each other. There *were* lots of Germans. There *was* a Canadian called Jonah and I did like him, in a vague way, in passing.'

He looks at me. 'Oh. Who else was there?'

I think about it. In my mind I flip through everybody on the beach.

'There was a man lurking around who might have been Moses. They said an old man came and paid our bills and checked us out, which meant nobody at the resort worried about us. They thought it was a bit weird, but they took the money and re-let the rooms. I never saw him.'

'Right.'

'The way they described it – at the time we thought they were talking about Gene, who was on the island with us, but now I can see it was Moses.'

He drives for a while, frowning. 'And there's no way that Gene could actually have *been* Moses?'

'Of course not. Moses is my father. I lived with him till I was sixteen, Chris. Gene's not Moses. And he's dead now, anyway.'

'Shit.'

'Apparently Moses isn't in charge any more. Martha kept talking about "our new leader". She didn't say his name.

I don't think she likes him. And he's gone with Cassandra and Daisy.'

'OK. So we'll meet him when we find them. See if you might have seen him lurking around the beach. It was probably someone who was in the shadows, you know, Esther. Watching you, reporting back and writing emails as you.'

I glance through the rest of the email thread. My bizarre messages alternate with Chris's befuddled ones.

'Seriously, Esther,' he wrote at one point. 'WTF?'

I put the phone down in between us and yawn.

'Do you mind,' I ask him, 'if I sleep for a bit? It's kind of . . .' I have to break off to stretch and yawn again. 'Catching up with me.'

'Go for it,' he says. 'I'll keep driving. If we don't hear from your friend, I'll . . . Well, I suppose I'll drive along the A30 until I hit the end.'

chapter forty-three

When I open my eyes, the car is not moving and it is nearly dark outside. It takes me a long time to remember everything, to process the fact that, first of all, I am not on the island, not lying on the sand, not with Ed, Katy and the others. Nor am I at home.

Nor have I found my daughter.

There is a rancid taste in my mouth, and I notice that I am dressed in a bizarre work outfit. Chris, I think. Chris is my ally in all this. I look for him, but the driver's seat is empty.

I think about Jean, bereaved in Asia. She is doubly bereaved now. I hope her children are strong like she is, and I hope she lets them look after her.

I wonder what has happened in Mark and Cherry's street in Montauk, what the ramifications are. I picture Cherry hugging Hannah and Aaron, reunited with them at last. My stomach contracts in jealousy.

The car is in a sparsely filled car park. It is not big

enough to be a motorway service station. I open the door and stretch my legs out to stand up.

I am completely disorientated. This could be any time of the day or night. The light is grey, and there are clouds overhead. I shiver in my stupid blouse, which is far too flimsy for the British spring evening, and leave the car door open as I walk back and forth. My legs complain about being used, and I remember that they have spent twenty-nine days on a tropical island and forgive them for wobbling.

The car is parked facing an expanse of tarmac and a grass verge, but when I turn around I see that, in fact, there is a Costa coffee shop and a Little Chef behind us. This is a standard pit stop. I should go to the loo.

I wobble towards the coffee shop, blinking and trying to regain my focus. It is all about Daisy. I have been away from her for so long that the image of her face in my mind is unreliable. I think of her with Cassandra, somewhere in the West Country, and I see a three-year-old with chubby cheeks and a solemn face. Then I see a five-year-old in a school photograph. A girl of seven walking somebody's dog. A baby, smiling at me for the first time. Try as I might, I cannot grasp the real Daisy, now-Daisy: I have lost the Daisy who is even now somewhere in the country with Cassandra and a person I don't know, being told intensively that I hate her, but that God loves her.

When I come back from the loo, pleased that in my woozy state I did not automatically head across the grass verge and dig a hole, island-style, I am still unable to focus. Chris is standing beside the car, looking at me with wide eyes.

'You're there!' he says.

'Yes,' I agree.

'You left the car door wide open. I thought . . .'

I try to understand what he thought. If only my brain would work.

'You thought Cassandra had come and got me,' I say.

'Yes. I did.'

'She wouldn't, though.' My mental faculties are beginning to come back. 'Their whole point is that I am cast out. They wouldn't have me back now if I wanted to come. But I still belong to them in some way, so they can take my child.' I glance at him. He looks stressed, his face tight. 'Sorry,' I say. 'I just went to the loo. I was a bit disorientated.'

'Yeah. You've been out of it for ages. Here, I got you a coffee, on the off chance that you might wake up. It's in the car.'

'Thanks.'

'I know you say you don't like coffee. But you knocked back that last one and I think you could do with it.'

I get into the car and take a sip from the paper cup that is in the cup-holder next to my seat.

'I like it again.'

'Good girl.'

I look at him. 'Good girl?'

We both smile, sad little forty-something smiles.

'Want me to drive?' I ask.

'Er,' he says. 'No. Thanks. Really, not. That would be a terrible idea.' He starts the engine again. 'There was a text,' he says. 'From that woman, I'm guessing.'

'From Martha?' That wakes me up a bit.

'Yes, but it was signed "Sarah".'

'She said she'd do that. She didn't need to sign it anything.'

'According to her, we need to go to St Ives.'

I look at him. 'St Ives? Daisy's in St Ives?'

'Have a look.' He nods to the phone, and I pick it up and find the text for myself.

'Hello c,' it says. 'You need to find a place called Saint Ives. That is all I know. I wish you luck, from sarah.'

I text back at once, just saying 'Thank you a million times sarah xx.' I imagine the phone beeping inside her bra.

'Martha's life is screwed,' I remark.

We head out of the services and back on to the dual carriageway.

'Where are we, anyway?' I ask. 'Not on the M5 any more?'

'A30,' Chris says. 'We're still absolutely miles from St Ives. Do you remember?'

I know exactly what he is talking about.

'As it was our honeymoon, I haven't managed to block it out entirely.'

'Me neither.'

We both smile, thinking of the first four days of our marriage. I was heavily pregnant, and Chris was putting a brave face on our future, enthusing about our little family with unconvincing zeal, betrayed by his panic-stricken eyes. We carefully did all the things we were supposed to do, looking at art and walking on beaches, eathing fish and chips and ice cream, admiring the lifeboat.

'Do you remember,' I say, 'sitting in that café on the main street, watching crowds and crowds of people walking past outside? We said that if you sat there long enough, you'd end up seeing everyone you'd ever met.'

'Were you secretly wondering how come, out of all those people in the world, we'd managed to end up sitting there with each other?'

I laugh. 'Probably. We should have been admiring the artistic Cornish light and looking into one another's eyes in optimistic bliss. Not scoping out the exits.'

'At least we know our way around a bit.'

'I hope it's not as busy now as it was then.'

Hours later, I stare out of the window. We are on a narrow road now, following brown signs for day visitors to St Ives. The light is starting to fade. The road twists and turns.

I start staring at everyone we drive past, just in case.

chapter forty-four

It is nearly night-time. This has been the longest, strangest day of my life, and it is nearly over.

'We have to go and sit in one of those places where everyone walks past the window,' I say urgently, as we skitter down the steep hill from the car park into the town. 'Even in the dark, we'd see her.'

'I know,' he agrees. 'Hey, this is going to be weird, but we'll need to book into a place to stay tonight too.'

'Yes, sure. Whatever. I've got some cash. No cards, though. Lost them in the adventure.'

'It's fine. Overdrawn, but I'm sure I can stretch to a B and B.'

'Separate rooms.'

'Fuck, yes.'

We hardly say a word as we make our way into the town. St Ives is a funny little place: insanely pretty, hilly, with an odd quality to the air and the light that you really do not find in other places. I try to tell myself that Daisy, too, is breathing this strange fresh air from the Atlantic. This is a small town, and my baby is in it.

'Why do we believe what Martha says?' I ask suddenly, as we come to the end of a street of terraced houses and find ourselves beside the library, and the people.

Chris looks at me.

'Are you serious?'

'I know we have no choice. Nothing else to go on. But she's Philip's wife and she does as she's told. What if he's told her to send us down here, to one of the most remote places in the country, to get us out of the way?'

'Esther. Shut up. There's no point.'

'I'm going to call her. On that number she texted from, the phone she keeps in her bra just so she can have a secret from that twat of a husband. See if she answers.'

'Why? That's not going to do you any good at all, is it?' His voice is hard, the way it used to be. 'Just don't think it. There's fuck-all else we can do. We'll find the cheapest, scuzziest bed and breakfast we can here, and then we'll go and sit in a café in one of those busy places and get some food and a drink. God knows, we need a drink. And watch the people walking by.'

We end up checking into a nicer hotel than Chris threatened, simply because it has a 'Vacancies' sign up and is close to the town centre.

The carpet is blue and patterned, and the air inside feels rarified and stifling. We look at one another complicity, and Chris hits the bell on the small reception desk with a pedantic hand movement that makes me giggle inappropriately.

'We need two single rooms, please,' he says clearly.

'Yes, that's fine.' The woman is years younger than we are, with white-blonde hair and black roots. I see her looking at us, trying to assess our relationship. She pushes two forms across the desk. 'If you could each fill one of these in. I'll need to authorise a credit card. Will you be paying separately?'

'No,' I say at once. 'Together.' I turn to Chris. 'Sorry. I'll pay you back when I get my cards replaced.'

'It's fine.' He hands his card to the woman. 'This one's on me. Call it alimony, if you like.'

She looks from me to him and then turns to the card machine. When we hand back the forms, she studies them.

'I would have said brother and sister,' she says, 'if you hadn't just mentioned alimony. Alimony's something to do with being married, isn't it?'

'Something to do with it,' I agree.

'We used to be married,' Chris tells her.

'But now we're friends,' I add.

She raises her eyebrows. 'Is it not possible to be both at once?'

'Some people manage it,' Chris says. 'Apparently.'

We go to our rooms, which are next door to one another. It is very odd having nothing but a phone to my name, and I realise I will need to buy a toothbrush and other items that I should consider essential but that I managed to live without for twenty-nine days in the very recent past.

Chris bangs on the wall. I knock back.

'Have a shower,' he shouts. 'Then we'll go out, and get looking.'

It is properly dark by the time we sit down, at a window table in a restaurant in what we judge to be the busiest part of St Ives. We are beside the harbour, but the lights reflected in the still black sea do nothing for me. There are not enough people walking past. I stare at all of them.

'You need to eat,' Chris says, pushing a menu into my hands. 'Come on. Order a pizza.'

'It's good that there aren't as many people walking by as there were last time we were here,' I say. 'Isn't it? I was thinking it was bad because if there were more people there'd be more chance of Daisy being one of them. But that's not true, is it?'

'No. It's not true. Now, choose a pizza or I'll choose for you.'

It is a strange feeling, being hungry and nauseous with dread at the same time. I order a vegetable pizza, garlic bread and a salad, and as soon as it is put in front of me, I flash on to a scene from the island, in which Mark is saying: 'Pepperoni pizza with extra jalapenos, garlic bread, and salad with ranch dressing.'

I hear my own voice countering: 'Vegetable pizza with an enormous side salad and garlic bread, and a large glass of white wine.'

I have no idea if we ever had that conversation, or if I have made it up. Either way, I make a token effort to appreciate my extraordinary luck in having my dream meal in front of me, tell myself to be optimistic, and start gently with a piece of lettuce.

Chris is drinking his wine before eating anything. I am too nervous to sip mine: it has been many weeks since I had an alcoholic drink, and I do not want to mess up the clarity of my mind even further. When I try to remember the last drink I had, I settle on the beer that I drank as I swapped stories with Katy in Paradise Bay, a few days before my birthday. That seems like an innocent and long-ago era.

I was on an island, stuck in a place where no one ever lives, thinking I was out of the human race for ever. Now I am in a crowded seaside town eating pizza, watching waves of humanity drifting past the door, looking for my lost child. The two scenarios are equally unreal.

Girls pass the window. They are sometimes her age, sometimes around the right height. Many of them have her light brown hair. I strain around, looking obsessively at every person. None of these girls is Daisy. I know that Cassandra would be much easier to spot, and she does not pass either. Any of the passers-by could, of course, be the famous 'new leader'. I also imagine Moses to be around somewhere. Any one of the elderly men who is passing this window, and there are several, could be him. I focus on a man standing opposite the window, his head turned away from me, wearing a fisherman's jumper and chatting to a woman. He has short grey hair and is the right height. Before I can get a look at his face, he is gone.

People struggle by, walking sideways to the wind, their hair blown all over the place, their clothes flapping about. It is absolutely dark, and the clouds are low, but there is so much electric light around that I hardly notice.

'Where is she?' I say. The pizza is giving me energy. 'Where is Daisy? Where the hell is my baby?'

Chris puts down his fork. 'We need to call the police now, Esther. You know we do. I should have done it back in Hampshire.'

'Yes. Because they've abducted her.'

'Of course they have, and like you say, they might not even be in this town. They could be anywhere in the country. Or the world. When you were at your house, did you check for her passport?'

I feel sick. 'No.'

The very idea makes me take a reflexive sip of wine. It is sour and wonderful on my tongue, so I take another.

'You're right,' I say. 'They have still got me feeling guilty, like it's all my fault. But it's not, is it? It's theirs. Daisy belongs with us, and the police can help with that.'

I pour the story out to a sympathetic, if baffled, police officer. He writes it all down and asks us to come back in the morning when more people are on duty, or to call them if we see Daisy or if anything else happens.

'See?' says Chris, as we walk back to the hotel. 'He'll help us. Straight after breakfast we'll go and talk to his boss.'

I am surprised at how relieved I am. 'Good call,' I say. 'Doing that.'

Chris squeezes my arm. 'Hey. Occasionally I can get it right.'

I wake to the sound of seagulls shrieking impossibly loudly very close to my head. This time I know exactly where I am. I check my phone, and discover that it is eight o'clock.

I bang on the wall.

'Chris! It's morning!'

There is a muffled acknowledgement.

I stand under the hot shower, appreciating every drop of it. I shampoo my hair, and use a whole miniature bottle of conditioner once again. I wash myself carefully, recoiling at the condition of my skin, and feel ready for the day, though it would be nice to have some clean, crisp clothes to put on, rather than the bizarre HR manager's outfit I picked out yesterday in my hallucinatory shock.

'Today I will see my daughter,' I say confidently. I need to believe it.

We are sitting in the hotel's quiet dining room, drinking coffee and waiting for our substantial breakfasts to arrive, when my phone rings.

I grab it.

'Martha,' I say, looking at the display. 'Hello?' I say into it.

'Catherine.'

My heart sinks. 'Philip.'

'Where are you?'

'I'm at home,' I say. 'Waiting for my girl. Chris is coming up to collect her this morning. That was the arrangement, wasn't it? She'll be back there, with Cassandra, won't she?'

I am perfectly in control of myself, because everything is at stake. If he guesses we are in St Ives, I will lose her.

'What did you say to Martha, when you were here?'

'That is none of your business and you know it.'

'You've agitated her.'

'Yes, she's not allowed to have feelings, is she?'

'Catherine.'

'Sorry. Look, just give Daisy to Chris when he gets there. You will, won't you?'

I can hear the smile in his voice. 'Of course. Why is your number on this phone?'

'Why shouldn't it be? Martha said she'd contact me when Daisy got back.'

'Hmm. That's what she says too. We'll wait to hear from you.'

I throw the phone on to the table. 'Tosser. He was checking up on us, but he can't prove anything. I hate him.'

'Your ex-fiancé.'

'Lucky escape, in many senses.'

'Let's get back to the police.'

It is raining this morning, and we hurry towards the little police station. We are about halfway there, crossing a road on a treacherous corner, when the phone rings once more.

'It's him again,' I say, looking at the display. I press the button. 'What?'

'Cathy?'

'Martha? Are you OK?'

'Did he just call you?' She sounds scared. 'What did he say? I was very careful about deleting the text messages.'

'Yes, you did well. He didn't know anything. He was just sniffing around.'

Her voice drops. I have to stop and put my finger in my ear to hear her. The wind is wailing around me, and I turn in to the wall for shelter.

'He was talking to them, Cathy. They're in St Ives, but

they're worried because you haven't been hanging around here. They don't like it that they don't know where you are. As far as I can tell, they're at a café on the beach in the rain, because they're waiting for a taxi that's going to collect them there. Then they're going somewhere else. I couldn't work out where.'

'In a café on the beach in the rain,' I repeat.

'It *is* raining with you, is it?'

'Yes. Yes it is. Martha, you're amazing. Thank you so much. When this is over . . .'

I hear her brave smile down the phone. 'Yes,' she says. 'Yes, I know. Now go and find her.'

There are several beaches in St Ives. Chris stops the first person we see, a man walking two small dogs.

'Excuse me, mate,' he says. 'We're meeting someone in a café on the beach. That's all they said. Where do you think that'd be?'

The man purses his lips.

'Got to be Porthminster or Porthmeor,' he says. 'One or the other. You should have got them to be more specific. Porthminster.' He points. 'That's nearest. It's over there. Porthmeor, right over that way.'

'Cheers,' Chris says, and the man walks on.

'One each?' I ask. 'We don't have much time.'

'Yes. You get Porthminster. I'll get the other one. Call me.'

The rain stings my face as I run to the beach. There are not many people around. I pass a few women with push-chairs, a couple of runners and several people walking dogs.

When I step on to the beach, I note that it is wide and sandy. I will never be impressed by a beach again, so I spend no time admiring. No one is on the sand at all.

They are cowards. That hits me like a wave. Throughout my adult life, everything I have done has been about escaping their power, but if I am not afraid of them, they are powerless.

And I am not afraid of them. I am furious, but I am not scared.

The sea is heaving in the worsening storm, with huge choppy waves pitching up and down. As I walk towards the café, I see a woman leaning off the back of its covered balcony, looking across the beach to the water.

She has straight hair that was once blonde but is now a silvery grey. She looks like me, but she is older and perhaps a little odder.

I stand on the sand and watch her turn away from the sea. She is talking to someone who is sitting at a table inside the café. I write a text to Chris. 'Porthminster,' I say. 'Now.'

I walk around to the doorway and step inside the café.

It is a smart restaurant, one of those airy ones with floorboards and wicker chairs. A blonde girl with flawless skin comes towards me with a professional smile, holding a menu.

'Breakfast?' she says. 'Table for one?'

I smile back, forcing my skinny face into some sort of rictus grin, and say, 'I'm just looking for some friends. Could I check out there?'

She says, 'Of course,' and wanders off.

I edge around the corner, on to the terrace. Three of the tables are occupied. The one above the beach has three people sitting at it, and one of them is – actually is – my baby.

I stand frozen to the spot and drink in the sight of her. Her hair is tied back in a single plait, a recognised Village style. It does not suit her. Her face, however, is Daisy's face. Her nose is slightly turned up. Her mouth, when she is not smiling, looks sulky. She is not smiling.

They have dressed her in a knee-length blue skirt, a white jumper and a pink anorak. She has wellies on her feet. She is with them, and she should be with me.

I cannot wait for Chris. I cannot call the police. This is my daughter, and I have found her, and any second they are going to try to bundle her into a car and take her away.

I start to walk across the terrace to them. Then I run.

'Daisy!' I shout. Cassandra turns to me, startled. 'Daisy!' I yell again.

Daisy looks up, and our eyes meet, and she grins and gets to her feet.

Cassandra grabs her arm and stops her coming towards me. I watch Daisy trying to shake her off, watch Cassandra tightening her grip. They struggle. The third person at the table is looking at me. I have paid that person no attention at all. It is, I suppose, the famous new leader. From the corner of my eye I can see that it is not Moses.

I glance at the figure.

The world spins and contracts, and I grab the back of someone's chair to avoid falling over.

I was assuming the cult's new leader would be someone I didn't know. I presumed he would be a man. That was the way it made sense. I am still running for my daughter, reaching out for her, grabbing her, but I am unfocused. I am completely thrown off my stride by the discovery that the new leader, the third person in the group, the mastermind of the whole affair, is Katy.

chapter forty-five

I pull Daisy away from Cassandra, who does not let go. Daisy starts to cry. I hug her tightly to me.

'It's all right,' I say, into her hair. For a second, all I want to do is to drink in the smell of her, her presence, her very Daisyness. 'I'm sorry, darling. So sorry. I've been desperate to find you.'

She cannot speak. Her face is red and she is sobbing into my shoulder. I keep her against me, using all my strength. Cassandra, I see, is furious. She is tugging at Daisy, harder and harder. I hit her to get her away. Then I turn my attention to the new leader.

'Katy?' I say. 'What the hell?' I am trying to work it out. 'I knew someone was from the Village. I had no idea it was you.'

She sighs. She is still thin, like she was on the island, but the desperation has gone from her eyes, and she is utterly self-possessed.

'Oh, Catherine,' she says. 'Martha sent you here, did she? I knew we should have dealt with her properly.

Philip said he had her under control, but his problem is that he forgets she could conceivably act of her own free will.'

'To be fair to him, that rarely happens,' says Cassandra, who has retreated from Daisy for the moment, but is glaring at me, and clearly planning.

'It doesn't matter what happened,' I say. 'I've got my daughter back. She's back where she belongs, and you are never going to see her again. Never, ever.'

'You think?' Katy raises her eyebrows.

'I know it.' I look round, waiting for Chris. 'Daisy, are you OK? Everything they've told you about me is a lie, OK? I'll explain what's happened when we get away from here.'

Daisy looks scared. She moves away from me slightly.

'That's right, sweetheart,' says Cassandra. 'Remember? I know it's hard for you. But remember what we said.'

Katy turns to me. 'You idiot, Catherine. Blundering in. Upsetting the poor girl. Never mind, Daisy. Here.' She takes a polar bear out of a handbag and passes it to her. Daisy snatches it and clutches it tight.

'I told you about Poley,' I remember.

'You told me lots of things,' Katy agrees. 'You were very helpful.'

'You're the new leader Martha talked about.'

'She didn't mention my name? We had her well trained in that respect, if in no other.'

'The woman you had the relationship with, and broke up with, all of that.' I look at Cassandra. 'Was that my *mother*?'

Katy looks at Cassandra and they both laugh.

'No, you idiot,' Cassandra says. 'I cannot believe you are my child, and that you could be so stupid. That was a story to make you like her. And to make sure you didn't see her as anything connected to the Village. She was undercover. You know?'

Daisy has disengaged from me completely. I look at her. She is gazing away, miserable, out to sea.

'Moses killed Samad,' I say. I am stalling, waiting for Chris and, I hope, the police. 'He sorted out the guest house so no one would miss us.' I step closer to Daisy. She edges away from me.

'Bravo. Moses has his uses, bless him. I obviously sorted out the trip and disposed of the lighters and so forth. We'd been waiting for you to go away, by the way. Keeping an eye. As soon as you booked your grand holiday in Malaysia, and kindly told everyone you'd ever met about it, we started planning. It was nice of you to go somewhere so remote.'

I look at Cassandra. 'But why? Why do all that so you could get my daughter?'

She shrugs. 'You owe me a daughter. And you know full well that if Villagers leave, that means they are dead. Which in turn means that their children need guidance and guardianship from us. It's not Daisy's fault you ran away. She deserves the same chances you had.'

'You were talking on the satellite phone.'

'I could have killed Jean for finding that,' Katy says, rolling her eyes. 'I nearly did, actually, but then I remembered I had no particular quarrel with her. Everyone thought it was yours, or Mark's or Ed's, anyway. No one dreamed it was me. Even though I had to be the one to find the water to bring you back to life. I thought that would be a giveaway, but no, apparently not.'

'Katy,' I say quickly, because I have to know. 'How on earth did you fix up the whole trip? I mean, it was Samad's idea.'

'Samad was susceptible to being fed ideas. More than that, though, he was susceptible to money. Oh, Cathy. It's incredibly easy to bribe someone in a poor country, you know. I suggested what he might like to do, then paid him handsomely to do it and let him think it was all his idea. I probed him about deserted islands until he told me the right one. Then I arranged it all. Didn't you wonder why he was providing such a sumptuous lunch and he never asked any of you for a penny?'

The waitress is approaching. I look at her quickly, begging her silently to call the police. Then I realise I can do it myself. I reach into my pocket for my phone. Katy holds it up: it has been expertly pickpocketed.

'Sorry,' she says.

'But who are *you*?' I ask. 'Why did you do all that, to get my daughter? Why?'

'Who am I?' asks Katy. 'Who do you think I am, Catherine? You're Catherine. You're dead, it's official. It said so in the paper. Then I came along. Katy. I'm you, of course.' She puts a hand on Cassandra's arm. 'This is my mother. And this.' Her other arm is suddenly around Daisy's shoulder. 'This is my daughter, Daisy.'

'Everything OK?' says the waitress, apparently oblivious to what is happening. 'Can I get anything for anyone?'

'Just a cappuccino for our friend,' says my birth mother with a smile, and the waitress nods and leaves.

'You're mad,' I spit. 'Both of you. Come on, Daze. We're going home.'

'What do you say to that, Daisy?' asks Katy. 'Where's your home, darling?'

Daisy looks miserable. She keeps her mouth tightly shut.

'Come on,' Cassandra prompts her.

'Home is God's Village,' she says eventually, and bursts into tears.

'Oh, don't be so ridiculous,' I say to all of them. I take Daisy by the arm and pull her away.

Everything happens at once.

A car pulls up in front of the café. Chris runs up the steps and on to the terrace. A police siren comes closer and closer. Katy and Cassandra perform what looks like a practised movement, and take Daisy between them to the steps of the café. I run after them. Chris stops them in the doorway. They fight him off. Katy kicks him, and he falls over backwards, down the steps.

In slow motion, I see them moving Daisy to the waiting car. She is protected by both of them. The engine is revving up, and it is ready to go. The police car is not here yet.

I do the only thing I can do to save my baby. I grab a bread knife from a shelf, where it is resting beside three baguettes, and just as they have got my crying, screaming daughter to the car, I plunge it into Katy's back.

There is blood everywhere. The world stands still. I have stabbed somebody and I am covered in blood. Daisy is standing looking at me, stricken, and she is screaming and screaming.

I know, suddenly, that I have lost her. She has watched me commit a murder. I am a murderer. The fact that I did it solely to stop Katy taking her away from me will not change anything; in fact, it will probably make it worse, because I know that Daisy will think it was her own fault in some way.

Katy and Cassandra wanted me to do this. This way, I lose Daisy completely and for ever.

Katy is on the ground, unmoving. The knife is still sticking out of her back. The waitress is shouting for help. The police car pulls up. There is nothing I can do. I cannot pretend I did not do this. There is no possible escape.

I watch Chris take three strides towards Daisy and pull her into his arms. She collapses in to him and he cradles her, turning her away from the gruesome scene.

The policeman, who is not the nice man we spoke to yesterday, immediately starts talking into his radio. He looks worried. He has a little black beard. I walk towards him. Cassandra is staring at Katy. The waitress says the word 'ambulance' behind me.

My legs give way. I collapse. There is a chair behind me, so I end up sitting in it. When I look up, Chris and Daisy have gone.

Cassandra has started to talk to the policeman.

'It was her.' Her voice is bald, icy. 'She did it. She stabbed her. In the back. She murdered her.'

He looks at me. I know he is going to arrest me, and, indeed, he does.

chapter forty-six

They have won. I sit in a cell, and the only thing I care about is the fact that I have lost her. I do not care at all about being in custody. I am not interested in what will happen when I go to court. I could not care less about the media scrum that I know is going on, now that the press has finally caught up with our story. I am sure they will be getting it all wrong.

I like the peace and quiet. I like the food that appears from time to time. I like being able to sit down and look at a wall. Since I cannot have Daisy, I like not having anything.

Days pass. They tell me that Katy is alive, that I did not stab her as deeply as the amount of blood might have suggested. Apparently I missed her heart and all the other important stuff. That, I think, is a shame. I should have pushed the knife in harder.

They have won. Chris has got Daisy for now, but they beat me. From the moment I walked out of there, they wanted to destroy me, and now, years later, they have done it.

A nice man tells me that charges are being dropped and I am free to go. I do not understand this, and I do not bother to think about it either. I do what he tells me to do, and eventually I find myself outside, breathing the fresh air. People shout and thrust cameras in my face. They want me to tell my story. I look around, panic-stricken, and then I see Chris. Chris, and Ed. They come towards me, and take one of my arms each, and they escort me to a car and put me in the back. We drive away.

'What's happened?' I say. I have not focused on anything, properly, since I saw the look on Daisy's face as Katy fell.

'You're free,' Ed says, turning in the front passenger seat. This, I notice, is Chris's car, the same one we drove to Cornwall in.

'Why, though?'

'Because Katy's made a full recovery,' says Chris. 'Though you still don't get to go round stabbing people in the back with bread knives. And because the whole story came out, thanks to Ed here. And those Americans. And the Australian woman. Once that whole episode came to light – can you imagine how the press love the "stranded" element of the story? When it became clear that there was a hell of a lot more stacked up against them than there was against you, and Katy wasn't in a position to press charges, they decided to let you go. But Esther – you should know all this. Didn't they explain it to you?'

I shrug. 'I didn't listen. Where are we going? Where's Daisy?'

'Daisy's in Brighton,' says Ed, 'with Chris's mum. Everything's going to be OK.'

I think of her face. 'It's really not,' I tell him.

I am out of prison, but they have still won.

chapter forty-seven

Four weeks later

'Daisy,' I say. 'You know Ed.'

'Hi, Daisy,' says Ed. He is shifting around from foot to foot, looking from my face to hers, and back again. 'It's lovely to see you again. Are you OK?'

She shrugs. 'Yeah.'

I look at her. She tells me she is all right. I am not sure that she will ever actually get over what has happened to her over the past two months. We have come to Scotland to get away from home and to spend some time together. She barely spoke to me on the train.

'You know when we were on the island? Your mum did not stop talking about you. Not once. Seriously.'

Daisy smiles a sad smile. I take her hand and squeeze it. She looks up at me. People pass by, parting to walk around us. Waverley station is busy in the summer, it turns out.

'Didn't you?'

'I'm afraid I didn't.'

She nods. She is still pale and scared, and I am constantly eaten alive by fear about what this whole episode might have done to her psyche.

'Good,' she says. 'That's one good thing.'

'I've got the motor,' Ed says. 'If you'd like to follow me, ladies, I'd be honoured to drive you to your destination.'

I sit in the back, hoping Ed won't take offence at this. I cannot bear to be away from Daisy for the moment. I sit in the middle of the back seat of what I assume to be Ed's parents' car; it is a black four-wheel drive and so shiny and well-hoovered that it looks and smells brand new. Daisy sits beside me, her thigh pressing against mine. In the four weeks that I have been home, she has refused to speak to me about anything that has happened. She will not tell me what they said to her at the Village. She refuses to address what I did in St Ives.

'I did it because I was desperate,' I told her, making a shaky effort to hold myself together. 'Because they were going to bundle you into that car and I had no idea how Dad and I would find you again. I did it because it was the only thing I could do to stop them.'

'Yeah,' she said, looking away from me. 'I know.'

She has grown up. She does not want to go out walking dogs any more. All the pony posters have come down from her bedroom walls. She wants to read scary books now, or stare into space. Often I find her appearing to watch television, her eyes unfocused and her gaze clearly turned inwards.

'Mum,' she says quietly, just after Ed points out

Edinburgh Castle to us. 'Is this going to be OK? Not a trap?'

I push her hair off her face.

'Darling,' I say. 'I am absolutely, completely certain it's not a trap. Ed is one of the good guys. We're going to have a nice time staying at his mum and dad's house. It's a bit of a holiday. We can both relax and start to feel normal again. They live in the countryside and there'll be no one around but us and them.'

'And Daddy?' Her face is so anxious that I want to cry. 'He's on his own.'

'Daddy's fine,' I tell her. 'You know he's fine. No one's going after Daddy.'

'Are you and Dad going to stay friends?' Daisy whispers.

'Yes, we are,' I tell her firmly. She has asked me this time and time again: I have always given her a firm 'yes', and oddly enough, it is true. I set off on my trip to Asia, a million years ago, hating Chris with what felt like a passion that would endure for ever. Now I could not imagine a better friend. Saving your child from the clutches of religious madwomen is, it seems, a bonding experience, even for us. We did it together, and we seem to have developed a respect for one another that we never had before. 'Don't worry,' I say. I have said this so many times. Daisy's world has been rocked to its foundations, and she has been seeing a counsellor about her fears, which include the specific fear that she will be snatched from her bed at night by strangers who tell her her mummy doesn't love her any more.

'Daisy,' says Ed, as he drives out of the city and takes

a big road heading north. 'You have had a hell of a time. What can we do while you're here that would cheer you up? Would you like to go horse-riding? Or we could take a boat out? Fishing? Tennis? Or we could just spend loads of time watching telly and playing games and messing about?'

I see him looking at her in the rear-view mirror. He smiles, and she smiles tentatively back at him.

'Yes please,' she says quietly. 'That. The one with the telly and the messing about.'

Ed's parents are distantly welcoming to me, and make an enormous fuss of Daisy.

'Well, hello, young lady!' says Ed's mum, or 'call me Patricia', as she says to Daisy, so I assume it applies to me too. 'You've been through the wars rather, I hear, is that right?'

I watch Daisy nod solemnly. 'It actually did feel like a war,' she says. 'I just wanted it to stop. And Mummy and Daddy came and rescued me. But Mummy had to hurt someone to get her off me and that got Mummy into trouble.'

'Yes,' says Patricia. 'Well, she did what a mother has to do. And thank goodness it's worked out. Esther, welcome – Edward will show you to your room. He said you wanted to be in with Daisy?' I nod. Daisy nods so hard I worry she will harm her neck. 'Well, I have to say, that's a first. Normally I've had to lay down the law about the boys bringing lady friends home and sharing a room. Never before has one actively *not* wanted to share a bedroom with him.'

'Oh, Ed and I are just friends,' I say firmly, and I see her raise her eyebrows and say nothing. Her husband walks into the room. 'Malcolm and I are off to dinner with friends,' she adds airily, 'but Edward will look after you. Patch and Alice might call in, you never know.'

Malcolm snorts. 'In case you don't speak Patricia-ese, that means Patch and Alice will definitely be calling in to get a good look at you, as will the twins and possibly David too. They're all curious to meet you, I'm afraid, Esther. The famous Esther. We've had our share of reflected glory, as the parents who didn't even notice their son was missing for a month.'

'Oh, right,' I say. 'Um. I look forward to meeting Patch and Alice too. I've heard a lot about everyone.'

It comes out, I fear, sounding sarcastic, and I catch Ed sniggering.

Daisy falls asleep more quickly than she has done since the whole affair began. It helps, I think, that we are in an old-fashioned bedroom tucked into the eaves, with ancient dark-wood floorboards, a dormer window and a sturdy wash basin in a corner.

'It's like a bedroom in a book!' she exclaimed when she saw it, and went and sat on one of the high beds with iron bedsteads, both of which had floral counterpanes pulled tightly across them. I knew what she meant: it is an evacuee's room from a war story.

I sit at her side until I am certain she is sleeping. It is only seven o'clock, and the light outside is like midday; I am glad she is allowing her watchfulness to waver for a while. I creep out of the room, leaving the door wide open, and down the small set of wooden stairs, followed by the much wider carpeted ones that lead down to the hallway.

This is the grandest house I have ever been in, and as soon as I see Ed, I burst out laughing, knowing we are alone.

'This is your family pile?' I say, and I hug him tightly, burying my face in his chest. 'God, it's weird, you having clothes on, you know. So lovely to be back with you again.'

'Don't let my mother hear you saying that. It took me weeks to convince her that you weren't the worst woman in the world. She kept saying, "Of course you didn't realise what she was like, because she had designs on you! I know what women are like, Edward. You don't." It was only when it said in the paper that it was all Katy and Cassandra's fault that she believed me.'

'She's nice, though. She was nice to Daisy and that makes her OK with me.'

'She loves little girls. Never got one of her own, as she still likes to remind us at every opportunity.'

'How's it been?'

'All right. Anti-climactic. From the moment we got off the island and nobody was anything more than mildly surprised and inconvenienced to see us back. When we were there, it felt like our disappearance must be the most gigantic mystery, and everyone must have been scouring the oceans for us. I know I used to say no one would be missing me, but after a week or so I was pretty sure they had to be, because I thought they would have been alerted by the huge amount of publicity about the rest of you disappearing. But they weren't. And then we get back and it all starts to fall into place because of Daisy. Bloody Katy.'

'Did they try to find us?' I ask. 'Piet and Jonah, I mean. You thought they might.'

'They both emailed, separately, after the publicity. Both feeling bad about not trying harder. The guys at Paradise Bay told them I'd checked out. My bag was gone. They were a bit confused, but they both thought I'd gone off somewhere with you.'

'Which you had.'

'In a way.'

I nod, and follow him into the enormous kitchen/dining room, where I sit at a huge pine table and watch Ed make gin and tonics with great care.

'Here you go,' he says. 'Welcome, and it's lovely to hang out with Daisy. She's gorgeous, and you got her back. I think she's going to be fine. Thanks for coming, Esther. I'm really glad you did.'

I smile at him. 'Thanks.' I want to say 'thanks, sweetheart' or something similar, but I am too shy, suddenly, for endearments. 'I wanted to come here all along, you know. But I had to be sure Daisy was ready for a trip. She is, by the way. I think getting away from Brighton and doing something with me is exactly what she needed. This is the first time she's slept peacefully since . . .' My voice tails off.

'I know.'

I take a sip of my drink. 'This is perfect,' I tell him. 'Thank you.' I hold up my glass and we clink. 'To Gene,' I say, and Ed nods solemnly. Gene was the real casualty of our expedition. It has been too easy to forget that he died: Jean has not answered any letters or emails directly, but she spoke out to the press, which I know she must have hated, to support my story. I want to fly over and see her in Brisbane as soon as I can afford it.

I am aware that I am being slightly too polite. I feel awkward. It took being abandoned off the east coast of Malaysia for me to drop my defences, and now they are back and tripled. I cannot relax with Ed, partly because I am attempting to quash a fierce desire, and I do not believe that he reciprocates it. When we were on the island, I spent almost all the time shaking him off and retreating into myself, while he was by far the strongest of any of us. Ed and Jean were the ones who kept us going. We thought, at the time, that it was Katy. She was pulling our strings, in her manic Village way.

Because I pushed him away, however, and never took any of our many opportunities to sneak into the jungle together, never did anything more than kiss him, he has probably moved on from thinking about me that way. He was not spoiled for choice out there: now, doubtless, he is. I am a damaged older woman with a child in tow. I am his friend, and that is all.

'So,' he says, sitting opposite me and grinning. He looks nice in a grey T-shirt, with more muscles than he used to have. Being clean-shaven suits him. In fact he looks like a model. 'Katy. She stepped in and took your identity. Where did she come from? Do we know?'

'Apparently they started doing some outreach with addicts and homeless people. That was where Cassandra met Katy. She rescued her and Katy went at it with a convert's zeal. She and my mother deposed Moses, which

I cannot imagine, because that place was all his, and Katy took over. I don't know what her original name was. But she stepped into my shoes. Cassandra must have loved that. A new daughter, and one who wasn't going to run out on her.'

'And the island thing?'

I smile. 'That just proves how crazed the two of them were together. Once they discovered – however they did, I have no idea – that I was going there, they got a huge plan in place.' I have managed to piece most of this together after the event, with Martha's help. Martha has been wonderful, and now that Cassie has vanished and Katy is out of action, she is in the process of daring to leave the Village. Philip doesn't know yet. 'She'd actually been to the island before she engineered my meeting with her, waiting for the boat. Planted the satellite phone there.'

Ed shakes his head and sips his drink.

'No wonder she found the water supply and saved us all. Nice of her to let us almost die before she did it.'

'I know. She wasn't meant to leave it that long. It was just for fun, according to Martha. She waited for us to find the spring, and when we didn't, she had to step in and do it herself. Enjoyed seeing us suffer, I imagine.'

Ed puts his feet up on the chair next to him. He has green socks on.

'So she was you. Does that freak you out?'

'Of course it does. She'd been living as me for twenty years. Sometimes I think I should have made the connection between Katy and Cathy, my original name, but then I realise how ridiculous that is. But it makes complete sense that Cassie replaced me, because that's how crazy they are in there. And also that they made an elaborate plan to grab my child to get their twisted revenge on me. That, I knew they were going to do. They try that one with everyone. I think that they particularly had it in for me, though, because I'd always been such a good girl and had tried so hard, so when I ran away they were extra furious. Martha said they were raging and Moses swore revenge on me. But when Katy arrived, the dynamic changed and Moses ended up being sidelined. It was him, did I tell you that? Who paid for our rooms and took our bags away. God knows what he did with them. Not Gene at all, and not a cover story by that poor boy, the way we thought it was. Moses, sent to do Cassandra and Katy's dirty work. Impossible.'

'You never spoke about your childhood when we were on the island,' Ed says. I look away.

'I wish I had. I wonder how she'd have reacted. She never spoke about hers either, did she? I never did because I wanted to keep part of myself back. The stories that people did tell, particularly Cherry and poor old Gene, were very particular parts of their lives. There's loads of all of you that was kept hidden. I was happy to talk about my divorce because it's tangential and trivial, almost. Talking about that was fine.'

Ed is fiddling with his drink, looking down at the table.

'I wish you'd told me, you know,' he says. 'Not that it matters. But I wish you had.' He suddenly shakes his head and smiles. 'Anyway, this has certainly made me see how dull I am. Everyone else has much more interesting lives than I do. I'll be the boring one in the corner.'

'You could never be boring,' I tell him, and I mean it.

'You were the strong one. Not Katy, and definitely not me. You were amazing. I never heard you being grumpy. You never cried, you never seemed to get irritated with anyone, not even Mark. That's a huge thing, Ed. You have no idea.'

He smiles.

'I had you with me,' he says. 'Cheesy, but true. Clichéd, but what the hell. I was stranded on a desert island with the woman of my dreams – and an assortment of oddballs, admittedly. So none of it really mattered.'

I laugh, assuming he is joking, but when I look into his face – strong, handsome, still deeply tanned – I see that he is not.

'Really?' I say, moving closer to him.

He puts his arms around me and draws me in.

'Really.'

epilogue

We make our way to the appointed diner. It is lunchtime, and the Manhattan pavements – the sidewalks – are a ballet of people knowing where they are going and not bumping into each other as they do it.

We are clearly tourists.

'It should be right here,' says Ed, map in hand. I follow his gaze.

'There it is!' says Daisy, pointing. She is right: it is on the next corner.

'Daisy,' says Ed. 'You're quite something with the maps. You're better than your mum and me by a factor of at least a million.'

'I know,' she says with a grin.

The floor is checked with black and white tiles. This is an extremely upmarket burger restaurant, with booths and a high ceiling. Daisy loves it. She skips on the spot as she takes in the scene: the clanking of dishes, the clatter of cutlery, the echoing voices.

Ed and I are here with Daisy. We are a little unit. He is

my boyfriend. I grin whenever I think of the word. Nine years my junior, handsome and apparently in love with me, stabbing former cult-member that I am. Having Ed is the thing that has got me back on my feet.

Mark and Cherry are there already, sitting in a booth. They shout and wave us across. I am grinning all over my face at the sight of them. When we were on the island, I thought I would never want to see my fellow castaways again, yet now I look on them as long-lost friends.

They are both dressed like New Yorkers: Cherry is back to being her polished gorgeous self, her eyebrows barely there, her hair honey-blonde and shorter than it used to be, cut in a gamine bob. She is wearing skinny jeans and a white shirt, and I immediately feel sweaty and unkempt. Mark is in a polo shirt and chinos.

They both jump to their feet, and we all embrace. I squeeze both of them tightly.

'This is Daisy,' I say afterwards, an arm around her shoulders. 'Daisy, my actual daughter. I may have mentioned her once or twice.'

'Well, hello, Daisy,' Cherry says. 'We heard all about you in Malaysia. Your mom missed you so very, very much. And look at you – such a beautiful big girl.'

Daisy grins. 'Hello,' she manages to say. She looks at me for reassurance, and I take her hand and squeeze it.

'I have a little girl too,' Cherry continues, 'but she's younger than you. She's only five, and she's with her daddy this weekend. I missed her so very, very much too. And her brother.'

'What's her name?' Daisy asks shyly. Cherry beams, sits on the banquette and shuffles over, patting the spot next to her. Daisy obediently sits there, looking at me first to check. I nod and smile.

'Her name,' Cherry says, 'is Hannah. Her brother's name is Aaron. He's just three . . .'

Soon Daisy is discussing our trip out here, the aeroplane, the hotel. Cherry asks her if she had already seen Manhattan in the movies.

'We call them films,' Daisy tells her.

I turn to Mark. 'How are things with you, then, Marky Mark?' I say. I feel far more relaxed with him here, in this Manhattan restaurant, than I ever did in Malaysia.

He considers the question carefully and ushers me down to the end of the booth, where we are out of Cherry's earshot. Ed slides in next to him.

'Things are acceptable,' he says quietly. 'Cherry has a new lease of life, as you can see. She and Tom split the moment she got home, kids have shared residency, and she's picked herself up and taken the view that she has been given another chance in life. She's a different person, actually. She's open about everything, and it's only now I see her like this that I realise how much of a front she used to put on. Naturally our relationship, such as it was, is well and truly over, but she's a dear, dear friend.

'Me . . . not so good. Antonia decided we should "give it another go", "work on us", all of that. She's honourable, you know? Not a quitter. I felt like the worst turd on earth. It lasted a month or so, and *then* we quit.'

'The worst turd on earth? Blimey.'

'I know! That's something, isn't it? Don't even imagine what that would look like. But yeah, it's been shit. My kids are that much older than Cherry's, they actually went through Daddy being missing, the whole discovery that I was in Malaysia with Cherry-the-neighbour rather than being where I was meant to be, the assumption that we'd waltzed off to start again without a word. And then the return with the tail between the legs. I don't think Antonia believed, for a long time, that we were genuinely stuck on that island. She can be pretty scathing. She was entirely convinced that we eloped together and had second thoughts, and nothing I could say convinced her otherwise. Until the whole business with you and Katy came out. So I should thank you for corroborating my story.

'But I'm trying to get back on my feet. I rented an apartment in Queens. I'm a weekend dad, a McDonald's-and-the-zoo type. As I said, Cherry's become my best friend, though we try to keep that under the radar as far as our kids are concerned, particularly mine, because they don't like it that she still lives across the street from them, as Tom was the one to leave the family home. I'm building it up, with them. The older two pretty much hate me and I'm not looking forward to their therapy bills. But that's us. It's been a million times worse for you. Daisy is bearing up, isn't she? She's adorable, and exactly like you. Your "mini-me". I was expecting a timid little thing, considering.'

'It hasn't been easy,' I say in a low voice. Daisy is still chatting to Cherry, very animatedly telling her everything we have seen in Manhattan so far. Cherry is acting as if it were all new to her, and I love her for that. 'It's taken all summer,' I continue, 'to get her confidence up. It's been hellish for her. I go away for the holidays, promising to come back rested and less tetchy, and I don't come back at all. Then her "grandma" shows up, and she goes to stay with this grandma, is whisked away to a little town hundreds of miles away and bombarded with "Mummy doesn't love you" and talk of God. The stuff of horror films and nightmares, in fact. It culminated with the thing the world knows about. Where I had to fly at Katy with a knife. Watching her mother, who apparently doesn't love her, and who's been gone for weeks and weeks and weeks, suddenly showing up and doing that was incredibly hard. But that's Daisy. She deals with things, she always has done. She's the strongest person I know. She's been so brave. She started getting back to her old self when we went to stay at Ed's parents' place in Scotland and just ate amazing food and watched telly and played Monopoly for a week. And now, I think she's coming out of it. I'll feel guilty for the rest of my life.'

'How about you? Are you OK, apart from that?'

'Oh,' I say. 'I'm all right. I feel a bit stupid that I didn't twig about Katy. I thought she was my friend. But looking back on it, she knew what was going on and when we were going to be picked up. Apparently she was scared the night we saw that other boat, because it wasn't part of the plan. They'd chosen that island because nothing ever went that way, so when something did, and Cherry started swimming to it, she was afraid that she might actually reach it. That was why she plunged in.'

'But the next morning, real rescue came. We thought the night boat had sent someone out in the day. Was that wrong?'

'I think the night boat freaked Katy out, so she called in the rescue boat sooner than planned.'

'Sooner!'

'I know.'

'Any idea how long she was planning to prolong our sojourn?'

'Another week or so, I think.'

'Jeez.'

'She kept us alive because that was her job. Keeping me out of the way long enough for them to get their hands on Daisy. She could have killed me easily, any time, but the whole point was that I needed to suffer by losing my daughter, because that was what I had inflicted on Moses and Cassandra.'

'That's pretty insane,' Mark says. He takes a bottle of wine from the cooler on the table and pours each of us a glass. I see that Cherry has already ordered Daisy a Coca-Cola, a drink she is not technically allowed. 'Esther, you can't actually blame yourself for not working it out. You can't expect that sort of unhinged behaviour from complete strangers.'

'I spent ages vowing never to go away again. Then I thought, that's a bit ridiculous. It's a freaky thing that happened because of my background. Normally, having children doesn't preclude anyone from travelling. So I decided that I *can* go travelling, and I will. But I'm going to bring her with me, for the moment.'

'And Katy? Did she recover?'

'Completely, though I think she was in hospital for a while. I was glad she did, purely because it meant they let me go. If I'd actually killed her, I'd be in prison for manslaughter for a long time. I can't bear to think about that, and I make a point of not thinking about it, because it didn't happen. Cassandra managed to get away from the St Ives police then and there, because they were busy arresting me and looking after Katy. I have no idea where she went. She never showed up again, anywhere. Which is unnerving. Then Katy was being investigated for the abduction, and skipped bail and hasn't been heard from since either. The two of them have melted away. Unfortunately.'

Mark exhales deeply. 'Yeah. Not your ideal outcome.'

'The Village, meanwhile, are under huge pressure from the police. At least things are going to change there. I hope.'

Soon we are talking about other subjects. Gene was dead before he got to the mainland and Jean went home and found that her other son, Steve, had switched off Ben's life support when his parents never returned.

'He thought we'd lost our minds and were sitting gibbering in Asia somewhere,' Jean reported when I spoke to her. 'And how far off the mark was he? Not much. It was almost a relief. If you can call losing two of your very dearest people in one go a relief. I'm old, you know. I can live out the rest of my days. I have no requirement to be happy. I might even go over to visit you all, in New York and England, one of these days.'

I look around the table. We are all thin, but less thin than we used to be. None of us look like the desperate castaways we once were. It is strange that we have slipped back into a life we thought had been taken from us for ever. Yet everything is different.

We are all raising our glasses, clinking them, saying 'cheers', when something catches my eye outside the window.

It is nothing, I tell myself. I did not see anything. There are people passing us, because we are in the centre of Manhattan. Millions of people walk these streets, every day. Some of them are bound to have short dark hair. Many of them will be thin: they will be thin because they are New Yorkers, not because they chose to spend weeks on a deserted island in Asia. Some of them will, by the law of averages, have a look of Katy about them, move in the way she moves, share her essence in some indefinable way. I just saw someone like that.

Perhaps I will always feel like this. I will probably see her in crowds, occasionally. I will always be nervous about Daisy when I do not have her right next to me. I look at her again, talking to Cherry about some band they both like, laughing. She is fine now. She is here, with me, and everything is all right.

I look out of the window again. There is no sign of the person I just saw, the face that looked in, right at us, for a fraction of a second. That is because it was the face of a passing New Yorker. There is nothing, I tell myself, to worry about. Nothing at all. It is all over.